Starfire

Starfire

Dale Brown

An Imprint of HarperCollins*Publishers*

STARFIRE. Copyright © 2014 by Air Battle Force, Inc. All rights reserved. Printed in the United States of America. No part of this book may be used or reproduced in any manner whatsoever without written permission except in the case of brief quotations embodied in critical articles and reviews. For information address HarperCollins Publishers, 10 East 53rd Street, New York, NY 10022.

HarperCollins books may be purchased for educational, business, or sales promotional use. For information, please e-mail the Special Markets Department at SPsales@harpercollins.com.

FIRST HARPERLUXE EDITION

HarperLuxe™ is a trademark of HarperCollins Publishers

Library of Congress Cataloging-in-Publication Data is available upon request.

ISBN: 978-0-06-232638-6

14 ID/RRD 10 9 8 7 6 5 4 3 2 1

I used to dream about being chosen to be an astronaut in the U.S. National Aeronautics and Space Administration and someday walking on the moon or doing experiments on a space station orbiting Earth. I thought there was nothing better than being in NASA . . .

. . . until the advent of private companies, universities, and individuals with the vision and determination to think outside the government-controlled bureaucratic box, accept the risks, and get the job of space travel done.

This novel is dedicated to the innovators, entrepreneurs, and the just plain bold and brash visionaries who have struck out against all odds to make manned spaceflight by nongovernmental entities a reality. What could be better than flying in space on a spacecraft you and *your company* designed and built?

As always, your comments are welcome at readermail@dalebrown.info. I can't promise to reply to every e-mail, but I read every one.

Cast of Characters

SKY MASTERS AEROSPACE INC. PERSONNEL

HUNTER "BOOMER" NOBLE, Ph.D., spaceplane pilot and chief of aerospace engineering

HELEN KADDIRI, Ph.D., president and chairman of the board

JASON RICHTER, colonel, U.S. Army (ret.), Ph.D., vice president and chief of technology development

SONDRA EDDINGTON, student spaceplane pilot, Battle Mountain, Nevada

ARMSTRONG SPACE STATION PERSONNEL

KAI RAYDON, brigadier general, U.S. Air Force (ret.), station director

TREVOR SHALE, station manager

VALERIE LUKAS, chief of combat operations

JESSICA "GONZO" FAULKNER, lieutenant colonel, U.S. Marine Corps (ret.), chief of flight operations, spaceplane pilot

DR. MIRIAM ROTH, chief medical director

HENRY LATHROP, aerospace tactical weapons officer

CHRISTINE RAYHILL, terrestrial weapons/surveillance officer

ALICE HAMILTON, engineering officer

LARRY JESSOP, life-support techniciam

THE WHITE HOUSE, WASHINGTON, D.C.

KENNETH PHOENIX, president of the United States of America

ANN PAGE, vice president of the United States and White House chief of staff

WILLIAM GLENBROOK, president's national security adviser

JAMES MORRISON, secretary of state

THOMAS TORREY, CIA director

PAULA ELLS, U.S. ambassador to the United Nations

ROBIN CLARKSON, special agent, U.S. Secret Service

WASHINGTON, D.C.

STACY ANNE BARBEAU, candidate for president of the United States

LUKE COHEN, Barbeau's campaign manager

THE PENTAGON, WASHINGTON, D.C.

FREDERICK HAYES, secretary of defense

HAROLD LEE, undersecretary of defense for space

TIMOTHY SPELLING, general, USAF, chairman of the Joint Chiefs of Staff

JASON CONAWAY, general, USAF, U.S. Air Force chief of staff

JOSEPH EBERHART, admiral, U.S. Navy, commander, U.S. Strategic Command

GEORGE SANDSTEIN, general, USAF, commander, Air Force Space Command, and deputy commander for space, U.S. Strategic Command

SCION AVIATION INTERNATIONAL, ST. GEORGE, UTAH

KEVIN MARTINDALE, president, former president of the United States of America

CHRIS WOHL, sergeant major, U.S. Marines Corp (ret.), ground ops leader

JAMES RATEL, chief master sergeant, U.S. Air Force (ret.), martial-arts instructor

JORGE "DICE" LUNA, ground-team member (logistics)

RICHARD "FLEX" ROSEN, ground-team member (intelligence)

BEN "RATTLER" SCOTT, ground-team member (weapons)

CALIFORNIA POLYTECHNIC STATE UNIVERSITY (CAL POLY) SAN LUIS OBISPO, COLLEGE OF ENGINEERING

BRADLEY J. MCLANAHAN, Battle Mountain, Nevada

LANE EAGAN, Roseburg, Oregon

KIM JUNG-BAE ("JERRY"), Seoul, United Korea

CASEY HUGGINS, Kansas City, Missouri

JODIE CAVENDISH, Brisbane, Australia

DR. MARCUS HARRIS, Ed.D., president, California Polytechnic State University, San Luis Obispo (Cal Poly)

DR. TOSHUNIKO "TOBY" NUKAGA, Ph.D., aerospace engineering professor, Cal Poly

RUSSIAN FEDERATION

GENNADIY ANATOLIYVICH GRYZLOV, president of the Russian Federation

SERGEI TARZAROV, president's chief of staff

VIKTOR KAZYANOV, minister of state security

GREGOR SOKOLOV, minister of defense

DARIA TITENEVA, foreign minister

ANDREI NARYSHKIN, United Nations ambassador

GENERAL MIKHAIL KHRISTENKO, chief of the general staff of the Russian armed forces

BRUNO ILIANOV, colonel, deputy air attaché, Russian embassy, Washington

YVETTE KORCHKOV, assistant and bodyguard to Bruno Ilianov

BORIS CHIRKOV, chief envoy, Russian Trade Mission, San Francisco, California

COLONEL MIKHAIL GALTIN, Elektron spaceplane commander

PEOPLE'S REPUBLIC OF CHINA

ZHOU QIANG, president of the People's Republic of China

COLONEL GENERAL SUN JI, chief of the general staff of the People's Liberation Armed Forces

UNITED NATIONS

SOFYAN APRIYANTO, president of the United Nations Security Council

Weapons and Acronyms

WEAPONS

9K720—Russian air-launched antispacecraft missile

B-1B Lancer ("Bone")—American long-range heavy bomber

BOHM ("bomb")—borohydrogen metaoxide, an oxidizer in advanced hybrid rocket engines

BOR-5 Buran—unmanned Soviet space shuttle

C-23C Sherpa—American short-haul cargo plane

Elektron—Russian spaceplane

Gvozd' **(Hobnail)**—Russian space-borne laser

Hydra—American space-based laser

Iskander—Russian short- to medium-range ballistic missile

Kingfisher—a constellation of American antispacecraft and ground-attack space-based weapons

"leopards"—Laser Pulse Detonation Rocket System, an advanced hybrid turbofan/scramjet/rocket engine

MiG-31D—Mikoyan-Gurevich-31D, Soviet and Russian advanced high-speed interceptor; the "D" model is used to launch antisatellite missiles

Mjollnir—"Thor's Hammer," American space-launched land-attack projectile

nantenna—nanoscopic rectifying antenna, used to convert light to electric power

Progress—Russian unmanned space transportation module

rectenna—rectifying antenna, a device that converts electromagnetic energy into direct current electricity

S-9, S-19, S-29—American single-stage-to-orbit spaceplanes

S-500S—Russian surface-to-air missile system capable of attacking spacecraft in low Earth orbit

scramjet—supersonic ramjet, an advanced air-breathing engine that can propel an aircraft beyond three times the speed of sound

Skybolt—American space-based free electron laser

SL-16—Russian heavy space launch rocket

Soyuz—Russian manned space transportation capsule

ACRONYMS

ACES—Advanced Crew Escape Suit, a light-duty space suit

CBP—Customs and Border Protection

CID—Cybenetic Infantry Device, a manned robot

COIL—Chlorine-Oxygen-Iodine Laser, an American laser system

DB—"duck blind," a known base or site with anti-spacecraft weapons

DEFCON—Defense Condition, a gradual escalation in readiness for nuclear war

EEAS—Electronic Elastomeric Activity Suit

EMP—Electromagnetic Pulse, a massive discharge of energy from a nuclear explosion that can damage electronics at long distances

ICBM—Intercontinental Ballstic Missile

JASSM—Joint Air-to-Surface Standoff Missile, an American long-range cruise missile

LCVG—Liquid Cooling and Ventilation Garment, worn under a space suit to keep the wearer comfortable

LOX—liquid oxygen

MC—Mission Commander, the "copilot" aboard a spacecraft

MHD—magnetohydrodynamic generator, produces electricity by spinning plasma through a magnetic field

MRE—Meals Ready to Eat, American field ration

NRL—Naval Research Laboratory

PAC-3—Patriot Advanced Capability, an American surface-to-air missile with an antiballistic-missile capability

PLSS—Primary Life-Support System—the backpack worn by astronauts that provides oxygen, power, and environmental controls

ROS—Russian Orbital Section, the Russian-built portion of the International Space Station

SAFER—Simplified Aid for EVA Rescue, an American device worn by astronauts conducting an EVA (Extra-Vehicular Activity) to maneuver back to safety if disconnected from a tether

SBIRS—Space-Based Infrared System, American next-generation missile detection and tracking system

SBR—Space-Based Radar, American advanced space and Earth surveillance system

UC—University of California college system

WCS ("wicks")—Waste Containment System, a commode used on spacecraft

Real-World News Excerpts

RUSSIA TO REVAMP AIR-SPACE DEFENSES BY 2020—Ria Novosti—Moscow—Russia will create a new generation of air and space defenses to counter any strikes against its territory by 2020 due to a potential foreign threat, the Air Force commander said on Tuesday.

"By 2030 . . . foreign countries, particularly the United States, will be able to deliver coordinated high-precision strikes from air and space against any target on the whole territory of Russia," Col. Gen. Alexander Zelin said, referring to the potential for new hypersonic and space-based offensive weapons.

"That is why the main goal of the development of the Russian Air Force until 2020 is to create a new branch of the Armed Forces, which would form the core of the country's air and space defenses to provide a reliable deterrent during peacetime, and repel any military aggression with the use of conventional and nuclear arsenals in a time of war," the general said.

"In line with the new air-space defense concept, we have already formed a number of brigades, which will be armed with S-400 and S-500 air defense systems," Zelin said at a news conference in Moscow.

The S400 Triumf (SA-21 Growler) is designed to intercept and destroy airborne targets at a distance of up to 400 kilometers (250 miles), twice the range of the U.S. MIM-104 Patriot, and 2 1/2 times that of Russia's S-300PMU-2.

The system is also believed to be able to destroy stealth aircraft, cruise missiles, and ballistic missiles, and is effective at ranges up to 3,500 kilometers (2,200 miles) and speeds up to 4.8 kilometers (3 miles) per second.

The fifth-generation S-500 air defense system, which is currently in the blueprint stage and is expected to be rolled out by 2012, would outperform the S-400 as well as the U.S. Patriot Advanced Capability-3 system.

"The S-500 system is being developed under a unique design . . . and will be capable of destroying hypersonic and ballistic targets," the general said.

Meanwhile, the Soviet-era MiG-31 Foxhound supersonic interceptor aircraft will most likely be used as part of the new air-space defense network, as was intended when it was designed.

"We are upgrading this system to be able to accomplish the same air-space defense tasks," Zelin said.

According to some sources, Russia has over 280 MiG-31 aircraft in active service and about 100 aircraft in reserve.

AEGIS BALLISTIC MISSILE DEFENSE INTERCEPTS TARGET USING SPACE TRACKING AND SURVEILLANCE SYSTEM—

U.S. Department of Defense, 13 February 2013—The Missile Defense Agency (MDA) and U.S. Navy sailors aboard the USS *Lake Erie* (CG 70) successfully conducted a flight test of the Aegis Ballistic Missile Defense (BMD) system, resulting in the intercept of a medium-range ballistic missile target over the Pacific Ocean by a Standard Missile-3 (SM-3) Block IA guided missile.

At 11:10 P.M. HST, (4:10 A.M. EST) a unitary medium-range ballistic missile target was launched from the Pacific Missile Range Facility, on Kauai, Hawaii. The target flew northwest toward a broad ocean area of the Pacific Ocean.

The in-orbit Space Tracking and Surveillance System-Demonstrators (STSS-D) detected and tracked the target, and forwarded track data to the USS *Lake*

Erie. The ship, equipped with the second-generation Aegis BMD weapon system, used Launch on Remote doctrine to engage the target.

The ship developed a fire control solution from the STSS-D track and launched the SM-3 Block IA guided missile approximately five minutes after target launch. The SM-3 maneuvered to a point in space and released its kinetic warhead. The kinetic warhead acquired the target reentry vehicle, diverted into its path, and, using only the force of a direct impact, engaged and destroyed the target.

Today's event, designated Flight Test Standard Missile-20 (FTM-20), was a demonstration of the ability of space-based assets to provide midcourse fire control quality data to an Aegis BMD ship, extending the battlespace, providing the ability for longer-range intercepts and defense of larger areas . . .

RUSSIAN SUPPLY SHIP DOCKS WITH ORBIT-ING SPACE STATION—Moscow (UPI)—July 28, 2013—An unmanned cargo ship has docked at the International Space Station to deliver nearly 3 tons of supplies, Russia's space agency said.

The Progress 52 spacecraft docked smoothly with the orbiting station Saturday, shortly after being launched from Russia aboard a Soyuz rocket. "The docking was carried out in automated regime as scheduled," a spokesman for the space agency Roscosmos said.

Russia's RIA Novosti news agency said the mission returned to the short 6-hour course to the space station. The previous supply mission took two days to rendezvous with the station. Before that, three space freighters—Progress M-16M, Progress M-17M and Progress M-18M—also delivered their cargo to the ISS in six hours.

Progress M-20M will bring some 2.4 metric tons of fuel, food, oxygen, scientific and medical equipment to the orbital outpost.

Fragments of Russia's Progress M-18M space freighter sank safely in the Pacific Ocean after reentering the atmosphere on Friday, a spokesman for the Russian mission control center said.

The spacecraft undocked from the International Space Station shortly after midnight Moscow time and started its final journey toward a remote location in the Pacific Ocean known as the "spacecraft cemetery."

EXPERIMENTAL SPACE PLANE COULD CUT SATELLITE COSTS—Ray Locker, USA Today, 13 November 2013—The Pentagon wants to cut the costs of putting satellites into space by creating a "space plane" that can fly into low Earth orbit and release satellites for about $5 million a launch.

Called the XS-1, the plane to be developed by the Defense Advanced Research Projects Agency (DARPA) would be capable of flying 10 times the speed of sound (Mach 10), and carry payloads between 3,000 and 5,000 pounds into orbit, according to documents released this week.

If developed, the plane would be capable of rushing smaller satellites into space and cutting the long lead times necessary to use conventional launchers, such as rockets. "Current space launch vehicles are very expensive, have no surge capability, and must be contracted years in advance (i.e., long call-up times)," DARPA records show . . .

. . . The XS-1 project follows a 10-year effort to build another hypersonic vehicle, called the Falcon HTV-2. According to a 2003 DARPA plan, the Falcon was intended to be capable of taking off "from a conventional military runway and striking targets 9,000 nautical miles distant in less than two hours. It could carry a 12,000-pound payload consisting of Common Aero Vehicles (CAVs), cruise missiles, small diameter bombs, or other munitions . . ."

PROLOGUE

Revenge is a kind of wild justice.
—SIR FRANCIS BACON

SACRAMENTO, CALIFORNIA
April 2016

"Ladies and gentlemen," the flight attendant said over the airliner's public-address system, "let me be the first to welcome you to Sacramento's Patrick S. McLanahan International Airport, where the local time is eight-oh-five P.M." She continued with the usual warnings about staying seated with seat belts fastened and watching for loose articles in the overhead bins as the airliner taxied to its assigned gate.

One of the first-class passengers, wearing a business suit and white oxford shirt with no tie, looked up from his magazine in surprise. "They named Sacramento International after General Patrick McLanahan?" he said to his companion seated beside him. He spoke with a very slight European accent, hard to pinpoint from which country he was from to the other passengers seated around them. He was tall, bald but with a dark well-groomed goatee, and ruggedly handsome, like a recently retired professional athlete.

The woman looked at him with amusement. "You did not know that?" she asked. She had the same accent—definitely European, but hard for the other passengers within earshot to pin down. Like her companion, she was tall, beautiful without being sexy, with pinned-up, long blond hair, an athletic figure, and high cheekbones. She wore a business suit that had been made to look unbusinesslike for travel. They most definitely looked like a power couple.

"No. You made the reservations, remember. Besides, the airport code on the ticket still says 'SMF,' back when it was Sacramento Metropolitan Field."

"Well, it is Sacramento-McLanahan Field now," the woman said. "Fits perfectly, if you ask me. I think it is a great honor. Patrick McLanahan was a real hero." The passengers across the aisle from the couple, although pretending not to eavesdrop, nodded in agreement.

"I think we do not know of half the stuff that guy did during his career—it will all be classified for the next fifty years at least," the man said.

"Well, what we *do* know is more than enough to get his name on the airport in the city he was born in," the woman said. "He deserves his own memorial in Arlington National Cemetery." More nods of agreement from those around the couple.

The tributes to Patrick McLanahan in the terminal building continued after they left the plane. The center of the main terminal had a ten-foot-tall bronze statue of Patrick on a six-foot tall pedestal, carrying a high-tech flight helmet under one arm and a handheld computer in the other hand—the toe of the statue's right boot was shiny from passersbys rubbing it for good luck. The walls were lined with photographs of Patrick depicting events throughout his entire military and industrial career. On display panels, children had drawn and painted pictures of EB-52 Megafortress and EB-1C Vampire bombers, with words like BOMBS AWAY, GENERAL! and THANK YOU FOR KEEPING US SAFE, PATRICK!

While waiting at the baggage carousel for their luggage, the man nodded toward an electronic billboard. "There is the ad for that tour of the McLanahan family bar and home, and his columbarium," he remarked. "I would like to see that before we leave."

"We do not have time," the woman pointed out. "The only flight from New York to Sacramento was

late, and we have to be in San Francisco by ten A.M.
The gravesite does not open until nine, and the bar
does not open until eleven."

"Rats," the man said. "Maybe we go early and see
if someone can open it for us." The woman shrugged
noncommitally and nodded.

They retrieved their luggage a short time later and
headed for the rental-car counters beside the baggage
carousels. On the way, the man stopped at a gift shop
and emerged a few minutes later with a large shopping
bag. "What did you get?" the woman asked him.

"Airplane models," the man replied. "One of the
EB-52 Megafortress, the one that General McLanahan
used when he first attacked Russia, and another of the
EB-1C Vampire, one of the bombers he used against
the Russian president's bunker after the American
Holocaust." The massive subatomic cruise-missile
attack against American air defense, intercontinental-
ballistic-missile, and long-range-bomber bases was
known worldwide as the American Holocaust, during
which over fifteen thousand Americans were killed.
Patrick McLanahan had led a counterattack against
Russian mobile intercontinental-ballistic-missile sites
and eventually against Russian president Anatoliy
Gryzlov's underground command bunker, killing
Gryzlov and putting an end to the conflict.

"I thought you already had models of all of McLanahan's experimental aircraft," the woman pointed out.

"I do," the man said, grinning like a young boy on Christmas morning, "but not this *big*! The largest of my models are one-forty-eighth scale, but these bad boys are *one-twenty-fourth* scale! Twice as big as my other ones!"

The woman shook her head in mock disbelief. "Well, you have to carry them," was all she said, and they proceeded to get in line for a rental car for the drive to their hotel in downtown Sacramento.

The next morning, both were up early. They dressed, had breakfast in the hotel dining room, went back to their room to pack, and were checked out and leaving the hotel in their rental car by seven thirty. The downtown streets of the capital city of the state of California on this weekend morning were quiet, with just a few joggers and merchants about.

The couple's first stop was at McLanahan's, a small bar and restaurant that had been popular with law enforcement officers since it opened just after the turn of the twentieth century. A relative had bought the property from Patrick McLanahan's sisters, the only surviving members of the family other than Patrick's son, Bradley, and turned the upstairs apartment into a small Patrick McLanahan museum. Downstairs it was still a bar and restaurant, but the owner had hundreds of framed photographs and newspaper clippings depicting events in Patrick McLanahan's life as well as the lives of those who served in the U.S. Air Force during the Cold War. "Closed," the woman observed. "Not open until eleven A.M. We have to be in San Francisco by ten."

"I know, I know," her companion said. "Let's try the columbarium."

The entrance to the newly redesigned section of Sacramento Old City Cemetery had a security access aisle with a CLOSED sign over it, but the couple found the gate open and an elderly man wiping down the table beside an X-ray machine. The man smiled and nodded as the couple approached. "Mornin', folks," he greeted them cheerfully. "Sorry, but we're not open for about another hour."

The European man did not try to hide his disappointment one bit. "We must be in San Francisco on important business by ten, and we will not have an opportunity to come back. I wanted so much to see the general's crypt."

The caretaker nodded, a little pang of regret in his eyes, then asked, "Where are you from, sir?"

"I am from Vilnius, Lithuania, sir," the man said. "My father was a colonel in the Lithuanian Air Force under General Palcikas when my country announced its independence from the Soviet Union, and he witnessed the events firsthand when the Russians invaded in retaliation. He told many stories of the incredible battles fought by Patrick McLanahan, Bradley Elliott, and the brave fighters of the secret task force code-named 'Madcap Magician' on behalf of my country. He talked about Patrick so often I thought we were related." The caretaker smiled at that. "And now here I am, standing outside his gravesite, anxious to say good-bye to our family's true hero, and I cannot." His face turned crestfallen. "Well, good day to you, sir," and he turned to depart.

"Wait," the caretaker said. The Lithuanian man turned, his face brightening. "I'm a docent here at the memorial." He thought for a brief moment, then said, "I can take you in to see the crypt. Just a quick look so we don't get a flood of people wanting to go inside, no pictures out of respect—"

"That would be wonderful, sir!" the Lithuanian man exclaimed. "Honey, did you hear that?" The woman seemed elated for her companion. "Just a quick look, no touching, no pictures. You have made my day, sir!" The caretaker let the couple in and closed the gate behind them.

"I need to look inside your bag," the caretaker said. The Lithuanian man had brought the large bag of model planes with him. "Our X-ray machine is off, and it'll take a long time to get it warmed up—"

"Of course, of course," the man said. He lifted up one of the large boxes. "An EB-52 Megafortress model. I already have one—"

"*Several,* you mean," the woman interjected with a smile.

"Yes, several, but not one this large!" He lowered the box into the bag and lifted the second box. "An EB-1 Vampire. I cannot wait to put them together."

The caretaker smiled and nodded. "This way, folks," he said. He launched right into his memorized guided tour: "Old City Cemetery was established in 1849, at the beginning of the California Gold Rush, and is the final resting place of over twenty-five thousand souls," he began. "The McLanahans were part of a large influx of fortune hunters and adventurers from Ireland. But they saw that their adopted little town was growing quickly and getting wild, so they gave up panning for gold and silver and took up law enforcement to help maintain law and order. Over five hundred McLanahans were Sacramento city police officers, including nine chiefs of police.

"This section of the cemetery, over an acre, holds the remains of seven generations of McLanahans, including four city mayors, two Roman Catholic bishops, one state governor, three United States congressmen, several general officers, and hundreds of men and women who served our nation all the way back to the Civil War. Patrick's father and mother were the last to be interred here because space finally ran out, and then the family and the General Patrick McLanahan Memorial Foundation built the columbarium for the general and his remaining family members."

They came to an area with two rows of marble walls. The wall on the left had eighteen-inch-square crypts, some already faced with markers; the wall on the right had a large mural etched into marble with an American flag, several large American jet-bomber aircraft flying toward the viewer from a central bald eagle, and the words of the John Gillespie Magee Jr.'s sonnet "High Flight" inscribed below the planes. "You will notice that each wall is eighteen feet high, eighteen inches thick, and the walls are eighteen feet apart," the docent said, "eighteen being the number of years the general was in the Air Force."

The caretaker gestured to the wall to the left, which was flanked with an American flag and another blue flag beside it with three silver stars. "Here is General McLanahan's final resting place," he said. The visitors looked wide-eyed and awestruck. At the top center of the marble wall was a simple blue metal plaque framed in silver with three silver stars on it. "His wife Wendy's crypt is beside his to the right, but her urn is empty because her ashes were scattered at sea. By executive order of President Kenneth Phoenix, for the first year after the general's inurnment here the columbarium had a military guard twenty-four hours a day—the president wanted a special place set aside for the general in Arlington National Cemetery in Washington, but the family did not want that. When the segregation of the McLanahan columbarium from the rest of the cemetery was completed, the guard was removed. On special occasions such as Patrick's birthday, anniversaries of some of his battles, or on occasions such as Veterans Day, we have volunteer sentries stationed here on duty to honor the general and America.

"To the left of the general's is the crypt of Patrick's brother, Paul, who was a Sacramento Police Department officer, injured in the line of duty, and then rebuilt by Sky Masters Inc. with high-tech limbs and sensors, then becoming a member of the secret antiterrorist task force called the 'Night Stalkers,'" the caretaker went on. "He was killed in a secret government contract operation in Libya; many of the facts of that operation are still classified. The other crypts on the top row are reserved for the general's two sisters and for several of the general's close friends and aides-de-camp, including Major General David Luger, who recently retired from active duty, and Brigadier General Hal Briggs, killed in action, where the plaque with the single silver star there is located. The spot directly beneath Patrick's and Wendy's is reserved for Patrick's son, Bradley, who currently is a student of aerospace engineering at California Polytechnic University, San Luis Obispo."

The docent turned and gestured to the opposite marble wall. "The general has a very large extended family, so this wall was built to house the remains of any other family members, friends of the general, or fellow general officers who wish to be inurned here," he went on. "It contains crypts as well, but until the first wall is filled, this beautiful carved limestone diorama covers the face. The diorama will be removed and relocated when . . ." It wasn't until then that the caretaker noticed that the Lithuanian man had set his bag down on the bench seat in between the marble walls and had slid the aircraft model boxes out. "What are you doing there, sir? Remember, no pictures."

"We are not here to take pictures, my friend," the woman said behind the caretaker. A fraction of a second later a cloth was pressed against the caretaker's mouth and nose. He struggled to get free, but the woman was surprisingly strong. The caretaker gasped as he inhaled a lungful of a very harsh chemical that smelled like mothballs. Within seconds he felt as if the columbarium were spinning, and his vision blurred, switching from color to black and white, and then began exploding in bursts of color. In thirty seconds the man's legs could not support his body, and he slumped to the ground.

He was awake long enough to see the Lithuanian man removing what looked like metal tools from the airplane-model boxes!

"*Eta shtuka prekrasno rabotayet,*" the man said in Russian. "That stuff works great."

"*Ya poluchayu nemnogo golovokruzheniye sebya,*" the woman said, also in Russian. She used a moist towelette to wipe the residue of the nerve agent from her fingers. "I am starting to get a little dizzy myself from the dimethyltryptamine."

In seconds the man had assembled two crowbars and a tool resembling a lug wrench from parts in the boxes. While he assembled the tools, the woman went out of the columbarium and returned a moment later rolling back a large ornate concrete planter. The man climbed onto the planter, the woman handed him a crowbar, and he began prying off the engraved marble stone covering the crypt of Lieutenant General Patrick Shane McLanahan.

"*Kamery videonablyudeniya vezde,*" the woman said. "Security cameras are everywhere."

"It does not matter," the man said. After breaking off several pieces of the thin stone, he finally managed to pop the engraved stone off the crypt, revealing a steel panel with two very large bolts that attached it to the marble. Using the lug wrench, he started loosening the bolts. "Notify the sleeper teams that we will be on the move shortly." The woman made a call using a disposable cell phone.

It did not take long to open the crypt. Inside they found a simple cylindrical aluminum urn, along with several letters sealed in see-through airtight containers, and several military decorations. The man picked one up. *"Proklyatiye!"* he swore. "I did not know the *ublyudok* received an Air Force Cross with a silver star!" The star signified receiving the Air Force Cross, the Air Force's highest award except for the Medal of Honor, five times. "One of them *had* to be for killing President Gryzlov. I guess they do not give Medals of Honor out to criminals."

"Let's get out of here," the woman said. "The network has been alerted."

It was over moments later. The contents of the crypt were loaded into the shopping bag, and the two Russians departed the cemetery, walking briskly back to their rental car but not running so as to not attract attention. They drove just a few blocks away, in an area already scouted out as having no security or traffic cameras nearby, and transferred to a different vehicle driven by a young man. Careful not to hurry or run any traffic lights or stop signs, they drove out of the city across the Tower Bridge into West Sacramento. They changed cars three more times in various areas around the city before stopping at a deserted fruit-stand gravel parking lot west of Davis, California, a place unlikely to have security cameras. The man approached a large dark sedan that had diplomatic license plates. A window rolled down; the man put the bags in through the window and returned to his car. The black sedan drove down an access road until reaching an onramp that took them onto Interstate 80 heading west toward San Francisco.

"*Ty polnyy durak,* Colonel," an older man in the front seat said. He had long white hair carefully styled in waves, a thick neck, wore a dark expensive-looking suit and designer sunglasses, and he spoke without turning around to address the persons in the backseat. "You are a complete fool, Ilianov," the man, named Boris Chirkov, said. Chirkov was the envoy in charge of the Russian consulate in San Francisco, coordinating all trade matters between the Russian Foreign Ministry, the American State Department, and businesses in the western United States. "You risk too much."

"I am under orders from President Gryzlov himself, Excellency," the man in the backseat, Bruno Ilianov, said. Ilianov was a Russian Air Force colonel and, officially, deputy air attaché assigned to the Russian embassy in Washington. Beside him sat a woman with jet-black hair, high cheekbones, and an athletic body, her sunglasses hiding dark eyes. "But I am happy to follow those orders. These Americans, especially the ones from his home city, treat McLanahan like a god. It is an insult to all Russians. The man who deliberately murdered President Gryzlov's father and bombed our capital city does not deserve to be lauded."

"You are—or shall I say, *were*, before you touched those bags—an official military representative of the Russian Federation, Ilianov," Chirkov said. "And you"—he turned to address the woman—"are a high-ranking security officer with diplomatic privileges, Korchkov. You both will lose your diplomatic credentials and be forced to exit this country forever, as well as being banned from entering all North Atlantic Treaty Organization and NATO-aligned countries. Less than six months in the United States, on your first major Kremlin posting overseas, and now you are nothing more than a common thief and vandal. Does your career mean so little to you?"

"The president has assured me that my future will be secure, sir," Ilianov said. "Even if I am arrested, all the Americans can do is deport me, which I will gladly see happen just to get away from this corrupt and decrepit country."

Ilianov was an idiot, Chirkov thought—Gennadiy Gryzlov discarded human beings like used tissues, and had done so for decades. But the world geopolitical situation was far more serious than Ilianov's brainless actions. This could completely destroy American-Russian relations, Chirkov thought—although, truth be told, those relations were already pretty bad right now. He knew Gennadiy Gryzlov's father, Anatoliy Gryzlov, had issued orders that killed tens of thousands of Americans and even hundreds of fellow Russians on Russian soil, and he had no doubt that his son was capable of similar unspeakable acts. Although Chirkov was the fourth-highest-ranking member of the Russian diplomatic delegation to the United States of America, Gryzlov's family was far wealthier and vastly more politically powerful than his own. Whatever Gryzlov had in mind beyond grave robbing, Chirkov probably couldn't stop him. But he had to try to dissuade him somehow.

Chirkov half turned in his seat. "What else is President Gryzlov planning, Ilianov?" he asked. "Defiling and looting a crypt is bad enough."

"When that crypt held the remains of Mother Russia's most murderous aggressor since Adolf Hitler, I am happy to participate," Ilianov said. "McLanahan is a criminal that murdered the president of my country. He does not deserve to be honored."

"That attack was a long time ago, and it was during a time of war."

"A war of McLanahan's making, sir, completely unauthorized and illegal," Ilianov said. Chirkov sat motionless, suppressing a shake of his head. Former Russian president Anatoliy Gryzlov had retaliated against an attack led by Patrick McLanahan by unleashing waves of nuclear-tipped supersonic cruise missiles and nearly wiped out America's entire land-based nuclear deterrent—along with several thousand Americans—in what became known as the "American Holocaust." McLanahan's subsequent nonnuclear attack on Russia with America's last remaining long-range bombers was the response, which left both nations with near parity in the numbers of nuclear warheads. The final attack, led by Patrick McLanahan himself, was against Gryzlov's alternate underground command post at Ryazan, a pinpoint strike that had killed the Russian president.

Whoever was responsible for starting the bomber war that led to the American Holocaust and the attack on Ryazan, McLanahan or Gryzlov, was debatable and probably pointless, but Gryzlov was definitely not an innocent bystander. A former commanding general of Russian long-range bomber forces, he had responded to an almost insignificant attack on Russian air defense sites by unleashing nuclear warheads and killing thousands of Americans in a sneak attack. These were not the actions of a sane man. When McLanahan captured a

Russian air base in Siberia and used it to stage attacks on Russian mobile ballistic-missile sites, Gryzlov ordered another nuclear cruise-missile attack . . . but this time *targeting his own Russian air base!* His obsession with killing McLanahan resulted in the deaths of hundreds of Russians at Yakutsk, but McLanahan escaped and killed Gryzlov several hours later by bombing Gryzlov's alternate and supposedly secret command post.

"Give me the urn and the other items, Colonel," Chirkov insisted. "I will return them at the appropriate time, and I will explain that you acted out of extreme emotion and have been sent back to Moscow for grief counseling or something that will hopefully arouse a little bit of sympathy."

"With respects, sir, I will not," Ilianov said in a toneless voice.

Chirkov closed his eyes and shook his head. Ilianov was a brainless stooge of Gennadiy Gryzlov and would probably die before handing over the things he had stolen. "What will the president do with them, Colonel?" he asked wearily.

"He said he wishes to place the urn on his desk and use it as an ashtray," Ilianov said, "and perhaps pin McLanahan's medals inside his commode whenever he urinates. He deserves nothing less than a proper place of honor."

"You are behaving like a child, Colonel," Chirkov said. "I urge you to reconsider your actions."

"The first President Gryzlov was forced to respond to McLanahan's aggression or face more attacks and more killing," Ilianov said. "McLanahan's actions may or may not have been authorized, but they were certainly sanctioned by President Thomas Thorn and his generals. This is but a small example of what President Gryzlov intends to do to restore honor and greatness to the Russian people."

"What else are you planning to do, Colonel?" Chirkov repeated. "I assure you, you have already done quite enough."

"The president's campaign against the memory of General Patrick McLanahan has only just begun, Excellency," Ilianov said. "He intends to destroy every institution of which McLanahan ever had any part. Instead of celebrating and memorializing the life of Patrick McLanahan, America will soon curse his name."

Chirkov's encrypted cellular phone beeped, and he answered it, saying nothing, then terminated the call a few moments later. "The American secretary of state was notified by the Federal Bureau of Investigation of the robbery in Sacramento," he said tonelessly. "Your henchmen will probably be arrested within the hour. They will talk eventually." He half turned again in his seat. "You know that if the American FBI obtains a warrant from a federal judge, they can enter your premises in Washington, and because your activity was not an official act you can be arrested and prosecuted. Diplomatic immunity will not apply."

"I know, Excellency," Ilianov said. "I did not really think the Americans could react so quickly, but I planned for this in case I was discovered. I have already arranged for a private jet to take me from Woodland, California, to Mexicali, and from there home via Mexico City, Havana, Morocco, and Damascus. Diplomatic security forces are standing by to assist with local customs." He handed the consul a card. "Here is the address of the airport; it is not far from the freeway. Drop us off, and you can continue to the consulate in San Francisco, and we will be on our way. You can deny all involvement in this matter."

"What else do you have planned in this escapade of yours, Colonel?" Chirkov asked after he handed the card to the driver, who entered the address into the car's GPS navigator. "I sense it is a lot more serious than a burglary."

"I will not jeopardize your diplomatic status or career by involving you any further in the president's activities, Excellency," Ilianov said. "But you will know it when you hear of the incidents, sir . . . I guarantee it." He produced the aluminum urn from his large grocery bag, running his fingers across the three silver stars on the side and the shield of the U.S. Space Defense Force on the lid. "What a joke," he muttered. "Russia has had a true space defense force for almost ten years, while this unit was never activated, except in McLanahan's twisted brain. Why did we fear this man so much? He was nothing but a work of fiction, both alive and dead." He hefted the urn experimentally, and a puzzled expression crossed his face. "You know, I have never seen cremated human remains before . . ."

"Please, do not further desecrate the man's remains," Chirkov said. "Leave them alone. And reconsider leaving them with me. I can concoct some sort of story that does not implicate you, and the president's anger will be directed toward myself, not you. Russian thieves and hooligans did the deed, but when they tried to sell them on the black market, we caught them and are holding them under arrest in the consulate. Sincere apologies, return of the artifacts, promises to prosecute those responsible, and an offer to pay to repair the damage and restore the columbarium should be sufficient to satisfy the Americans."

"I do not wish to implicate you any further, Excellency," Ilianov repeated, "and I have no wish to return these things or restore that bastard's monument to himself. Hopefully, having these things not properly interred will result in McLanahan's soul wandering the universe for all eternity."

That, Chirkov thought, was *exactly* what he was afraid of.

Ilianov hefted the urn once again. "It is much lighter than I thought," he muttered, then twisted off the lid. "Let us see what the great General Patrick Shane McLanahan looks like after taking his last sauna bath at one thousand degrees Centigrade."

Chirkov did not turn to look, but stared straight ahead and fought to hide his disgust. But he soon became puzzled after several long moments of silence, and he turned to look over his shoulder . . .

. . . to see the Russian air force colonel's face as white as a consulate dinner tablecloth, his mouth open as if trying to speak. "Ilianov . . . ?" The colonel looked up, his eyes as round and big as saucers, and now Chirkov saw Korchkov's face with an equally shocked expression—very, very unusual for such a highly trained security officer and assassin. "What is it?"

Ilianov was stunned into silence, his mouth still hanging open. As he shook his head in utter disbelief, he slowly tilted the open urn toward Chirkov . . .

. . . and that's when the Russian ambassador could see that the urn was completely empty.

ONE

Go to the edge of the cliff and jump off.
Build your wings on the way down.
—RAY BRADBURY

MCLANAHAN INDUSTRIAL AIRPORT, BATTLE MOUNTAIN, NEVADA

Several days later

"Is the guy asleep, Boomer?" the flight surgeon monitoring the crew's physiological datalink radioed. "His heart rate hasn't changed one bit since we put him on the monitors. Is he freakin' dead? Check on him, okay?"

"Roger," Hunter "Boomer" Noble, the aircraft commander on this flight, replied. He left his seat, climbed back between the two side-by-side cockpit seats, walked through the airlock between the cockpit and cabin, and entered the small four-person passenger compartment. Unlike the more familiar orange full-pressure space suit worn by the two passengers on this flight, Noble's tall, lanky, athletic body was covered in a skintight suit called an EEAS, or Electronic Elastomeric Activity Suit, which performed the same functions as a traditional space suit except it used electronically controlled fibers to compress the skin instead of pressurized oxygen, so it was much easier for him to move about the cabin than it was for the others.

Noble, his mission commander and copilot, retired U.S. Marine Corps pilot Lieutenant Colonel Jessica "Gonzo" Faulkner, and the two passengers were aboard an S-19 Midnight spaceplane, the second of three versions of the United States' single-stage-to-orbit aircraft that had revolutionized space flight when the first, the S-9 Black Stallion, was made operational in 2008. Only three of the S-19s had been built, in favor of the larger experimental XS-29 Shadow spaceplanes. All versions of the spaceplanes could take off and land on runways built for commercial airliners, but each had special triple-hybrid engines that could transform from air-breathing supersonic turbofan engines to hypersonic supersonic ramjets to pure rocket engines capable of propelling the craft into Earth orbit.

Boomer walked up to the first passenger and checked him over carefully before speaking. Through his space helmet's visor he could see the passenger's eyes were closed and his hands folded on his lap. The two passengers were wearing orange Advanced Crew Escape Suits, or ACES, which were full pressure suits designed for survival in case of a loss of pressurization in the passenger compartment, or even in open space.

Yep, Boomer thought, this is one cool cucumber—his first trip into space and he was either sleeping or on the verge of it, as if he was on a wide-body airliner getting ready to take off for a vacation in Hawaii. His companion, on the other hand, looked normal for a first-time space passenger—his forehead glistened with sweat, his hands were clenched, his breathing rapid, and his eyes darted to Boomer, then out a window, then at his companion. Boomer gave him a thumbs-up and got one in return, but the man still looked very nervous.

Boomer turned back to the first passenger. "Sir?" he asked via intercom.

"Yes, Dr. Noble?" the first man replied in a low, relaxed, almost sleepy voice.

"Just checking on you, sir. The flight doc says you're *too* relaxed. You sure this is your first time in orbit?"

"I can hear what they're saying. And I don't think I'd forget my first time, Dr. Noble."

"Please call me 'Boomer,' sir."

"Thank you, I will." The man looked over at his companion, frowning at the man's obvious nervousness. "Is Ground Control worrying at all about my companion's vital signs?"

"He's normal for a Puddy," Boomer said.

"A what?"

"A Puddy—a first-time astronaut," Boomer explained. "Named after Don Puddy, the guy at NASA that used to give shuttle astronaut candidates the good news they'd been accepted to the astronaut training program. It's natural to be supernervous, even for veteran astronauts and fighter jocks—if I may say so, sir, it's kinda creepy to see someone as relaxed as you appear."

"I'll take that as a compliment, Boomer," the man said. "How long before takeoff?"

"The primary window opens in about thirty minutes," Boomer replied. "We'll finish the pretakeoff checks, and then I'll have you come up to the cockpit and take the right seat for takeoff. Colonel Faulkner will be in the jump seat between us. We'll have you go back to your seat here before we go hypersonic, but once we're in orbit you can go back up into the right seat if you wish."

"I'm perfectly happy to stay here, Boomer."

"I want you to get the full effect of what you're about to experience, and the cockpit is the best place for that, sir," Boomer said. "But the G-forces are pretty strong as we go hypersonic, and the jump seat isn't stressed for hypersonic flight. But when you unbuckle to come back up to the cockpit, sir, *that* will be a moment you'll never forget."

"We've been hooked up to oxygen for an awfully long time, Boomer," the passenger asked. "A few hours at least. Will we have to stay on oxygen on the station?"

"No, sir," Boomer replied. "Station's atmospheric pressure is a little lower than sea-level pressure on Earth or the cabin pressure on the spaceplane—you'll feel as if you're at about eight thousand feet, similar to cabin pressure on an airliner. Breathing pure oxygen will help purge inert gases out of your system so gas bubbles won't lodge in your blood vessels, muscles, your brain, or joints."

"The 'bends'? Like scuba and deep-sea divers can get?"

"Exactly, sir," Boomer said. "Once we're on station you can take it off. For those of us who do space walks, we go back to prebreathing for a few hours because the suits have an even lower pressure. Sometimes we even sleep in an airlock sealed up with pure oxygen to make sure we get a good nitrogen flush."

Takeoff was indeed thirty minutes later, and soon they were flying north over western Idaho. "Mach one, sir," Boomer radioed back on intercom. "First time going supersonic?"

"Yes," the passenger said. "I didn't feel anything abnormal."

"How about Mach two?"

"We just went *twice* the speed of sound? That quickly?"

"Yes, sir," Boomer said, the excitement obvious in his voice. "I like to loosen up the 'leopards' at the beginning of every mission—I don't want to find out at Mach ten or Mach fifteen that there might be a problem."

" 'Leopards'?"

"My nickname for the hybrid turbofan-scramjet-rocket Laser Pulse Detonation Rocket System engines, sir," Boomer explained.

"Your invention, I believe?"

"I was the lead engineer for a very large team of Air Force engineers and scientists," Boomer said. "We were like little kids in a candy store, I swear to God, even when the shit hit the fan—we treated a huge 'leopards' explosion as if we tossed a firecracker into the girls' lav in high school. But yes, my team developed the 'leopards.' One engine, three different jobs. You'll see."

Boomer slowed the Midnight spaceplane down to midsubsonic speed and turned south over Nevada a short time later, and Jessica Faulkner came back to help the passenger into the mission commander's seat on the right side of the cockpit, get strapped in, and plug her suit's umbilical cord into a receptacle, and then she unfolded a small seat between the two cockpit seats and secured herself. "How do you hear me, sir?" Faulkner asked.

"Loud and clear, Jessica," the passenger replied.

"So that was the 'first stage' of our three-stage push into orbit, sir," Boomer explained over the intercom. "We're at thirty-five thousand feet, in the troposphere. Eighty percent of Earth's atmosphere is below us, which makes it easier to accelerate when it's time to go into orbit. But our tanker has regular air-breathing turbofan engines, and he's pretty heavy with all our fuel and oxidizer, so we have to stay fairly low. We'll rendezvous in about fifteen minutes."

As promised, the modified Boeing 767 airliner emblazoned with the words SKY MASTERS AEROSPACE INC on the sides came into view, and Boomer maneuvered the Midnight spaceplane in position behind the tail and flipped a switch to open the slipway doors overhead. "Masters Seven-Six, Midnight Zero-One, precontact position, ready, 'bomb' first, please," Boomer announced on the tactical frequency.

"Roger, Midnight, Seven-Six has you stabilized precontact, we're ready with 'bomb,' cleared into contact *position, Seven-Six ready,*" a computerized female voice replied.

"Remarkable—two airplanes traveling over three hundred miles an hour, flying just a few feet away from one another," the passenger in the mission commander's seat remarked.

"Wanna know what's even more remarkable, sir?" Boomer asked. "That tanker is unmanned."

"What?"

"Sky Masters provides various contract services for the armed forces all over the world, and the vast majority of their aircraft, vehicles, and vessels are unmanned or optionally manned," Boomer explained. "There's a human pilot and boom operator in a room back at Battle Mountain, watching us via satellite video and audio feeds, but even they don't do anything unless they have to—computers do all the work, and the humans just monitor. The tanker itself isn't flown by anybody but a computer—they load a flight plan into the computer, and it flies it from start-taxi to final parking without any human pilots, like a Global Hawk reconnaissance plane. The flight plan can be changed if necessary, and it has lots of fail-safe systems in case of multiple malfunctions, but the computer flies the thing all the way from start-taxi to engine shutdown back at home base."

"Amazing," the passenger said. "Afraid your job will be given to a computer someday, Dr. Noble?"

"Hey, I'd *help* them design the thing, sir," Boomer said. "Actually, the Russians have been sending Soyuz and unmanned Progress cargo vessels up to the International Space Station for years, and they even had a copy of the space shuttle called Buran that did an entire space mission unmanned. I think I'd rather have a flight crew if I was flying into orbit on a Russian spacecraft, but in a few years the technology will be so refined that passengers would probably never notice."

As the passenger watched in absolute fascination, the spaceplane glided up under the tanker's tail, and a long boom steered by small wings lowered from under the tail down toward the spaceplane. Guided by green flashing director lights and a yellow line painted under the tanker's belly, Boomer moved forward under the tail until the green director lights went out and two red lights illuminated.

"How do you tell when you're in the right position, Boomer?" the passenger asked.

"There's a certain 'picture' between the tanker's belly and the windscreen frame that you learn to recognize," Boomer replied. "Not very scientific, but it works every time. You get a feel for it and recognize if you're too close or too far away, even at night."

"You do this *at night?*"

"Of course," Boomer said matter-of-factly. "Some missions require night ops, and of course it's always night where we're going." As he was speaking, Boomer pulled off a tiny bit of power, and all forward motion stopped. "Midnight Zero One, stabilized in contact position, ready for contact," he radioed.

"Roger, Zero One," the female-voiced computer replied. A nozzle extended from the end of the boom, and moments later they heard and felt a gentle *CL-CLUNK!* as the tanker's nozzle slid into the slipway and seated itself in the refueling receptacle. *"Showing contact,"* the computer voice reported.

"Contact confirmed," Boomer said. On intercom he said, "All I do now is follow those director lights and stay on the tanker's center line."

"If the tanker is fully computerized, shouldn't the receiver aircraft be able to do a rendezvous by computer as well?" the passenger asked.

"It can—I just prefer to fly the thing in myself," Boomer said.

"Impressing the VIP on board, right?"

"After what you'll see today, sir," Boomer said, "I and my meager flying skills will be the *least* impressive things you'll see on this flight."

"You said 'bomb,' not 'fuel,'" the passenger said. "We're not taking on fuel?"

"First we're taking on a special liquid oxidizer called *B-O-H-M*, or borohydrogen metaoxide, 'bomb'—basically, refined hydrogen peroxide," Boomer said. "Our engines use BOHM instead of liquid oxygen when we switch to pure rocket engines—it's impossible, at least with today's technology, to transfer supercooled liquid oxygen from a tanker aircraft. 'Bomb' is not as good as cryogenic oxygen, but it's much easier to handle and far less costly. We don't take on any 'bomb' before takeoff to save weight; we'll take on jet fuel last so we have the maximum for the mission."

It took over fifteen minutes to download the thick oxidizer, and another several minutes to purge the transfer system of all traces of BOHM oxidizer before switching over to begin transferring JP-8 jet fuel. Once the jet fuel began transferring to the Midnight spaceplane, Boomer was visibly relieved. "Believe it or not, sir, that was probably the most dangerous part of the flight," he said.

"What was? Transferring the BOHM?" the passenger asked.

"No—making the switch from BOHM to jet fuel in the tanker's transfer system," Boomer admitted. "They rinse the boom and plumbing with helium to flush all the 'bomb' out before the jet fuel moves through. The boron additives in the oxidizer help create a much more powerful specific impulse than regular military jet fuel, but mixing BOHM and jet fuel, even in tiny amounts, is always dangerous. Normally, the two mixed together needs a laser for ignition, but any source of heat, a spark, or even vibration of a certain frequency can set it off. The experiments we did at Sky Masters and at the Air Force test centers made for some spectacular explosions, but we learned a lot."

"Is that how you got your nickname, 'Boomer'?"

"Yes, sir. Perfection requires mistakes. I made a ton of them."

"So how do you control it in the engines?"

"The laser igniters are pulsed, anywhere from a few microseconds to several nanoseconds, to control the detonations," Boomer explained. "The stuff goes off, believe me, and it's massive, but the specific impulse lasts just an instant, so we can control the power . . ." He paused, long enough for the passenger to turn his helmeted head toward him, then added, ". . . most of the time."

They could virtually feel the second passenger in the back stiffen nervously, but the passenger in the front seat just chuckled. "I trust," he said, "that I won't feel a thing if something goes wrong, Dr. Noble?"

"Sir, an uncontrolled 'leopards' explosion is so big," Boomer said, "that you won't feel a thing . . . even in your *next* life." The passenger said nothing, but just did a big nervous "GULP."

The JP-8 transfer went much faster, and soon Colonel Faulkner was helping the front-seat passenger to get strapped into his seat in the back beside the plainly still-nervous second passenger. Soon everyone was seated and the crew was ready for the next evolution. "Our tanker is away," Boomer said, "and as planned he's dropped us off over southwestern Arizona. We'll make a turn to the east and start our acceleration. Some of the sonic boom we'll create might reach the ground and be heard below, but we try to do it over as much uninhabited area as we can to avoid irritating the neighbors. We're monitoring the flight computers as they finish all the checklists, and we'll be on our way."

"How long will it take?" the first passenger asked.

"Not long at all, sir," Boomer replied. "As we briefed on the ground, you'll have to deal with the positive G-forces for about nine minutes, but they're just a bit more than what you'd feel taking off aboard a fast bizjet, strapped into a dragster, or on a really cool roller coaster—except you'll feel them for a longer period of time. Your suit and the design of your seat will help you stay conscious—in fact, you may 'red out' a little because the seat is designed to help keep blood in your brain instead of the G-forces pulling it out, and the more pressure you get, the more blood will stay."

"How long will we have to stay in orbit before we can chase down the space station?" the passenger asked. "I've heard it sometimes takes days to link up."

"Not today, sir," Boomer said. "The beauty of the spaceplane is that we're not tied to a launch pad set on one particular location on Earth. We can make our own launch window by adjusting not only our launch time but changing our insertion angle and position relative to our target spacecraft. If we needed to, we could fly across the continent in just a couple hours, refuel again, and line up on a direct rendezvous orbit. But since we planned this flight so long ago, we could minimize the flying, gas up and go, and save fuel just by planning when to take off, when and where to refuel, and being in the right spot and right heading for orbit. By the time we finish our orbital burn and coast into our orbit, we should be right beside Armstrong Space Station, so there's no need to chase it down or use a separate Hohmann transfer orbit. Stand by, everyone, we're starting our turn."

The passengers could barely feel it, but the S-19 Midnight made a sharp turn to the east, and soon they could feel a steady pressure on their chests. As directed, they sat with arms and legs set against the seats, with no fingers or feet crossed. The first passenger looked over at his companion and saw his chest within his partial-pressure space suit rising and falling with alarming speed. "Try to relax, Charlie," he said. "Control your breathing. Try to enjoy the ride."

"How is he, sir?" Gonzo asked on intercom.

"Hyperventilating a little, I think." A few moments later, with the G-forces steadily rising, he noticed his companion's breathing became more normal. "He's looking better," he reported.

"That's because home base reports he's unconscious," Boomer said. "Don't worry—they're monitoring him closely. We'll have to watch him when he wakes up, but if he got the anti-motion-sickness shot as he was directed, he should be fine. I'd hate to have him blow chunks in his oxygen helmet."

"I could've done without that last bit of detail, Boomer," the conscious passenger said wryly.

"Sorry, sir, but that's what we have to be ready for," Boomer said. He was astonished that the passenger didn't seem to be having one bit of difficulty breathing against the G-forces, which were now exceeding two Gs and steadily increasing as they accelerated—his voice sounded as normal as back on Earth. "Battle Mountain may adjust his oxygen levels to keep him asleep until the medics are standing by."

"My home base won't like that," the passenger pointed out.

"It's for his own good, believe me, sir," Boomer said. "Okay, everybody, we're approaching Mach three and fifty thousand feet, and the 'leopards' are beginning to transform from turbofan engines to supersonic combustion ramjets, or scramjets. We call this 'spiking,' because a spike in each engine will move forward and divert the supersonic air around the turbine fans and into ducts where the air is compressed and mixed with jet fuel and then ignited. Because there are no spinning parts in a scramjet as there are in a turbofan engine, the maximum speed we can attain goes to around fifteen times the speed of sound, or about ten thousand miles an hour. The scramjets will kick in shortly. We'll inert the fuel in the fuel tanks with helium to avoid having unspent gas in the fuel tanks. Stay ahead of the Gs."

This time, Boomer did hear some grunts and deep breaths over the intercom as moments later the engines went completely into scramjet mode and the Midnight spaceplane accelerated rapidly. "Passing Mach five . . . Mach six," Boomer announced. "Everything looks good. How are you doing back there, sir?"

"Fine . . . fine, Boomer," the passenger replied, but now it was obvious that he was fighting the G-forces, clenching his stomach and leg muscles and pressurizing a lungful of air in his chest, which was supposed to slow blood flowing to the lower parts of his body and help keep it in his chest and brain to help him stay conscious. The passenger looked over at his companion. His seat had automatically reclined to about forty-five degrees, which helped his blood stay in his head since he couldn't perform the G-crunches while unconscious. "How . . . how much . . . longer?"

"I hate to break it to you, sir, but we haven't even gotten to the fun part yet," Boomer said. "The scramjets will give us the maximum velocity and altitude while still using atmospheric oxygen for fuel combustion. We want to conserve our BOHM oxidizer as long as possible. But around sixty miles' altitude— three hundred and sixty thousand feet—the air will get too thin to run the scramjets, and we'll switch to pure rocket mode. You'll feel . . . a little push then. It won't last long, but it'll be . . . noticeable. Stand by, sir. Another ninety seconds." A few moments later, Boomer reported: " 'Leopards' spiking . . . spiking complete, scramjets report full shutdown and secure. Stand by for rocket transition, crew . . . back me up on the temp and turbopump pressure gauges, Gonzo . . . standing up the power, now . . . good ignition, rockets throttling up to sixty-five percent, fuel flows in the green, throttles coming up . . ." The passenger thought he was ready for it, but the breath left his lungs with a sharp *BAARK!* at that moment . . . "Good primary ignition, nominal turbopump pressures, all temps in the green, stand by for one hundred percent power, here we go . . . ready . . . ready . . . now."

It hit like a car crash. The passenger felt his body crushed backward into his seat—thankfully the computer-controlled seat was anticipating it, simultaneously reclining, cushioning, and bracing his body weight against the sudden force. The nose of the Midnight felt as if it was aimed straight up, but that feeling lasted only a few moments, and soon he had no idea of up or down, left or right, forward or backward. For a moment he wished he was unconscious like his companion, unaware of all these strange, alien forces battering his body.

"One-six . . . one-seven . . . one-eight," Boomer announced. The passenger was not quite sure what any of that meant. "Passing four-zero . . . five-zero . . . six-zero . . ."

"Are . . . we . . . doing . . . okay, Boomer?" the passenger asked, trying with all his might to suppress the growing darkness in his vision that indicated the beginning of unconsciousness. He pretended he was a bodybuilder, flexing every muscle in his body, hoping to force enough blood into his head to keep from dropping off.

"We're in . . . in the green, sir," Boomer replied. For the first time in this entire damned flight, the passenger thought, he could detect a hint of pressure or strain in Hunter Noble's voice. His tone was still measured, still succinct and even official, but there was definitely a worried edge to it, signifying even to a newbie space voyager that the worst was yet to come.

Crap, the passenger thought, if Hunter Noble— probably America's most oft-traveled astronaut, with dozens of missions and thousands of orbits to his credit—is having trouble, what chance do *I* have? I'm getting so tired, he thought, trying to fight the damned G-forces. I'll be okay if I just relax and let the blood flow out of my brain, right? It won't hurt me. The pressure is starting to make me a little nauseous, and for God's sake I don't want to barf in my helmet. I'll just relax, relax . . .

Then, moments later, to his complete surprise the pressure ceased, as if the turnscrews on the vise that had been pressing on his entire body simply disappeared after just a few minutes. Then he heard the surprising, completely unsuspected question: "You doing okay this splendid morning back there, sir?"

The passenger was somehow able to reply with a curt and completely casual, "It's morning, Dr. Noble?"

"It's morning somewhere, sir," Boomer said. "We have a new morning every ninety minutes on station."

"How are we doing? Are we doing okay? Did we make it?"

"Check out your detail, sir," Boomer said. The passenger looked over and saw the man's arms floating about six inches above his still-unconscious, reclined body, as if he were sleeping while floating on his back in the ocean.

"We're . . . we're weightless now?"

"Technically, the acceleration of gravity toward Earth is equal to our forward velocity, so we're in effect falling but never hitting the ground. We are hurtling toward the Earth, but Earth keeps on moving out of the way before we hit it, so the net effect feels like weightlessness," Boomer said.

"Say what?"

Boomer grinned. "Sorry," he said. "I like saying that to Puddys. Yes, sir, we're weightless."

"Thank you."

"We're currently cruising past Mach twenty-five and climbing through one hundred twenty-eight miles' altitude up to our final altitude of two hundred and ten miles," Boomer went on. "Course corrections are nominal. When we stop coasting at orbital speed, we should be within ten miles of Armstrong at matching speed, altitude, and azimuth. It looks very cool, sir, very cool. Welcome to outer space. You are officially an American astronaut."

A few moments later Jessica Faulkner drifted back to the passenger cabin, her eyes still alluring behind the closed visor of her space-suit helmet. The passenger had seen plenty of astronauts floating in zero-G on television and movies, but it was as if this was the first time he had seen it in person—it was simply, utterly unreal. He noticed her movements were gentle and deliberate, as if everything she touched or was about to touch were fragile. She didn't seem to grasp anything, but she used a few fingers to lightly touch the bulkheads, ceiling, or deck to maneuver herself around.

Faulkner checked on Spellman first, checking a small electronic panel on the front of his space suit that displayed conditions in the suit and the wearer's vital signs. "He looks okay, and his suit is secure," she reported. "As long as his gyros don't tumble when he wakes up, I think he'll be fine." She drifted over to the first passenger and gave him a very pretty smile. "Welcome to orbit, sir. How do you feel?"

"It was pretty rough when the rockets kicked in—I thought I was going to pass out," he replied with a weak smile. "But I'm doing all right now."

"Good. Let's get you unbuckled, and then you can join Boomer in the cockpit for the approach. He might even let you dock it."

"*Dock the spaceplane?* To the space station? *Me?* I can't fly! I haven't hardly driven a *car* in almost eight years!"

Faulkner was unstrapping the passenger from his seat, using tabs of Velcro to keep the webbing from floating around in front of them. "Do you play video games, sir?" she asked.

"Sometimes. With my son."

"It's just a video game—the controls are almost identical to game controllers that have been around for years," she said. "In fact, the guy who designed them, Jon Masters, probably did that on purpose—he was a video-game nut. Besides, Boomer is a good instructor.

"Now, the secret to maneuvering around in free fall is remembering although you don't have the effects of gravity, you still have mass and acceleration, and those need to be counteracted very carefully, or else you'll end up pinging off the walls," Faulkner said. "Remember that it's not the weightless feeling you feel floating in the ocean, where you can paddle to move about—here, every directional movement can be countered only by opposing the acceleration of mass with opposite and *equal* force.

"Once we're on station, we use Velcro shoes and patches on our clothes to help secure ourselves, but we don't have those yet, so you'll have to learn the hard way," she went on. "Very easy, gentle movements. I like to just *think* about moving first. If you don't consciously think about a movement before you do it, you'll launch yourself into the ceiling when your major muscles get involved. If you just *think* about getting up, you'll involve more minor muscles. You'll have to overcome your mass to start moving, but remember that gravity isn't going to help you reverse directions. Try it."

The passenger did as she suggested. Instead of using his legs and hands to push up off the seat, he merely thought about getting up, with light touches of a few fingers of one hand on a handhold or seat armrest . . . and to his surprise, he started to float gently off the seat. "Hey! It worked!" he exclaimed.

"Very good, sir," Faulkner said. "Feel okay? The first time in zero-G upsets a lot of stomachs."

"I'm fine, Jessica."

"The balance organs in your ears will soon have no 'up' or 'down' direction and will start feeding your brain signals that won't correspond to anything you see or feel," Faulkner explained. The passengers had been briefed on all this back home, but they had not undergone any other astronaut training such as simulated zero-G work underwater. "It'll be a little worse once you get to station. A little nausea is normal. Work through it."

"I'm fine, Jessica," the passenger repeated. His eyes were as wide as a young child's on Christmas morning. "My God, this feels incredible—and incredibly weird at the same time."

"You're doing fine, sir. Now, what I'm going to do is step aside and let you maneuver yourself toward the cockpit. I could try to guide you into your seat, but if I'm not perfectly aligned and not applying the right amount and direction of force, I'll spin you out of control, so it's better if you can do it. Again, just *think* about moving. No hurry."

Her suggestions worked. The passenger completely relaxed his body and faced the hatch connecting the cockpit with the passenger cabin, and barely touching anything, he started to drift toward the hatch, with Boomer watching his slow progress over his right shoulder, a pleased smile visible though the visor of his oxygen helmet. In no time, the passenger had floated right up to the cockpit hatch.

"You're a natural at this, sir," Boomer said. "Now Gonzo will unhook your umbilical cord from the passenger seat and hand it up to me, and I'll plug it into the mission commander's seat receptacle. You need to gently hold on to the hatch while we get you hooked back on. Again, don't kick or push anything—gentle touches." The passenger heard and felt the tiny puffs of conditioned air in his partial-pressure suit shut off, and soon the umbilical hose appeared. Boomer reached across the cockpit and plugged it in. "Hear me okay, sir? Feel the air-conditioning okay?"

"Yes and yes."

"Good. Getting into the seat is the tricky part, because it's a kinda tight fit. The technique is to slowly, carefully, bend at the waist and lift your thighs toward your chest, like you're doing a stomach crunch. Gonzo and I will maneuver you over the center console and into your seat. Don't try to help us. Okay, go ahead." The passenger did exactly as he was told, curling his body slightly, and with only a few unexpected bumps and swerves he was over the very wide center console and into the seat, and Faulkner fastened his lap and shoulder straps for him.

"Are you sure we didn't pass each other in the hallways at NASA astronaut training in Houston, sir?" Boomer asked, his smile visible through his oxygen helmet's visor. "I know veteran astronauts who get all hot, sweaty, and grumpy doing what you just did. Very good. Here's your reward for all that work." And he motioned outside the cockpit . . .

. . . and for the first time, the passenger saw it: planet Earth spread out before him. Even through the relatively narrow cockpit windows, it was still marvelous to behold. "It's . . . it's incredible . . . beautiful . . . my God," he breathed. "I've seen all the photos of Earth taken from space, but they just don't compare with seeing it myself. It's magnificent!"

"Worth all the hoops you had to jump through to get up here, sir?" Gonzo asked.

"I'd do it a hundred times over just to get the chance," the passenger said. "It's extraordinary! Damn, I'm running out of adjectives!"

"Then this is a good time to get back to work," Boomer said, "because things will be getting a little busy here. Take a look."

The passenger looked . . . and saw their destination in astonishing splendor. It was almost thirty years old, mostly built of 1970s technology, and even to an untrained eye it was starting to show signs of age despite minor but fairly consistent upgrading, but it still looked amazing.

"Armstrong Space Station, named after the late Neil Armstrong, of course, the first man to step foot on the surface of the moon, but everyone who's anyone calls it Silver Tower," Boomer said. "It started out as a semiclassified Air Force program, combining and improving on the Skylab space-station project and President Ronald Reagan's Space Station Freedom project. Freedom eventually became the American contribution to the International Space Station, and Skylab was abandoned and allowed to reenter and burn up in Earth's atmosphere, but the military-funded space-station program kept going in relative secrecy—as secret as you can keep a three-billion-dollar monstrosity like this that orbits the earth. It's basically four Skylabs connected together and attached to a central truss, with enlarged solar arrays and improved docking, sensors, and maneuvering systems, tailored more to military applications than to scientific research."

"It looks fragile—kinda spindly, like those modules will fall off any second."

"It's as strong as it needs to be up here in free fall," Boomer said. "It's certainly not as sturdy as a building that size on Earth, but then again, it doesn't need to be. All of the modules have small computer-controlled thrusters that move all the pieces together, because station revolves around its axis to keep antennas pointed toward Earth."

"The silver coating is really supposed to protect against ground-based lasers?" the passenger asked. "Has it ever been hit by a laser? I've heard Russia hits it with a laser every chance they get."

"It gets hit all the time, and not just from Russia," Boomer said. "So far it doesn't seem to have done any damage; the Russians claim they are just using lasers to monitor station's orbit. Turns out the silver material—aluminized spray-on polyimide—is good protection against micrometeorites, solar wind, and cosmic particles as well as lasers, and it's a good insulator. But the best part for me is being able to see station from Earth when the sun hits it just right—it's the brightest object in the sky except for the sun and moon, and can sometimes be seen in daytime, and can sometimes even produce shadows at night."

"Why do you call it 'station' instead of 'the station'?" the passenger asked. "I've heard a lot of you guys say it that way."

Boomer shrugged against his seat harness. "I don't know—someone started saying it that way in the first months of Skylab, and it stuck," he said. "I know most of us think of it as more than just a collection of modules or even as a workplace—it's more like an important or favorite destination. It's like I might say, 'I'm going to Tahoe.' 'I'm going to station' or 'I'm going to Armstrong' just sounds . . . right."

As they got closer to the station, the passenger motioned toward the station. "What are those round things on each of the modules?" he asked.

"Lifeboats," Boomer replied. "Simple aluminum spheres that can be sealed up and jettisoned away from station in case of an accident. Each holds five persons and has enough air and water to last about a week. They can't reenter the atmosphere, but they're designed to fit inside the cargo bay of any of the spaceplanes, or they can be towed to the International Space Station and the survivors transferred. Every module has one; the Galaxy module, which is the combination galley, exercise room, entertainment room, and medical clinic, has two lifeboats."

He pointed to the lowermost center module, smaller than the others and attached to the "bottom" of the lower center module, pointing Earthward. "So that's Vice President Page's creation, eh?"

"That's it, sir: the XSL-5 'Skybolt,'" Boomer said. "A free-electron laser with a klystron, or electron amplifier, powered by a magnetohydrodynamic generator."

"A what?"

"Power for station is generated mostly by solar cells or by hydrogen fuel cells," Boomer explained, "neither of which produces enough power for a multimegawatt-class laser. A nuclear reactor on Earth uses the heat from the fission reaction to produce steam to turn a turbine generator, which is not doable on a space station because the turbine would act like a gyroscope and upset station's steering and alignment systems—even the flywheels on our exercise bikes do that. The MHD is like a turbine-style power generator, but instead of spinning magnets producing an electron flow, the MHD uses plasma spinning within a magnetic field. The power generated by the MHD is massive, and the MHD generator has no moving or spinning parts that can affect station's orbit."

"But the catch is . . . ?"

"Creating plasma requires heating ion-producing substances to high temperatures, far past the steam state," Boomer said. "In space, there's only one way to produce that level of heat, and that's with a small nuclear reactor. Naturally, a lot of people are wary of nuclear anything, and that goes double if it's flying overhead."

"But nuclear reactors have been orbiting Earth for decades, right?"

"The MHD generator was America's first nuclear reactor in space in twenty years, and is by far much more powerful than anything else up here," Boomer replied. "But the Soviets had launched almost three dozen satellites that used small nuclear reactors to generate electricity using thermocouples until the USSR went broke. They never squawked about their nuclear reactors, but when the USA launched one MHD generator after the USSR canceled their program, they go berserk. Typical. And they're still squawking, even though we haven't fired Skybolt in aeons."

The passenger studied the Skybolt module for a moment, then remarked, "Ann Page designed all that."

"Yes, sir," Boomer said. "She was just a young female whippersnapper engineer and physicist when she produced the plans for Skybolt. No one took her seriously. But President Reagan wanted a 'Star Wars' missile defense shield, and he had scared up the money, and Washington was frantically looking for programs to start up so they could spend all that money before it went to some other program. Dr. Page's plans got into the right hands at the right time; she got the money, and they built Skybolt and stuck it on Armstrong in record time. Skybolt was Dr. Page's baby. She even talked her way into attending partial astronaut training so she could go up in the shuttle to supervise installation. They say she lost thirty pounds of 'executive spread' in order to be chosen for astronaut training, and she never put it back on. When her baby said its first words, it shook the world."

"And that was almost thirty years ago. Amazing."

"It's still state of the art, but if we had the funds, we could probably improve it considerably in efficiency and accuracy."

"But we *could* reactivate Skybolt now, couldn't we?" the passenger asked. "Improve it, modernize it, yes, but load it up with fuel and fire it now, or in fairly short order?"

Boomer turned and regarded his passenger for a moment with some surprise. "You're serious about all this, aren't you, sir?" he finally asked.

"You bet I am, Dr. Noble," the passenger replied. "You bet I am."

A few minutes later they had moved within a few hundred yards of Armstrong Space Station. Boomer noted the passenger's eyes growing bigger and bigger as they closed in. "Kinda feels like you're in a tiny rowboat paddling up beside an aircraft carrier, doesn't it?"

"That's *exactly* what it feels like, Boomer."

Boomer unstowed a wireless device that actually did resemble a familiar console game controller and positioned it in front of the passenger. "Ready to do more than be a passenger, sir?" he asked.

"You're serious? You want *me* to fly this thing up to the space station?"

"We *could* let it drive in automatically, and the computers do a fine job, but where's the fun in that?" He repositioned the controller over in front the passenger. "I have a feeling you'll do fine."

He entered commands into a keyboard on the center console, and a target appeared on the windscreen in front of the passenger. "The right control moves the spaceplane forward, backward, and side to side—we don't bank like an aircraft, but just move laterally," Boomer went on. "The left control is a little different: twisting the knob yaws the spacecraft around its center, so you can point the nose in a different direction than the spaceplane's direction of travel; and you can adjust the spaceplane's vertical position by pulling up on the knob to go upward vertically, or push down to move downward. Manipulating the controls activates thrusters—tiny rocket engines—positioned all around the spaceplane. Normally we would pay close attention to how much fuel we use for the thrusters to do a docking—another reason why the powers that be prefer we use the computer for docking, since it's generally better and more fuel-efficient at docking than us mere mortals—but for this trip we loaded plenty of extra fuel on station so we can top the tanks before we leave and everything is cool.

"So, sir, your task is to manipulate the controls to keep the aiming reticle you see before you centered on the docking target on station, which is that big 'zero' you see on the docking module. As you close in, director lights will flash and you'll see more hints on what to do. Big mention here: Remember that station rotates along its long axis once every ninety minutes, so the antennas and windows are always pointed toward Earth as it orbits, but as long as you follow the director signals it will compensate for that. Remember also that not only do you need to spear the target, but you need to align the spaceplane as directed by the director lights, and you also need to control your forward speed so you don't ram the space station and break Midnight, which would be bad for all involved."

"I'll try not to do that," the passenger said weakly.

"Thank you, sir. As Jessica instructed you when moving yourself around in zero-G, gross movements are bad, and slight movements and corrections are good. We have found that *thinking* about a movement is usually enough to activate a measured, proper minor-muscle response. You seemed to have that concept well in hand when getting into your seat this morning, so I have full confidence that you will be able to do the same when maneuvering our spaceplane for docking." The passenger responded with a very noticeable nervous swallow.

"Your director indicators are telling you that you are closing at twelve inches per second, you are thirty yards low, ten yards right, range one hundred thirty-three yards, and sixteen degrees left of course for alignment," Boomer went on. "When we get within fifty yards we'll gradually decrease the closure rate so at five yards we'll be less than three inches per second. You need to get within less than one degree in yaw and dead-on in heading and altitude and less than one inch per second to plug the bull's-eye, or we'll abort the approach and try again."

"Want to warn the station, Boomer?" Faulkner asked on intercom. She was now seated on the jumpseat between Boomer and the passenger.

"I think we'll be fine, Gonzo," Boomer replied.

Boomer could see the passenger swallow nervously, even through his space suit and helmet. "Maybe we'd better not . . ." he said.

"I think you'll do fine, sir," Boomer repeated. "You have the touch."

Boomer noticed the passenger straightening his body and gripping the controller even firmer than before, and he put a hand on his left arm. "Wait, sir," he said. "Wait. Just wait. Take a deep breath, then exhale slowly. Seriously. Take a deep breath, sir." Boomer waited until he could hear the passenger take a deep breath then let it out. "Very good. The key to this maneuver is visualization. Visualize the approach before you even touch the controls. Visualize what the controls will do when you touch and activate them.

Can you visualize what each control and input will do? If you can't, don't activate it. Positively determine long before you make a move that what you are about to contemplate doing is what you really want to do. Map it out in your mind before you hit any switch. Never be surprised by what happens when you press a switch. Expect that whatever happens when you press a switch is *exactly* what you intended to do; and if it's not, identify *immediately* why it didn't happen the way you wanted it, and *fix it*. But don't overreact. All reactions and counterreactions should be deliberate, measured, and intentional. You should know *why* you are moving a thruster, not just *where* and *how much*. Let's do it, sir."

The passenger responded . . . by doing exactly nothing, which was in Boomer's opinion the best thing to do. The Midnight was already coasting to a nearly perfect rendezvous, and the passenger was very much aware that the technology that had gotten him this far was probably far better than were his own meager powers to complete, so he wisely decided to let the automated maneuver complete its evolution, study what extra needed to be done—if anything—and then complete it, if he could.

Armstrong Space Station loomed closer and closer to the spaceplane Midnight, filling the tiny, narrow windscreen with its impressive bulk and obliterating all other visual inputs . . . except the important ones, which were the computer-generated images on the multifunction display in front of both the aircraft commander and passenger. The proper alignment with the dock on the space station was apparent—it was which controls to touch and adjust to correct the spaceplane's movements that required some consideration.

"I can't start the spaceplane's lateral motion," the passenger mumbled, the frustration evident in his voice. "I keep on hitting the switch, but nothing happens."

"The correction you applied is in there—you just need to let it happen, sir," Boomer said. His voice began to sound less military and more like a shaman or spiritual guide. "Nice, easy, gentle, smooth inputs. Remember: Even one little twitch of your thumb on the vernier controls generates hundreds of pounds of rocket thrust that alters the orbit of a spacecraft weighing hundreds of thousands of pounds, traveling at over twenty-five times the speed of sound hundreds of miles above Earth. Visualize the movement of the spacecraft, and visualize the corrective actions necessary to correct the flight path, then apply the necessary control inputs. Reacting without thinking is evil. Take command."

The passenger took his hands off the controls, letting the controller float before him on its tether, and he closed his eyes and took a couple of deep breaths. When he opened them, he found that all of the inputs he had entered were indeed starting to register. "How about that?" he murmured. "I'm not a complete moron."

"You're doing great, sir," Boomer said. "Remember there's no atmosphere or roadway to create friction, and gravity would take several dozen orbits to take effect, so whatever corrections you put in have to be taken out. These readouts here tell you how much correction you applied and in what direction, which is how much you need to take out. Also remember how long it took for your inputs to apply, so that will give you an accurate gauge about when to take them out."

The passenger was definitely in the zone now. With the controller in his lap, oriented the same way as the spaceplane itself, he barely touched the knobs with his fingertips. As they closed in on the bull's-eye, the forward speed ever so slightly decreased, so by the time the crosshairs hit the bull's-eye, forward speed had almost reached zero inches per second.

"Contact," Boomer announced. The passenger's shoulders visibly relaxed, and he let the controller float from his fingers. "Latches secure. The spaceplane is docked. Congratulations, sir."

"Don't do that to me again, would you mind, Dr. Noble?" the passenger asked, looking up and taking several relieved breaths of air, then releasing the hand controller as if it was a piece of radioactive weaponry. "All I could think about was crashing and all of us being stranded in orbit."

Boomer held up another controller, identical to the first. "I had your back, sir," he said with a smile. "But you did excellent—I didn't touch anything. I didn't tell you this, but we normally need at least zero-point-three feet per second forward speed to get the docking mechanism to latch—they latched for you with less than that."

"That's not going to relax my nerves any, Boomer."

"Like I said, sir, you have the touch," Boomer said. "Gonzo is going to get us ready to transfer to station. She'll get your companion ready first, and some crewmembers from station will transfer him first, and then we'll go. Normally we'd seal off the airlock from the cockpit while we get the transfer tunnel in place, in case there's a leak or damage, but everyone's in a space suit, so even if there's an accident or malfunction, we'll be all right."

Boomer and the passenger turned and watched as Faulkner produced a checklist, attached it to a bulkhead with Velcro, and got to work. "The Midnight spaceplane has a small cargo bay, larger than the S-9

Black Stallion's but not anywhere near as large as the space shuttle, but it was never really designed for docking or carrying cargo or passengers—it really was just a technology demonstrator," Boomer explained. "We turned it into a workhorse later on. In front of the passenger module is an airlock that allows us to dock with Armstrong or the International Space Station and to transfer personnel or cargo back and forth without having to go into space."

"Go into space?" the passenger repeated. He pointed out the cockpit windows. "You mean, you had to *go out there* to get on the station?"

"That was the only way to get to the space station in the S-9 Black Stallion and early S-19 Midnight," Boomer said. "Sky Masters designed the airlock between the cockpit and cargo-bay with the pressurized transfer tunnel system, so now it's easier to get from the spaceplane to station. The S-9 is too small for an airlock, so transferring means a spacewalk. It's a short and sweet spacewalk. It wasn't far, but it was sure spectacular."

"Cargo-bay doors coming open," Gonzo reported. They could hear a gentle rumble on the spaceplane's hull. "Doors fully open."

"Looks like your cargo-bay doors are fully open, Boomer," a voice said on intercom. "Welcome to Armstrong."

"Thank you, sir," Boomer replied. To the passenger he said, "That's Trevor Shale, the station manager. All of the personnel on Armstrong Space Station right now are contractors, although just about all are prior military, with lots of experience in space operations, and about half have worked on station in the past. We open the cargo-bay doors to vent excess heat from the spaceplane." On intercom he said, "Pretty good docking approach, wouldn't you say, sir?"

"Don't get a cramp patting yourself on the back, Boomer," Shale radioed.

"It wasn't me or Gonzo: it was our passenger."

There was a long, rather uncomfortable pause; then, Shale responded with a wooden, "Roger that."

"He didn't sound pleased," the passenger observed.

"Trevor didn't like the idea of you docking Midnight, sir," Boomer admitted. "The station director, General Kai Raydon, retired Air Force, approved the idea; they left it up to me."

"I would think that overruling your station manager would not be a good thing, Boomer."

"Sir, I think I know and understand the reason why you're doing all this," Boomer said as he monitored the progress of attaching the transfer tunnel to the airlock. "You're here to prove an important point, and I am all for that. It's a tremendous risk, but a risk I think needs to be taken. If you're willing to do it, I'm willing to do as much as I can to water your eyes, and thereby water the eyes of the world. If I may say, sir, I just need you to have the courage to tell the world what you did on this trip and what you've seen, over and over and over again, in every possible venue, all around the world. Your words will ignite the world to the excitement of space travel far more than mine could ever do." The passenger thought about that for a moment, then nodded.

"Transfer tunnel connected and secure," Gonzo reported. "Sealing the airlock."

"So Gonzo is in the airlock by herself, sealed off from the cockpit and the passenger module?" the passenger asked. "Why do you do that?"

"So we don't depressurize the entire spaceplane in case the tunnel fails or isn't sealed properly," Boomer replied.

"But then Gonzo . . . ?"

"She's in a partial-pressure suit and could probably survive the loss of pressure," Boomer said, "but she and Mr. Spellman would have to spacewalk to get to the station, which she's done many times in training, but of course Mr. Spellman would have to endure on his own. It's hazardous, but she's done it before. Mr. Spellman would probably survive it just fine—he's a pretty healthy dude . . ."

"Jesus," the passenger said. "It boggles the mind to think of how many things can go wrong."

"We work through it and make improvements all the time, and train, train, train, and then train some more," Boomer said. "But you just have to accept the fact that it's a dangerous game we're playing."

"Clear for station unseal," Shale said.

"Roger. Armstrong, Midnight ready for station-side unseal," Boomer said. He pointed at the instrument panel's multifunction display, which showed air pressure in the spaceplane, on the station's docking module, and now inside the transfer tunnel linking the two. The tunnel pressure read zero . . . and just then, the pressure inside the tunnel slowly began to rise. It took almost ten minutes for the tunnel to fully pressurize. Everyone watched for any sign of the pressure dropping, indicating a leak, but it held steady.

"Pressure's holding, Boomer," Shale reported.

"I concur," Boomer said. "Everyone ready to equalize?"

"I'm good, Boomer," Gonzo replied. "The second passenger is too."

"Clear to open her up, Gonzo."

They felt a slight pressure in their ears as the spaceplane's higher cabin pressure equalized with the station's slightly lower pressure, but it wasn't painful and lasted just an instant. A moment later: "Transfer hatches open, second passenger on his way through."

"Copy that, Gonzo," Boomer said. He started to unstrap from his seat. "I'll unstrap first, sir," he told his passenger, "and then I'll get into the airlock while you unstrap, and I'll steer you out and up." The passenger nodded but said nothing; Boomer noticed a rather distant expression on the first passenger's face and wondered what he was thinking about so hard. The hard stuff was done—all he had to do now was float around the big station, look around, and be a space tourist until it was time to go home.

But after Boomer unfastened his lap and shoulder restraints and was about to float out of his seat, the passenger held his arm. "I want to do it, Boomer," he said.

"Do what, sir?"

The passenger looked at Boomer, then motioned out the right side of the cockpit with a nod of his head. "Out. That way."

The passenger could see Boomer's eyes flash through his helmet in disbelief, even alarm, but soon a pleased smile spread across his face. "You really want to do it, sir?" he asked incredulously.

"Boomer, I'm doing several incredibly amazing things today," the passenger said, "but I know that I'll be mad at myself if I return to Earth having passed it up. We've done enough of that oxygen prebreathing, haven't we? There's no danger of getting the 'bends,' is there?"

"Sir, a case of decompression sickness might be the *least* hazardous aspect of a spacewalk," Boomer said, his mind racing through the checklist in his head to see what might prohibit this. "But to answer your question: yes, we've been prebreathing pure oxygen for over four hours, so we should be good." He clicked open the ship-to-station intercom. "General Raydon? He wants to do it. Right now. Out the cockpit and through the station's airlock, not the tunnel."

"Stand by, Boomer," replied a different voice.

"That's the second guy on station that seems exasperated talking with you, Boomer," the passenger observed once again with a smile.

"Believe it or not, sir, we talked about this too," Boomer said. "We truly wanted you to have the full experience. That's why we put you in a full ACES advanced crew escape system space suit instead of a more comfortable partial-pressure suit—it's rated for short EVAs, or extra-vehicular activities. You sure your folks back at home base will like what you're about to do?"

"They may not like it at all, Boomer," the passenger said, "but they're down there, and I'm up here.

Let's do it." As if signaling concurrence, a moment later a mechanical arm extended from a hatch on another side of the docking module, carrying a device resembling a ski-lift chair and two cables in a mechanical claw.

Boomer flipped a few switches, then checked his passenger's space-suit fittings and readouts before giving him a pat on the shoulder and a confident, approving nod. "I like the cut of your jib, sir," he said. "Here we go." Boomer hit the final switch, and with several loud, heavy *SNAPs* and a loud whir of motors, the canopies on both sides of the cockpit of the S-19 Midnight spaceplane opened wide.

Before the passenger could realize it, Boomer was up and out of his seat, floating completely free of the spaceplane with only one thin strap securing him to anything, looking like some kind of unearthly Peter Pan in his skintight space suit and oxygen helmet. He grasped one of the cables on the remote-controlled arm and plugged it into his suit. "I'm back up," he said. "Ready to come down." The robot arm lowered Boomer level with the outside of the passenger's side of the cockpit. "I'm going to disconnect you from the ship, connect you to me and to the hoist, and plug you into this umbilical, sir," Boomer said. In a flash it was done. "All set. How do you hear?"

"Loud and clear, Boomer," the passenger replied.

"Good." Boomer helped the passenger up and out of his seat, which was much easier than getting in because it was now completely open. "We can't stay out long because we're not very well protected from microme-teorites, cosmic radiation, temperature extremes, and all that happy space stuff, but it'll be a fun ride while it lasts. Umbilicals are clear, Armstrong. Ready to hoist." The robot arm began to slowly pull them up and away from the spaceplane, and then the passenger found himself floating free in space over and above the dock-ing module . . .

. . . and within moments, the entire structure of Armstrong Space Station was spread out before them, gleaming in reflected sunlight. They could see the entire length of the structure, see the large laboratory, living, mechanical, and storage modules both above and below the truss, and the endless expanses of solar cells at both ends of the truss that seemed to spread out to infinity—he could even see persons looking at them through large observation windows on some of the modules. "Oh . . . my . . . God," the passenger breathed. "It's beautiful!"

"It is, but that ain't nothing," Boomer said. He grasped the back of the passenger's space suit and pulled him so he pivoted down . . .

. . . and the passenger got his newest glimpse of planet Earth below them. They could all hear him gasp in utter wonderment. "Good Lord!" he exclaimed. "It's incredible! It's magnificent! I can see almost the entire continent of South America down there! My God! It looks totally different than through the cockpit windows—I can really sense the altitude now."

"I think he likes it, General Raydon," Boomer said. He let the passenger marvel at planet Earth for about another minute, floating free of the harness; then said, "We don't dare stay out here any longer, sir. Reel us in, Armstrong." With the passenger still facing toward Earth, the robot arm began to retract back toward the space station, pulling the two men along. Boomer pulled the passenger upright just before arriving at a large hatch. He floated up to the hatch, unlocked and opened it, floated into the opening, secured himself with a strap to the inside of the airlock, attached another strap to the passenger, and carefully maneuvered him inside the station's airlock. Boomer detached them both from the umbilicals, released them outside, then closed and dogged the hatch. He hooked himself and the passenger up to umbilicals in the airlock while waiting for the pressure to equalize, but the passenger was absolutely dumbstruck and said not a word, even after the interior airlock door opened. Technicians helped the passenger remove his space suit, and Boomer motioned to the airlock exit.

As soon as the passenger exited the airlock, Kai Raydon, a trim, athletically built man with silver crew-cut hair, chisel-cut facial features, and intense, light blue eyes, snapped to attention, adjusted a wireless headset microphone to his lips, and spoke: "Attention on Armstrong Station, this is the director, all personnel be advised, the president of the United States of America, Kenneth Phoenix, is aboard station." Raydon, station manager Trevor Shale, Jessica Faulkner, and several other space-station personnel stood at attention, as best they could while looping their toes under footholds, as ruffles and flourishes and then "Hail to the Chief" played on the station's public-address system.

TWO

*The fear of death is more to be
dreaded than death itself.*
—PUBLILIUS SYRUS

ARMSTRONG SPACE STATION

"As you were, ladies and gentlemen," President Kenneth Phoenix said when the music ended. "I'd kiss the deck if I knew which way it was." The assembled station personnel laughed, applauded, and cheered for several long moments.

"I'm Kai Raydon, station director, Mr. President," Kai said, floating over to Phoenix and shaking hands. "Welcome to Armstrong Space Station, and congratulations on having the courage to be the first sitting head of state to travel in Earth orbit, and now being the first sitting head of state to do a spacewalk. How are you feeling, sir?"

"I'm completely blown away, General Raydon," Phoenix said. "I've seen and done things I've only dreamed of doing, thanks to you and your people. Thank you for giving me this incredible opportunity."

"We gave you the opportunity, as we have with every president since Kevin Martindale, but *you* chose to take it," Kai said. "A lot of folks are saying this is all a political stunt, but the bravery you've shown today clearly tells me it's a lot more than politics." He turned to those beside him. "May I present the station manager Trevor Shale, the operations chief Valerie Lukas, and of course you've met Jessica Faulkner, our head of flight operations." The president shook their hands, at the same time finding it wasn't easy to do while in zero-G—the simple gesture threatened to launch him up against the ceiling.

"Dr. Noble and Colonel Faulkner did an excellent job getting me up here, General Raydon," the president said. "Spectacular trip. Where is Dr. Noble?"

"He has a little bit of flight planning to do for your return, sir, and he is also supervising spaceplane refueling and servicing," Raydon said. "Boomer is director of aerospace development at Sky Masters Aerospace, which is the prime contractor for Armstrong Space Station, and he probably has work to do for them, too. He is also the company's chief spaceplane pilot, and he has six students going through his training program. He's a busy boy."

"Knowing him, Mr. President, he's probably taking a nap," Jessica interjected with a smile. "He likes to make himself out to be the cool space jock, but he's been planning the flights and checking the spacecraft for this visit for a week."

"Well, his work paid off," the president said. "Thank you all for an amazing trip."

"We have about an hour before your broadcast, so we have time for a tour and a light refreshment if you'd like."

"A tour would be great, General Raydon," Phoenix said. "But first I'd like to check on Agent Spellman, my Secret Service detail."

"Trev?" Raydon asked.

"Got it," Shale said, putting a wireless mic to his lips. A moment later: "Agent Spellman is awake in sick bay, sir," Shale responded. "Unfortunately he's not handling unusual Gs very well. Physically he was the top-qualifying member of your detail who volunteered to go with you on this mission, Mr. President, but there's no direct correlation between athletic abilities and your ability to operate with abnormal pressures and kinesthetic sensations on your body. We'll have to consult the aerospace medical team to find out how best to get him back to Earth. I don't believe we've ever taken a completely unconscious person through reentry before."

"He's the real mark of courage on this mission," Phoenix said. "Volunteering for this was way beyond the call, and that's saying a lot for the Secret Service. Let me go visit him first, and then the tour if there's time."

Raydon led the way through the connecting tunnel to the first module. "I'm sure Boomer and Jessica explained moving about in free fall to you in depth, sir," Raydon said. "You'll see some of the more experienced crewmembers flying around the larger modules like Superman, but for the newcomers, I have found that using one or two fingers to push yourself around, using the handholds and footholds, and taking it nice and slow works best."

"I'm sure I'll have a few bruises to show off when I get home," Phoenix said.

They emerged from the connecting tunnel into what appeared to be a circular wall of cabinets, with a circular passageway through the middle. "This is the storage and processing module," Raydon explained. "Follow me." He gently floated up through the center passageway, using handholds on the edge of the cabinets, and the president and the others followed. The president soon found a dozen circular rows of cabinets arrayed through the module, like pineapple slices in a can, with large man-sized gaps between them. "Supplies are brought in through the airlocks on the upper and lower ends, assembled or processed as necessary, and stored here. The sick bay is in the module above us."

"I'm starting to get a little dizzy from all the references to 'up' and 'above,'" the president admitted. "I have no sensation of either."

"'Up' and 'down' refer to the direction you happen to want to go," Faulkner said. "You can have two crewmembers side by side, but one will be pointing one way, and the other another way, so it's all relative. We use every surface of the modules for work, so you'll see astronauts 'hanging' from the ceilings while others are working on the 'floor,' although 'ceiling' and 'floor' are of course completely relative."

"You're not helping my vertigo, Gonzo."

"Let us know if your dizziness starts to physically manifest itself, sir," Jessica said. "Unfortunately, it's something that takes time getting used to, and you won't be here that long. As we said, it's not unusual at all to start experiencing some queasiness shortly after moving around in free fall."

"I'm fine, Jessica," the president said, but this time he wondered how long that would last.

On their way to Galaxy, the combination galley, exercise, study, clinic, and entertainment module, the president stopped several times to shake hands with station personnel, and the stopping and restarting greatly helped his maneuvering skills. Although Raydon had announced that the president was aboard, most of the technicians he met seemed absolutely shocked to see him. "Why do some of the men and women aboard the station seem surprised to see me, General?" Phoenix finally asked.

"Because I chose not to inform the crew until I did just as you came through the airlock, sir," Raydon replied. "Only myself, Trevor, the Secret Service, a few officials at Sky Masters Aerospace, and the Midnight spaceplane flight and ground crew knew. I felt security was paramount for this event, and it's too easy for station personnel to communicate with Earth. I expect the messages to family and friends to be spiking soon, but by the time word gets out, you'll be on TV worldwide."

"And the time of your address was chosen so when you made your broadcast, you would not be in range of any known Russian or Chinese antisatellite weapons for several orbits," Trevor Shale said.

The president's eyes widened in surprise—that revelation definitely got his attention. *"Antisatellite weapons?"* he asked, astonished.

"We know of at least a half-dozen sites in northwestern and eastern Russia and three sites in China, sir," Raydon said. "This station has self-defense weapons—short-range chemical lasers and missiles—but the Kingfisher antiballistic-missile and anti-antisatellite systems in Earth orbit aren't yet fully operational again, so the spaceplane had no protection, and we didn't want to take any chances."

"Why wasn't I told about this!" the president exclaimed.

"It was my call, sir," Raydon said. "Frankly, in my opinion, the threat from antisatellite weapons is far down the list of the life-threatening dangers you face on this mission—I didn't want to give you anything more to think about." The president tried to say something, but his mouth only wordlessly opened. "By the time you depart, you'll be in range of just one site," Raydon went on, "and Boomer is planning the deorbit path of the spaceplane to avoid most of the others. You'll be as safe from antisatellite weapons as we can make you."

"You mean, you have been planning for this trip on the assumption that some foreign government would actually try to attack the spaceplane or the space station while I'm aboard them?" Trevor and Raydon's silence and expressions gave Phoenix his answer. The president could do nothing else but shake his head for several moments, staring at a spot on the bulkhead, but then he looked at Raydon with a wry smile. "Are there any *other* threats I haven't been told about, General Raydon?" he asked.

"Yes, sir—the list is longer than my arm," Raydon said directly. "But I was notified that the president of the United States wanted to visit Armstrong Space Station, and I was ordered to make it happen, and we succeeded. If my orders were to attempt to deter you from coming up here, I think I could have delivered a very long list of very real threats to your family, your administration, and to members of Congress that would have succeeded in getting this mission canceled as well." He motioned to the end of the connecting tunnel. "This way, Mr. President."

Unlike the storage and processing module and the tiny spaceplane cockpit and passenger module, the Galaxy module was light, warm, and airy. The walls of the module were lined with a variety of stand-up desks and pub-style tables with the ubiquitous footholds, many computer monitors and laptops, exercise bicycles, and even a dart board. But the greatest numbers of station personnel were clustered around a three-by-five-foot picture window, snapping pictures and pointing at Earth. A large computer monitor showed what part of Earth the space station was overflying, and another screen showed a list of names that had reserved a space at the window for taking pictures of their hometown area or some other Earth landmark.

"Highly trained and skilled astronauts who had to work their tails off to get up here—and their main form of entertainment is looking out the window?" the president remarked.

"That, and sending e-mails and doing video chats with folks back home," Raydon said. "We do a lot of video chat sessions with schools, colleges, academies, Scouts, and ROTC and Civil Air Patrol units, along with the media and family and friends."

"That must be a very good recruiting tool."

"Yes it is, for both the military and getting kids to study science and engineering," Raydon agreed.

"So in a sense, my coming up here may have been a bad idea," the president said. "If kids learn that any healthy person can travel up to a space station—that they don't have to study hard sciences to do it—maybe those kids will just turn out to be space tourists."

"Nothing wrong with space tourism, Mr. President," Shale said. "But we're hoping the kids will want to design and fly newer and better ways to get into space, and perhaps take it all the way to the moon or the planets in our solar system. We don't know what will spark a young imagination."

"Don't worry, Mr. President," Raydon said. "I think you being here will have a very profound effect on people all over the world for a very long time."

"Sure; the kids will be saying, 'If that old fart can do it, I can do it,' eh, General?" the president deadpanned.

"Whatever it takes, Mr. President," Valerie Lukas said. "Whatever it takes."

The president was surprised to find Agent Charles Spellman in a strange linen sleeping-bag-like cocoon, Velcroed vertically to the bulkhead—he looked like some sort of large insect or marsupial hanging from a tree. "Mr. President, welcome," a very attractive dark-haired, dark-eyed woman in a white jumpsuit said, expertly floating over to him and extending a hand. "I'm Dr. Miriam Roth, the medical director. Welcome to Armstrong Space Station."

The president shook her hand, pleased that he was getting steadily better at keeping body control in free fall. "Very nice to meet you, Doctor," Phoenix said. To the Secret Service agent he asked, "How are you feeling, Charlie?"

"Mr. President, I am so sorry about this," Spellman said, his deep monotone voice not masking the depth of his chagrin. His face was very puffy, as if he had been in a street fistfight, and the faintest whiff of vomit nearby was unmistakable. "I have never in my life been seasick, airsick, or carsick—I haven't had so much as a stuffy nose in years. But when that pressure hit me, my head started to spin, and before I knew it, it was lights-out. It won't happen again, sir."

"Don't worry about it, Charlie—I've been told that when it comes to motion sickness, there's them that have and them that will," the president said. To Roth, he asked, "The question is: Will he be able to return to Earth without getting another episode?"

"I think he will, Mr. President," Miriam said. "He is certainly healthy, easily on a par with anyone on this station. I gave him a little shot of Phenergan, a long-time standard antinausea medicine, and I want to see how he tolerates it. In fifteen minutes or so, I'll let him get out of the cocoon and try moving about station." She gave Spellman a teasing scowl. "I think Agent Spellman failed to take the medications I prescribed before takeoff as he was advised."

"I don't like shots," Spellman said gruffly. "Besides, I can't be medicated while on duty, and I never get sick."

"You've never been in space before, Agent Spellman," Miriam said.

"I'm ready to get out now, Doc. The nausea has gone away. I'm ready to resume my duties, Mr. President."

"Better do as the doctor says, Charlie," the president said. "We've got the return flight in just a few hours, and I want you one hundred percent for that." Spellman looked immensely disappointed, but he nodded, saying nothing.

They made their way through yet another connecting tunnel, longer this time, and entered a third
module, lined with computer consoles and large-
screen, high-definition monitors. "This is the command module, Mr. President, the top center module
on the station," Raydon said. He floated over to a large
bank of consoles manned by six technicians. The technicians were floating before their consoles in a standing position, their feet anchored in place by footholds;
checklists, clipboards, and drink containers with straws
protruding were Velcro'd securely nearby. "This is the
sensor fusion center. From here we collect sensor data
from thousands of civil and military radars, satellites,
ships, aircraft, and ground vehicles, and combine them
into a strategic and tactical picture of the world military threat. Armstrong Space Station has its own radar,
optical, and infrared sensors, with which we can zoom
in on targets in both space and on Earth within range,
but mostly we tap into other sensors around the globe
to build the big picture."

He floated across the module to four small unmanned
consoles behind two sets of three consoles and computer screens, also unmanned. "This is the tactical
action center, where we employ the space-based weaponry," Raydon went on. He put a hand on a technician's
shoulder, and the man turned and smiled broadly at the

president. "Mr. President, I'd like to introduce you to Henry Lathrop, our aerospace-weapons officer." The two men shook hands, with Lathrop grinning ear to ear. Lathrop was in his late twenties, very short, very slim, wearing thick glasses and sporting a shaved head. "Henry, explain what it is you do here."

Lathrop's mouth dropped open as if he hadn't expected to say anything to the president—which he hadn't—but just as Raydon was about to be concerned, the young engineer pulled it together: "Y-yes, sir. Welcome to station, Mr. President. I am the aerospace-weapons officer. I control station's weapons designed to work in space and in Earth's atmosphere. We have some kinetic weapons available, but the Skybolt laser is not active per presidential order, so my only weapon is the COIL, or Chlorine-Oxygen-Iodine Laser."

"What can you do with it?" the president asked.

Lathrop gulped, a bit of panic in his eyes now that he had to answer a direct question from the president of the United States. But he was in his element, and he recovered quicker than before: "We can defend ourselves from space debris out to a range of about fifty miles," Lathrop said. "We also use it to break up larger pieces of debris—the smaller the debris, the less danger it is to other spacecraft."

"And can you use the laser to protect the station from other spacecraft?"

"Yes, sir," Lathrop said. "We have radar and infrared sensors that can see oncoming spacecraft or debris out to a range of about five hundred miles, and we can tie into other military or civilian space sensors." He pointed to a computer monitor. "The system is now on automatic, which means the COIL will automatically fire if the sensors detect a threat meeting certain parameters. We set it to manual as you were arriving, of course."

"Thank you for that, Mr. Lathrop," the president said. "So the laser can protect the station and break up space debris, but that's all? Didn't you once have the capability of attacking targets on Earth?"

"Yes, sir, we did," Lathrop said. "The Skybolt laser was powerful enough to destroy light targets such as vehicles and planes, and disable or damage heavier targets such as ships. The Kingfisher weapon garages held guided kinetic payloads that could attack spacecraft or ballistic missiles, and also precision-guided projectiles that could reenter Earth's atmosphere to attack targets on the ground or at sea."

"Do we still have those Kingfisher garages? I know President Gardner was not in favor of them—he used them more as bargaining chips with the Russians and Chinese."

"President Gardner allowed seven of the garages to reenter Earth's atmosphere and burn up," Lathrop said. "Another thirteen garages were retrieved and are stored on station's truss. Ten garages are still in orbit but are inactive. They are periodically retrieved, refueled, serviced, and placed back into orbit by the spaceplanes so we can study their long-term effectiveness and make design changes, but they are not active at this time."

"The COIL laser is different than Vice President Page's laser?" Phoenix asked.

"Yes, sir, it is. We are prohibited from using any weapons with a range of more than approximately sixty miles, and Skybolt, the free-electron laser, can attack targets in Earth's atmosphere and on the surface out to a range of about five hundred miles, so it's currently inactivated."

"Inactivated?"

"Not active, but capable of being activated if necessary," Raydon said.

"In fairly short order?" the president asked.

"Henry?" Kai asked.

"We would need some expertise from Sky Masters or other contractors," Lathrop said, "and a few days to bring the MHD's reactor online."

"And an order from you, sir," Raydon added. "Controversy over Skybolt nearly cost us the entire military space program."

"I remember very well," Phoenix said. "I aim to fix that. Please continue, Mr. Lathrop."

"The COIL uses a mixture of chemicals to produce laser light, which is then magnified and focused," Lathrop went on. "We use different optics than the Skybolt free-electron laser to focus and steer the laser beam, but the process is very similar. We use radar and infrared sensors to continually scan around station for objects that might be a hazard—we can detect and engage objects as small as a golf ball. The COIL has a normal maximum range of three hundred miles, but we've detuned the laser by eliminating some of the reflectors that increase laser power, so we're right at the legal limit."

"Can you show me how the sensors work?" the president asked. "Perhaps do a mock attack on an Earth target?"

Lathrop looked panicked again, and he turned to Raydon, who nodded. "Show the president how it's done, Henry," he said.

"Yes, sir," Lathrop said, the excitement quickly growing on his face. His fingers flew over a keyboard on his console. "We occasionally do attack drills on a series of targets that are continually tracked and are prioritized." The largest computer monitor came to life. It showed a large area of the earth with the space station's track and position approaching the North

Pole from eastern Siberia. There was a series of circles around several spots in Russia.

"What are those circles, Mr. Lathrop?" the president asked.

"We call them 'Delta Bravos,' or duck blinds," Lathrop replied. "Locations of known antisatellite weapons. The circles are the approximate radius of action of the weapons there."

"We're coming awfully close to that one, aren't we?"

"We fly over many of them in a day, located in Russia, China, and several countries aligned with them," Lathrop said. "That particular one is Yelizovo Airport, a MiG-31D fighter base that we know has antisatellite weapons they can launch from the air. They routinely fly patrols from there and even practice attack runs."

"They *do*?" the president asked incredulously. "How do you know if it's a real attack or not?"

"We scan for the missile," Kai explained. "We can see the missile and have less than two minutes to launch defensive weapons or hit it with the lasers. We scan them and analyze any signals they transmit, and we can study them by radar and optronics to find out if they're getting ready to do something. They almost always track us on long-range radar, but every now and then they'll hit us with a target-tracking and missile-guidance radar."

"Why?"

"Try to scare us, try to get us to hit them with Skybolt or an Earth-attack weapon, so they can prove how evil we are," Trevor said. "It's all cat-and-mouse Cold War nonsense. We usually ignore it."

"It does keep us on our toes, though," Valerie added. "Command, this is Combat, simulated target designated Golf Seven will be in range in three minutes."

"Prepare for simulated Skybolt engagement," Raydon said. "Attention on station, simulated target engagement in three minutes. Operations to the command module. All crewmembers go to combat stations and report. Secure all docks and hatches. Off-duty personnel report to damage-control stations, suit up, and commence prebreathing. Simulate undock Midnight."

"What is that about, General?" the president asked.

"Off-duty personnel have damage-control responsibilities," Kai said. "Up here, that may mean doing a spacewalk to retrieve equipment or . . . personnel lost in space. Prebreathing pure oxygen for as long as possible allows them to put on an ACES space suit and do their rescue duties, even if it means a spacewalk. They might need to do a lot of repair and recovery operations in open space. For the same reason, we also undock whatever spacecraft we have on station to use as lifeboats in case of problems—we would use the lifeboat spheres and await rescue by a spaceplane or commercial transport." The president swallowed hard at those grim thoughts.

"Command, this is Operations, request permission to simulated spin up the MHD," Valerie Lukas said from her place on the bulkhead, observing the mock engagement.

"Permission granted, simulate spinning up the MHD, make all preparations to engage simulated terrestrial target." It was like a tabletop play rehearsal, the president noted: everyone was saying their parts, but no one was actually moving or doing anything.

"Roger. Engineering, this is Operations, simulate spinning up the MHD, report activation and fifty percent power level."

"Operations, Engineering, Roger, simulated spin up the MHD," the engineering officer, Alice Hamilton, reported. A few moments later: "Operations, Engineering, the MHD is simulated active, power level at twelve percent and rising."

"Command, this is Operations, the MHD is simulated online."

"Command copies. Combat, what's our simulated target?"

"Simulated terrestrial target Golf Seven is a deactivated DEW Line radar site in western Greenland,"

Lathrop said. "Primary sensor data will be from SBR. Stand by for secondary sensor source." His fingers flew over his keyboard again. "Simulated secondary sensor source will be USA-234, a radar-imaging satellite, which will be above Golf Seven's horizon in sixty seconds and will be in range of the target for three-point-two minutes."

"What does all that mean, General?" President Phoenix asked.

"We can fire Skybolt fairly accurately with our own sensors," Kai explained. "The SBR, or Space-Based Radar, is our primary sensor. Station has two X-band synthetic aperture radars for Earth imaging. We can scan long swaths of Earth in 'stripmap' mode, or use 'spotlight' mode to zero in on a target and get precise pictures and measurements, down to a few inches' resolution.

"But because we're shooting at such a great distance, traveling hundreds of miles a minute, for even greater accuracy we can tie into any other sensors that happen to be in the area at the same time," Kai went on. "USA-234 is a U.S. Air Force radar-imaging satellite that takes radar pictures and transmits them to the National Reconnaissance Office in Washington. We are lucky enough to be a user of the images, so we can request that the satellite focus in on that particular target. We can merge the satellite's images with our own to get a more accurate look at the target."

Lathrop entered more commands, and on a large monitor to the left of the main monitor there appeared an overhead still photograph of the simulated target, a remote radar site with a large radome in the center, several communications pointed in different directions, and several long, low buildings surrounding the radome. "This is what it looks like in a recent overhead photo," he said. A few moments later the photo disappeared and was replaced by a different image, this one showing a dot surrounded by an H-shaped box against a mostly black background. "This is the radar image from the reconnaissance satellite. The background is black because snow doesn't reflect radar energy very well, but the buildings show up nicely."

"Operations, Engineering, MHD is at simulated fifty percent," Alice reported.

"Roger, Engineering," Valerie said. "Combat, this is Operations, we're at fifty percent, simulate open Skybolt engagement circuits, weapons tight, prepare to engage."

"Roger, Operations, simulating opening Skybolt engagement circuits, weapons tight."

Another few moments later the image changed again, and this one looked very much like the photograph they saw, with an occasional cloud drifting across the image. Lathrop used a trackball to precisely center the image on the screen. "And this is with station's telescopic electro-optical sensors added to the radar image," he said. "Operation, this is Combat, positive identification on simulated target Golf Seven, tracking established, we're locked on and ready."

"Roger, Combat," Valerie said. "Command, Operations, we're locked on. MHD status?"

"MHD at one hundred percent in ten seconds."

"Roger," Valerie acknowledged. "Request permission to simulate transferring Skybolt to Combat and engage."

"This is Command," Raydon said. "You are cleared to transfer Skybolt control to Combat and simulate engage target. Attention on station, this is the director, we are simulate engaging terrestrial target with Skybolt."

"Roger, Command, Operations acknowledges we are cleared simulate engage target. Combat, Operations, Skybolt is cleared to simulate engage, weapons simulate released."

"Roger, Ops, weapons simulate released." Lathrop pressed a single key on his keyboard, then looked up. "That's it, Mr. President," he said. "The system will wait for the optimal time to fire and then keep firing until it detects that the target is destroyed or until we drop below the target's horizon. There are actually two lasers involved other than the main laser: the first measures the atmosphere and issues corrections to the mirror to correct for atmospheric conditions that might degrade the laser beam; and the second tracks the target as station flies past and helps to focus and precisely aim the main beam."

"Thank you, Henry," Kai said. Lathrop looked exceedingly relieved to return to his console after nervously shaking the president's hand. "As you can see, Mr. President, only one tactical crew station is manned, because our Kingfisher weapon garages have not been reactivated. But if they were, the sensor fusion operators detect, analyze, and classify any threats they see, and those threats appear on these four monitors, used by myself; Valerie, my chief of combat operations; the aerospace tactical-weapons officer, and the terrestrial-weapons officer. We can then respond with our own space-based weapons, or direct Earth-based ground, naval, or air responses."

"What are the Kingfisher weapon garages?" the president asked. "I remember President Gardner was not fond of them."

"The Kingfisher weapon system is a series of spacecraft that we call 'garages,' in low Earth orbit," Kai said. "The garages are controlled from here and can also be controlled from U.S. Space Command head-quarters on Earth. The garages have their own sensors, thrusters, and control systems, and they can be programmed to dock with station for refueling and rearming. Each garage carries three antisatellite- or antiballistic-missile weapons and three Earth-attack precision-guided weapons."

"I remember Gardner *really* hating those things," the president remarked. "When that one attack missed and took out that factory, I thought he was going to kill someone."

"Well, President Gardner didn't cancel the program, just put it in mothballs," Kai said. "A full-up Kingfisher constellation has thirty-six Trinity garages in orbit, so that every part of Earth has at least three garages overhead at any moment, similar to the GPS navigation system. It's all controlled right from here, or from U.S. Strategic Command headquarters."

"General Raydon, this is the part of the Space Defense Force I never understood: why have all this orbiting Earth?" President Phoenix asked. "This is very much like command centers already existing on Earth, and in fact it looks identical to an Airborne Warning and Control System radar aircraft. Why put the same thing in space?"

"Because we're much more secure and protected here in space, which makes it ideal for any command center, sir," Raydon replied.

"Even with a list of dangers as long as your arm, as you put it, General?"

"Yes, sir, even with all of the dangers of traveling in space," Raydon said. "The enemy is less likely to completely blind the United States with an orbiting command center. The enemy could destroy a base, ship, or AWACS radar plane, and we'd lose that sensor, but we can grab sensor data from elsewhere, or use our own sensors, and quickly fill the gap. Plus, because we're orbiting Earth, we're less likely to be successfully attacked. Our orbit is known, of course, which makes finding, tracking, and targeting us easier, but at least for the near term, attacking this station is far more difficult than attacking a ground-, ship-, or air-based command center. The bad guys know where we are and where we will be, but at the same time we know precisely when their known antisatellite bases would become a possible threat if an attack was launched. We track those known sites constantly. We also scan for unknown attack bases and prepare to respond to them."

"I think in a broader sense, sir," Trevor Shale said, "that manning the station and making it an operational military command post, rather than just a collection of sensors or laboratories, is important for the future of America's presence in space."

"How so, Mr. Shale?"

"I compare it to the westward expansion of the United States, sir," Trevor explained. "At first, small bands of explorers went out and discovered the plains, the Rockies, the deserts, and the Pacific. A few settlers ventured out after them, lured by the promise of land and resources. But it wasn't until the U.S. Army was sent out and established camps, outposts, and forts that settlements and eventually villages and towns could be built, and the real expansion of the nation began.

"Well, Armstrong Space Station is not just an outpost in Earth orbit, but a real military installation," Shale went on. "We're much more than computers and consoles—we have twelve men and women aboard who monitor and can control military operations across the globe. I think that will encourage more adventurers, scientists, and explorers to come to space, just like the presence of a U.S. Army fort was of great comfort to settlers."

"Space is a lot bigger than the Midwest, Mr. Shale."

"To us in the twenty-first century, yes, sir," Trevor said. "But to an eighteenth-century explorer who first sets eyes on the Great Plains or the Rockie Mountains,

I'll bet it felt like he was standing at the very edge of the universe."

The president stopped to think for a moment, then smiled and nodded. "Then I think it's time to take it to the next level," he said. "I'd like to talk with my wife and Vice President Page, and then get ready for my address."

"Yes, sir," Raydon said. "We'll put you in the director's chair." The president carefully maneuvered himself over to Raydon's console and wedged his feet into the stirrups underneath, standing before the console but feeling as if he were floating on his back in the ocean. The large monitor in front of him came to life, and he saw a tiny white light under a small lens at the top of the monitor, and he knew he was online.

"You finally stopped gawking around and decided to give us a call, eh, Mr. President?" Vice President Ann Page asked, her face visible in an inset window on the monitor. She was in her midsixties, thin and energetic, with long hair unabashedly allowed to stay naturally gray, tied up off her collar. Until recently, with all of the cuts in the U.S. budget, Ann had taken on many tasks in the White House along with her duties as vice president: chief of staff, press secretary, national security adviser, and chief political adviser; she had finally ceded most of those additional duties to others, but continued to be Ken Phoenix's closest political adviser and confidante as well as White House chief of staff. "I was starting to get a little worried."

"Ann, this is an absolutely incredible experience," Ken Phoenix said. "It's everything I imagined it would be, and a whole lot more."

"I'll have you know that I've had one justice of the Supreme Court standing by round the clock to administer the oath of office, in case any of the thousands of things that could go wrong *did* go wrong," Ann said. "I will continue to insist on that long after your return."

"Very wise decision," the president said. "But I'm fine, the trip up was incredible, and if I'm doomed to turn into a meteorite on the return, at least I know the nation will be in good hands."

"Thank you, sir."

"It's been just amazing, Ann," the president went on. "Dr. Noble let me dock the spaceplane."

The vice president blinked in surprise. "You did? Lucky dog. I've never done that, and I've ridden in the spaceplanes several times! How was it?"

"Just as most everything else in space: just *think* about something and it happens. It's hard to believe we were traveling *five miles* a second but talking about moving the spaceplane by just inches per second. I didn't really have a sense of altitude or speed until we did the spacewalk and I saw Earth under—"

"*The what?*" Ann exclaimed, her eyes bugging out in shock. "You did a *what?*"

"Ann, you were the one who first told me about how you got to the station from the early spaceplanes," the president said. "Dr. Noble mentioned it again to me as we were disembarking, and I decided to go for it. It only lasted a couple minutes."

The vice president's mouth was hanging open in complete surprise, and she had to physically shake herself out of her stunned speechlessness. "I . . . I don't believe it," she said finally. "Are you going to mention that to the press? They'll flip . . . even harder than they're *already* going to flip."

"Probably the same reaction when a sitting president took the first ocean-liner voyage, or the first ride in a locomotive, or a car, or an airplane," the president said. "We've been flying in space for decades—why is it so hard to conceive of a president of the United States traveling in space or doing a spacewalk?"

Vice President Page momentarily went back to her near-catatonic state of utter disbelief, but shook her head in resignation. "Well, I'm glad you're all right, sir," Ann said. "I'm glad you're enjoying the trip and the view and the"— she swallowed again in disbelief before continuing—". . . spacewalking, sir, because I think we're in for a real shit-storm when you get back." The president freely encouraged Ann to speak her mind, both in public and private, and she took every opportunity to do just that. "The cat's out of the bag already—folks from station must've already phoned home to let others know you arrived, and word is spreading like wildfire. The presser will be a real stunner, I'm sure." As all the astronauts did, Ann referred to Armstrong Space Station as "station." "I hope you're ready for it."

"I am, Ann," the president said.

"How do you feel?"

"Very good."

"No vertigo?"

"A tiny bit," the president admitted. "When I was a kid I had a mild case of anablephobia—fear of looking up—and that's kind of what it feels like, but it goes away quickly."

"Nausea? Queasiness?"

"Nope," the president said. Ann looked surprised, and she nodded admiringly. "My sinuses feel stuffed, but that's it. I guess that's because fluids don't flow downward like normal." Ann nodded—she and Phoenix's wife, a medical doctor, had talked at length about some of the physiological conditions he might encounter even during a short stay on station. She had avoided talking about some of the psychological ones that some astronauts experienced. "It's irksome, but not bad. I feel okay. I can't say the same for Charlie Spellman."

"Your Secret Service detail that volunteered to go up with you? Where is he?"

"Sick bay."

"Oh, Christ," Ann murmured, shaking her head. "Wait'll the press finds out you're up there without your detail."

"He's looking better. I think he'll be good for the return flight. Besides, I don't think any assassins will make their way up here."

"True enough," Ann said. "Good luck with the press conference. We'll be watching."

The president was then connected to his wife, Alexa. "Oh my God, it's good to see you, Ken," she said. Alexa Phoenix was ten years younger than her husband, a pediatrician who had left her private practice when her husband became the surprise choice of President Joseph Gardner to be his running mate. Her olive complexion, dark hair, and dark eyes made her look Southern European, but she was a surfer girl from southern Florida through and through. "Sky Masters Aerospace called and told me you have arrived on the station. How are you? How do you feel?"

"Okay, hon," the president replied. "A little stuffy, but okay."

"I can see a tiny bit of facial edema—you're already starting to get your space moon-face," Alexa said, framing her face with her hands arrayed in a circle.

"Is it noticeable already?" the president asked.

"I'm teasing," his wife said. "You look fine. It's a badge of honor anyway. Will you be okay for your presser?"

"I feel good," the president said. "Wish me luck."

"I've been wishing you luck every hour of every day since I agreed to this crazy little trip of yours," Alexa said, a tiny hint of vexation in her voice. "But I think you'll do great. Knock 'em dead."

"Yes, ma'am. I'll see you at Andrews. Love you."

"I'll be there. Love you." And the connection was terminated.

About fifteen minutes later, with Kai Raydon, Jessica Faulkner, and Trevor Shale standing beside him, the world got to watch the most amazing sight most of them had ever seen: the image of the president of the United States in space. "Good morning, my fellow Americans and ladies and gentlemen watching this broadcast around the world. I am broadcasting this press conference from Armstrong Space Station, orbiting two hundred miles above Earth."

A small window on the monitor showed the White House press room . . . and the place exploded into near bedlam. Several reporters shot to their feet in absolute surprise, dropping tablets and cameras; several women and even a few men gasped in horror, holding their heads in disbelief or biting knuckles inserted into their mouths to stifle their outcries. Finally a staffer stepped before the reporters and waved them back to their seats so the president could continue.

"I flew here just a few minutes ago aboard a Midnight spaceplane, a spacecraft much smaller than the space shuttle but able to take off and land like an airplane and then blast itself into orbit and dock with Armstrong or the International Space Station," the president went on. "Needless to say, it was an amazing voyage. It has been said that planet Earth is nothing more than a spacecraft itself, with all the resources it has always had and will ever have already loaded on board by God, and seeing our planet from space against the backdrop of billions of stars really makes you realize how important our commitment to protect our spaceship called Earth really is.

"I am grateful to the personnel aboard Armstrong and to the folks at Sky Masters Aerospace for making my trip successful, safe, and awe-inspiring," the president said. "With me are the station director, retired Air

Force general and space veteran Kai Raydon; the station's manager and veteran shuttle mission commander, Trevor Shale; and the chief of flight operations and the copilot aboard the spaceplane, retired Marine Corps colonel Jessica Faulkner. The spaceplane pilot, Dr. Hunter Noble, is busy planning our return, but I thank him for allowing me some unique and wondrous views as well as plenty of opportunities to experience the challenges of flying and working in space. You will not find a more professional and dedicated group of men and women anywhere in the world than the ones who man this facility. It's been almost thirty years since this station became operational, but although it's starting to look its age and is in need of some upgrades, it is still in orbit, still operational, still making a contribution to our nation's defense, and still caring for its crew.

"I must admit that my staff and I purposely misled the White House press corps over the past several days: I did want to conduct a press conference, but I didn't say where it was going to be," the president said with a slight smile. "I know the rumors were that I was going to secretly go to Guam to meet with residents and military members and inspect the repairs ongoing to Andersen Air Force Base following the attack by the People's Republic of China last year. But I had this opportunity to take this remarkable voyage, and after consulting with my wife, Alexa, and my children, as well as Vice President Page—who as you know is an experienced astronaut herself—my staff and cabinet, congressional leaders, and my doctors, I decided to accept the risks and do it. I will be returning to Washington in just a few hours aboard Midnight. I thank the ones I consulted for their advice and prayers, and for keeping my trip a secret.

"The purpose of this trip is simple: I want America to return to space," the president went on. "Our work on the International Space Station and Armstrong has been outstanding over the years, but I want to expand it. Mr. Shale compared outposts in space to forts built on the American frontier to help and support settlers moving west, and I think that is an excellent comparison. The future of America is in space, just as westward military expansion across North America was key to America's future in the eighteenth century, and I want that future to begin right now. I am here, talking to you from space, to prove that an average person with a little courage and heart, as well as a fairly trim waistline and good genetics, *can* travel into space.

"Armstrong Space Station is a military outpost, and it is in need of replacement, but I want our return to space to be much more than just the military—I want ours to include more scientific research and industrialization as well," President Phoenix went on. "I have been briefed and have seen plans for amazing systems and industries permanently operating in Earth orbit and beyond, and I will challenge the Congress and the federal government to support and assist private industry to deploy and advance these incredible innovations.

"For example, as you may know, debris in space is a big problem for satellites, spacecraft, and astronauts—a hit by even a tiny particle traveling over seventeen thousand miles an hour can cripple a ship or kill a spacewalker. I have seen patented plans by American companies to venture into debris fields and use robots to retrieve large damage-causing pieces. I have even seen plans for a space recycling program: spent or malfunctioning satellites and jettisoned boosters can be retrieved, the unused propellant captured, the solar panels and electronics salvaged and repaired, and the batteries recharged and reused. They are even talking about having a space-based facility in orbit that can rebuild and repair spacecraft and place them back into service—no need to waste the time, energy, manpower, and dollars to bring the satellite all the way back to Earth when there's a crew on a space station ready to do the work.

"Those are only two of the many projects I have seen, and I have to tell you: after the briefings, and especially after coming up here and traveling in space, I feel as if I'm standing at the starting line of the great westward land rush, the reins in my hand and my family, friends, and neighbors beside me, ready to start a new life and take on the future. I know there will be dangers, setbacks, disappointments, loss, injury, and death. It's going to cost a lot of money, private as well as public money, and I'm going to cancel, postpone, or downsize a lot of other programs to make resources available for systems that I feel will take us well into the twenty-second century. But after coming up here, seeing what is being done and learning what can be done, I know it's imperative—no, it's *vital*—that we get started immediately.

"Now, my ride back to Washington leaves in a couple hours. I want to check on Special Agent Spellman to see how he's doing, have a meal with the dedicated personnel aboard this facility, tour around a little more so I can work on my zero-G free-fall movement technique, and then catch a ride back to Earth, but I'd be happy to take a few questions from the White House press corps back in the press briefing room in the White House in Washington." He looked at the monitor before him, at the slack-jawed, stupefied expressions of the correspondents, and he had to stifle a smile. "Jeffrey Connors of ABC, why don't you start us off?" The correspondent rose shakily to his feet. He looked at his notes and realized he hadn't written anything else down except the questions about Guam that he assumed he would be asking. "Jeff?"

"Uh . . . Mr. . . . Mr. President . . . how . . . how do you feel?" the reporter finally stammered. "Any . . . any adverse effects of the launch and weightlessness?"

"I've been asked that question about a hundred times in the past couple hours," the president replied. "Every now and then I get a little shot of vertigo, as if I was in a tall building and glanced out the window and suddenly felt as if I was falling, but it passes quickly. I feel good. I guess other first-timers in free fall— weightlessness—don't do as well. My Secret Service detail, Special Agent Spellman, is in sick bay."

"Excuse me, sir?" Connors asked. The shocked, bewildered expressions of the other correspondents instantly vanished—they smelled fresh news blood in the water. "You have a Secret Service agent *up there with you?*"

"Yes," the president acknowledged. "It's required, of course, and Earth orbit is no different. Special Agent Charles Spellman volunteered to accompany me on this trip. That was way, way beyond the call of duty."

"But he's not well?"

"If I may, Mr. President?" Kai Raydon interjected. The president nodded and motioned to the camera.

"I'm retired brigadier general Kai Raydon, formerly of the U.S. Space Defense Force and now an employee of Sky Masters Aerospace and the station director. The stresses of space flight affect persons differently. Some people, like the president, tolerate the G-forces and weightlessness very well; others don't. Special Agent Spellman is in top physical condition, on a par with anyone who has ever traveled up to Armstrong, but his body was temporarily intolerant to the forces and sensations he experienced. As the president said, he's recovering very well."

"Is he going to be able to take the stress of returning to Earth?" another reporter asked.

"I'd have to refer to our medical director, Dr. Miriam Roth," Kai said, "but Special Agent Spellman is looking good to me. I think he'll do fine on the return after some rest and antisickness medication."

"He'll be *medicated*?" another correspondent retorted. "How is he going to perform his duties if he's medicated?"

"It's a standard drug used by almost all station personnel experiencing symptoms of space sickness," Kai said. It was clear he was not comfortable being the target of all these rapid-fire, rather accusatory questions. "Persons using Phenergan can continue all their normal duties in a very short time."

Now the correspondents were tapping quickly on their tablets or scribbling quickly on their notepads. President Phoenix could see the rising irritation in Kai's face and quickly stepped in. "Thank you, General Raydon. How about Margaret Hastings from NBC?" the president asked.

The well-known and longtime White House chief correspondent got to her feet, her eyes narrowed in a way that millions of American viewers recognized as the veteran reporter preparing to dig in her claws. "Mr. President, I must say, I am still in a state of absolute shock," she said with a distinctive Boston accent that she never lost despite her years in New York and Washington. "I simply cannot fathom the extraordinarily extreme level of risk to the nation you took by traveling up to the space station. I am simply at a complete loss for words."

"Miss Hastings, life has risks," the president said. "As I mentioned to Vice President Page, I'm sure a lot of people felt that a sitting president should not have taken the first ride on a motor vessel, locomotive, automobile, or airplane—that it was simply too risky and the technology so new that it wasn't worth placing the president's life needlessly in jeopardy. Yet now all that is routine. Theodore Roosevelt was the first president to fly in an airplane, and that was less than ten years after Kitty Hawk. Americans have been flying in space for almost sixty years now."

"But this is completely different, Mr. President!" Hastings exclaimed. "Space is infinitely more dangerous than flying in an airplane . . . !"

"You can say that now, Miss Hastings, in the second decade of the twenty-first century, when airplanes have been around for over a hundred years," the president interjected. "But at the beginning of the twentieth century, I'm sure many realized that flying was infinitely more dangerous than riding in a carriage or on horseback, and certainly too dangerous to risk the president's life when he could just as easily take a carriage, train, or ship. But I know that space travel has advanced to the point where we need to exploit it to help our country and mankind to grow, and the way I chose to do it is to take this trip."

"But that is not your job, Mr. President," Hastings said indignantly, as if she was lecturing a young boy. "Your job is to run the executive branch of the government of the United States of America and be the leader of the free world. The location of that very important job is in Washington, D.C., sir, not in outer space!"

"Miss Hastings, I've watched you on television for years," the president responded. "I've seen you report from chaotic, shattered urban battlefields, from blood-soaked crime scenes, from disaster areas with looters running through the streets threatening you and your crew. Are you telling me that reporting from the eye of a hurricane was necessary for your job? You went out into one-hundred-twenty-mile-an-hour winds or put on a flak vest and helmet and stepped out into the middle of firefights for a reason, and I think that reason is to drive home the message you wanted to give to your audience.

"Well, I'm doing the very same thing by coming up here," Phoenix went on. "I believe that America's future is space, and I wanted to drive home that point by accepting the invitation to fly up here and do it. I wanted to experience what's it's like to suit up, fly in space, feel the G-forces, see Earth from two hundred miles up, do a spacewalk, look at this magnificent . . ."

The shock and bedlam in the White House press room erupted once again, and the members of the press corps who were seated shot to their feet as if pulled by a puppeteer with strings. *"Do a spacewalk?"* they all exclaimed as if in unison. *"You did a spacewalk . . . ?"*

"It lasted two, maybe two and a half minutes," the president said. "I stepped out of the spaceplane's cockpit, was hoisted up atop—"

"You were in the spaceplane's cockpit?" Hastings shouted.

"I had the opportunity to sit in the cockpit during docking, and I took it," the president said. He decided right then not to tell them that it was *he* who did the docking. "I had been told by Vice President Page that the way they first had to transfer to the station from the early models of the spaceplane was via a spacewalk. We were prepared for it, and there was no more danger in it than any other astronaut experiences."

"But you're not an astronaut, Mr. President!" Hastings shouted again. "You're the *president of the United States*! You're not paid to take risks like that! With all due respect, Mr. President . . . are you completely *insane*?"

"He's not insane, Hastings," Kai Raydon retorted, angered by her unprofessional outburst. "And now that he's had the courage to fly into orbit, he most certainly *is* an astronaut—a pretty damn good one, it turns out. He proved that any healthy, teachable, level-headed individual can become an astronaut if he so chooses, without years of physical training or scientific or engineering education."

The bedlam seemed to subside, as if Raydon was a middle-school teacher admonishing his class to settle down and get to work, but the president could see that group of reporters was getting pretty riled up, and he was ready to wrap this up. "Any more questions?" he asked.

Another well-known television anchor seated in the front row got to his feet. "Mr. President, these space industrial proposals sound interesting, but they also sound expensive, as I'm sure everything dealing with space can be. You have been campaigning for well over a year on fiscal responsibility and paying for every new government program. How do you propose to pay for all this? You said you were going to cancel, postpone, or downsize other programs. Which ones?"

"I'm planning on targeting programs that I feel are costly, unnecessary, bloated, outdated, and wasteful, Mr. Wells," the president said. "I have a long list of proposals that I will present to the congressional leadership. The three categories that make up eighty percent of the national budget—entitlements, defense, and discretionary spending—all need to be addressed. Modernizing our nation's defense and preparing for the challenges of the twenty-second century is my absolute priority."

"So you're going to build space weapons by cutting Social Security, Medicare, Medicaid, and the Affordable Care Act?" a reporter asked.

"I want to stop adding more government entitlement programs, and I want to see real reforms in all entitlement programs so they can survive the century," the president responded. "I think we can find cost savings when we do real reforms, which we can use to modernize defense. The same can be said about the military itself. One example would be a significant reduction of nuclear weapons in the American arsenal." He could see another flurry of tapping and scribbling, and digital recorders moved closer to the speakers set up in the press briefing room. "I am going to propose that we reduce the number of nuclear warheads on alert from the current level of approximately seven hundred down to about three hundred."

The level of excitement in the press briefing room began to rise again. "But, Mr. President, don't you think with what's happened in the South China Sea and western Pacific—China setting off a nuclear depth charge, firing on ships, downing our aircraft, and attacking Guam, not to mention Russia's military resurgence—that this is the absolute worst time to be reducing our nuclear deterrent?"

"You've answered your own question, Mr. Wells," the president said. "We currently have about seven hundred nuclear warheads ready to strike within a few hours' time, but exactly what have they deterred? Russia, China, and other nations in response have all grown stronger and bolder. And when we retaliated, what kind of weapons did we use to stop them? Precision-guided nonnuclear weapons launched from aircraft and spacecraft.

"I feel the nuclear deterrent is no longer relevant and should be drastically downsized," the president repeated. "The Russians took care of a lot of the downsizing during the American Holocaust, of course, with a horrendous loss of American lives. But there has been a lot of talk about replacing the bomber and intercontinental-ballistic-missile fleet, and I'm not going to endorse that. I propose that the strategic nuclear submarine fleet be the only forces on day-to-day nuclear alert, and it will be reduced so that only four strategic nuclear ballistic-missile submarines will be on alert, two in the Pacific and two in the Atlantic, with four more ready to put to sea on short notice. A few tactical air forces stationed on land and sea will be poised to generate forces for nuclear alert within a few days, if needed."

The shocked, incredulous expressions on the correspondents' faces had returned—the reporters who were not texting back to their editors on handheld devices were making stunned comments to their colleagues, the noise level quickly rising. The president knew that this news conference was all but over, but he had a few more bombshells to let loose: "Not all the cuts will be from defense, but most will," he went on. "I propose to decrease the number of Army and Marine Corps personnel and weapon systems such as tanks and artillery, reduce the number of aircraft-carrier battle groups down to eight, and cancel future purchases of ships such as the Littoral Combat Ship and aircraft such as the F-35 Lightning fighter-bomber."

"But, Mr. President, don't you feel that you're gutting the military at a time when we should be gearing up the military to prepare to oppose adversaries such as China and Russia, both of whom have attacked us repeatedly in recent years?" a correspondent asked. "Are you going to replace these canceled weapon systems with something else?"

"Yes, in two key twenty-first- and twenty-second-century national security imperatives: space, and cyberspace," the president replied. "I will propose that the bulk of American long-range offensive military systems be deployed from space or Earth orbit, and the bulk of our defensive military systems be deployed from cyberspace. The United States should dominate both realms, and I am going to see to it that America does exactly that. If we fail to do this, we will quickly and inevitably lose, and that's not going to happen on my watch. America will dominate space and cyberspace like we used to dominate the world's oceans. That is my mission, and I will expect Congress and the American people to support me. Are there any other questions for me?"

"Yes, sir, I have many," Margaret Hastings said. "What exactly do you mean by 'dominating' space and cyberspace? How do you intend to dominate them?"

"For one: by no longer tolerating the actions that have persisted over the past several years and are almost considered part of the price of doing business," Phoenix said. "For example, I am told that American companies, government agencies, and military computers detect intrusions and outright attacks on a daily basis from governments all over the world, either sponsored by a government entity or done directly by a government. That will no longer be tolerated. A computer attack will be treated like any other attack. The United States will respond appropriately to any cyberattack.

"I am also told that American reconnaissance satellites are hit by lasers to blind or destroy optics; that jamming satellites are placed into orbit near our satellites to disrupt them; and that American GPS signals are jammed on a regular basis. I am told that several nations hit this very station on a daily basis with lasers, microwaves, and other electromagnetic forms of energy to try to damage or disrupt operations here. That will no longer be tolerated. Any such attack will be dealt with accordingly. We will closely monitor Earth orbit for any signs of possible interference or attack by any nation or entity. An American satellite in orbit, as well as the orbit itself, is sovereign American territory, and we will defend it just like any other American resource."

"Excuse me, sir," Hastings said, "but did you just say that you consider *Earth orbit* American property? Do you mean to say that no other nation can put a spacecraft into orbit if the United States already has a satellite in that orbit?"

"That's exactly what I'm saying, Miss Hastings," Phoenix said. "A common technique for attacking American space assets is to launch an antisatellite weapon into the same orbit, chase it down, and destroy it when within range. That is how the Russians destroyed our Kingfisher weapon garage after knocking parts of it out of commission with directed-energy weapons, with the loss of an American astronaut. Any spacecraft launched into the same orbit as an American satellite will be considered a hostile act and will be dealt with appropriately."

The bedlam that was growing and threatening to go out of control in the White House Press Briefing Room did not subside this time, and the president knew that it probably wouldn't for a very long time. "Thank you, ladies and gentlemen, thank you," the president said, ignoring the upraised hands and shouted questions. "I think it's time to share a meal with the astronauts aboard station . . ." He turned to Raydon, smiled, and added, ". . . my *fellow* astronauts, and prepare to return to Washington. Good night from Armstrong Space Station, and may God bless the United States of America." He saw so much clamor on the monitor that he doubted if anyone heard his sign-off.

"Good speech and good responses to questions, Mr. President," Vice President Ann Page said a few moments later after her image reappeared on the director's station monitor in the command module. "A lot of veteran astronauts have trouble doing press conferences down on Earth, let alone just minutes after arriving in space for the first time. I didn't leak any parts of the military restructuring, as you requested, so everyone in the world got it all at once. The phones are even now ringing off the hook. Are you going to take any calls up on station?"

Phoenix thought about it for a moment, then shook his head. "I'm going to call Alexa, and then I'm going to sit down with the space station crew, try some of their food, check on poor Charlie Spellman, check out a little more of station, and prepare for the return flight. We talked about responses to several questions we anticipate reporters and heads of state will ask, and I'll let you handle those until I get back and get checked over by the docs. The last thing I want to do is spend my last couple hours on station talking on the phone."

"I hear you, sir," Ann said. "I'll take the calls from heads of state, then the major media outlets. You enjoy yourself up there. No more spacewalks, okay, sir? Go through the docking tunnel like the rest of us mere space travelers."

"If you insist, Miss Vice President," President Phoenix said with a smile. "If you insist."

THREE

The mere apprehension of a coming evil has put many into a situation of the utmost danger.
—MARCUS ANNAEUS LUCANUS

THE WATERGATE HOTEL
WASHINGTON, D.C.

That same time

"Of course I saw it!" former U.S. senator, Senate majority leader, and secretary of state Stacy Anne Barbeau exclaimed on the phone, staring dumbstruck at the large high-def television in her hotel suite. "Get the senior staff in here right now!"

Despite being in her early sixties, Stacy Anne Barbeau was still a beautiful, energetic, ambitious woman and a veteran politician. But those in the know knew that Barbeau was not a sweet Louisiana magnolia—she was a venus flytrap, using her beauty and southern charms to disarm and disable men and women alike into lowering their defenses and submitting to her wishes, willingly clamped tightly between her ruby-red lips. The whole world had known for a decade that she had presidential ambitions, and now those ambitions had been transformed into a high-powered, well-funded campaign that had maintained a small but consistent lead in the race against incumbent president Kenneth Phoenix . . .

. . . a race that had just been turned on its ear with that unexpected news conference from space.

Barbeau's Washington campaign headquarters occupied an entire floor in the Watergate Hotel and office building. She had just returned to her hotel suite from a fund-raising dinner and turned on the news to watch the press conference, full of energy and excitement over another successful appearance. Now she stood in complete shock, listening to the stunned and flabbergasted commentators trying to make sense of what they had just seen: the president of the United States speaking to the world from Earth orbit.

Luke Cohen, Barbeau's campaign manager and chief adviser, was the first to dash into her hotel suite. "That had to be faked or CGI'd," he said breathlessly. Cohen, a tall, thin, good-looking New Yorker, had been Barbeau's chief of staff during her years as Senate majority leader and as secretary of state. "No president of the United States would ever be stupid enough to fly into space, especially six months before an election!"

"Shush, I'm listening," Barbeau said. Cohen turned away to answer his cell phone while she listened to the commentary.

"CNN," Cohen said at the next break. "They want five minutes."

"They can have two," Barbeau said. An aide whose only job was to record every word that came out of Barbeau's mouth rushed in, tablet computer at the ready. "It was the most audacious, sensationalist, dangerous, and irresponsible election-year stunt I have ever seen in my thirty years in Washington," she recited. "President Phoenix is risking the safety and security of the entire nation and the free world with this reckless act. I seriously question his judgment, as should all Americans. For the good of the nation, as soon as he returns, he should undergo a series of medical and psychological examinations to check to see if he has suffered any ill effects of traveling in space, and if any are found he should immediately thereupon resign his office." The aide tapped a button, and the words were sent to Barbeau's chief speechwriter, who would put together talking points for her and the campaign's spokespersons within minutes.

"Luke, assign a researcher to find out the symptoms of every known sickness or affliction that astronauts can suffer," Barbeau went on, "and then I want him to watch every second of every public appearance Phoenix makes to see if he exhibits any of those symptoms." Cohen had his cell phone out in a flash and issued the instructions. "So what do you think the feedback will be?"

"I agree with your points, Miss Secretary," Cohen said. "At first, I think most voters will think it's cool and exciting that the president flew into space and did a spacewalk, talk about his bravery, et cetera. But shortly thereafter, maybe by the time the morning talk shows start discussing this and people start to learn more about the dangers and risks, they might question his judgment and his ability to hold the office. The pressure to resign might be intense."

"If he thinks he's going to start gutting the military to pay for his fancy space weapons and cyberwarfare stuff, he's sadly mistaken," Barbeau said. "Take away two aircraft-carrier battle groups? Over my dead body. I want to build *more* carrier battle groups, not take them down! I want to go to shipyards, Navy groups, air bases, and veterans groups and talk about what the effect of doing away with two carrier battle groups will have on the economy as well as national defense. Cut the size of the nuclear deterrent in half? Cut tanks and fighters? Maybe he's already suffering some kind of space sickness. He's just committed political suicide. I'm going to see to it that he pays a price for this stunt."

"I can't believe he started talking about entitlement reform," Cohen said. "That's okay to do before the convention if you're in a primary race, but he's already got the nomination. No one is challenging him."

"He's going to regret that too," Barbeau said acidly. "Find out how much one of those spaceplanes and that space station costs, and then find out how many people it will disadvantage if everyone loses even ten percent of their benefits to pay for a spaceplane that ninety-nine-point-nine percent of Americans will never even see, let alone fly. Find out what it cost to fly his butt up there and back, and then compute how much education, infrastructure, and medical research we could have done but for the president's joyride."

Stacy Anne Barbeau stepped over to a large mirror in her suite and examined her makeup. "You think you made history today, Mr. President?" she said. "You think you're a big astronaut hero? You made the biggest blunder in your political career, buster, and it's going to cost you. I'll see to that." She looked at Cohen through the mirror. "Luke, make sure there's someone in Makeup ready for me and that my TV studio is ready to feed, and tell CNN I'll be ready in five."

THE KREMLIN, MOSCOW
RUSSIAN FEDERATION

That same time

"*Chelovek deystvitel'no bezumno!* The man is truly insane!" Russian president Gennadiy Gryzlov thundered at the television in his office at the Kremlin. "Phoenix thinks he is going to control all of outer space? He will soon learn just how wrong he is!"

Just forty years old, Gennadiy Gryzlov was the son of the former president Anatoliy Gryzlov, and his career paralleled his father's to a great extent. Gennadiy Gryzlov had graduated from the Yuri Gagarin Military Air Academy and attended basic flight instruction at Baronovsky Air Base in Armavir and bomber flight training at Engels Air Base in southwestern Russia, and had been selected to attended command leadership school in Moscow just two years later. He wanted nothing more than to follow in his beloved father's footsteps, and determined to do so without his family's extensive government and petrochemical industry connections.

But shortly after completing command leadership school in Moscow but before he returned to Engels

Air Base to take command of the 121st Guards Heavy Bomber Regiment, a Tupolev-160 Blackjack supersonic bomber unit, an event happened that changed his life forever: Engels Air Base was attacked by an American unmanned stealth bomber called an EB-1C Vampire, a heavily modified supersonic B-1 Lancer bomber, destroying dozens of Russian bombers awaiting orders to take off and destroy a nest of terrorists in Turkmenistan. Hundreds were killed in the air raid, including many of Gryzlov's closest friends and fellow aviators. Both father and son were devastated and spent more than a month attending funerals and memorial services and planning how to rebuild the base and the bomber force.

It was never officially revealed, but the elder Gryzlov told his son who he thought planned the air raid: an American Air Force general by the name of Patrick McLanahan, acting without orders or authority from the American White House or Pentagon. Both men turned their sadness at the devastation into a white-hot burning desire for revenge against McLanahan.

With the destruction of Engels Air Base, Gennadiy shifted his focus from flying bombers and, with the help of his father, attended the Alexander Mozhaysky Military Space Academy in St. Petersburg, with a slot already reserved for him at the Cosmonaut

Training Center at Star City. But his training there too was interrupted. An American bomber unit attacked a Russian defensive antiaircraft battery in Turkmenistan . . .

. . . and, it was soon discovered, the raid was planned and ordered by Major General Patrick McLanahan, again without proper authority from his superior officers.

That raid, Gennadiy knew, had pushed his father over the edge. President Gryzlov recalled all bomber crewmembers and sent them to Belaya Air Base in Siberia for training. Gennadiy was able to use his father's influence to stay at Mozhaysky, but he carefully followed the activities of the vast array of long-range aircraft at Belaya and other bases like Irkutsk, Aginskoye, and Yakutsk, including sleek Tupolev-22 Backfires, reliable turboprop-powered Tupolev-95 Bears, supersonic Tupolev-160 Blackjacks, and Ilyushin-62 aerial refueling tankers. Something big, Gennadiy knew, was going to happen.

In late summer 2004, it did. Waves of Russian long-range bombers attacked American air defense and early-warning radar sites in Alaska and Canada with AS-17 "Krypton" antiradar missiles and AS-16 "Kickback" supersonic attack missiles, then launched AS-X-19 "Koala" long-range hypersonic cruise missiles with micro-yield nuclear warheads against intercontinental-ballistic-missile launch control centers, bomber bases, and command and control bases in the United States. The United States lost almost its entire land-based ballistic missile force, a large portion of its strategic bomber fleet, and tens of thousands of military personnel, family members, and civilians in the blink of an eye.

It soon became known as the "American Holocaust."

Gennadiy was happy and pleased with the bravery of his fellow heavy-bomber crewmembers—many of whom were lost over the United States and Canada—and proud of his father for finally striking a decisive blow against the Americans. He hoped McLanahan was under one of those nuclear warheads. In the meantime, all training at Mozhaysky was canceled, and Gennadiy was ordered to report to Aginskoye Air Base in southern Russia to stand up a new bomber regiment where more Tupolev-160 Blackjack bombers that were being refurbished and returned to service would be sent. Russia was beginning to go on a war footing, and Gennadiy was happy that he was not going to be stuck in school while other brave Russian aviators would be going toe-to-toe against the Americans.

The preparations for war with the United States had hardly begun when the unthinkable happened.

Yakutsk Air Base in Siberia was overrun and captured by a small force of American commandos, and
the United States began flying long-range bombers
and aerial refueling tankers from the base. Within
days, American bombers were roaming most of Russia
from Yakutsk, hunting down and destroying Russian
mobile intercontinental-missile launchers and underground launch control centers with ground-penetrating
precision-guided cruise missiles and bombs.

Gennadiy was not surprised to learn that the bomber
force was led by none other than Patrick McLanahan.

President Anatoliy Gryzlov was forced to make a
fateful decision: to destroy Yakutsk before the American
fleet could devastate the mobile ballistic-missile force,
the mainstay of Russia's strategic deterrent. He ordered
bombers to launch nuclear-tipped AS-X-19 Koala cruise
missiles against the American-occupied base, without first warning the Russians still being held there.
Although most of the cruise missiles were shot down by
American air-to-air missiles and by a sophisticated airborne laser system installed on a few B-52 bombers, a
few managed to hit the base, killing hundreds, Russians
and Americans alike, who were unlucky enough not to
make it to hardened underground shelters.

Gennadiy felt sorry for his father, who had been
forced to make an awful decision and kill Russians

to prevent the widespread destruction of the nation's prized ICBM force. He wanted so badly to be with his father and lend him some moral support, but the elder Gryzlov was undoubtedly safe and secure in one of over a dozen alternate command centers in western and central Russia. Gennadiy's greatest concern now was for his base and his regiment, and he ordered all non-essential personnel into shelters, fearing an American counterattack, and an acceleration of preparations for the Blackjack bombers that would hopefully be arriving shortly.

Gennadiy was deep into organizing his regiment and planning their activities when he received the devastating news the next morning: an American bomber task force of modified B-1 and B-52 bombers had blasted their way past western Russia's sophisticated air defense network and attacked Ryazan Alternate Military Command Center, 120 miles southeast of Moscow. The devastation was complete . . . and Gennadiy's father, the center of his universe, the man he wanted nothing more than to emulate, had been blown into dust. He made immediate arrangements to head back to Moscow to be with his mother and family, but before he left Aginskoye he learned that his mother, upon hearing the news about her husband, had committed suicide by an overdose of sleeping pills . . .

. . . and, once again, he learned that the commander of the bomber task force that killed his father, and thereby also his mother, was General Patrick McLanahan. The rogue American aviator had been promoted to lieutenant general shortly after the attack and made a special adviser to the new/former president of the United States, Kevin Martindale, placed in charge of rebuilding the long-range strike force.

Gennadiy Gryzlov turned into a different man after that day. He resigned his commission and left the military. He'd always had a high level of energy, but now his personality became more akin to that of a whirling dervish. He took control of his family's oil, gas, and petrochemical companies and had them positioned perfectly when oil prices began to skyrocket in the later part of the first decade of the twenty-first century, and he became one of the wealthiest men in the western hemisphere. He remained a bachelor and became one of the most popular and recognizable playboys in the world, pursued by wealthy women and men everywhere. He translated his wealth, popularity, and good looks into political capital and was appointed minister of energy and industry and deputy premier of Russia in rapid succession, then elected prime minister by the Duma even though he had never served in the legislature, aligning himself for higher office.

He ran for president thereafter and was elected to the office by more than 80 percent of the voters in the 2014 elections.

But now the face of the tall, handsome young man, easily the most photographed male face on planet Earth, was contorted in a mixture of disbelief, rage, and resolve. Sergei Tarzarov, the president's chief of staff, trotted into Gryzlov's office when he heard the president shouting. "Get Sokolov and Khristenko in here on the double," Gryzlov shouted to his chief of staff, his longish dark hair whirling around his head as he stomped around his office. "I want some answers, and I want them *now!*"

"Yes, sir," Tarzarov said, and he picked up a phone in the president's office. Tarzarov was almost a generation older than Gryzlov, a thin and unimposing-looking man in a simple brown suit, but everyone in the Kremlin knew the former intelligence officer and minister of the interior was the power behind the presidency and had been so since Gennadiy's father was in office. "They saw the broadcast and are already on the way, sir," he reported a few moments later.

"Why, that smug, preening, clueless bastard—I will show him how to make a statement to the world," Gryzlov snapped. "It was nothing but an election-year stunt. I hope it blows up in his face! I hope he dies in a fireball during reentry. Then the American government will be in a state of complete chaos!"

"Receiving data from the ministry of defense," Tarzarov reported after checking his tablet computer. "Minister Sokolov ordered an update of our space offensive and defensive forces and ground, air, and naval forces that support space operations. He and General Khristenko will brief you as soon as they arrive."

"Why the hell did we not know that Phoenix was going to fly to that space station?" Gryzlov shouted. "We know what that bastard does almost before *he* knows it, and we have plants, eavesdroppers, listening devices, cameras, and informants all over Washington. Get Kazyanov in here too. No, get the entire security council in here." Tarzarov made another phone call and reported that Viktor Kazyanov, the minister of state security, Russia's top espionage and counterintelligence service, was also already on the way to the president's office.

"Mr. President, Phoenix has got to be totally crazy to pull off a stunt like that," the minister of defense, Gregor Sokolov, said as he quickly strode into the president's office a few minutes later. "If he was not damaged goods before he blasted off, the cosmic radiation and lack of oxygen will surely get to him—if he really did all the things he claimed to do, and all of this is not an elaborate election-year fake—and then the American space program will be deader than it was after the space shuttle *Challenger* blew up."

"Shut up, Sokolov," Gryzlov said. "The fact is, he did it, and I want to know how, I want to know why I didn't know about it, and I want to know what we can do if he starts doing all the shit he says he is going to do—and I want to know it *right now!*"

Tarzarov stepped over to Gryzlov, turned his back to the others in the room, and said in a soft voice, "It is perfectly all right to have a rant when I or no one else is in the room, Gennadiy, but when the national security staff arrives you should contain yourself." Gryzlov's head snapped over to his chief of staff and his eyes flared, but when his angry visage met Tarzarov's steady, warning gaze, he relaxed and nodded. "And do not make your comments personal. You need the support of your cabinet, not their resentment."

"I want answers, Sergei," Gryzlov said, lowering his voice but only slightly. "I want answers I should have had days ago!" But he turned away from Tarzarov, gave Sokolov a slight bow of his head in apology, then returned to his desk and pretended to look over some dispatches on his tablet computer.

The meeting of Gryzlov's national security advisers began several minutes later, with Foreign Minister

Daria Titeneva joining Gryzlov and the others in the conference room adjoining the president's office. Chief of the general staff General Mikhail Khristenko was the first to speak, using a tablet computer to wirelessly present photographs and data slides on a large flat-screen computer monitor: "If you will allow me, sir: I double-checked the records, and in fact the American Strategic Command, who oversees all military space operations, did inform our embassy in Washington through the air attaché's office that they would be launching an S-19 Midnight spaceplane to Armstrong Space Station."

Gryzlov looked as if he was going to explode again, but Tarzarov spoke first: "Minister Titeneva?"

"I was not informed," Titeneva, a veteran foreign-affairs officer with dark hair and eyes and a full but attractive body, responded. "Urgent and emergency messages are routed to my office immediately, but routine messages are sent to my staff office in charge of such matters, and they are included in the two summary reports I receive each day. A spaceplane goes to the space stations or into orbit many times a month—such flights are considered routine."

"Perhaps your office should be notified every time such a flight occurs," Tarzarov suggested.

"That may be a good idea for the military, Mr. Tarzarov, but I see no reason for the Foreign Ministry to be so advised unless the military or state security thinks the flight might be a threat to the homeland or our allies," Titeneva said, obviously piqued about being challenged by the chief of staff in a meeting of the full security council. "The main reason we demanded that the United States notify us of the flights at all is because its boost into orbit could resemble an intercontinental-ballistic-missile launch. They are certainly not obligated to give us the passenger list."

"You will instruct your office to notify you whenever one of those spaceplanes is set to launch, Minister," Gryzlov said angrily. "Then you will notify me immediately, with details about its departure and return dates and times, destination, and purpose. I will not allow those damned things to just flit about overhead and not know anything about it!" He turned to the minister of state security. "Kazyanov, do you not keep track of the whereabouts of the president of the United States?" he asked. "How in hell can the president of the United States make a television broadcast from space and apparently no one in this entire damned city know anything about it?"

"We do our best to track the president of the United States, major officials, and senior military officers, sir," Viktor Kazyanov, a tall, bald, and powerful-looking former army colonel, replied. Like the director of national intelligence in the United States, the recently created Ministry of State Security was meant to combine domestic, international, and military intelligence, presidential and embassy protection, and border security activities under one cabinet-level officer who reported directly to the security council.

However, the intelligence services were reluctant in the extreme to share information and lose access to the office of the president. It was well known that the directors of the Federal Security Service (once known as *Komitet Gosudarstvennoy Bezopasnoti,* or KGB), the Foreign Intelligence Service, the Presidential Security Service, and the Chief Directorate for Intelligence of the General Staff (*Glavnoe Razvedivatel'noe Upravlenie,* or GRU) reported directly to the president through the chief of staff: very often Kazyanov was the last to know anything. "But we cannot know precisely where the American president is every minute of every day," Kazyanov said. "The American press all believed he was on his way to Guam for this press conference, and that was where we were waiting for him. If he is going to leave the capital for any length of time, we know about it."

"Well, I would say he has left the capital, would you not?" Gryzlov retorted derisively. "Are you not watching the White House and Capitol all the time?"

"Any movement of the president, vice president, cabinet officials and their deputies, and senior-level military officers and defense officials triggers a warning to us, sir," Kazyanov said. "The president and any official that travels with a large contingent, or any information we receive on movement plans, triggers an alert. If they do not, we may not know about their movement. Obviously, this trip was kept under very tight secrecy, with minimal security protocols to avoid attracting attention."

"It is imperative that you come up with the means for discovering when one of those spaceplanes is going to make a flight and who and what is aboard it, Kazyanov," Gryzlov said. "If they fly so routinely, maybe their security procedures are starting to break down. You must also think of ways to be alerted to movement of major American officials other than by the size of their retinue. Be prepared to brief the council on your suggestions at next week's regular meeting." It was obvious by his expression that Kazyanov didn't like being barked at, even by the president, but he nodded assent. Gryzlov turned back to General Khristenko. "Continue, General."

"Yes, sir," the chief of the general staff said. He called up a silent replay of President Phoenix's press conference. "My staff studied the video of Phoenix's press conference and some video that was shot after the press conference of Phoenix having a meal with some cosmonauts, and based on these preliminary images my staff feels that it is indeed President Phoenix and he is aboard a spacecraft in Earth orbit, experiencing real weightlessness, and looks very healthy and not suffering from any ill effects of space flight or weightlessness. The other persons in the video were identified as retired brigadier general Kai Raydon, engineer and astronaut Trevor Shale, and retired U.S. Marine Corps lieutenant colonel and astronaut Jessica Faulkner, a spaceplane pilot.

"Most likely he did travel to Earth orbit on the spacecraft reported to our embassy by U.S. Strategic Command, an S-19 spaceplane, nicknamed 'Midnight,'" Khristenko went on, switching slides to a photograph of the spaceplane. "It carries a crew of two and up to five thousand kilos of cargo. It apparently has a pressurized module in its cargo bay that has seats for as many as four passengers."

"I do not care about its seating capacity, General," Gryzlov said acidly. "What kind of threat is this spacecraft to Russia?"

"It represents a technology that we are still several years away from developing: the ability to take off from almost any commercial runway in the world, fly into low Earth orbit, dock with the space stations or perform various activities in space, reenter Earth's atmosphere, and land again on any runway—and do it all again just a few hours later," Khristenko said. "It has a sophisticated propulsion system that uses readily available jet fuel and hydrogen-peroxide oxidizer. It can dock with the space station and deliver supplies or personnel almost on demand. If it stayed in the atmosphere, it could fly from its base in the western United States to Moscow in less than three hours."

"Three hours!" Gryzlov exclaimed. "And then deliver a nuclear weapon right on top of our heads!"

"To our knowledge, sir, the spaceplanes have only deployed nonnuclear weapons in space," Kazyanov said, "but one such weapon, the so-called Thor's Hammer, did successfully reenter Earth's atmosphere and destroyed a target on the ground."

"That is when we argued to put the Space Preservation Treaty in place, sir," Foreign Minister Titeneva said. "The treaty bans any weapons based in space that can attack targets on Earth. Russia, China, and all of the other space-capable countries have ratified the treaty except the United States, although they appear to be abiding by it."

"Damn it, Daria, I want weapons such as that banned . . . only as long as it takes *us* to build them ourselves!" Gryzlov said. He ran a hand through his thick hair. "And we have no technology similar to this spaceplane?"

"We had built a reusable spacecraft years before the Americans built their space shuttle," Minister of Defense Sokolov said. "The Elektron spaceplane was boosted into orbit atop an SL-16 booster and could land on a runway—it was even armed with guided missiles. We built several of the spacecraft, but their operational status is unknown. The Buran spaceplane was very similar to the American space shuttle. We built five of them and performed one successful flight before the empire dissolved. Three more Burans are in various states of completion; the other completed spacecraft was destroyed in a ground accident."

"And look what has happened: we let the Americans gain the advantage over us in space," Gryzlov said. "So put them back into operation and get them flying right away, and if we have built them once before, we can build them again. I want as many as possible put into immediate production."

"Phoenix is a fool if he really plans to degrade his army and navy in favor of space weapons," Sokolov said. "And he can build all the cyberweapons he wants—while our troops overrun his cities."

"It looks to me like Phoenix will not abide by any space treaty for long," Gryzlov said. "If he wants to industrialize space, he will want to defend it. If we cannot get him to agree not to militarize space, and he wins reelection and goes ahead with this plan, what do we have to counter such moves? What can we use to attack his spacecraft?"

"Our most potent antisatellite weapon currently deployed is the S-500 'Autocrat' surface-to-air missile system, sir," Khristenko said. "Its maximum target altitude of five hundred kilometers and a maximum range of seven hundred kilometers put it well within range of the American's military space station. The system is mobile and easily moved and set up, so it can be fired and then moved to evade counterstrike or quickly be placed under the orbital path of a target. The S-500 is also very capable against hypersonic attack missiles, stealthy aircraft, low-flying aircraft or cruise missiles, and ballistic missiles. It is by far the most capable surface-to-air missile system in the world."

"Finally, some good news," Gryzlov said.

"The one problem with the S-500 is we have built very few of them so far, sir," Sokolov said. "There are only twelve batteries in service, stationed around Moscow, St. Petersburg, and Vladivostok for defense against stealth aircraft and cruise missiles."

"*Twelve?*" Gryzlov retorted loudly. "We should have *twelve thousand* of them! You will get the funding to build ten a month, and I want several to be deployed to every Russian military base in the world! I want that space station and every Western spacecraft in Russia's crosshairs around the clock! Go on."

"The next viable antisatellite system, and the most flexible, is the MiG-31D antisatellite missile carrier," Khristenko said, changing the slide again. The slide showed a picture of a large twin-tailed muscular-looking jet fighter. "It has a top speed of almost three times the speed of sound and a maximum altitude of over thirty thousand meters. It employs the 9K720 *Osa* missile, which is the same missile as on the Iskander theater ballistic missile. The MiG-31 is directed toward its target by ground radar stations and deploys the missile as it climbs through twenty thousand meters. The *Osa* missile optionally carries a micronuclear warhead, so one missile would probably be sufficient to knock the American space station out of the sky. The *Osa* missile steered by the MiG-31's radar is capable against other aerial targets as well."

"That is good," Gryzlov said. "How many do we have active right now, General?"

"There are only thirty of the antisatellite missile carriers in service right now, sir," Khristenko replied. "Two squadrons in the west and one in the far east."

"When in hell did we stop building military equipment?" Gryzlov moaned. "What else?"

"The MiG-31 first flew over forty years ago," Khristenko said. "Its radar has been updated, but not for several years in favor of newer fifth-generation fighters. In its antisatellite role the MiG-31's range is limited to only about eight hundred kilometers. But the 9K720 missile has a range of four hundred kilometers, sufficient to reach any American spacecraft in low Earth orbit."

"Can we build more?"

"We currently have about two hundred and fifty MiG-31s in the inventory, sir," Khristenko said. "About one hundred are active."

"More than *half* the inventory is inactive?" Gryzlov complained again. "If our country is awash in oil money, why have we been allowing half our aircraft to be inactive?" Khristenko did not answer. "Then turn all of the active MiG-31s into antisatellite missile carriers," Gryzlov said. "I assume you have other fighters that can take over the interceptor role from the MiG-31s?"

"Of course, sir."

"I want a full report on the conversion, and I want an estimate of how long it will take to build more of the S-500s," Gryzlov ordered. "What about space assets?"

"We have the Soyuz man-rated cargo spacecraft and the Progress unmanned cargo spacecraft, sir, along with the Proton medium-lift and Angara heavy-lift launch rockets," Khristenko replied. "We have extensive experience with resupply missions to the International Space Station."

"That is all? *Supply missions?*"

"Sir, Russia has been heavily supporting the International Space Station, especially since the Americans stopped flying their shuttle," Sokolov said. "We needed no other outpost in Earth orbit since we have unlimited access to the Russian Orbital Section of the ISS for scientific experiments."

"But it is not a Russian space station," Gryzlov said. "Do we have any plans whatsoever to build our own military space station? Whatever happened to our own space station projects? We had several, and now we have none?"

"Yes, sir," Khristenko replied. "The project is called Orbital Piloted Assembly and Experiment Complex. Before the International Space Station is decommissioned and allowed to reenter the atmosphere, Russia would detach its Russian Orbital Section modules and mount them on a central truss with solar panels and positioning thrusters. The station will be used to assemble spacecraft for moon or Mars missions, conduct experiments, and—"

"When is this supposed to take place?"

"In about five years, sir," Sokolov replied.

"*Five years?* That is unacceptable, Sokolov!" Gryzlov shouted. "I want the plans for this station to be advanced. I want this to happen as quickly as possible!"

"But we have agreements with nine nations for the use of those modules on the International Space Station, sir," Foreign Minister Titeneva said. Gryzlov's eyes flared at this interruption. "The partnership has already paid Russia for their use and to support the ISS. We cannot—"

"If the United States will not cancel this domineering plan to militarize and industrialize Earth orbit, all partnerships and agreements regarding outer space are null and void," Gryzlov said. "Do you understand me? If Phoenix persists with this outrageous plan, Russia is going to push back. Everyone here had better understand: Russia is not going to allow any one nation to dominate outer space. That bastard Kenneth Phoenix has just thrown down the gauntlet: Russia is picking it up, and we *will* respond . . . starting *right now!*"

Gryzlov dismissed the meeting with a wave of his hand, and soon he and Tarzarov were alone. "I am tired of always having to light a fire under these career bureaucrats' asses," Gryzlov said, lighting a cigar. "We may need to update the list of replacement ministers again. Titenov's name is at the head of the list to be replaced. How dare she challenge my wishes? I do not care what protocols are in place—what I want is what I want, and her job is to get it for me."

"Now that you have given them their orders, let us see how they respond," Tarzarov suggested. "If they fail to get the money from the Duma and start military construction projects, you have good reason to replace them. As I said, Gennadiy, do not make this personal."

"Yes, yes," Gryzlov said dismissively.

Tarzarov checked his smartphone for messages. "Ilianov is here."

"Good. Get him in here," Gryzlov said. A moment later Tarzarov, carrying a box of items, escorted Bruno Ilianov and Yvette Korchkov into the president's office, then put the box on the president's desk. "I hear you were successful, Colonel, even though your workers were arrested," he said, rising from his desk to greet them. Ilianov was wearing his Russian Air Force uniform. Making no attempt to be circumspect, Gryzlov ran his eyes up and down Korchkov's body as she approached. She was dressed in a dark business suit, tailored to accentuate her curves and breasts, but she wore spiked high heels that were more suited to a cocktail party than business in the office of the president of Russia. Korchkov returned Gryzlov's appreciative gaze without expression. He turned his attention back to Ilianov and extended his hand. The Russian colonel took it, and Gryzlov held the hand, keeping Ilianov close to him. "The capture of your men is unfortunate, Colonel," he said. "I hope they can hold their tongues."

"It does not matter, sir," Ilianov said. "Our story will hold up. They are known burglars and Russian nationalists who wanted revenge on General Patrick McLanahan. They gave the items to other unknown expatriates. If they do talk and implicate me, I will deny everything. You can support their sentiments but will launch an investigation, terminate me, and offer to pay for repairs. The American media's ridiculously fast news cycle and general ignorance for anything except sex and violence will quickly sweep the whole episode away."

"It had better, Colonel," Gryzlov warned. He returned to his desk, dumped the items from the box onto its top, picked up the urn, hefted it, then looked at Ilianov. "Empty?"

"Exactly so, sir," Ilianov said. "What does that mean?"

"It means someone already flushed him down the sewer," Gryzlov said acidly, "depriving me of the opportunity to do so." He glanced over the remaining items. "So. This is all that remains of the great Patrick Shane McLanahan, aerial assassin," he said.

"Not quite all, sir," Ilianov said. "His immediate family. Two sisters and a son."

"I do not order the assassination of women, Colonel," Gryzlov said, glancing again at Korchkov. He knew the Russian beauty was a highly trained *Spetsgruppa Vympel* commando, specializing in close-quarters killing . . . *intimately* close quarters. "But all the rest of McLanahan's possessions are forfeited to me. Have you located the son?"

"He is making no attempt to hide his whereabouts, sir," Ilianov said. "He posts regularly to social media—the entire planet knows where he is and what he does. We have so far detected no evidence of security surrounding him."

"Just because he does not post anything about a security detail on Facebook does not mean it doesn't exist," Gryzlov said. "I hope you have picked more reliable men to carry out this task."

"There is no lack of men willing to carry out these operations, sir," Ilianov said. "We have selected the best. They are in position now and are ready to strike. My men will make it look like the son killed himself while drinking and freebasing cocaine, and I will be sure that the details are in every newspaper and television show in the world. I will also make it clear that the son got hooked on drugs and alcohol because of his father's neglect, and that the father had similar dependency and emotional problems."

"Very good," Gryzlov said. He took a deep drag of his cigar, using the interlude to look Korchkov up and down again. "Why not send Captain Korchkov?" he asked. "I am sure young McLanahan would wear a nice big smile on his face . . . the instant before his life was snuffed out." Korchkov remained completely expressionless, her hands folded in front of her body, her legs almost shoulder width apart in a very ready, athletic stance.

"The men I have selected will have no difficulties, sir," Ilianov said. "Sending the captain back to the United States to get McLanahan would be like using a sledgehammer to crack an egg."

"Just see to it that it gets done, Colonel," Gryzlov said. "I have waited long enough to seek my revenge on Patrick McLanahan. I want everything that belonged to him dead and destroyed. All that remains of him is his son and his reputation, and I want both shattered."

"Yes, sir," Ilianov said. "I will report on the success of my team tomorrow."

"It had better be successful, Colonel," Gryzlov said. "I want the McLanahan name stained beyond repair." He gave Korchkov another glance, wondering if he should tell her to stay or contact her later, then waved a hand. "You have your orders, Colonel. Carry them out." Ilianov and Korchkov turned and left without a word.

"This is no business for a president of the Russian Federation, sir," Tarzarov said after the two had departed.

"Perhaps not, Sergei," Gryzlov said, his face hard and foreboding through a cloud of cigar smoke, "but it is certainly the business of the son of Anatoliy Gryzlov. Once McLanahan's son has been eliminated, I can turn full attention to rebuilding our nation and putting it back on the path to greatness. We have been raking in the natural resources money and stuffing it under the mattress for too long, Sergei—it is time to start spending it and taking our rightful place in the world as a true superpower."

CALIFORNIA POLYTECHNIC UNIVERSITY
SAN LUIS OBISPO, CALIFORNIA

That same time

"How freakin' cool was that?" exclaimed Bradley McLanahan. He and four other students were in their professor's office in the Reinhold Aerospace Engineering Building on the sprawling campus of the California Polytechnic University, San Luis Obispo, known simply as Cal Poly, near California's central coast, watching TV on one of the computers in the office. "The president of the United States is up in orbit on Armstrong Space Station! If he can do it, I sure as hell can!" The other students nodded in agreement.

Brad McLanahan was close to finishing his first year as an aerospace engineering student at Cal Poly. Everything in his life, from his body to his education to his experiences, all seemed to be just a little bit more than average. He was a little bit taller, heavier, and better-looking than average, with blue eyes and blond hair that had grown a bit longer than most engineering students on campus wore theirs. His grades were probably a bit better than average, just good enough to be accepted to the college of engineering at Cal Poly, which accepted fewer than one-third of all applicants. Thanks to a generous trust and benefits of a sizable life insurance policy from his deceased parents, Brad was in a better financial situation while in college than most other students: he rode a nice bicycle to school from his off-campus house in San Luis Obispo and even occasionally flew his father's turbine Cessna P210 Silver Eagle airplane from the nearby airport, all while knowing that he would have no college tuition or student loan bills from his undergraduate or graduate education.

"We couldn't have timed this any better, Brad," said Lane Eagan. Fifteen-year-old Lane was from Roseburg, Oregon, graduating from homeschooled high school after just two years with a stratospheric grade-point average, and was accepted to Cal Poly with a four-year scholarship. Small, a little pudgy, and wearing thick glasses—he looked like the classic Hollywood version of a nerd—Lane looked up to Brad like a big brother. Lane was a freshman attending the college of electrical engineering, specializing in computer and microchip design and programming. "I hope Professor Nukaga likes our proposal."

"I still think we should have gone with the space-junk idea, Bradley," said Kim Jung-bae. Jung-bae—everyone called him "Jerry" because he liked Jerry Lewis movies, a nickname he used proudly—was from Seoul, United Korea, who transferred after two years at Pohang University of Science and Technology to study in the United States. Tall and thin, he spent as much time on the basketball court as he did in an engineering laboratory. Jerry was a mechanical engineering student, specializing in robotics and power storage technologies. "You know Nukaga: he does not care for the military stuff as much."

"Starfire is not a military program, Jerry," said Casey Huggins. Casey was also a freshman four-year

scholarship winner to Cal Poly. A water-skiing accident when she was a young girl left her paralyzed from
the waist down, so academics became a large part of
her life. She fought to keep her weight down by using a
manually powered wheelchair to get around Cal Poly's
very large six-thousand-acre campus, and competing
in adaptive sports such as wheelchair basketball and
archery. Casey was an electrical engineering student,
specializing in directed-energy projects. "We're using
some military hardware, but it's not a military program." Jung-bae shrugged, not entirely convinced but
not willing to provoke another argument.

"I like Jerry's space-debris idea too, but especially after
hearing President Phoenix's little speech there, I think
we should stick with our proposal, mates," said Jodie
Cavendish, sweeping her long blond hair back off her
shoulders, then nervously twisting it back around across
her breasts. Jodie was from Brisbane, Australia, and
although she looked like a tall, trim, blue-eyed Southern
California surfer girl, lived very close to the ocean back
home, and loved sailing, surfing, and paddleboarding,
she loved more than anything else to study and experiment, and could be found either in a laboratory or the
library on a computer. She was close to finishing her two-
year exchange-student scholarship program between Cal
Poly and Queensland University of Technology, studying

mechanical engineering with a specialty in advanced materials and nanotechnology. "Besides, we've spent too much time rehearsing our yabber."

"Like Jodie said, I'm good with either idea, and we can pitch the space-debris idea too—we're prepared," Brad said. "But now, with that speech and that challenge, I think Starfire will be a winner."

"Do you now, Mr. McLanahan?" they heard a man say, and into the office raced Toshuniko Nukaga, Ph.D., professor of aerospace engineering at Cal Poly. Born, raised, and educated in Berkeley, California, Nukaga, known in academic circles as well as to his close friends as "Toby," did nothing slowly, whether it was bicycle racing, giving lectures, or writing and presenting yet another paper on another breakthough in the world of aerospace science. Sixty years old and retired from the aerospace industry, Nukaga was one of the most-sought-after experts on new aircraft and spacecraft design. He'd had his choice of positions on the board of directors or leadership of hundreds of companies and universities around the world, but he had chosen to spend his remaining years before retirement in California's Central Valley, imparting his knowledge and yearning to explore and question conventional wisdom to a new generation of engineers and thinkers.

"Good afternoon, Dr. Nukaga," Brad said. "Thank you for seeing us so late in the afternoon."

Nukaga had checked his e-mail on his desktop computer, removed his tablet computer from his backpack, and put it on its charging stand by the time Brad had finished speaking. He nodded, acknowledging the young man's gratitude, then sat back in his chair, tapping his fingertips together to keep himself in motion despite being seated. "You're welcome. Let's hear your 'winner,' Mr. McLanahan."

"Yes, sir," Brad said. "I recently found out that Sky Masters Aerospace in Nevada has put out a request for proposals to universities and companies for a new generation of space projects. It seems that companies like Sky Masters have been working with the Phoenix administration, because the president just proposed the very same thing in his address from Armstrong Space Station. Sky Masters wants—"

"Did you say, the president addressed the nation *from the military space station?*" Nukaga asked incredulously. "He is up in orbit *right now?*"

"Yes, sir," Brad replied. "He just concluded a press conference too. He was feeling pretty good, weightless and everything. I guess his Secret Service guy didn't do as well."

"What in the world is a president of the United States doing on a *military space station?*" Nukaga remarked rather bitterly. "It seems extremely irresponsible to me. There are a thousand incidents that could happen and a hundred illnesses he could contract, some of which could affect his mind, and he is the commander in chief of a nuclear-armed military. It's madness." He fell silent for a moment, then waved a hand, erasing the topic from his mind. "Please continue, Mr. McLanahan."

"We are requesting computer-, mechanical-, and aerospace-engineering-lab space and resources for twelve weeks this summer for a project that hopefully can be put into orbit and tested before the end of the year," Brad said. "We call it Project Starfire."

Nukaga's eyebrows raised in amusement. "Your name, I assume, Mr. McLanahan?"

"It was mine, sir," Lane Eagan said proudly.

"Of course, Mr. Eagan," Nukaga said, hiding a slight smile behind two fingertips tapping against his lips. He had at first distrusted the young man—boy, really—because his parents both held multiple doctorates and were very wealthy, aggressive, hard-charging research scientists, and he believed Eagan's success was mostly due to his parents' strong, driving influence. But that definitely did not turn out to be the case. Although young Eagan slipped back easily into a teenager's persona now and then, he truly was a gifted young man who would no doubt hold his own collection of doctorates, exceeding his parents' impressive credentials, before long.

The professor erased all hint of a smile, turned stony once again, then said, "Indeed. So why don't you continue the presentation, Mr. Eagan?"

"Yes, sir," Lane said without skipping a beat. Just like that, the teenager was gone, replaced by a serious young scientist-to-be. "As you well know, sir, the idea of generating power from the sun from a spacecraft in Earth orbit and transmitting the electricity to Earth has been proposed for many years, but we think we've overcome the technical hurdles and can design a commercially feasible space-based solar-power station."

Nukaga looked at Casey and Jodie. "Since your team has Miss Huggins, I assume your spacecraft uses some sort of directed energy, such as microwaves," he observed. "Miss Huggins?"

"Not exactly, sir," Casey said. "Most research on the subject of space-based solar-power production used microwaves or lasers to transmit the solar-collected electricity to Earth. Lasers have some political roadblocks. Microwaves are very efficient and can transmit a lot of energy very quickly. But microwaves require a large nantenna, or transmitting antenna—as large as a square kilometer or more in area—and an even larger rectenna, or receiving antenna, perhaps ten times as large as the transmitting antenna. Our associates around the world and we here at Cal Poly have developed a maser: a microwave laser. We are able to wiggle and collimate a beam in the microwave spectrum so it's possible to squeeze a lot of energy into a smaller, more focused beam. It has some of the best characteristics of a microwave and a visible-light laser, using much smaller antennas, and is far more efficient. In addition, maser rectennas that transform the microwave energy into electricity are smaller, fairly portable, and can be set up almost anywhere."

"Besides, sir, the main components and power-generation equipment are already up on Armstrong Space Station," Brad said. Nukaga looked at Brad and narrowed his eyes disapprovingly at the interruption, but let him continue. "The Skybolt laser is a free-electron laser pumped by a klystron powered by a magnetohydrodynamic generator. We can introduce the microwave cavity into the laser itself, and use the collected electricity from Starfire to power the laser, so we don't have to use the MHD. We can even use Skybolt's aiming and control systems."

"That monstrosity should have been removed from orbit years ago and allowed to burn up on reentry," Nukaga said. He gave Brad another scowl, as if the space-based laser belonged to him. "Do you see any problems with shooting maser beams from space, Miss Huggins?" he asked.

"There are many potential political roadblocks, sir," Casey replied. "The Space Preservation Treaty of 2006 seeks to eliminate all offensive space weapons. Specifically, it mentions directed-energy systems capable of producing greater than one megajoule of energy at a range of more than one hundred kilometers. The Skybolt laser on Armstrong Space Station has attacked targets in space, the atmosphere, and even on Earth, at ranges far greater than one hundred kilometers, with far more energy." Nukaga wore a very sour expression—obviously he knew very well about what the space-based laser had done and was most displeased about it.

"After the reactivation of the Skybolt missile defense laser aboard Armstrong Space Station, as well as the deployment of Kingfisher space-based interceptors, the treaty was presented again and passed in the United Nations General Assembly in 2010," Casey went on. "The Security Council sought to codify the treaty; the United States under the Gardner administration chose to abstain rather than veto it, and the treaty passed. Although it has not been ratified by the U.S. Senate, the United States has—at least up until now—chosen to abide by it. Therefore, if the maser-power transmission concept is seen by the United Nations as potentially a space weapon, it couldn't be used unless the United States simply ignored the treaty."

"Which I sincerely hope is *not* done," Nukaga added. "What other problems have you overcome in this project? Miss Cavendish, since you are the advanced-materials student, why don't you continue?" They all knew that Nukaga would never allow just one member of the team to give a presentation like this, so they all had to be equally familiar with the proposal and prepared to give it at any time.

"Yes, sir," Jodie said. "The weight of standard silicon photovoltaic cells is simply a deal killer—it would take hundreds of shuttle-sized spacecraft, which we do not have except for some Russian spacecraft, which we probably couldn't use, or expendable heavy-lift launch vehicles to put enough photovoltaic panels on the spacecraft to make this work. But we and our partners have developed a solar-cell capture technology using multiwidth nanotubes applied to a flexible conducting substrate that could allow the construction of a mile-long photovoltaic cell for the same launch cost as a single furlable silicon solar cell designed to fit inside the shuttle, with several times the power-generation capacity."

For the first time in the meeting, Nukaga momentarily stopped fidgeting, and the change was instantly noticed by all of the students, even young Lane. "Interesting," the professor commented as he resumed his finger tapping. "An organic carbon nanotube that is more efficient than a silicon cell?"

"It's not a carbon nanotube, sir," Jodie said. She smiled, leaned forward, then said in a low conspiratorial voice, "It's a multiwidth inorganic titanium dioxide nanotube-structured optical nantenna."

Nukaga's eyebrows arched, just for a heartbeat, but to the students around him it felt as if a firecracker had gone off in the room. "Interesting," he repeated, although all the students could detect a slightly breathless tone in his voice. "An optical nantenna."

"Yes, sir," Jodie said. "Using inorganic nanotubes, we've designed a way to convert sunlight into electricity at efficiencies thousands of times greater than silicon solar cells. Even better, the structures are hundreds of times lighter and stronger than silicon solar cells."

He tried very hard to hide his surprise, but Toshuniko Nukaga was starting to look as if he might slip out of his chair. "Interesting," he managed to repeat, but his finger tapping had completely ceased. "You have fabricated such a structure?"

"I haven't done it yet, sir," Jodie said, "but I've spoken and corresponded with researchers in Cambridge and Palo Alto, and we could do it here, in our own labs, with the proper support. And, thanks to our team leader, Brad, we have access to researchers all over the world."

"And what are the advantages of this inorganic nanotube structure, Mr. Kim?" Jerry seemed to have a little bit of trouble answering a question about an area of engineering with which he wasn't as familiar as some of the others, so Nukaga turned to Brad. "Perhaps you can assist Mr. Kim, Mr. McLanahan?"

"Energy production vastly greater than silicon solar cells, but with far less weight," Brad replied. "Plus, the solar arrays fix themselves."

"How do they do that?"

"Because the substrate upon which the nanotubes are built is not metal, but flexible sol-gel material that not only allows electrons to flow from the nanostructure to the collection system with greater efficiency, but acts as a shock absorber," Brad said. "If the solar array is hit by orbital debris, the break is electrochemically reconnected, like damaged skin. It forms a kind of scar tissue, like human skin, which is not as photovoltaic as the original, but at least the array is still functional. Plus, the defensive lasers aboard Armstrong Space Station could be used to deflect debris that might seriously damage the nantennna arrays."

"Defensive lasers? I hardly think so," Nukaga remarked. "Continue."

"The titanium-dioxide nanotubes are impervious to cosmic radiation and the solar wind, and the sol-gel substrate can handle large changes in temperature with only minimal and temporary changes in conductivity," Brad said. "The structures we can put together can be enormous, perhaps stretching as far as several kilometers. This will allow us to eventually conduct several energy shots to different spots all around the globe in one orbit."

Nukaga was obviously not impressed with Brad's response—it was a huge oversimplification of a very complicated process that the team needed to have nailed down before the university was asked to grant thousands or even millions of dollars to research. "And how would deployment of Starfire work?" Nukaga asked. He turned to Jerry. "Start us off, Mr. Kim."

Jung-bae frowned as he collected his thoughts, but pressed ahead with only a short delay. "One of our imperatives in this project was a size limitation, sir," Jerry said. "The S-19 Midnight spaceplane, our preferred delivery vehicle for the space-based components, can carry a payload of approximately nine thousand pounds in its cargo bay, with some rather small size dimensions. That was a problem at first. Even using expendable boosters along with the spaceplanes, it would take many years, perhaps even decades, to build Starfire."

"And how did you solve this? Nine thousand pounds seems like a lot, but not when you have to build an entire expansive spacecraft from scratch."

"It would not be from scratch, sir," Jerry said. "Our proposal specifies the use of Armstrong Space Station, the International Space Station, or China's . . . China's . . ." Again he had trouble searching his memory.

Nukaga glanced at Brad, silently allowing him to assist. "China's Tiangong-2 space laboratory, sir," he said.

"Why these spacecraft? Mr. Eagan?"

"Because except for Tiangong, the others are old and ready to be changed to unmanned platforms, sir," Lane said. "Armstrong is almost thirty years old and ten years past its design service life. The ISS is twenty years old and approaching its design limit—it has been scheduled for deorbit in five years."

"And Tiangong-2?"

"The Chinese are expected to launch Tiangong-3 in just a few weeks, sir," Lane said. "We think they wouldn't mind letting their laboratory be used for this project. If Starfire works as planned, we'll be able to shoot electricity into the most remote regions of China—even to the top of the Himalayas!"

"What other problems lie ahead? Miss Cavendish?"

"It's a matter of getting the nantenna, capacitors, control equipment, microwave cavity, and maser-beam generators and associated equipment up to the station," Jodie said. "We estimate that we can get all the panels up into orbit in just ten missions in the spaceplanes, or four if we use expendable rockets."

"That seems extraordinary," Nukaga remarked. "How did you estimate that, Miss Huggins?"

"That's based on Jodie's estimate of the thinness of the nantennas and the dimensions of an S-19 Midnight spaceplane's cargo bay, sir," Casey replied. "We compute that one rolled-up nantenna array five hundred meters long and thirty meters wide can fit in the Midnight's cargo bay, well within weight limits because the nanotube structure will be so light. Our original design calls for a total of eight of these panels. We'd then need two more flights to bring up the extra equipment."

"That seems unrealistically optimistic, Miss Huggins. Mr. McLanahan?"

"We propose using a lot of the equipment that's already aboard Armstrong Space Station for this project, sir," Brad said. "Armstrong is particularly well suited for our project because it already has a lot of the beam-control hardware, capacitors, and aiming systems we need for the maser. It's all already up there—we don't have to launch it, just update software and some of the hardware. It's a lot better than having all that stuff burn up after being deorbited."

"It seems a lot is riding on the government letting you use their space station for your project," Nukaga pointed out.

"I've been in contact with the folks at Sky Masters Aerospace, who are Armstrong Space Station's caretakers until they figure out what they're going to do with it," Brad said. "They are open to Project Starfire. They want to see our data and results before they commit, but they like the idea of acquiring the space station for themselves, privatizing it, and putting it to work."

"I think Sky Masters Aerospace is a front for the Central Intelligence Agency or even for a secret government spy unit," Nukaga said. "I have a bad taste in my mouth every time I hear that name." Yet he nodded, almost imperceptibly, but to the students it was a very good sign. "Tell me about the ground portion of your project, Mr. Kim," Nukaga said. "I've heard a lot about the on-orbit parts, but very little about the ground systems and the challenges you're working around."

Kim seemed to struggle with the answer once again, but after a moment he replied, "Sir, the ground collection system includes a two-hundred-meter steerable rectenna, alternators, positioning controls, environmental systems, and a way to either store the direct current output from the rectenna or integrate the output into the local electrical grid."

"A two-hundred-meter rectenna?" Nukaga remarked. "Not exactly suited for the Himalayas, is it, Mr. Eagan?"

"The rectenna's size is based on the beam-control system currently aboard Armstrong Space Station, sir," Lane said. "It's forty-year-old technology, probably updated a few times but not to current standards. I haven't seen their code yet, but I'm sure I can improve the software to make the pointing and focusing more accurate, and then we can build a smaller rectenna. The maser beam doesn't expand as much as a microwave beam, and side lobe propagation is vastly lower and tunable."

"Regardless, sir, the ground systems are far smaller than any other type of power-generating plant," Brad interjected. "We don't use any natural resources other than sunlight, and there's more electricity potential from one day's worth of sunlight than all the electricity generated around the world in one year."

"That will look good on a website, Mr. McLanahan, but I'm not interested in a sales pitch now," Nukaga said rather irritably, now openly showing his displeasure at Brad's interruptions. He fell silent, thinking, then resumed his finger tapping. "And what sort of progress have you made so far?" he asked after a few moments.

"Jodie and Casey have drawn up the plans for the nantenna and maser and can start fabrication as soon as we get the go-ahead for the laser and materials lab and funding," Brad replied. "They also have plans for miniaturization so it can fit in a spacecraft, but our focus is on demonstrating that an inorganic nanotube nantenna is technically feasible. They feel confident they can do it by the end of summer."

"The end of summer?" Nukaga exclaimed. "Engineering complex nanotube structures in just a few months' work?"

"I've been working on inorganic nanotubes for over four years, sir," Jodie said, "but mostly by myself back in Australia. Brad sought me out based on my presentations over the years. He brought our team together, and he's still seeking out experts and scientists from all over the world to assist. Things are happening quickly."

Nukaga nodded slightly, then indicated to Brad that he could continue. "Jerry and I have plans to integrate the control, power, environmental, communications, and sensor systems, but we don't have the spacecraft, so we're still spread out," Brad said. "Lane has the software already written for the spacecraft control systems and ground-system rectenna controls, and is ready to start debugging and burning chips once we get the go-ahead. He already has software project outlines for Armstrong's beam-control units, but Sky Masters hasn't released their software to us yet, so it's just an anticipatory outline."

"And you have done all this on your own time, in between your classes and other responsibilities?" Nakuga remarked. "And except for Mr. Kim you are all freshmen, no?"

"Jodie is a third-year undergrad, sir," Brad replied. "Lane, Casey, and I are freshmen."

Nakuga nodded slightly, obviously impressed. "Where do you intend to get a spacecraft, Mr. McLanahan?"

"Sky Masters Aerospace out in Battle Mountain, Nevada, sir," Brad replied. "I've already got a Trinity module identified and on loan, and as soon as we have lab space I can have it shipped to us. It's not flyable, but it's an actual spacecraft, not just a mock-up or scale model."

"Trinity?"

"It's one of several different versions of Sky Masters Aerospace's autonomous orbital maneuvering vehicles, used by the Space Defense Force a few years ago," Brad explained. "It's placed into orbit by a Midnight spaceplane. It has its own targeting sensors, or it can take targeting data from a Kingfisher weapon garage or from Armstrong Space Station; it can autonomously refuel from Armstrong or another unmanned servicing module; it can—"

"'Targeting'? 'Weapon garage'?" Nukaga interrupted. "These are all space weapons?"

"Well, Trinity is a multipurpose orbital module, but yes, sir, it is used in a variety of space-based weapons," Brad said. He was hoping to not bring up the fact that Trinity was a space weapon to Nukuga—the professor was a well-known and moderately activist antiwar guy—but in his excitement to pitch the project and get the lab space, he said the words that hopefully would not kill this project.

Nukaga began blinking in some confusion. "I didn't know you were building a space weapon, Mr. McLanahan," he said.

"We're not, sir," Brad said, his confidence eroding quickly like a slow leak on a bicycle tire. "Starfire is an orbiting power plant based on Armstrong Space Station. We felt we had to not only design the components of the power plant but figure out ways to safely and efficiently get all the components into orbit using current technology. We can demonstrate that if we—"

"I'm not comfortable at all with cooperating with a company that produces space weapons," Nukaga said stiffly, staring accusingly at Brad. "If this company gets the information on your Starfire and then decides to use the technology to develop more space weapons, this university would be complicit in an arms race in space. Technology that could beam maser energy to a rectenna on Earth can certainly be used to disable a spacecraft or even destroy targets on the ground."

"Sky Masters Aerospace is offering a fifty-million-dollar grant for new orbital spacecraft technology, Dr. Nukaga," Brad said. "I think even just a piece of that would be extremely good for the university. We're hoping that getting the lab space and time in the directed-energy and computer labs will show the university's commitment to the project and help get part of that grant money."

"Money isn't the only consideration here, Mr. McLanahan," Nukaga retorted indignantly . . . but he briefly glanced away, silently acknowledging the fact that landing a big piece of a multimillion-dollar grant would certainly be good for the school—and for his own prestige, of course. "How did you happen to come across this Trinity module, Mr. McLanahan?" he asked.

"My father used to be the chief operations officer at the company, sir," Brad said. "I worked there for a short time, and I still have friends there. I stay in contact with the guys in the engineering and flight-test departments, and I hope to work there some day."

" 'Used to be'? Your father's retired?"

Brad swallowed hard, and when his mouth opened, no sound came forth.

"His father was killed, sir," Lane said in a soft voice. Nukaga looked at the young man, then back to Brad's blank expression, still confused.

"Dr. Nukaga, Brad's father was General Patrick McLanahan," Casey said, the tone in her voice making it plain that she couldn't believe he didn't know— Bradley McLanahan, the son of the great aerospace warrior General Patrick McLanahan, was a sort of minor celebrity on campus.

It finally dawned on Nukaga what had just transpired, but his expression of shock and embarrassment lasted only a moment. "I . . . my apologies, Mr. McLanahan," he said finally, straightening in his chair and looking at a spot on the wall over Brad's shoulder. "I did not know this." Still looking away, he cleared his throat, then motioned for the folder in Brad's hand. "I will look over your project, present it to the projects committee, and inform you as quickly as possible," he said as Brad gave him the folder. "Thank you all." The students shuffled to their feet and departed. "Mr. Kim. A word please."

"We'll be at the Starbucks at the Market, Jerry," Casey whispered to Jung-bae as they headed out. Jerry nodded, then returned to his seat.

Nukaga waited a few moments until he was sure the outer office was clear; then: "It seems to me you were not very well prepared for this presentation, Mr. Kim," he said. "I receive several dozen requests for sponsored summer lab space every spring for just three slots. The teams that I invite to make a personal presentation spend hundreds of hours in preparation and are all at the top of their games. But you did not seem to be so this afternoon. Can you tell me why, Mr. Kim?"

"I am afraid I cannot, sir," Jerry said. "A little stage fright perhaps."

"I hardly think so, Mr. Kim," Nukaga said. "If granted, this will be your third sponsored lab project in two years, in a school where only a third of the engineering students get even one. You are the top undergraduate engineering student in South Korea and one of the outstanding minds in the world. I'm pleased you chose Cal Poly, but you belong at MIT or Stanford."

Jerry averted his eyes for a moment, then looked at Nukaga. "Actually, sir . . . *you* are the reason I am here," he said. "I have followed your career for many years."

"Then why aren't you in aerospace engineering, son?" Nukaga asked. "We could be working side by side if you weren't on the mechanical engineering side of the campus. I've only had you for a few classes in all the years you've been here."

"Mechanical engineering was chosen for me by my corporate and government sponsors back home, sir," Jerry said. "Out of respect for them, I did not change my major. My second major was chosen for me by my parents, and my minor had to be in a nonscience field, so I chose business. But once I graduate and accept my credentials back home, I will be free to pursue other specialties, and I intend to come back here for my master's degree and doctorate under your tutelage."

"That would be outstanding, Jung-bae," Nukaga said. "I can almost guarantee your acceptance. I would even consider transferring to Stanford if you wanted to get your doctorate there instead—they've been hounding me for years to join their faculty and perhaps even be the dean of the college of engineering." Jerry's eyes widened in surprise, and he broke out into a very happy grin.

"But let's get back to this so-called Starfire project, son," Nukaga went on. "I'm confused. You're on a graduate-school level, but you're hanging out with a bunch of underclassmen. Mr. Eagan is almost young enough to be your son. None of those kids are on your intellectual level. What gives? Even if you liked the project—which to me seems you do not—why aren't you at least leading it? You have a freshman leading it, and he's not even the smartest one on the team." Jerry shrugged his shoulders and cast his eyes away. Nukaga paused, then winked conspiratorially at Jerry when the student's eyes came back to his. "Is it Miss Cavendish, Jung-bae? She certainly is a cutie. I would even volunteer to carry Miss Huggins in and out of her wheelchair, if you know what I mean."

Kim did not react at all to the personal remarks about his fellow students. He shrugged again, a childish motion that Nukaga was beginning to find irritating for such a gifted student. "I . . . I respect Mr. McLanahan, sir," he finally responded.

"McLanahan? Respect what about him? He's just a freshman aerospace engineering student with good but unremarkable grades. I didn't know he is Patrick McLanahan's son, but that hardly matters to me—in fact, it takes him down a notch as far as I'm concerned. His father was a rogue airman who always seemed to skate free of demotion, if not prison, after causing all manner of heinous international incidents without proper orders. I myself am sure it was his actions that precipitated the Russian air attack on the United States that killed tens of thousands."

"Perhaps Mr. McLanahan is not the best engineering student at Cal Poly, sir, but he is . . . is a team builder," Kim said. "He not only came up with the idea for Starfire, but he put together an incredible team, steered us through Tuckman's four stages of group development—forming, storming, norming, and performing—and coached us through our presentation to you. If he does not understand something or encounters a problem, he finds someone to explain the science to him, and they always end up joining his team. As you will see when you read the presentation, sir, Mr. McLanahan has amassed a sizable and quite impressive list of students, faculty, scientists, and engineers from all over the world willing to contribute to the project."

"This is the college of engineering, Jung-bae, not a frat house," Nukaga said. "Mr. McLanahan would be well advised to work on his grades a little more and do a little less glad-handing." He frowned, then went on: "And I'm very wary of the connection between Mr. McLanahan and this military defense company in Nevada. I will not have the college of engineering at Cal Poly become the crib of some new technology of death and destruction—I don't care if they give us the *entire* fifty million dollars." That certainly wasn't true, but Nukaga was standing on principle, not the university's political reality. He thought for a moment, then nodded resolutely. "I will read the proposal and present it to the committee," he said, "but I will also recommend approval for whatever resources you need."

"Thank you very much, sir," Jerry said.

Nukaga nodded again, a signal that the meeting was over. Jerry got to his feet, as did Nukaga. He extended a hand, and Jerry shook it. "I will tell you that the main reason I will recommend this project is because you are on it, Jung-bae," the professor said. "I wish it was your name at the top of the project leadership list, but having you on McLanahan's team is good enough for now. I think having you on the project will ensure getting a sizable portion of that seed money from that Nevada defense contractor."

"Thank you again, sir," Jerry said, bowing.

"But I will also make a strong suggestion to you, Jung-bae: if it appears that this Sky Masters Aerospace outfit wants to weaponize your technology in any way, I strongly urge you to leave the team and report to me," Nukaga said. "Money or no money, I will not allow this university to become a weapon technology factory. There are quite enough universities in this country willing to prostitute themselves for a little money, but I will not allow Cal Poly to be one of them." He paused for a moment, then asked, "Tell me, Jung-bae: did you have an alternative project to present to me in lieu of this Starfire thing?"

"Yes, sir, I did."

Nukaga's eyes widened in interest, and he motioned him back inside his office. "Favor me with another fifteen minutes of your time, Mr. Kim," he said. "I want to know all about it."

FOOD PROCESSING AND CAMPUS MARKET BUILDING
CAL POLY

A short time later

"I blew it, guys," Brad said. He and his fellow Starfire team members were sitting at a table on the patio of the Starbucks at the Campus Market. The Food Processing building was an unattractive warehouse-looking structure, but its southeast side had been attractively remodeled with a coffee shop and a store where students could buy fresh and prepared food and a wide variety of other items, and it had a large sunny outdoor seating area that was popular with the students and faculty. "I shouldn't have mentioned details about the Trinity module. Now Nukaga thinks we're going to build a death ray. Sorry."

"He was going to find out eventually when he read our proposal, Brad," Jodie said. "No worries. It's apples."

"You know, I noticed that your accent and slang almost completely disappear when you're talking to professors like Nukaga," Casey said. "How do you do that, Jodie?"

"I can do lots of accents, or none at all," Jodie said. She switched to a thick Russian one. "*Kak vam nravit- sya etot?* How do you like this one?"

"I think your Australian accent and slang are funny, Jodie," Lane said, giggling.

"I'm funny how—you mean funny like I'm a clown, I amuse you? I make you laugh?'" Jodie said in her best Brooklyn accent, convincingly impersonating Joe Pesci's character, Tommy DeVito, in the movie *Goodfellas* and being careful to take out the four-letter words. "'I'm here to amuse you?'" Lane giggled again, the scientist gone, replaced by the young schoolboy. Jodie switched to her thickest Australian accent and added, "Crikey, mates, but I could eat a horse and chase the jockey." The others looked at one another, then at Jodie. "It means, 'I'm hungry.' Let's get something to eat."

"I'm going to the library," Lane said, suddenly rising to his feet and snatching up his laptop backpack. In the blink of an eye the schoolboy was gone, replaced by the serious scientist. "See you guys later."

"Have dinner with us, Lane," Casey said. "We're just going to wait to see if Jerry shows."

"No thanks," Lane said. "My mom and dad will come get me from there. Besides, I have a history paper to finish." Brad blinked at that last statement but said nothing.

"When's it due?" Casey asked.

"A couple weeks," Lane said, "but I can't stand to have any unfinished projects sitting around." He put on his best Australian accent and said, "G'day, mates. Don't you blokes be gettin' rotten now, right-o?"

Jodie wadded up a napkin and threw it at him. "Bloody bodgie, dag!"

Lane headed toward University Avenue, toward the Robert E. Kennedy Library, just a few short blocks away. Brad caught up with him a few moments later. "I'll walk with you, Lane," Brad said, his own laptop backpack looped over one shoulder.

"You don't have to walk with me, Brad," Lane said. "I'm not a kid."

"You're fifteen," Brad said. "Besides, we talked about the buddy system. Always find a safety officer or someone you know who will walk with you."

"I see kids all the time walking around town by themselves."

"I know, and it's not smart," Brad said. "Find a buddy. Call me if you can't get a campus volunteer or security guard." He looked and saw Lane smile, obviously glad that Brad was coming with him and lecturing him about personal safety. "What was all that junk about a history paper due? I know for a fact that you finished *all* your coursework for *all* your classes for the *entire year* months ago, and with straight A's to boot."

"I know," Lane admitted after a moment. "I just . . ."

"Just what?"

"Nothing."

"Spill it, Lane."

"It's just . . . I think you guys would have a better time at the Market if I wasn't there," Lane said. "I . . . I get the feeling you guys can't . . . you know, have fun because 'the kid' is with you."

"That's bull, Lane," Brad said. "We're all friends. We're doing what we want to be doing. The girls go off and do whatever they do all the time. If they want to hang with us, they do it." They walked along in silence for a minute or so, and then Brad added, "But it must be tough to be a fifteen-year-old surrounded by adults."

"Nah. I'm used to it," Lane said. "I don't ever remember Mom and Dad treating me like a little kid or a teenager, like they do my friends or other kids. I feel way older than I am, and have ever since I finished elementary school. But I've seen you guys at Starbucks or downtown when I wasn't with you, and you look like you're having a really great time. When I'm with you, you're all . . . I don't know, restrained, uptight, making sure you don't say or do anything to upset or corrupt the youngster."

"Listen, we're all buddies," Brad said. "We—" And suddenly, just as they reached the trees on University Avenue surrounding the parking lot across the street from the library, he jumped, because someone had dug fingernails into his ribs and yelled, "BOO!" behind him. Brad whirled around and found Jodie Cavendish giggling hysterically, and soon Lane joined in. "Jeez, Jodie, I nearly crapped my pants!"

"You have to learn to be more aware of your surroundings, mate," Jodie said. "The world is a rough place, even little Cal Poly. I thought I'd walk with you." To Lane she said, "I know all about Brad's buddy policy, and I thought he shouldn't be out on the mean streets of Cal Poly alone."

"The buddy policy is meant for Lane," Brad said, but when Jodie gave him a soft smile and a wink, he added, "but the company is nice. What about Casey?"

"We gave up on Jerry—I'm sure he's on the basketball court," Jodie said. "Casey got a call from her boyfriend du jour and is heading back to the dorm for God knows what. I wonder what Dr. Nukaga wanted with Jerry?"

"Jerry thinks Dr. Nukaga is badass," Lane said.

"So does half the engineering world, Lane," Brad said. "I know Jerry's bummed that we didn't pick his ion-accelerator space-debris cleanup idea to present to Dr. Nukaga. Maybe he's presenting it to him now."

"Can you do two sponsored lab projects at the same time?" Jodie asked.

"If anyone can do it, Jerry can," Brad said.

They crossed North Perimeter Street, entered the library, and made their way to the café on the ground floor. "Remember, don't go off wandering around the campus by yourself, Lane," Brad said. "Call your parents to pick you up, or give me a call."

"Yes, Uncle Brad," Lane whined, but he gave Brad a fist bump and smiled, glad to have someone looking out for him, and he trotted off to his favorite computer terminal.

"Can I buy you a cup of coffee, Jodie?" Brad asked after Lane disappeared.

"Why don't I buy you a glass of wine at my place?" she responded. "I'm parked across from Reinhold."

"So am I. Sounds good," Brad replied.

It was a short two-block walk to the parking lot. They climbed into Jodie's little sedan and headed northwest up Village Drive to the Poly Canyon Village apartment complex. She parked in the large north parking structure, and they walked a short distance to her apartment. The complex resembled a small town square, with several five-story apartment buildings, some with retail stores on the first floor, surrounding a large common area with benches, chairs, and picnic areas. The elevator was not working, so they had to walk the stairs to Jodie's third-floor apartment.

"C'mon in, mate," she said, throwing the door wide open for him, then bringing her laptop over to a desk and plugging it in for recharging. Inside, Brad found a small but comfortable one-bedroom apartment with a bar surrounding a small but functional kitchen, and a combination living room/breakfast nook/dining area. The living room also served as Jodie's office and computer room; Brad was not surprised that she had no television. Through a sliding-glass door, a small patio overlooked the common area, and there was even a peek of the city of San Luis Obispo off in the distance.

"These apartments are very nice," Brad commented.

"Except when the west breeze kicks up and you get a whiff of the university stockyards," Jodie said. "We might do a lot of engineering work here, but you can always tell what Cal Poly's roots were: agriculture and livestock." She poured two glasses of Chardonnay from a bottle in her refrigerator and offered one to him. "Weren't you thinking of moving up here next year? Lots of engineering students stay at Poly Canyon."

"I have an application in for here and Cerro Vista, but everyone wants up here, so I'm probably way down on the list, and it is a longer bike ride," Brad said. "I haven't heard either way."

"Not going to get a car anytime soon?"

"I've been too busy to even think about it," Brad said. "And with the bike I get a little exercise in every day."

"Where do you live?" she asked. "It's funny; we've been working together for months, but we don't see each other except on campus."

"Not far. Down Foothill across Highway One, past Foothill Plaza."

"That's a long ride, I think," Jodie said. "How do you like it?"

Brad shrugged. "It's not bad. It's a little rancherito, about an acre fenced off from the rest of the neighborhood. The surrounding neighborhoods are a little wild sometimes. It belongs to a friend of my dad. He's retired from the Marine Corps, I think, but he's always traveling, so I stay in his house and take care of the place. I've never even met the guy—we just correspond by e-mails. It's quiet most of the time, I never see the owner, and it's fixed up nice."

"A bohemian bachelor-party pad, then?" Jodie asked with a smile.

"I don't know the owner, but I know he used to be a drill instructor or something," Brad said. "I don't do parties in his place. Just my luck he'd blow into town during a party and he'd kick my ass. I'm not a partying guy anyway. I don't know how any of these freshmen can have all these crazy parties, especially during the week. I'd never get anything done."

"You're at Cal Poly, mate," Jodie said. "We are an amateur party school compared to the UCs or USC."

"What about Australian universities?"

"Without doubt, you blokes are amateur partiers compared to even our most stately schools," Jodie replied. "We Aussies work our brains out to get into the best schools with the best scholarships, then do nothing but rage on once we're out of the house and away to uni."

"So you turned into a party girl too?"

"Not me, mate," Jodie said. "I actually went to uni to get an education. I had to get out of there and go to a regular American school so I could get some work done."

"But you go back pretty soon, don't you?"

"Right before Christmas," Jodie replied with a sigh and a sip of wine. "Our first semester back home starts in February."

"That's too bad. Starfire should be just heating up then, if our project goes forward."

"I know," Jodie said. "I'll still help via the Internet, and I want to be there when we flip the switch and beam the first watts to Earth, but I really want to stay to see the project launched. I've applied for grants and scholarships to extend, but nothing's come through yet."

"You'd have to pay your own tuition, room, board, and books?" Brad asked.

"Yes, and American universities are big bikkies compared to Aussie schools, especially for out-of-staters," Jodie said. "My parents are battlers, but I've got five brothers and sisters all younger than me. I had to get scholarships or not go to uni at all."

"Maybe I could help," Brad said.

Jodie fixed her eyes on Brad over the rim of her wineglass. "Why, Mr. McLanahan, are you cracking up to me?" she asked after taking a sip.

"What?"

"No worries, Brad," Jodie replied. "I would never borrow money from anyone, especially from a cobber. It's just not in me." Brad's eyes narrowed for about the sixteen-millionth time. "From a friend, you mug. I'd never borrow money from a friend."

"Oh." He hesitated for a moment; then: "But if it was to keep you here to finish Starfire, then it would be an investment in the project, not a loan, right?"

She smiled at him again, trying to discern any hidden intent in his words, but finally shook her head. "Let's see what happens with all my applications and with the project, mate," Jodie said. "But you're lollies to offer. More wine?"

"Just a little, and then I need to go back to Reinhold to get my bike and head home."

"Why not stay and I'll fix us something?" Jodie asked. "Or we can go to the Market and pick up something." She stepped closer to Brad, put her wineglass down, leaned forward, and placed a soft kiss on his lips. "Or we can skip tea and have a little naughty."

Brad gave her a light kiss in return, then said, "I don't think I need an Australian slang dictionary to decipher that one." But, to her immense disappointment, he averted his eyes. "But I've got a girl back in Nevada," he said.

"I've got a bloke or two back home, mate," Jodie said. "I'm not talking about a relationship. We're two mates far from home, Brad—I'm just a little farther from home than you are. I think you're spunk, and I've seen you perving me—"

"What! No, I haven't . . . what?"

"I mean, you are hot, and I've seen you checking me out," Jodie said with a smile. "I'm not saying we get married, mate, and I'm not going to steal you away from your soul mate . . . at least, not right away, or permanently . . . maybe." She reached up to take his hand, glancing briefly at the hallway to her bedroom. "I just want to . . . what do you Yanks call it, 'hook up'?" Brad blinked in surprise, and didn't—couldn't—say anything. She read the hesitation in his face and body language and nodded. "That's okay, mate. Don't blame a sheila for trying . . . or trying again, later."

"I think you're sexy, Jodie, and I love your eyes and hair and body," Brad said, "but I'm just not wired for hooking up, and I want to see if I can make a long-distance relationship work. Besides, you and I work together, and I don't want anything to spoil that."

"That's okay, Brad," she said. "I think we're both adult enough to keep working together even if we have a naughty or two, but I respect your feelings." She saw Brad's serious face break out into a grin, then a chuckle. "Stop making fun of my accent and slang, you wowser!"

He laughed aloud at the new slang word. "I thought I'd heard all the Aussie slang words, Jodie! I've heard ten more new ones just today!"

"You making fun of my accent again, Mr. McLanahan?"

"Sorry."

Jodie thumbed her nose, then said in a very deep voice, " 'Don't apologize: it's a sign of weakness.' "

"Hey! You do John Wayne too! *War Wagon*, right?" He clapped.

"Thank you, sir," Jodie said, taking a bow, "except it was *She Wore a Yellow Ribbon*. Now let's get out of here before I jump your bones, drongo!"

It was just starting to get dark by the time they drove back to the parking lot outside the Reinhold Aerospace Engineering building. "I'd be happy to drive you home and pick you up again in the morning, Brad," Jodie said as Brad got out of her car, retrieved his backpack, and crossed over to the driver's-side window. "All you have to do is buy brekkies."

"I assume that means 'breakfast,'" Brad said with a smile. She rolled her eyes in mock exasperation. "I may take you up on that offer when the weather is lousy, but I'll be okay. It's not too dark yet."

"Anytime, mate," Jodie said. She was pleasantly surprised when Brad leaned toward her through the open window and gave her a light kiss on the lips. "Anytime at all, Brad," she added with a smile. " 'Night." She put the car in gear and pulled away.

"Am I the luckiest SOB on the planet?" he asked half aloud to himself. He dug his keys out of his jeans, removed the locks from his Trek CrossRip hybrid road/cross-country bicycle, activated the headlight and the red-and-white-flashing LED safety lights he had arrayed all around the bike, strapped on his helmet and turned on its lights, secured his backpack with the waist strap, and headed off on his two-mile ride home.

Traffic was busy on the major avenues, but San Luis Obispo was a very bike-friendly town, and he only had to dodge inattentive motorists just once or twice on the fifteen-minute ride before reaching the house. The three-bedroom, one-and-a-half-bath, single-story home was situated in the center of a one-acre lot, with a detached two-car garage beside it; the lot was surrounded by an old but well-maintained wooden fence. In this busy and rather congested neighborhood, it was a little reminder of the expansive farming estates and numerous small ranches that dominated the area before the university swelled the population.

Brad carried his bike inside the house—the garage had been broken into many times, so nothing of value was kept in it—and even inside the house, he locked it up with a big ugly-looking chain and oversize padlock. The neighborhood wasn't crime-ridden, but kids were always jumping the fences, peering through the windows, and occasionally trying the doors, looking for something easy to snatch, and Brad hoped that if they saw the bike chained up like that they'd move on to easier pickings. For the same reason, he kept his laptop's backpack out of sight in his closet and never left the laptop out on the desk or kitchen table, even if he was in the yard or going to the store a few blocks away.

He rummaged through the refrigerator, looking for leftovers. He vaguely remembered his father, a single dad after the murder of his mother, making macaroni and cheese with sliced hot dogs for his son quite often when he was home, and that always made Brad feel good, so he always had a half pot of the stuff in the fridge.

Damn, Jodie felt good too, he told himself. Who knew the friendly but normally quiet Aussie science geek wanted stuff like "hooking up"? She was always so serious in class or in the lab. Who else, he wondered, was like that? Casey Huggins was a little more rambunctious but was pretty serious most of the time as well. He started going down the list of the few women he knew, comparing them to Jodie . . .

. . . and then he whipped out his cell phone, realizing that the main reason he hadn't hooked up with Jodie or anyone else was probably waiting for him to call. He speed-dialed her number.

"*Hello, this is Sondra,*" the message began. "*I'm probably flying, so do your thing when you hear the beep.*"

"Hi, Sondra. Brad," he spoke after the tone. "It's almost eight. Just wanted to say hi. We made the pitch today for Starfire. Wish us luck. Later."

Sondra Eddington and Jodie Cavendish, it turned out, were very similar to each other, Brad realized as he found the pot of macaroni. Both were blond-haired and blue-eyed; Sondra was a little taller, not quite as thin, and several years older. Although Jodie was a student and Sondra had already graduated with bachelor's and master's degrees in business along with a number of pilot's certificates, both were professionals in their own domains: Jodie was a master in a laboratory, while Sondra was completely comfortable and highly proficient in an airplane—and soon to be spaceplane, once she finished her training in Battle Mountain—cockpit.

And, most of all, both were not hesitant to speak their minds and tell you exactly what they wanted, whether it was professional or personal, and definitely on every level of personal. How in the heck do I attract women like this? Brad asked himself. It had to be just plain ol' dumb luck, because he certainly didn't . . .

. . . and at that moment he heard the scrape of a shoe against the wooden kitchen floor and sensed rather than saw a presence behind him. Brad dropped the pot onto the floor and whirled, finding two men standing before him! One was holding a backpack, and the other had one as well, along with a rag in his right hand. Brad half stumbled, half jumped backward against the refrigerator in surprise.

"*Neuklyuzhiye ublyudok,*" the first man growled at the other in what Brad thought was Russian. "Clumsy idiot." He then casually pulled an automatic pistol with a silencer affixed to the muzzle from the waist of his pants, held it level at his waist, and aimed it at Brad. "Do not move or cry out, Mr. McLanahan, or you will die," he said in perfectly good English.

"What the fuck are you doing in my house?" Brad said in a shaky, broken voice. "Are you robbing me? I don't have anything!"

"*Otpusti yego, durak,*" the first man said in a low voice. "Put him down, and do it right this time."

Advancing with amazing speed, the second man whipped something out of his waistband and swung it. Brad's vision exploded into stars, and he never remembered the object hitting his temple or his body crumpling to the floor like a sack of beans.

FOUR

Be like the fox who makes more tracks than necessary,
some in the wrong direction. Practice resurrection.
—WENDELL BERRY

SAN LUIS OBISPO, CALIFORNIA

"Finally you did something right," the first man said in Russian. "Now watch the back door." The second man put the bludgeon back inside his pants, pulled out a silenced pistol, and took a position where he could watch the backyard through the kitchen window curtains.

The first man started to set out objects from his backpack on the dining room table: small bags containing small pea-sized white chunks of powder, black- and soot-stained spoons, butane lighters, rolled-up one-hundred-dollar bills, votive candles, a bottle of 151-proof rum, and hypodermic needles and syringes. After they were arrayed on the table just as an addict might organize his works, the first man dragged Brad over to the table, took off his left athletic shoe and sock, and began deeply poking his foot between his toes with a hypodermic needle, drawing blood. Brad moaned but did not awaken.

He heard a shuffle of feet on the floor behind him. *"Molchat', chert by tebya pobral,"* the first attacker said in Russian through his teeth. "Silence, you clumsy fool. Pick your damned feet up." He then started to pour the rum over Brad's face and mouth and down the front of his shirt. Brad coughed, moaned, and spit out the strong liquid. "Shit, he is almost awake already," he said. He retrieved a lighter and put his finger on the igniter. "Clear the way and let's get the hell out of—"

Suddenly the man felt his body rise up off the floor as if he had been sucked up by a tornado. He caught a glimpse of his assistant crumpled and bleeding on the floor by the back door, before he felt himself being spun around . . . until he was face-to-face with one of the most fearsome, twisted, malevolent human visages he had ever seen in his twenty years of doing assassinations for the Federal Security Bureau of the Russian government, once known as the KGB, or *Komitet Gosudarstvennoy Bezopasnosti,* the Union of Soviet Socialist Republics' security bureau. But he saw the face only for an instant before a massive fist came out of nowhere and crashed into his face right between his eyes, and he remembered nothing after that.

The newcomer let the unconscious Russian drop four feet to the floor, then stooped down to check on Brad. "Jesus, kid, wake up," he said, checking that Brad's airway was unobstructed and his pupils didn't indicate a concussion. "I'm not going to carry your fat ass." He pulled out a cell phone and speed-dialed a number. "It's me," he spoke. "Cleanup at the ranch. Shut 'er down." After ending the call, he began slapping Brad's face. "Wake up, McLanahan."

"Wha . . . what . . . ?" Brad's eyes finally opened . . . and then they opened wide in complete surprise when he saw the newcomer's face. He recoiled in shock and tried to wriggle free of the man's grasp, but it was far too strong. *Shit! Who are you?*"

"The bogeyman," the man said, perturbed. "Where's your school stuff?"

"My . . . my what . . . ?"

"C'mon, McLanahan, get your shit together," the man said. He scanned the dining room and front hallway and noticed the closet door half open with a backpack on the shelf. "Let's go." He half dragged Brad out the front door, grabbing the backpack off the shelf before he hurried out the door.

A large black SUV was parked on the street near the entry gate. Brad was pushed against it and held in place by a hand on his chest as the man opened the right rear passenger door, then grabbed him by his shirt and threw him inside. Someone else pulled him farther inside as the fearsome-looking man slid in, the door slammed shut, and the SUV sped off.

"What the fuck is going on?" Brad shouted. He was squeezed tightly between the two very large men, and the squeeze seemed very deliberate. "Who—"

"Shut the hell up, McLanahan!" the man commanded in a low, menacing voice that seemed to cause the seats and windows to vibrate. "We're still in the middle of the city. Passerbys can hear you." But soon they were on Highway 101 heading northbound.

The second man in the backseat had moved back to the third row, so Brad was in the second row with the big stranger. Neither said a word until they were well out of the city. Finally: "Where are we going?"

"Somewhere safe," the stranger said.

"I can't leave. I've got work to do."

"You want to live, McLanahan? If you do, you can't go back there."

"I've got to," Brad insisted. "I have a project that could put an orbiting solar power plant into operation within a year." The stranger looked over at him but said nothing, then began working on a smartphone. Brad looked at the man as the light from the smartphone illuminated his face. The glow created deep furrows in the man's face, obviously caused by some sort of injury or illness, perhaps a fire or chemical burn. "You look familiar," he said. The man said nothing. "What's your name?"

"Wohl," the man said. "Chris Wohl."

It took a few long moments, but finally Brad's face brightened. "I remember you," he said. "Marine Corps sergeant. You're a friend of my father."

"I was never a friend of your father," Wohl said in a low voice, almost a whisper. "He was my commanding officer. That's all."

"You own the house I'm staying in?" Wohl said nothing. "What is going on, Sergeant?"

"Sergeant Major," Wohl said. "Retired." He finished what he was doing on the smartphone, which plunged his scarred face back into darkness.

"How did you know those guys were in the house?"

"Surveillance," Wohl said.

"You're watching the house, or me?" Wohl said nothing. Brad paused for a few moments, then said, "Those guys sounded Russian."

"They are."

"Who are they?"

"Former Federal Security Bureau agents, working for a guy named Bruno Ilianov," Wohl said. "Ilianov is an intelligence officer, with an official posting as a deputy air attaché in Washington with diplomatic credentials. He reports directly to Gennadiy Gryzlov. Ilianov was on the West Coast recently."

"Gryzlov? You mean, Russian president Gryzlov? Related to the former president of Russia?"

"His oldest son."

"What do they want with me?"

"We're not sure," Wohl said, "but he's on some sort of campaign against the McLanahans. He had agents break into your father's crypt and steal his urn and other items inside."

"*What?* When did this happen?"

"Last Saturday morning."

"Last Saturday! Why didn't anyone tell me?" Wohl did not answer. "What about my aunts? Were they told?"

"No. We have them under surveillance as well. We think they're safe."

"Safe? Safe like me? Those guys had guns and they got into the house. They said they'd kill me."

"They tried to make it look like an accident, a drug overdose," Wohl said. "They were sloppy. We detected them a couple days ago. We haven't detected anyone around your sisters. They might not know about them, or they might not be targets."

"Who's 'we'? Are you the police? FBI? CIA?"

"No."

Brad waited several moments for some elaboration but never received any. "Whom do you work for, Sergeant Major?"

Wohl took a deep breath and let it out slowly. "Your father belonged to several . . . private organizations before he took over at Sky Masters," he said. "Those organizations did contract work for the government and other entities, using some new technologies and weapon systems designed for the military."

"The Tin Man armor and Cybernetic Infantry Device manned robots," Brad said matter-of-factly. Wohl's head snapped over in surprise, and Brad could feel rather than see the big man's breathing slow to a stop. "I know about them. I was even trained in the CID. I piloted one back in Battle Mountain. Some Russians tried to assassinate my father. I squished them up inside a car."

"Shit," Wohl murmured under his breath. "You've piloted a CID?"

"Sure did," Brad said with a big smile.

Wohl shook his head. "Liked it, didn't you?"

"They shot up my house looking for my father," Brad said, a little defensively. "I'd do it again if I had to." He paused for a few moments, then added, "But yes, I did. The CID is one heck of a piece of hardware. We should be building thousands of them."

"The power gets to you," Wohl said. "Your father's friend—and mine—General Hal Briggs got drunk on it, and it killed him. Your father ordered me to do . . . missions with the CID and Tin Man outfits, and we were successful, but I could see how the power was affecting me, so I quit."

"My father didn't die in a CID robot."

"I know exactly what happened out on Guam," Wohl said. "He disregarded the safety of his unit and even his own son to strike back at the Chinese. Why? Because he had a bomber and weapons, and he decided on his own to use them. It was nothing but a pinprick . . ."

"The Chinese gave up right after the strike, didn't they?"

"Some Chinese military and civilian leaders staged a countercoup days after the attack," Wohl said. "It had nothing to do with your attack. It was a coincidence."

"I guess you're the expert," Brad said. Wohl shook his head but said nothing. "Who do you work for, Sergeant Major?" Brad repeated.

"I'm not here to answer a bunch of questions, McLanahan," Wohl snapped. "My orders were to intercept the hit team and keep you safe. That's it."

"I'm not leaving campus, Sergeant Major," Brad said. "I've got a lot of work to do."

"I don't give a shit," Wohl said. "My orders are to keep you safe."

"Orders? Whose orders?" No reply. "If you're not going to answer, then I'll speak to your boss. But I can't leave school. I just started." Wohl remained silent. After a few minutes, Brad repeated, "How long did you work for my father?"

"For a while," Wohl said after a few moments. "And I didn't work *for* him: I was under his command, his noncommissioned officer in charge."

"You don't sound happy about it."

Wohl glanced in Brad's direction, then turned back and looked out the window, and was silent for several long moments; then, finally: "After . . . after your mother was killed, your father . . . changed," Wohl said in a quiet voice. "In all the years I've known him, he was always a guy on a mission, hard-charging and kick-ass, but . . ." He took another deep breath before continuing: "But after your mother was killed, he took on a meaner, deadlier edge. It was no longer about protecting the nation or winning a conflict, but about . . . killing, even killing or threatening Americans, anyone who stood in the way of victory. The power he was given seemed to be going to his head, even after he quit Scion Aviation International and got the corporate job at Sky Masters. I put up with it for a while until I thought it was getting out of control, and then I quit."

"Quit? Why didn't you try to help him instead?"

"He was my commanding officer," Wohl responded woodenly. "I do not counsel superior officers unless they request it."

"That's bullshit, Wohl," Brad said. "If you saw my dad was hurting, you should have helped, and screw that superior-officer shit. And I never saw any of that other stuff. My dad was a good father, a volunteer, and a dedicated executive who loved his family, his community, his country, and his company. He wasn't a killer."

"You never saw it because he shields you from all that," Wohl said. "He's a different guy around you. Besides, you were a typical kid—your head was up and locked in your ass most of the time."

"You're full of it, Sergeant Major," Brad said. He again caught a glimpse of Wohl's heavily lined face in the glare of an oncoming truck's headlights. "What happened to your face?"

"None of your business," Wohl grumbled.

"You've been spying on me for who knows how long, and I can't ask you one lousy personal question?" Brad asked. "I think you were in the Marine Corps too long."

Wohl half turned to Brad as if he was going to argue with him, but did not, and turned back toward the window. After a few moments, he took a deep breath and let it out slowly. "The American Holocaust," he said finally. "You've heard of it, I assume?"

"Sarcasm, Sergeant Major? It doesn't suit you, and it's inappropriate. Tens of thousands were killed."

"Your father planned and executed the American counterattack," Wohl said, ignoring Brad's remark. "Waves of bombers spread out over much of western and central Russia, hunting down mobile intercontinental ballistic missiles. I was his noncommissioned officer in charge at Yakutsk, the Siberian air base he commandeered."

It took a few seconds, but then Brad recognized the name of the air base, and his mouth dropped open in surprise. "Oh, *shit*," he breathed. "You mean . . . the base that was *hit by Russian nuclear cruise missiles?*"

Wohl did not react, but fell silent again for several moments. "Obviously I didn't get a lethal dose of radiation—I was wearing Tin Man battle armor—but I had the greatest exposure to radiation of anyone except General Briggs," he said finally. "Forty-seven survivors from that Russian underground shelter died from radiation-caused diseases over the years. It's just taking a bit longer for me."

"My God, Sergeant Major, I'm sorry," Brad said. "The pain must be terrible." Wohl glanced over at Brad, a little surprised to hear the tone of empathy coming from the young man, but he said nothing. "Maybe that's what killed General Briggs. Maybe the radiation made him take risks. Maybe he knew he was dying and decided to go out fighting."

"Now look who's the expert," Wohl murmured.

They followed Highway 101 north, occasionally taking side roads and doubling back, looking for any signs of shadowing. Every few minutes when they found a highway overpass they pulled over, and one of the men in the SUV would get out, carrying what looked like very large multilensed binoculars. "What's he doing, Sergeant Major?" Brad asked.

"Searching for aerial pursuers," Wohl replied. "We know the Russians employ unmanned aircraft to spy on military bases and other classified facilities over the United States, and Gryzlov was a Russian Air Force officer. He would definitely have that kind of hardware. He's using infrared binoculars that can detect heat sources in the air or on the ground for several miles." A few minutes later the man reentered the SUV, and they were back on their way.

About an hour after leaving San Luis Obispo they turned in at the airport road outside the city of Paso

Robles. The driver entered a code into an electronic lock, and the tall chain-link gate opened to admit them onto the airport grounds. They drove along quiet, dark taxiways, illuminated only by small blue lights on the edges, until coming to a large aircraft hangar surrounded on three sides by another chain-link fence, with only the aircraft entrance to the parking ramp and taxiway open. This time, instead of a code, the driver pressed a thumb against an optical reader, and the lock opened with a quiet buzz.

The interior of the very large hangar was dominated by a gray General Atomics MQ-1B Predator remotely piloted aircraft parked on the left side of the hangar. The words CUSTOMS AND BORDER PROTECTION and the agency's shield were emblazoned on the front side of the aircraft, but this definitely didn't look like a government facility. Brad went to look it over, but a guy wearing jeans and a black T-shirt and carrying a submachine gun slung in a quick-draw rig on his shoulders moved between him and the Predator and stood with his hands crossed before him, silently and plainly warning him to stay away.

Brad walked back over to Chris Wohl, who had been speaking with the men that were in his SUV and some others. In the half illumination of the hangar he could get a better look at the deep etchings on Wohl's face, and he could also see skin damage around his neck and on both hands. "What is this place, Sergeant Major?" he asked.

"Someplace safe, for now," Wohl replied.

"Who are these—"

"I'm not going to answer questions right now," Wohl said gruffly. "If you're supposed to know any more, you'll be told." He motioned to a cabinet along one wall near the Predator. "There's coffee and water over there if you want. Don't go near the aircraft again." He turned away from Brad and began speaking with the others again.

Brad shook his head and decided to head over to see if they had anything to eat, regretting not taking Jodie up on any of her offers—meals or otherwise. He found a bottle of cold water in a refrigerator, but instead of drinking it, he put it on the side of his head to soothe the impact area where the Russian had clubbed him. A few minutes later he heard an aircraft of some kind outside the hangar, approaching the area, sounding as if it was moving very quickly. Wohl and the other men stopped talking and turned toward the hangar door as the aircraft sounds outside became a bit quieter as the engines were pulled back to idle. Just as Brad was going to go back to Wohl and ask him what was going on, the lights dimmed even further and the bifold hangar door began to open.

After the door was fully opened, a twin-tailed C-23C Sherpa small cargo aircraft taxied inside. It had an American flag and a civil N-number on the tail, but no other military markings, and it was painted jet black instead of the usual gray. It taxied right inside the hangar with its big turboprop propellers turning, and Brad, Wohl, and the others were forced to back away as the aircraft moved all the way inside. Directed by a linesman with a submachine gun on a shoulder rig, it taxied forward until it was signaled to stop, and then the engines cut off. The big bifold hangar doors started to motor closed as soon as the engines began to wind down. The smell of jet exhaust was strong.

A moment later a passenger door on the left side of the aircraft behind the cockpit windows opened up, and there appeared a big soldier-looking guy wearing a suit and tie—and with the noticeable bulge of a weapon under his jacket—followed immediately by a shorter man with a suit but no tie, rather long gray hair, and a neatly trimmed gray beard; at the same time the cargo door/ramp on the rear of the aircraft began to motor open. Wohl and the other men stepped over to the second newcomer, and they all shook hands. They spoke for a few moments, and then Wohl nodded toward Brad, and the second newcomer approached him, unbuttoning his jacket.

"Mr. Bradley James McLanahan," the newcomer said in a loud, dramatic, very politician-sounding voice when he was still several paces away. "It's been a long time. You probably don't remember me. I certainly wouldn't have recognized you."

"I don't remember you, sir, but I sure recognize you: you're President Kevin Martindale," Brad said, not trying to mask his surprise and confusion. Martindale smiled broadly and looked pleased that Brad recognized him, and he stuck out his hand as he approached. Brad shook it. "It's nice to meet you, sir, but now I'm even more confused."

"I don't blame you one bit, son," the former president said. "Things are happening fast, and folks are scrambling to keep up. Then this incident with you in San Luis Obispo popped up, and we had to react." He squinted at the bruise on the side of Brad's head. "How's your head, son? You have a very nasty bruise there."

"It's fine, sir."

"Good. I, of course, asked the sergeant major what we should do when we detected the break-in, and he said extract you, I said yes, and so he did. He is extremely effective at things like that."

"I didn't see what he did, but I'm here, so I guess he must be," Brad said. "If the sergeant major works for you, sir, then can you tell me what's going on? He hasn't told me a thing."

"He wouldn't tell you anything even if he had a car battery wired to his testicles, son," Martindale said. "Neither would any of the men in this hangar. I guess I'm the head honcho of this outfit, but I really don't run it. He does."

"He? He who?"

"Him," Martindale said, and he motioned to the cargo ramp of the aircraft just as it emerged. It was a Cybernetic Infantry Device—a manned robot, developed for the U.S. Army as a battlefield replacement for a standard infantry platoon, including the latter's mobility, versatility, and all of its firepower—but it was unlike any CID Brad could remember. This one somehow seemed sleeker, lighter, taller, and more refined than the one Brad had piloted a few years back. The twelve-foot-plus-tall robot had a large torso that sloped from broad shoulders to a slightly thinner waist, more slender hips, and rather spindly-looking arms and legs attached to the torso. There were sensors mounted seemingly everywhere—on the shoulders, waist, and arms. The head was a six-sided box with sloped sides and no eyes but only sensor panels on every side. It seemed slightly taller than the one Brad had piloted.

The sensory experience of piloting a Cybernetic Infantry Device was nothing like Brad had ever felt before. First he got his nervous system digitally mapped and uploaded to the robot's computerized control interface. He then climbed into the robot through the back, lay spread-eagled onto a rather cold, gelatinous conducting mat, and stuck his head inside a helmet and oxygen mask. The hatch was sealed behind him, and everything went dark and quickly became a little claustrophobic. But within moments he could see again . . . along with mountains of data derived from the robot's sensors being presented to him visually and inserted into his body's sensory system, so he was not just reading information on screens, but images and data were appearing in his consciousness, like a memory or actual inputs from touch, vision, and hearing. When he started to move, he found he could run with amazing speed and agility, leap several dozen feet, kick down walls, and overturn armored vehicles. A dazzling array of weapons was interfaced with the robot, and he could control all of them with breathtaking speed and pinpoint accuracy.

"A CID," Brad remarked. "It looks brand-new. New design too."

"It's the first copy of a new model CID force we plan on deploying," Martindale said.

"Cool," Brad said. He waved at the robot. "Who's the pilot? Charlie Turlock? She taught me how to pilot one a couple years ago." To the CID he said, "Hey, Charlie, how are you? Are you going to let me take it for a spin?"

The CID walked up to Martindale and Bradley, its movements frighteningly humanlike despite its size and robotic limbs, and in an electronic humanoid voice said, "Hello, son."

It took a few moments for Brad to realize that what he had just heard was the real thing and for the realization to sink in, but finally Brad's eyes widened in surprise and shock and he shouted, *"Dad?"* He reached out to the CID, unsure of where to touch it. "My God, Dad, is it *you?* You're alive? *You're alive!*"

"Yes, son," Patrick McLanahan said. Brad still couldn't figure out where to touch the robot, so he had to settle for clutching his own abdomen. He started to sob. "It's okay, Bradley," Patrick said finally, reaching out and embracing his son. "My God, it's so good to see you again."

"But I don't get it, Dad," Brad said after several long moments in his father's embrace. "They . . . they told me you had . . . had died of the injuries . . ."

"I did die, son," Patrick said in the electronically synthesized voice. "When they pulled me from the

B-1 bomber back on Guam after you landed the B-1, I *was* clinically dead, and everyone knew it, and that's the word that was passed around. But after you and the other crewmembers were evacuated to Hawaii, they loaded me onto an ambulance and started resuscitation, and I made it back."

"They . . . they wouldn't let me stay with you, Dad," Brad said between sobs. "I tried to stay with you, but they wouldn't let me. I'm sorry, Dad, I'm so sorry, I should have demanded—"

"It's okay, son," Patrick said. "All casualties had to wait for assessment and triage, and I was just one more casualty out of hundreds that day. Local medics and volunteers took over the casualties, and the military guys and contractors were taken away. They kept me alive in a small clinic off base for a day and a half, parked far away from everything. The first responders to arrive were locals, and they didn't know who I was. They took me to another little clinic in Agana and kept me alive."

"But how . . . ?"

"President Martindale found me, a couple days after the attack," Patrick said. "Sky Masters could still track me through the subcutaneous datalink. Martindale was monitoring all of Sky Masters Inc.'s activities in the South China Sea region and had a plane sent to

Andersen Air Force Base to collect intelligence and data on the attack. They eventually found me and secretly spirited me off to the States."

"But why the CID, Dad?"

"That was Jason Richter's idea," Martindale said. "You met Colonel Richter in Battle Mountain, I believe?"

"Yes, sir. He helped me do the programming so I could get checked out in piloting a CID. He's the head of operations for Sky Masters Aerospace now."

"Your dad was in critical condition and not expected to survive the flight back to Hawaii," Martindale said. "My aircraft that evacuated him had very few medical staff and no surgical or trauma-care equipment . . . but it did have a Cybernetic Infantry Device on board to help with rescue and recovery on Guam. Jason said the CID could help a victim breathe and control his other bodily functions until he made it to a hospital. Richter didn't know that victim was your father."

"Then . . . then you're okay, Dad?" Brad asked, at first happy. But he quickly realized that his father was far, far from okay, or else he would not still be aboard the CID with his only son standing in front of him. "Dad . . . ?"

"I'm afraid not, son," Patrick said. "I can't survive outside the CID."

"What?"

"I could possibly survive, Brad, but I'd definitely be on assisted breathing and heartbeat and probably in a vegetative state," Patrick said. Brad's eyes welled with tears, and his mouth dropped open in shock. Both the robot's hands reached out and rested on Brad's shoulders—its touch was light, even soft, despite its size. "I didn't want that, Brad. I didn't want to be a burden to my family for years, maybe decades, until they had the technology to heal me, or until I died. Inside the CID I was awake, functioning, and up and moving. Outside, I'd be in a coma, on life support. When I was inside the CID and awake, I had the choice: stay on life support, pull the plug, or stay in the CID. I decided I'd rather stay inside, where I could be of some service."

"You're . . . you're going to *stay inside* . . . *forever . . .* ?"

"I'm afraid so, son," Patrick said, "until we have the ability to heal all of the injuries I sustained." The tears rolled down Brad's face even harder now. "Brad, it's okay," Patrick said, and his softer, reassuring tone was evident even in the robot's electronic voice. "I should be dead, son—I *was* dead. I was given an extraordinary gift. It may not seem like life, but it is. I want you to be happy for me."

"But I can't . . . can't see you?" Brad reached up and touched the robot's face. "I can't touch you for . . . for real?"

"Believe me, son, I can feel your touch," Patrick said. "I'm sorry you can't feel mine, other than the cold composites. But the alternatives for me were unacceptable. I'm not ready to die yet, Brad. This may seem unnatural and unholy, but I'm still alive, and I think I can make a difference."

"What about the memorial service . . . the urn . . . the death certificate . . . ?"

"My doing, Brad," President Martindale said. "As your father said, he was dead for a short time, in critical condition, and not expected to live. No one except Richter thought putting an injured man in the CID would work for more than a few days at most. Once we got back to the States, we tried several times to remove him from the CID so we could get him into surgery. Every time we tried, he arrested. It was . . . like his body didn't want to leave it."

"I was pretty messed up too, Brad," Patrick said. "I saw the pictures. There wasn't much left of me."

"So what are you saying? You're being *healed* by the CID? How can that work?"

"Not healed, but more like . . . sustained, Brad," Patrick said. "The CID can monitor my body and brain, deliver oxygen, water, and nutrients, handle waste, and control the interior environment. It can't fix me. I might get better over time, but no one knows. But I don't need a healthy body to pilot the CID or employ its weapons."

Brad realized what his father was saying, and it made his skin crawl and his face contort in disbelief despite the joy he felt at talking to his father again. "You mean . . . you mean you're just a *brain* . . . a brain operating a *machine* . . . ?"

"I'm alive, Brad," Patrick said. "It's not just a brain operating a machine." He tapped on his armored chest with a composite finger. "It's *me* in here. It's your father. The body is messed up, but it's still *me*. I control this machine, just like you did back in Battle Mountain. The only difference is that I can't just dismount when I want to. I can't get out and be a regular dad. That part of my life was destroyed by that Chinese fighter's cannon shells. But I'm still me. I don't want to die. I want to keep on working to defend our country. If I have to do it from inside this thing, I will. If my son can't touch me, can't see my face anymore, then that's the penalty I get for accepting life. It's a gift and a penalty I happily accept."

Brad's mind was racing, but slowly he began to understand. "I think I get it, Dad," he said after a long silence. "I'm happy you're alive." He whirled to face Martindale. "It's *you* I don't get, Martindale. How could you not tell me he was alive, even if he was inside the CID?"

"I run a private organization that performs high-tech intelligence, counterintelligence, surveillance, and other high-risk operations, Brad," Martindale said. He noticed Chris Wohl starting to make a move toward Brad and shook his head, warning him away. "I'm always looking for personnel, equipment, and weapons to perform our job better."

"That's my father you're talking about, not some fucking piece of hardware, sir," Brad snapped. Martindale's mouth dropped open in surprise at Brad's retort, and Wohl looked angry enough to chew off a piece of the cargo plane's propeller. Brad noticed something he hadn't noticed before: two locks of gray hair had curled over Martindale's forehead above each eye, resembling inverted devil's horns. "You're starting to sound like some kind of Dr. Frankenstein mad scientist."

"I apologize, Brad," Martindale said. "As I said, all the doctors we spoke with didn't expect your father to make it. I really didn't know what to tell the White House, you, your aunts . . . hell, what to tell the whole *world*. So I made a suggestion to President Phoenix: we don't tell anyone that your father was still alive inside the CID. We had the memorial service in Sacramento. When your father passed, which we truly believed was imminent, we'd inurn his remains for real, and the legend of Patrick McLanahan would finally be put to rest." Martindale looked up at the Cybernetic Infantry Device beside him. "But as you can now see, he didn't die. He's managed to shock and surprise the hell out of us once again. But what could we do? We already buried him. We had the choice of telling the world he's alive but living inside the CID, or not telling anyone anything. We chose the latter."

"So why tell me now?" Brad asked, his head still reeling. "I believed my father was dead. You could have kept him dead, and I could have remembered him as he was before the attack."

"Several reasons," Martindale said. "First, the Russians stole your father's cremation urn, and we have to assume they opened it and found it empty—we never dreamed anyone would ever steal it, and we thought it was going to be a short time before it was needed, so unfortunately we didn't put anyone else's remains in it. We thought the Russians could use that fact to pressure President Phoenix or even make the fact public, and then he'd be forced to respond."

"You know what they say about assuming," Brad said acidly.

Patrick put an armored hand on Brad's shoulder. "Easy, son," the electronic voice said softly. "I know this is a lot to process, but you still need to show some respect."

"I'll try, Dad, but right now it's a little difficult," Brad said bitterly. "And second?"

"The Russians came after you," Patrick said. "That was the last straw for me. I was in a facility in Utah when all this went down, and I asked to be with you."

"A facility?"

"Storage facility," Patrick said.

"A storage facility?"

"We can talk more on the plane on our way back to St. George," Kevin Martindale said. "Let's load up and—"

"I can't leave here, sir," Brad said. "I'm about to finish my first year at Cal Poly, and I just made a presentation for a summer lab project that could land the engineering department a big grant from Sky Masters Aerospace. I can't just leave. I'm leading a big research and development team, and they're all counting on me."

"I understand, Brad, but if you return to San Luis Obispo and Cal Poly you'll be too exposed and vulnerable," Martindale said. "We can't risk your safety."

"I appreciate the sergeant major getting me out of there, sir," Brad said, "but—"

"I asked that you be pulled out, son," Patrick interrupted. "I know it'll be a complete disruption of your life, but we just don't know how many Russian agents are or could be involved. Gryzlov is just as crazy as his father, and he could be sending in dozens of hit teams. I'm sorry. We'll put you in protective custody, build you a new identity, send you someplace to finish your education, and—"

"No way, Dad," Brad said. "We have to figure out another way. Unless you hog-tie me and throw me in the back of your cool cargo plane there, I'm going back, even if I have to hitchhike."

"I'm afraid that's not possible, Brad," Patrick said. "I can't allow it. It's too dangerous. I need you to—"

"I'm an adult now, Dad," Brad interrupted, finding it a little amusing to be arguing with a twelve-foot-tall robot. "Unless you take my constitutional rights away from me by force, I'm free to do whatever I want to do. Besides, I'm not afraid. Now that I know what's going on—at least a little bit more than what I knew just a couple hours ago—I'll be more careful."

Kevin Martindale leaned toward Patrick and said, "Sounds like a damned McLanahan to me, all right," he commented with a smile. "What are you going to do now, General? Looks like the immovable object has met the irresistible force."

Patrick remained silent for several long moments. Finally: "Sergeant Major?"

"Sir?" Wohl responded immediately.

"Meet with Bradley and your team and come up with a resolution to this dilemma," Patrick said. "I want to know the risks and your assessments as to how to reduce or mitigate those risks to Bradley's person if he returns to that university campus. Report back to me as soon as possible."

"Yes, sir," Wohl responded, pulling out his cell phone and getting to work.

"Brad, you are not going back to school until this is settled to my satisfaction, and if necessary, to ensure your compliance, I *will* hog-tie you and throw you in the baggage compartment—and it won't be *that* plane's compartment, but one a lot smaller," Patrick went on. "Sorry, son, but that's the way it's going to be. Looks like we're staying here for the foreseeable future." He paused, silently scanning his onboard computer displays for information. "There's a motel not far from here with a restaurant, Sergeant Major," he said. "They're showing plenty of vacancies. I'll have Kylie get you rooms and send you the info. Stay there for tonight and we'll come up with a game plan in the morning. Have one of the men bring back some food for Bradley, please."

"Yes, sir," Wohl responded, and he turned and departed.

"But what are *you* going to do, Dad?" Brad asked. "You can't check into a motel."

"I'll be secure enough right here," Patrick said. "I don't need hotel beds or restaurants anymore, that's for sure."

"Then I'll stay here with you," Brad said. The CID was motionless and silent. "I'm staying here with you," Brad insisted.

"The McLanahans getting reacquainted," Martindale said. "Lovely." He pulled out a smartphone and read the display. "My jet is landing. As soon as it taxies over, I'm going back to St. George and sleep in my own bed for a change. You can work out the details of how to deal with the younger McLanahan, General." He paused, and everyone fell silent, and sure enough they could hear the sound of an approaching jet outside the hangar. "My ride has arrived. I wish you gents well. Keep me advised, General."

"Yes, sir," Patrick's electronically synthesized voice replied.

"Good night, all," sad Martindale, and he turned on a heel and departed, followed by his security detail.

Patrick spoke into midair through the CID unit's extensive communications system: "Kylie?"

A few moments later: *"Yes, sir?"* replied "Kylie," an automated voice-recognition electronic personal assistant that was given the same name as Patrick's real-life assistant back at Sky Masters Inc.

"We need two motel or hotel rooms nearby for tonight, and maybe three more for tomorrow and the next day for the sergeant major's team," Patrick said. "I'll be staying here tonight; 'Policeman' is heading back to headquarters." "Policeman" was the code name for President Martindale.

"Yes, sir," Kylie responded. *"I have already received 'Policeman's' updated itinerary. I will send lodging information to the sergeant major right away."*

"Thank you," Patrick said. "Out." To Brad he said, "Pull up a chair, son. I can't wait to start getting caught up." Brad found bottles of water in the small refrigerator. The CID extended a thick extension cord from a compartment on his waist, plugged it into a 220-volt outlet, stood up straight, then froze in place. Brad brought a chair and the water over to the CID. Inside the robot, Patrick couldn't help but smile at his son's expression. "Pretty weird, isn't it, Brad?" he said.

" 'Weird' doesn't even begin to describe it, Dad," Brad said, shaking his head, then placing a cold bottle against the swelling bruise on his head. He studied the CID carefully. "Do you sleep okay in there?"

"Mostly nap. I don't need much sleep. Same with food." He reached into another armored compartment on his waist and withdrew a curved container that looked like a large hip flask. "Concentrated nutrients infused into me. The CID monitors my blood and adjusts the nutrient mix." Brad was just sitting there, shaking his head slightly. "Go ahead and ask me anything, Brad," Patrick said finally.

"What have you been doing?" Brad asked after a few moments to clear his swimming consciousness. "I mean, what does President Martindale have you do?"

"Most of the time I train with Chris Wohl's and other direct-action teams using a variety of weapons and devices," Patrick said. "They also use my computers and sensors to plan possible missions and do surveillance." He paused for a moment, then said in a very obviously somber tone, "But mostly I stand in a storage locker, plugged into power, nutrients, medication, waste disposal, and data, scanning sensor feeds and the Internet, interacting with the world . . . sort of. Digitally."

"You stay in a storage locker?"

"Not much reason for me to be walking around unless we're in training or on a mission," Patrick said. "I creep people out enough already, I think."

"No one talks to you?"

"During training or operations, sure," Patrick said. "I put together reports of things I see and submit them to Martindale, and we might discuss them. I can instant-message and teleconference with just about anybody."

"No, I mean . . . just talk with you, like we're doing now," Brad said. "You're still *you*. You're Patrick McLanahan."

Another pause; then: "I was never one for chitchat, son," he said finally. Brad didn't like that response, but he said nothing. "Besides, I didn't want anyone knowing it's me in the CID. They think it's unoccupied when in storage and that a bunch of pilots show up to train with it. They don't know it's occupied twenty-four/seven." He saw the look of absolute sorrow in his son's face and desperately wanted to hold him.

"Doesn't it get . . . you know, kind of rank in there?" Brad asked.

"If it does, I can't detect it," Patrick said. "But they put me in a different CID periodically."

"They do? So you *can* exist outside the CID?"

"For very short periods of time, yes," Patrick said. "They change dressings, give me medications if I need them, check stuff like muscle tone and bone density, then lower me into a clean robot."

"So I *can* see you again!"

"Brad, I don't think you'd want to see me," Patrick said. "I was pretty busted up, sitting in the windblast of that shot-up B-1 bomber for so long. By the way, thank you for bringing us back safely."

"You're welcome. But I'd still like to see you."

"We'll talk about that when the time comes," Patrick said. "They give me a couple days' warning. I'm on life support while I'm outside."

Brad looked even more dejected than before. "What is all this for, Dad?" he asked after a long silence. "Are you going to be some sort of high-tech killing machine, like the sergeant major says you've become?"

"The sergeant major can be a drama queen sometimes," Patrick said. "Brad, I've seen the importance of the gift of life, because it was almost taken away from me. I know how precious life is right now. But I also want to protect our country, and I have an extraordinary ability to do that now."

"So what then?"

For a moment Brad thought he saw his father shrug his huge armored shoulders. "Honestly, I don't know," Patrick said. "But President Martindale has been involved in creating many secret organizations that defended and advanced American foreign and military policies for decades."

"Any you can tell me about?" Brad asked.

Patrick thought for a moment, then nodded. "You've seen the Predator with the Customs and Border Protection shield on it, but I think you've noticed that the guards and other personnel here are not CBP. It's one way to do surveillance within the United States but maintain complete deniability. It gives the White House and Pentagon a lot of room to maneuver."

"Sounds illegal as hell, Dad."

"Probably so, but we do a lot of great work as well that I feel kept the world from going to war several times," Patrick said. "President Martindale and I were involved in a defense contractor company called Scion Aviation International, providing contract aerial surveillance and eventually attack services to the U.S. military. When I joined Sky Masters, I lost track of what Scion was doing, but now I know he's kept the operation going. He does a lot of antiterrorist surveillance work all over the world, on contract to the U.S. government."

"Martindale is starting to creep me out, Dad," Brad said. "He's like a cross between a greasy politician and a generalissimo."

"He's the kind of guy who thinks outside the box and gets the job done—the ends always justifies the means with him," Patrick said. "As U.S. vice president, Martindale was the driving force behind using experimental high-tech planes and weapons being developed at the secret test sites at Dreamland and other places in what he called 'operational test flights,' and as U.S. president, he created the Intelligence Support Agency that covertly supported the CIA and other agencies in operations all around the world, including within the United States."

"Again, Dad, it sounds totally illegal."

"Nowadays, perhaps," Patrick responded. "During the Cold War, the politicians and commanders were looking for ways to accomplish the mission without violating the law or the Constitution. The law prohibited the CIA from operating within the U.S., but civilian surveillance and intelligence *support* groups were not illegal. Their definition, identity, and purpose were kept purposefully hazy."

"So what do *you* want to do, Dad?" Brad asked.

"I've been given something I could never repay: the gift of life," Patrick said. "I owe something to President Martindale for giving me that gift. I'm not saying I'm going to be his hired gun from now on, but I'm willing to follow this path to see where it leads me." Brad had a very concerned expression on his face. "Let's change the subject. One of the things I monitor every day is *you*, at least your digital life, which these days is pretty extensive. I can access your social media sites, and I can access some of the security cameras on campus as well as the security cameras in your house and out at the airport in the aircraft hangar. I've been keeping an eye on you. You haven't done much flying or much of anything else except school stuff. Busy with the Starfire project, I see."

"We pitched it to Dr. Nukaga this afternoon," Brad said. It was good to see him brighten up as he started talking about school, Patrick thought. "As long as I didn't put the idea in his head that it's secretly a military project, which it's not, I think we have a good shot. One of our team leaders, Jung-bae Kim, gets along really well with Nukaga. He might be our ace in the hole."

"Your entire team is pretty remarkable," Patrick said. "Lane Eagan's parents are world-class researchers, and he's probably smarter than both of them put together. Jodie Cavendish was a superstar high school science student in Australia. She's received a dozen patents before she's finished her first year of college."

Brad's face fell once again. "I guess you have a lot of time to surf the Internet, don't you, Dad?" he remarked in a quiet, sad tone.

This time, Patrick unplugged himself, went over to his son, put his armored arms around him, and held him. "I don't want you to feel sorry for me or pity me,

Brad," he said after several long moments. He went back to his spot, plugged himself in, then stood up straight and froze. "Please don't. As I said, I feel very connected to you because I can watch you and check up on you online. I've even tweeted you a couple times."

Like a flashbulb going off, Brad's face illuminated in astonishment. "You have? Who are you? What's your Twitter name?"

"I don't have one. I'm invisible."

"Invisible?"

"Not visible to a user or to other visitors." Brad looked skeptical. "I have the ability to monitor any-one's accounts on social media sites without 'friending,' Brad. A lot of government agencies and even compa-nies have the ability. I search posts for key words, and I leave messages for you. Sometimes it's just a 'like' or one or two words. I just like keeping tabs on you. I'm content to just watch and read."

Despite his son's initial unease at the thought of unknown persons, companies, or government agen-cies having access to his social media posts, Patrick thought that this was the happiest Brad looked since he emerged from the Sherpa. "You know something, Dad? I've always had the feeling, not very strong but just kind of deep down in the back of my head, that you were watching me. I thought it was a religious or spiritual thing, like it was your ghost or you were up in heaven or something. I think that of Mom too."

"You were right. I *was* watching you . . . even digitally speaking with you. And I think Mom does watch over us too."

"Damn. Trust your feelings, I guess," Brad said, shaking his head in disbelief.

"Let's talk about Cal Poly."

"I've got to go back, Dad," Brad said. "I *am* going back. Starfire is too big of a deal. If you've been looking in on me, you know how big it is."

"I know you've been working really hard on it," Patrick said. "But I'm not going to let you go back until I know you're safe. The house you were in is being shut down—it's just too isolated."

"Then I'll live in the dorms and eat in the dining halls," Brad said. "They're plenty crowded. I don't know how much work I can get done there, but I have twenty-four/seven access to the Reinhold Aerospace Engineering building—I can work there."

"If anyone can think of a way to have you safely go back there, Chris Wohl will do it," Patrick said. "So how did you pick Cal Poly?"

"Best aerospace engineering school on the West Coast I could get into with my grades," Brad said. "I guess too much football, Civil Air Patrol, and Angel

Flight West charity flying in high school really affected my grades." He paused for a moment, then asked, "So it's no coincidence that there happened to be that rancherita available when I was looking for housing? Does it really belong to the sergeant major?"

"It belongs to Scion Aviation," Patrick said. "I felt it was easier to keep an eye on you there than in the dorms. So you really like Cal Poly?"

"Cal Poly is a great school, I like most of my professors, and it's well within range for the P210 so I can fly to Battle Mountain to visit Sondra Eddington when I can."

"You two hit it off pretty well, didn't you?"

"Yes, but it's tough going," Brad said. "She's always gone, and I have virtually no spare time."

"Still want to be a test pilot?"

"You bet I do, Dad," Brad said. "I've been staying in touch with Boomer, Gonzo, Dr. Richter, and Dr. Kaddiri at Sky Masters, and Colonel Hoffman at Warbirds Forever. They might be able to get me an internship at the Nevada Test Pilot School between my junior and senior years if I keep my grades up, and maybe Sky Masters will even sponsor me for a class slot, like Warbirds Forever is doing with Sondra training to fly the spaceplanes at Sky Masters." Warbirds Forever was an aircraft maintenance facility at Stead

Airport in Reno, Nevada, that also trained civilian pilots in a wide variety of aircraft, from old classic biplanes, multimillion-dollar bizjets, and retired military aircraft; Sondra Eddington was one of their instructor pilots. "A million and a half dollars for a master's degree and accreditation as a test pilot. I eventually want to fly the spaceplanes into orbit too. Maybe Sondra will be my instructor."

"Congratulations. I think you're well on your way."

"Thanks, Dad." Brad paused, looking the CID up and down, and smiled. "It's great to be able to talk with you again, Dad," he said finally. "I think I'm starting to get over the fact that you're sealed up inside a machine."

"I knew it was going to be hard for you at first and maybe later on too," Patrick said. "I considered not stepping out of the Sherpa, or not telling you it was me, just so you'd be spared the pain this has caused. President Martindale and I talked about it, and he said he'd play it any way I wanted. I'm glad I did tell you, and I'm glad you're getting used to it."

"I get a feeling that it's not really you in there," Brad said. "You say you're my dad, but how do I know that?"

"Do you want to test me?" Patrick asked. "Go ahead."

"Okay. You fixed something for me all the time for dinner that was simple for you and good for me."

"Mac and cheese with roasted sliced hot dogs," Patrick said immediately. "You especially liked the MRE version."

"Mom?"

"You scattered her ashes at sea off Coronado," Patrick said. "It was amazing: the ashes glistened like silver, and it seemed as if they never touched the water. They went skyward instead of downward."

"I remember that day," Brad said. "The guys with us were sad, but you didn't seem that sad."

"I know," Patrick said. "I believed that as commanding officer, I wasn't supposed to show sadness, fear, weakness, or sorrow, even regarding my own wife. That was wrong. I always thought you never noticed. Obviously, you did." After a moment's hesitation, he added, "I'm sorry, son. Your mother was an extraordinary woman. I never told you stories about what she did. I'm sorry about that too. I'll make it up to you."

"That would be cool, Dad." Brad motioned over his shoulder to the C-23C Sherpa. "Is that your airplane?"

"One of many in President Martindale's collection," Patrick said. "Surplus from U.S. Air Forces in Europe. It's the smallest cargo plane I can fit in. He's got a Boeing 737-800 freighter for overseas trips. He paints them all black despite how dangerous and illegal that is, and how screwed up it makes the plane's environmental control systems. He's been like that ever since I've known him: everything is a means of control and intimidation, even the color of paint on an aircraft, and screw the mechanical, social, or political ramifications."

"Are you ever going to tell Aunt Nancy and Aunt Margaret?" Brad asked.

"I will never say never, Brad, but for now I want my existence to be a secret," Patrick said. "You can't tell anyone either. Only President Martindale, President Phoenix, Chris Wohl, and a handful of others know. Not even Dr. Kaddiri and Dr. Richter at Sky Masters know, and their company is the prime contractor on the Cybernetic Infantry Devices. To everyone else, I'm just a call sign."

"What's that?"

There was a slight pause, then Patrick replied, " 'Resurrection.' "

"We think it can be done, sir," Chris Wohl said as he and his men entered the hangar early the next morning. He set a bag of breakfast sandwiches on the table in the conference room where Brad was sleeping.

Brad was awake instantly, and he followed Wohl and his men into the main hangar, where the CID was standing. "You came up with a plan so soon?" he remarked. "It's not even six A.M."

"The general said as soon as possible," Wohl said matter-of-factly. "We worked all night." To Patrick in the CID he said, "Sir, we downloaded maps of the campus and the surrounding area, and obtained information on the campus security police unit, city police, San Luis Obispo county sheriff's department, California Highway Patrol, and federal law enforcement agencies based in and near the city of San Luis Obispo. All agencies are very well staffed and trained. The campus police have an extensive camera surveillance system—virtually every door and hallway in the education and administration buildings, almost every street corner, and every exterior doorway in every other building on campus, have cameras and are recorded. Major crime on campus does not appear to be a big problem.

"There are approximately nineteen thousand students on campus," he went on. "The student population is primarily from California, primarily white, Hispanic, and Asian; only two percent of the student population is from other countries, and only fifteen percent of foreign students are from Eastern Europe.

The county is rural and hilly and does not appear to have a serious gang presence, although there are numerous reports of meth labs and marijuana farms in the countryside that are quickly eradicated by county, state, and federal agencies that appear to work closely with each other.

"Problems: Access to the campus and most all the buildings is not normally controlled, although the campus's buildings, labs, and classrooms can be remotely locked down electronically by campus security; and emergency communications via text messaging is excellent," Wohl continued. "However, because access is not controlled, it would be easy for my team to go on campus if necessary. Identifying an attacker or surveillance among all the students would be difficult, and countersurveillance tactics training should be mandatory so Bradley can identify a shadow. Weapons are not allowed on campus, and concealed-carry firearm permits are almost impossible to get in that county or the entire state for that matter, but there were a great number of reports of armed students. 'Policeman' might be able to help get a concealed-carry firearm permit. The county jail is less than two miles south, and the California Men's Colony, a minimum- and medium-security state prison, is less than three miles to the northwest. The

San Luis Obispo Regional Airport is four-point-two miles south.

"My recommendation, sir, based on our preliminary analysis, would be for your son to move back on campus as soon as possible, but not into the mass dormitories," Wohl concluded. "Our recommendation would be to have him move to the housing unit known as Poly Canyon. It is more like an apartment building complex, has fewer students, is farther away from the main campus, each building has its own dedicated full-time manager and full-time security team, and each floor has shifts of student resident assistants, so there appears to be a lot of eyes open twenty-four/seven. We estimate that he would have a moderate to good chance of survival if he gets some proper countersurveillance, self-defense, and weapons training, and carries a firearm."

"I'd love to do all that stuff!" Brad exclaimed. "When do I start?"

The CID remained motionless for several long moments, but it finally moved its head. "Excellent report, Sergeant Major," Patrick said. "Thank you."

"You're welcome, sir."

"Set up a training schedule for Bradley at a local gym or similar facility," Patrick said. "I believe Chief Ratel is still in the area. Get started as soon as possible. I'll contact 'Policeman' and have him work on a legal concealed-carry permit and getting into Poly Canyon. Train Brad on how to use and carry a gun anyway until we get a legal unlimited concealed-carry permit."

"Yes, sir," Wohl responded, and turned and went into the conference room with his teammates.

"Kylie." Patrick spoke into his communication system.

"Yes, sir?" the computerized assistant responded.

"I need immediate summer and full-year residency at Poly Canyon student housing on the California Polytechnic University, San Luis Obispo campus for Bradley McLanahan," he said. "I also need a nation-wide concealed-carry permit for Bradley, including authorization to carry on college campuses. Notify headquarters and 'Policeman' of this request—he may need to assist you to overcome any bureaucratic or political obstacles."

"Yes, sir."

"I'm still not totally comfortable with this, Brad," Patrick said after signing off from his electronic assistant, "but if we can get you into Poly Canyon and the sergeant major can get you trained up, I'll feel better. I'm hoping the Russians won't bother you or your aunts after encountering Sergeant Major Wohl, but we'll assume they'll come back and try again after they regroup and track you down, so we'll do everything we can to keep you safe and staying in school. I'm sure Gryzlov will send more teams after you as soon as you resurface, so we have just a short time to get you trained, and Chris and his team won't always be available to watch over you, so it's important to get trained up as soon as possible."

"Thanks, Dad," Brad said. He walked over to the CID and gave it a hug—thinking of the big robot as his father was becoming easier every minute. "That would be great. I'll work really hard at it, I promise. One of my team leaders lives in Poly Canyon, and if I didn't already have Sondra back home, I'd definitely like to be with her."

"Just remember to keep your eyes and ears open and listen to that little voice in the back of your head, the one that was telling you that your father was watching you," Patrick said. "It will warn you of danger."

"I will, Dad."

"Good. Go talk to the sergeant major and arrange with him to take you to a hotel in town until we can get your room set up on campus. You probably also need to get your story straight and talk with the police about what happened back at the rancherito. I'll be heading back to St. George tonight."

"Back into storage?"

"Back where I can check on my targets and get caught up again," Patrick said. "I'll be in touch, Brad. I love you, son."

"I love you too, Dad," Brad said. He gave the CID another hug, then went to the conference room and found Chris Wohl. "Thanks for doing that report so quickly, Sergeant Major," he said. "I didn't realize the campus was so safe."

"It's not," Wohl said, "at least not for you against Russian hit men."

Brad's smile disappeared. "Say what?" he asked with a stunned expression.

"Think about it, McLanahan: nineteen thousand students, probably five thousand more faculty and staff, crammed into an area less than three square miles," Wohl said. "Anyone can come and go around the clock anywhere on campus they please. There is just one sworn campus police officer per shift for every one thousand students, and they have no heavy weapons and no SWAT training. You're done with all of your freshman-year courses, so your class sizes will be smaller from now on, but you'll still be in classes and labs with dozens of kids."

"Then why did you recommend I go back?"

"Because I believe your father is being too protective—he would be very happy to just lock you away, stand you in a nice safe secure box like him, and have the world fed to you through the Internet," Wohl said. "He wouldn't care how miserable you'd be, because in his mind you'd be safe from the dangerous world he's lived and fought in almost all his life."

"So what do you care about what my father wants to do about me, Sergeant Major?" Brad asked. "I don't know you, and you don't know me. You said you're not a friend of my father. Why do you care?"

Wohl ignored the question. "The information I gave was accurate: it's a relatively safe campus and city," he said instead. "With some training, the danger can be managed, maybe even minimized." He gave Brad a big smile, which still looked pretty malevolent, and added, "Besides, now my men and I have you, and we got the go-ahead to build a training program to get your ass in shape and learn the proper way to look at the world. Every day, one hour a day."

"Every day? I can't train every day. I've got—"

"Every day, McLanahan," Wohl said. "You *will* train each and every day, rain or shine, sick or well, exams or dates, or I'll send you back to your father, and he'll happily lock you away inside the red rocks of southern Utah. You'll do weights and cardio for physical fitness; Cane-Ja and Krav Maga for self-defense; and classes and demonstrations of surveillance, countersurveillance, investigation, observation, and identification techniques." He made that evil smile once more, then added, "You thought Second Beast at the Air Force Academy was tough? You ain't seen nothin' yet, bubba." Wohl's smile disappeared, and he wore a thoughtful expression. "The first thing we need to do is give you your call sign," he said.

"A call sign? What do I need a call sign for?"

"Because I'm tired of calling you 'McLanahan"—too many syllables," Wohl said. "Besides, McLanahan is definitely your father until he kicks the bucket, and I don't think that's going to happen for a very long time." He looked at his teammates in the conference room with him. All three of them were tall, square-jawed, and heavily muscled, the Hollywood version of a Navy SEAL, which Brad thought they probably used to be. "What do you boys think?"

"Pussy," one said. He was the biggest of the three, well over six feet tall and well over two hundred pounds, with a thick neck, broad shoulders tapering to a thin waist, enlarging again to thick thighs and calves, then tapering again to thin ankles. He looked like a professional bodybuilder, Brad thought.

"Better yet, just give him to the chief. He'll chew him up and spit him out, the general will send him to St. George, and then we don't have to fuck with him."

"Flex, we got a job to do," Wohl said. "Keep your opinions to yourself. Dice?"

"Doughboy."

"Geek," said the third.

"Be nice to the young man," Wohl said, wearing that malevolent smile again. "He's had a most traumatic experience, and besides he's a hardworking engineering student."

"A brainiac, huh?" the one named Dice asked. "My kid used to watch a brainless cartoon called *Dexter's Laboratory* on TV, where this really smart kid gets bushwhacked by his dumb sister all the time. Let's call him 'Dexter.' "

"I still like 'Doughboy' better," the third said.

" 'Dexter' it is," Wohl announced.

"That's a lousy call sign," Brad said. "I'll pick my own."

"Dexter, call signs are earned, and they are picked by your teammates, not by yourself," Wohl said. "You haven't earned anything yet. But call signs can change, for the worse as well as for the better. Work hard and maybe we'll give you a better one."

"What's your call sign?"

"For you, it's 'sir' or 'sergeant major,'" Wohl said, looking at Bradley with serious menace. "You'd better get that right the first time." To his men in turn he said, "Dice, find us a safe and securable hotel to stay in, in San Luis Obispo, close to campus. Flex, get in contact with Chief Ratel and ask if he can set up a martial-arts, countersurveillance, and firearms training program for us ASAP." To Brad he said, "Let's see your shooting hand."

"Shooting hand? I don't have a shooting hand."

"Then which hand do you pick your nose with, Dexter? C'mon, we don't have all day." Wohl grabbed Brad's right wrist, and Brad opened his hand. "Jeez, tiny little hands just like your father. That's probably why he joined the Air Force—he didn't have hands big enough to hold even a friggin' girl's gun." He held the hand up so the third team member could see Brad's hand. "Rattler?"

"Smith and Wesson M and P .40 cal," the third team member said in a low, growling voice. "Or a peashooter."

"Forty-cal it is," Wohl said. "Get to it." The three team members pulled out cell phones and got to work. "One last thing, Dexter."

"I hate that call sign already," Brad said.

"I hate that call sign already, *sir*," Wohl corrected him. "I told you: do something worthy for the team and yourself, and you might get a better call sign. And start showing some respect for your superiors around here. I should've kicked your ass across the hangar for the way you spoke to President Martindale yesterday. I will next time, I promise you." Brad nodded and wisely said nothing.

"Now, we can do several things to help you detect and defend against danger, but we can't do very much for your friends," Wohl went on. "We've noticed that you don't really hang out with anybody but your research team of nerds on that Starfire project, which is good, but I want you to limit your time in public with anyone. If a hit team starts to target your friends to get to you, it could spell real trouble for everyone that we could not contain. Understand?"

"Yes," Brad said. He could feel the anger rising in Wohl's expression. "Yes, sir," he corrected himself.

"Good. Grab some breakfast, get your things together, and be ready to move out in ten minutes."

"Yes, sir," Brad said. He returned to the conference room and noticed that all the breakfast sandwiches were gone. "This is starting out to be a really shitty day," he murmured. But he looked back across the hangar and saw the CID unit with his father inside of it, and he smiled. "But my father is alive. I can't believe it. I'm living in a dream . . . but I don't care, because my father is *alive!*"

REINHOLD AEROSPACE ENGINEERING BUILDING
CAL POLY

The next morning

"Brad! What in heck happened to you?" Lane Eagan exclaimed when Brad entered the room. The others shot to their feet and gaped in horror when they saw the long, ugly bruise on the side of Brad's head and face—no amount of ice had yet been successful in hiding it, although the swelling had gone down considerably.

"Hi, guys," Brad said. They all came over to him, and he especially liked Jodie's concerned touches. "I'm okay, I'm okay."

"What happened to you?" Kim Jung-bae asked. "Where have you been? In a hospital? We have been worried sick about you!"

"You're not going to believe this, Jerry: I was involved in a home invasion the other night, after we made our presentation," Brad lied. Eyes popped and mouths dropped open in complete surprise. "Two guys broke into the house and whacked me on the side of the head with a club or baseball bat or something."

"*No shit?*" they all exclaimed. "What happened?"

"No idea," Brad lied. "I woke up and there were cops everywhere. Paramedics checked me over, I gave a report, and that's pretty much it. They found drug stuff on the kitchen table and thought that maybe some crackheads wanted a place to get high."

"Oh my God, Brad," Casey gasped, "thank God you're okay."

"I'm good, I'm good, Casey," Brad assured them. "My gyros tumble a little bit every now and then, but I can still ride the bike."

"Where are you staying?" Jodie asked, and Brad thought he detected a twinkle in her eye and the hint of an eager smile. "You're not going back to that house, are you, mate?"

"Heck no," Brad said. "The landlord had a fit. He's having workers move the furniture that didn't get smashed up, and he's going to board the place up. I'm not sure what he's going to do after that. I'm in one of the all-suites hotels on Monterey Street. I might be there until the semester's over and students blow town. I'm going to apply at Cerro Vista and Poly Canyon and try to avoid going into the summer dorms if I can."

"Good luck with that, mate," Jodie said. "Applications for Cerro Vista had to be in two months ago, and Poly Canyon's apps had to be in last year. You might have to live off campus again if you don't want to live in the dorms."

"Okay, all that's being worked, so let's get to business before we have to scurry off," Brad said, and their meeting got under way. It lasted only a few minutes, long enough for everyone to report their team's status, coordinate their lab schedules, and put in requests to Brad for supplies or information for the upcoming week, and then they hurried off to class.

Jodie walked along with Brad. "Are you sure you're all right, mate?" she asked. "That's the worst bruise I think I've ever seen."

"I'm good, Jodie, thanks," Brad said. "I wish I could say 'you should see the other guy,' but I was out cold."

"Why didn't you call me, Brad?"

"There just wasn't time, Jodie," Brad lied. "I was out like a light, and then I had to deal with the cops, the paramedics, and then the landlord."

"Then where were you all yesterday?"

"Sitting around with ice packs on my throbbing head, listening to my landlord shouting orders and ranting and raving about dopers and crime and the breakdown of society," Brad lied again. "Then he helped me find a hotel. My head hurt so much, I just crashed after that."

"Why don't you stop by my place after classes?" she asked. "You don't just want to go to a hotel by yourself, do you, with no one to look out for you?" This time, Brad didn't have to guess her intentions— she reached out and touched his hand. "What d'ya say, mate?"

His head was swimming a bit with all the stuff happening to him in the past few days, so his reply was a bit hesitant, and Jodie's smile dimmed. "That sounds great, Jodie," he said, and her smile returned. "But first I have an appointment after our lab session."

"Doctor's appointment?"

Brad decided he wasn't going to lie to this woman about everything if he could at all avoid it. "Actually, my landlord—the ex-Marine, I think I told you—he's setting up a training program for me. Physical fitness and self-defense." He wasn't going to tell Jodie about the countersurveillance and other spy training classes, or the weapons training—hey, he thought, *not* telling something is different from lying, right? "He thinks I'm too soft and need to do more to help myself in situations like home invasions."

"Wow," Jodie remarked, blinking in surprise. "You're right with this?"

"Sure," Brad said. "I spend too much time sitting on my ass—a little physical fitness will do me good. One hour a day. I can be over your place around seven."

"Perfect, Brad," Jodie said, her worried and perplexed expression quickly disappearing. "I'll fix us something for dinner. I can pick you up and take you around to your appointments if you don't feel well enough to ride the bike."

"I'm good so far, Jodie," Brad said. He actually liked the idea, but he didn't know what the gym would look like, and he wanted to get a feeling from Wohl and whoever his trainer was going to be before he brought others around. "But thank you." He gave her a hug and got a kiss on the cheek in return. "See you around seven."

"See ya, conch," Jodie said, and hurried off to her next class.

He received a lot of surprised and some shocked expressions as students on campus saw his big ugly bruise, and Brad actually considered buying some makeup until the thing healed, but kids on campus were fairly open and tolerant—and he sure as hell didn't want Chris Wohl or his team members to catch him with makeup on!—so he put the thought out of his head and tried to ignore the looks. Thankfully he didn't need narcotics to kill the pain, so he made it through his classes and his session in the engineering lab on the Starfire project without too much difficulty, only an occasional headache that subsided when he stopped thinking about it and concentrated on something else. Afterward he locked his computer backpack in a locker, retrieved his gym bag, then hopped on the bike and headed off to his first physical-fitness session.

The name of the place was Chong Jeontu Jib, written in both Korean and Latin characters, on the south side of town not far from the airport. It was a simple two-story frame building, old but maintained very well, with a yard fenced in with chain link that had some exercise equipment and weights in a small workout area. Beyond the fence in the back was a gun range set up against a large round dirt wall which formerly surrounded petroleum tanks that stored fuel during World War II bomber training missions. The window in front was covered from the inside with United Korea and American flags, and the glass front door was covered with a large U.S. Air Force flag. Inside he found a counter, and beyond that a large workout room with the floor covered in a blue gym mat. The walls were covered with all sorts of awards, trophies, photographs, and martial-arts weapons.

A short, thin man with a shaved head and gray goatee approached from a back room. "Dexter?" he called out. "This way." Brad walked around the counter and had just touched the mat when the man called out, "Don't touch the mat with your shoes on, and only with respect." Brad hopped off the mat onto a linoleum walkway. The second room was a little smaller than the first, with another blue gym mat on the floor, but instead of decorations and awards it had a weight machine, treadmill, boxing speed bag, punching bag, and posters of arrows pointing to various spots on a human body—Brad was sure he was going to know all he needed to know about that stuff before too long. There was a back exit and what looked like a locker room in the opposite corner.

"You're late," the man said. "I'll let you slide today because it's your first time here, but now you know where the place is, so don't be late again."

"I won't."

"I won't, *sir*," the man said. "The sergeant major told me you were in Civil Air Patrol and attended the Air Force Academy for a short time, so you know something about military courtesy. Employ it when you deal with me or anyone on the team. You'll know when you can address us any other way. Understood?"

"Yes, sir."

"Next time, show up ready to work out. I don't want to waste time waiting for you to change. This is not your private resort club where you can stroll in and out as you please."

"Yes, sir."

The man nodded toward the locker room door. "You got thirty seconds to change." Brad hurried toward the locker room across the blue mat. "Stop!" Brad froze. "Get back here." Brad returned. "Get off the mat." Brad stepped off the blue mat onto the linoleum. "Dexter, you are in a Korean *dojang,*" the man said in a low, measured voice. "The center of the *dojang,* the mat, is the *ki,* which means 'spirit.' You train to learn how to accept the spirit of martial arts, the merging of inner peace and outer violence, when you step on the mat, which means you must respect the spirit that resides over it. That means you never touch the mat wearing footwear, you are prepared for a workout and are not in street clothes unless the lesson calls for them, you get permission to enter and leave the mat from a master, and you bow at the waist facing the center of the mat before you step on the mat and before you step off. Otherwise, go around it. Remember that."

"Yes, sir."

"Now get moving." Brad trotted around the mat and returned wearing his workout gear in record time.

"My name is James Ratel," the man said when Brad returned, "but you don't have to worry about real names or call signs because I'm 'sir' or 'chief' to you. I'm a retired U.S. Air Force chief master sergeant, thirty-three-year veteran, last serving as chief master sergeant of Seventh Air Force at Osan Air Base, United Korea. I'm a master parachutist with over two hundred combat jumps in Panama, Iraq, Korea, and Afghanistan as well as dozens of classified locations, completed Army Ranger School, and I've got two Purple Hearts and a Bronze Star. I am also a fifth-degree black belt and master instructor in Cane-Ja, a fifth-degree expert black belt in Krav Maga, and a nationally certified firearms and baton instructor. Here I give private self-defense and firearms lessons, mostly to retired military. I expect one hundred and ten percent each and every second you are in my *dojang*. Give respect and you will get it in return; slack off and your hour with me will be pure living hell."

Ratel retrieved a small device with a neck strap and tossed it to Brad. "Self-defense training takes months, sometimes years, and the danger facing you is immediate," he said. "So you're being given this device. Wear it always. It works almost anywhere in the country with a cell signal. If you are in trouble, press the button, and myself or anyone on the team that might be nearby will be able to track you down and assist. More likely, given the adversaries you face, it'll help us locate your body faster, but maybe we'll get lucky." Brad gave Ratel a stunned expression.

"Now, since this is your first day, you're probably still hurting from being clubbed on the head, and you came in late, which I excused, we're just going to do a fitness evaluation today," Ratel went on. "I want to see your maximum number of pull-ups, crunches, dips, and push-ups until muscle failure, with no more than ninety seconds' rest in between, and your best time on a two-mile run on the treadmill." He motioned to the other side of the room where the treadmill and other exercise implements were waiting. "Get moving."

Brad trotted over to the exercise area on the other side of the room. He was thankful that he did so much bike riding, so he thought he was in pretty good shape, but it had been a long time since he had been in a gym, and he had never been fond of pull-ups. He started with those and managed six before he couldn't pull himself up again. The crunches were easy—he was able to do eighty-two of those before having to stop. Dips were fairly new for him. He got between a set of horizontal parallel railings, grasped them, extended his arms, lifted his feet off the linoleum, lowered his body as far as he could, then extended his arms again. He could manage only three of those, and the third was an arm-trembling strain to complete.

His arms were really talking to him now, so Brad decided to do the running test next, and he got no complaint from Ratel, who was watching and taking notes from across the room. Now he was more in his element. He cranked the treadmill up to a nine-minute-mile pace, and found it fairly easy. He used the time to rest his weary arm muscles for the push-ups, which he thought would be easy as well. After the two-mile run, his arms felt pretty good, and he dropped down for push-ups but found he could only manage twenty-eight of them before his arms gave out.

"Dexter, you wouldn't have been able to graduate from Air Force basic training with those numbers, let alone the Air Force Academy," Ratel told him after he trotted around the blue mat and stood before him. "Your upper-body strength is pitiful. I thought you were a high-school football player—you must've been a place kicker." In fact Brad was not just a high-school football place kicker but a punter, and could snap a football twenty yards. "We can work on that. But what bugs me the most about what you just did was your lousy stinking give-a-shit attitude."

"Sir?"

"You were dogging it on the treadmill, Dexter," Ratel said. "I get you're a bike rider and in pretty good shape aerobics-wise, but it looked like you were just taking it easy on the treadmill. You set a lousy nine-minute-mile pace—that's not even an 'average' score in basic training. I said I wanted your best time on a two-mile run, not your lackadaisical time. What's your excuse?"

"I needed to rest my arms before finishing the tests," Brad said. "I thought a nine-minute mile was pretty good for starters." With every word he spoke, the little man's tiny little eyes got angrier and angrier until they looked as if they were going to pop right out of his head. Brad knew there was only one allowable response: "Sorry, Chief. No excuse."

"You're damned right there's no excuse, Dexter," Ratel snarled. "I told you about respect. There's nothing respectful about only doing things half-assed. You don't show respect for me, and you sure as hell don't show it for yourself either. It's your first day here, and you haven't showed me one damned thing I can respect you for. You came late, you were not ready to work out, and you took it easy on yourself. You're not showing me squat, Dexter. One more session like this, and we might as well call this thing off. Get your stuff and get out of my sight." Brad retrieved his gym bag by the bathroom, and by the time he came back, Ratel was gone.

Brad felt like crap as he mounted his bike and pedaled back to Cal Poly, and he was still in a somber mood as he made his way to Poly Canyon and Jodie Cavendish's apartment. She gave him a big hug at the door, which he failed to return. "Uh-oh, someone's cranky," she observed. "C'mon in, have a glass of wine, and yabber at me."

"Thanks, Jodie," Brad said. "Sorry I smell like the bottom of my feet. I didn't shower or change after I left the gym."

"You're welcome to use the shower here if you'd like, mate," Jodie said with a wink. Brad didn't notice the obvious suggestion. He made his way to one of the bar stools at the counter surrounding the kitchen, and she poured a glass of Chardonnay and set it before him. "But it doesn't bother me. I like a bloke who smells like a bloke and not like a trough lollie." She waited a few seconds, but Brad said nothing. "You're not even going to ask what that is? Wow, you must've really come a gutser today. Tell me about it, love."

"It's not really that big a deal," Brad said. "I show up for this workout session, a little late, but he said the first time was excusable. The instructor is this retired hard-core chief master sergeant. He has me do this fitness test. I thought I did okay, but he harangues me for holding back and being lazy. I thought I did okay. I guess I didn't."

"Well, there's always next time," Jodie said. "Fitness instructors are trained to shock and awe their students, and I think he was putting a Clayton's on you. No worries, Brad—we both know you're in good shape, except for that bruise on your head. How do you feel? Your bruise still looks spewin.' Maybe you should skip these workouts until that goes away."

Brad shrugged. "I told them I'd do it, so I guess I'll keep on going until I pass out or my head explodes," he said. The last thing he wanted to do was incur Wohl's wrath for quitting right after day one. He sat back in his seat and directly looked at Jodie for the first time. "I'm sorry, Jodie. Enough about my new fitness instructor. How was your day?"

"Apples, mate," Jodie replied. She leaned toward him across the kitchen counter and said in the usual conspiratorial whisper she used when she had something unexpected to say: "I did it, Brad."

"Did what?" Brad asked. Then, studying her face and body language, he knew. "The inorganic nanotube structure . . . ?"

"Synthesized," Jodie said in a low voice, almost a whisper but a very excited one. "Right in our own lab at Cal Poly. Not just a few nanotubes, but *millions*. We were even able to create the first nantenna."

"*What?*" Brad exclaimed. "Already?"

"Mate, the nanotubes practically mesh by themselves," Jodie said. "They're not yet mounted on the sol-gel substrate, we haven't hooked it up to a collector or even taken it outside yet, but the first optical nantenna built out of inorganic nanotubes is sitting in the lab on the other side of this very campus . . . on *my* workbench! It's even thinner and stronger than we predicted. I'm getting e-mails from scientists all over the world who want to get involved. It's turning out to be one of the biggest advances in nanotechnology in years!"

"That's incredible!" Brad exclaimed. He took her hands in his, and they exchanged a kiss across the kitchen counter. "Congratulations, Jodie! Why didn't you call me?"

"You were already at your workout, and I didn't want to disturb you," she said. "Besides, I wanted to tell you in person, not over the phone."

"That's great news! We're a shoo-in to get the lab space and grant money now!"

"I hope so," Jodie said. "I might even qualify for a scholarship from Cal Poly—they wouldn't want me going back to Australia taking a breakthrough like this with me, would they?"

"You'll get a scholarship for sure, I know it," Brad said. "Let's go out and celebrate. Some place not too fancy—I still smell like a gym."

A sly smile crept onto her face, and she glanced very briefly at the hallway to her bedroom, obviously signifying the way *she* wanted to celebrate. "I already have dinner started," Jodie said. "It won't be ready for about fifteen minutes." She took his hand again and gave him a sly smile. "Maybe we can soap each other's backs in the shower?"

Brad smiled broadly and looked into her eyes, but shook his head. "Jodie . . ."

"I know, I know," she said. "I told you I was going to try again, and maybe again and again. She's lucky to have you, mate." She went to the refrigerator, retrieved the bottle of Chardonnay, and refilled his glass.

Brad heard his smartphone vibrate in his gym bag, retrieved it, and read the text message. "Well, how about that?" he remarked. "This is turning out to be a really great day after all."

"What is it, love?"

"I got a room at Poly Canyon," he said. Jodie wore an absolutely stunned expression. "Fifth floor at Aliso. I can move in tomorrow, and I can stay through the summer if we get the summer lab grant, and I can stay through my sophomore and junior years."

"*What?*" Jodie exclaimed.

"Is that good?"

"Aliso is the most sought-after residence building at Cal Poly!" Jodie explained. "They're closest to the shops and parking garage. And the top floors always fill up first because they have the best views of campus and the city! And they never allow students to stay at Poly Canyon over the summer, and you have to reapply every year and hope you keep your room. How in bloody hell did you manage that, mate?"

"I have no idea," Brad lied—he was sure his father and probably President Martindale pulled some strings and made it happen. "Someone must've taken pity on me."

"Well, good onya, mate," Jodie said. "You got yourself a pozzy there." She noticed Brad smiling at her Australian slang again, picked up a towel, snapped it at him, then went over and gave him a light kiss on the lips. "Stop perving me with those baby blues, mate, or I might just drag you into the sleep-out and make you forget all about what's-her-name in Nevada."

FIVE

*There never yet was a mother who
taught her child to be an infidel.*
—Henry W. Shaw

MCLANAHAN INDUSTRIAL AIRPORT
BATTLE MOUNTAIN, NEVADA

The next morning

"Masters Zero-Seven, McLanahan Ground, you are cleared to operate in Romeo four eight one three alpha and bravo and Romeo four eight one six November, all altitudes, squawk assigned codes, advise Oakland Center when departing the areas, contact tower, have a good flight."

"Roger, Ground," Sondra Eddington replied on the number one UHF radio. She read back the entire clearance, then switched to the tower frequency. "McLanahan Tower, Masters Zero-Seven, number one, runway three-zero, ready for takeoff."

"Masters Zero-Seven, McLanahan Tower, winds calm, runway three-zero, airspeed restricted to two-zero-zero knots while inside the Class Charlie airspace, cleared for takeoff."

"Masters Zero-Seven cleared for takeoff runway three-zero," Sondra replied. She taxied the big jet onto the runway, lined up on the center line, held the brakes, advanced the throttles slowly and smoothly, felt the kick when the engines went to zone-one afterburner, released brakes, smoothly advanced the throttles to zone five, and lifted off in just five thousand feet. She lowered the big jet's nose to quickly build up airspeed, retracted the landing gear and flaps, then brought the throttles back to 50 percent power to avoid busting the speed limit until they got out of McLanahan Industrial Airport's airspace, which would not take long at all.

"Good takeoff, Sondra," said Hunter Noble, Sondra's instructor on this training flight. He was in the rear seat of Sky Masters Aerospace's MiG-25UX, a tandem-seat Mikoyan-Gurevich supersonic fighter with no combat equipment, modified for extreme high-speed and high-altitude operations. The original Russian MiG-25RU was the fastest combat jet fighter in existence, capable of almost three times the speed of sound and sixty thousand feet altitude, but after being modified by Sky Masters Aerospace, the jet was capable of achieving almost five times the speed of sound and one hundred thousand feet. "Good timing on the brakes and power. Zone one with the brakes on is okay, but anything after that will shred the brakes."

"Roger, Boomer," Sondra said. In fighter-pilot parlance, a "Roger" after a critique from an instructor meant that the student already knew and identified the discrepancy. A "thank you" usually meant the student missed it and acknowledged a good catch by the instructor. "I got it."

"I show us clear of Class Charlie airspace," Boomer said. "Heading two-zero-zero will take us to the restricted area."

"Roger," Sondra said. In less than two minutes they were in R-4813A and B, two restricted military training areas in the Naval Air Station Fallon complex in north-central Nevada, leased to Sky Masters Aerospace and coordinated with the FAA's Oakland Air Traffic Control Center for high-performance aircraft testing. "I'm running the pre-high-altitude checklists now. Report when complete."

"Will do," Boomer said. The checklist prepared the crew to operate at extreme high altitudes, ones usually not attained by conventional fighters. It only took a few minutes. "Checklist complete. I show us inside R-4813A. Cleared when ready."

"I got it, Boomer," Sondra said. "Stand by." Sondra applied full power, slowly and smoothly advancing the throttles on the MiG-25 until they were at full zone-five afterburner, and then at Mach 1 she raised the nose until they were at sixty-degrees nose-up attitude and still accelerating. As the speed increased, the gravity forces increased, and soon both were grunting against the G-forces pressing against their bodies, trying to keep blood from draining out of their lungs and brains. Both pilots wore partial-pressure space suits and space helmets, plus high-tech electronic G-suits that covered their legs and lower abdomen with a contracting fabric to help keep blood from pooling in the legs from the G-forces—but it still took work to fight off the effects of the G-forces. Soon they were at sixty-thousand-feet altitude and flying well over four times the speed of sound, with over seven times the force of gravity pressing on their bodies.

"Speak to me, Sondra," Boomer said. "You . . . you doing okay?"

"I'm . . . fine . . . Boo . . . Boomer," Sondra said, but it was obvious she was struggling to deal with the G-loads on her body. Suddenly the MiG-25 heeled sharply to the left and nosed down.

"Sondra?" No response. The fighter's nose pointed Earthward. Just before he was going to take control,

Boomer felt and heard the throttles retard to idle in the descent and the wings rolled level.

"You okay, Sondra?" Boomer repeated.

"Yes." Over the intercom he could hear her breathing was a little labored, but otherwise sounded all right. "I'm okay."

Boomer watched the altimeter and airspeed read-outs carefully, making sure that Sondra had complete control of the aircraft. In the rear cockpit, he could take full control of the aircraft if necessary, but touching the controls would mean a failure for the pilot-in-command, and he didn't want to do that unless it was absolutely necessary. After losing just ten thousand feet, Sondra started to bring the nose back up to the horizon, and as the jet came level and the airspeed went subsonic, she fed in power to keep the altitude and airspeed stable. "How are you doing, Sondra?" Boomer asked.

"I'm good, Boomer," Sondra replied, and she sounded perfectly normal and in control. "I'll descend back to thirty thousand feet and we'll give it another try."

"We won't have enough fuel for another high-G high-altitude demo," Boomer said. "We can do a few high-speed no-flap approaches, and then call it a day."

"We have plenty of fuel, Boomer," Sondra protested.

"I don't think so, babe," Boomer said. "Let's do the high-ILS approach to Battle Mountain and do a no-flap power-off approach, do a missed at decision height, then do another for a full stop. Okay?"

"Whatever you say, Boomer," Sondra replied, the dejection in her voice obvious.

The high-speed instrument approaches simulated an approach in the Black Stallion or Midnight space-planes. The MiG-25 was an important step for aspiring spaceplane pilots, because it was the only aircraft that could simulate for brief periods the extremely high G-loads imposed on pilots during their ascent. G-loads of up to nine times the normal force of gravity could be generated in Sky Masters Aerospace's centrifuge on the ground, but the MiG-25 was a better platform because the pilot had to fly the aircraft while being subjected to the G-forces. Sondra executed the instrument approaches with typical precision, and the landing was dead on the numbers.

They parked the big jet, went to the life-support shop to turn in the space suits and electronic G-suits, debriefed the maintenance technicians, got a quick check by a doctor, then went back to the classroom to talk about the flight. Sondra wore a blue flight suit, tailored to accentuate her curves, and in her flying boots she stood even taller. She shook her straight blond hair loose as she poured herself a cup of coffee; Boomer, in an Air Force–style olive-drab flight suit, already had his bottle of ice-cold water.

"Preflight, takeoff, departure, approaches, landing, and postflight all good," Boomer said, referring to a notepad. "Talk to me about the climb-out."

"I was fine—I think I just pulled out too soon," Sondra said. "You always say, it's better to break off a high-G run earlier than later. I might've gotten a little antsy. I was fine."

"You didn't answer up when I called."

"I heard you just fine, Boomer," Sondra said. "I had my hands full. The last thing I wanted to do was get myself into a compressor stall or spin." Boomer looked at Sondra, who had looked away as she sipped her coffee, and decided to accept her response. The rest of the debriefing did not take long. They reviewed the next day's classroom and flight training objectives, then Sondra got on the phone to check messages, and Boomer went to his office to catch up on messages and paperwork and check in on the many laboratories and design offices that he supervised.

The afternoon began with a company operations executive staff meeting, which Boomer just barely tolerated, but it was was part of his new job as head of aerospace operations. The meeting was chaired by the company's new vice president of operations, Jason Richter, a retired lieutenant colonel and robotics engineer from the U.S. Army, who was hired to replace the late Patrick McLanahan. Jason was tall, trim, and athletic, with dark good looks. He had been hired by Sky Masters Aerospace for his engineering background, especially in the realm of robotics, but it turned out he was equally adept in management, so he was promoted to lead research and development at the company. Although he was more at home in a laboratory or design facility, he enjoyed the power and prestige of overseeing such a large number of some of the world's best and brightest minds.

"Let's get started," Richter said, starting the meeting precisely at one o'clock, as always. "Let's start with the Aerospace Division. Hunter, congratulations on successfully bringing the president to Armstrong Space Station and back safely. Quite an accomplishment." The others in the room gave Boomer a round of light applause—Hunter "Boomer" Noble was considered an eccentric character in the company's executive boardroom, not a serious one, and was therefore lightly tolerated. "The president apparently is not suffering any ill effects. Observations?"

"The guy did fantastic," Boomer said, silently acknowledging the positive feedback from his board-member colleagues but also noting the negative reactions. "He stayed calm and cool the entire flight. I was not too surprised when he agreed to do the docking, but I couldn't believe it when he wanted to do the spacewalk to the airlock. He acted as if he'd been in astronaut training for years. That kind of courage is extraordinary."

"We're already getting inquiries about flying the spaceplane, and there's been talk about funding for more S-19s and the XS-29," Jason said.

"I'm all for that," Boomer said, "but I think we need to bring in resources to start working seriously on the next series of space stations. Armstrong is hanging in there, but its days are numbered, and if Brad McLanahan's Starfire project goes forward, which I'm betting it will, Armstrong may be out of the military space-weapon business altogether. I've got two folks, Harry Felt and Samantha Yi, working on space-station stuff, mostly designing systems to update Armstrong. I'd like to put them in charge of a new design team, three or four persons to start, coming up with designs for new military and industrial stations in line with President Phoenix's proposals. We also need to get you and Dr. Kaddiri out to Washington right away to meet up with our lobbyists and find out who's in charge of this new push for space." He hesitated for a moment, then added, "Maybe you or Helen should volunteer to run it, Jason."

"Me?" Jason asked. "In Washington? I'd rather be buried up to my neck in the desert. But I like your ideas. Submit a proposal and a budget to me right away and I'll take it to Helen."

Boomer made a few taps on his tablet computer. "In your in-box now, comandante."

"Thank you. I knew you'd have something worked out already. I'll make sure Helen gets it today."

At that moment the company president and chief executive officer, Dr. Helen Kaddiri, entered the meeting room. Everyone rose to their feet as the tall, dark-eyed, fifty-two-year-old woman with very long dark hair tied in an intricate knot at the back of her neck and a dark gray business suit stood by the doorway. Helen Kaddiri was born in India but educated mostly in the United States, earning numerous advanced degrees in business and engineering. She had worked at Sky Masters for decades, partnering with Jonathan Masters to acquire the original failing aerospace company they worked for, and building it into one of the world's premier high-technology design and development companies. "Take seats, everyone, please," she said in a light, singsong voice. "Sorry to interrupt, Jason."

"Not at all, Helen," Jason said. "Have something for us?"

"An announcement," she said. She walked to the front of the room and stood beside Jason. "The board of directors has selected three projects to provide grants to this year, all of them at universities: State University of New York at Buffalo for a swarming satellite project; Allegheny College in Pennsylvania for a laser communications system; and the bulk of the award, twenty-five million dollars, going to California Polytechnic University, San Luis Obispo, for a very impressive orbiting solar-power-plant project." Another round of applause from the branch directors in the room.

"That project is being run by Brad McLanahan," Boomer said. "That kid's amazing. I ask the kid a question about some part of the project, and he says he doesn't know and he'll get back to me, and next thing I know I'm getting a phone call from some Nobel Prize laureate from Germany with the answer. He's got a list of experts and scientists on his team that'll water your eyes."

"We're already heavily investing in their project," Jason said. "We've already provided them with a Trinity module they're using for dimensions and mate-testing. When they start fabricating subsystems, they want to lift parts of the space-based system up to Armstrong Space Station on Midnight and Black Stallion, so they asked for things like dimensions of the cargo bay, systems, power, environmental, temperatures, vibration, et cetera. They've also asked to see computer code on the Skybolt aiming system—they want to use it to beam maser energy down to a rectenna on Earth, and their computer-team leader thinks he can improve the accuracy."

"They have their act together, that's for sure," Boomer added.

"I will give the universities the good news," Helen said. "That's it. Anything for me?"

"Boomer had a great idea: meet with President Phoenix and whoever's heading up this new space initiative, present them with some ideas, and find out what they're interested in doing," Jason said. "He also wants to form a team to start designing space stations, military and industrial. His proposal and budget are on my tablet."

"Good ideas, Boomer," Helen said. "Drop his proposal off to me in my office right after the meeting."

"Will do," Jason said.

"I also suggested you or Jason volunteer to head up the government space initiative if there's no one named yet," Boomer said.

"I have a job, thank you very much, and Jason is not going anywhere—I just got him here, after a lot of cajoling and harping," Helen said, smiling. "But a trip to Washington for us sounds good." She fielded a few more questions and comments, then departed. Jason continued to chair his meeting, going around the table getting reports from all of the operations branch directors, and it broke up about an hour later.

Jason walked up to Helen's office a few minutes later and knocked on the doorframe of the open office door. "I have that report for you," he said through the doorway, holding up his tablet computer.

"Come in, Jason," Helen said, working on her laptop at her desk. "Close the door." Jason did as she ordered, then walked over to her desk and initiated the file transfer from his tablet to her laptop.

"It's kind of a long file," he said. "You know Boomer—why say something in just two words when he can think of twenty?"

"That is fine," she said. "What shall we do while we are waiting?"

"I've got a few ideas," Jason said, smiling, and he leaned down and gave her a deep kiss, which she returned with equal enthusiasm. They kissed for several long, lingering moments. "I wish I could take your hair down right now," he said in a deep, quiet voice.

"I love watching your hair cascade down from being pinned up . . . especially if it comes down across my naked chest." She responded by pulling him down and giving him another deep kiss. "Are you free tonight? I haven't been with you in days."

"Jason, we should not be doing this," Helen whispered. "I am your boss, and I am over ten years older than you."

"I don't care how chronologically old you are," Jason said. "You are the most exotic, most alluring woman I've ever been with. Sex radiates from you like a laser. And you may be older than me, but I can barely keep up with you in bed."

"Stop it, you randy goat," Helen said with a smile, but she gave him another deep, lingering kiss in gratitude. She grabbed his face and gave it a playful shake. "I have that speech for the Lander County Chamber of Commerce meeting tonight, remember, and the city manager, planning-commission chair, and police chief want to talk afterward. I think it is about extending utilities to build more subdivisions near the airport and revising the letter of agreement with airport security, the county, and company security. I want to make sure housing stays well outside the airport noise zone, and I do not want our security officers tied down by the sheriffs in federal and state security agreements. Charles Gordon from the governor's office will be there too, and I want to talk with him about getting some seed money for an airport expansion."

"Damn."

"Why don't you come with me? Everyone knows you as the guy who designed and built the Cybernetic Infantry Device that saved the city from Judah Andorsen and the Knights of the True Republic—I am sure they would like to meet you."

"I'm not into politics," Jason said. "I'm into you. I don't think I could keep my hands off you."

"Oh, I think you have more impulse control than that, Jason," she said. "Besides, I am sure they would want to meet the future president and CEO of Sky Masters Aerospace."

"We need to talk about that some more, Helen," Jason said. He took a seat across from her. "I don't think I'm CEO material. You had to persuade me to take over as chief of operations after Patrick McLanahan was killed—"

"And you are doing a great job," Helen said. "Your team is the best in the business. You have only been in the position for a few months. It will become second nature before you know it. You need a little more business education, maybe an MBA to add to all the other degrees you have, but you are obviously a leader."

"I feel more at home in a lab, not behind a desk."

"Nobody says you have to stay behind a desk," Helen said. "Leaders do their thing in all sorts of ways. You know how to assign, delegate, and organize—that leaves you the time and ability to spend more time with your engineers as well as do all the things that CEOs have to do." She got up from her desk and stepped beside him, pressing her breasts against him as she knew he liked. "Come with me tonight. Afterward, if it's not too late, I would love to have you over."

"Thought you said we shouldn't be doing this."

"Oh, we should not," Helen said with a smile. Jason stood up, and they shared another deep, passionate kiss. "I might lose my job if the board found out that I was sleeping with one of my vice presidents, even though I cofounded the company." Another kiss. "You would definitely be fired, and you would probably be sued for your signing bonus." Yet another kiss.

"Stop talking now, please, Miss President," Jason said.

"Yes, Mr. Vice President," Helen said, and they kissed again, and this kiss lasted far longer than the others.

. . .

It was well past sunset when Boomer left the Sky Masters Aerospace facility and headed home. The formerly sleepy, isolated little mining settlement of Battle Mountain in north-central Nevada had undergone an incredible transformation in just the three years since Sky Masters Aerospace Inc. had relocated there from Las Vegas: the population had more than tripled, construction projects of all kinds were everywhere, and the unincorporated settlement—it had retained its mining-camp and railroad-way-point identity since its inception in the 1840s, even though it was the seat of Lander County—finally became Nevada's newest city and one of the fastest growing in the nation. Boomer rented a house in one of the newer subdivisions located between the airport and the new heart of the city, close enough to visit the new casinos and high-end restaurants when he wanted but convenient enough to commute to work, especially now that the morning commute on Interstate 80 to the airport seemed to be getting busier and busier by the day, thanks to the dozens of businesses that had sprung up in the area since Sky Masters Aerospace expanded its operations.

Boomer parked his Lincoln MKT in the garage, looking forward to a nice relaxing evening. He was a

regular at several of the new casinos in town, and hadn't had to pay for a meal or drinks in over a year—he was sure he had given the casinos plenty of money at the card tables to more than make up for the comps—but tonight was just going to be a down day. Maybe a little wine, maybe a movie, maybe—

"About time you got home," a voice said from the kitchen. It was Sondra Eddington, wearing nothing but one of Boomer's Sky Masters Aerospace Inc.'s T-shirts, her long blond hair draped just perfectly around her breasts as if she had arranged it that way—which, Boomer thought, she probably had. "I was about to start without you."

"I didn't know you'd be coming over," Boomer said.

"I was a little amped after flying this morning," Sondra said in a half-weary, half-teasing tone. "I tried a run and a hard workout at the gym, but I'm still a . . . little wired." She went over and gave him a kiss on the lips. "So I decided to drop by and ask to see if you knew any ways I can burn off a little energy?"

Boomer tried, but he couldn't help but let his eyes roam across her body, which made her smile. "Where's your car?" he asked.

"I parked it at the convenience store down the block," Sondra said. "I've seen too many people from Sky Masters in your neighborhood, and I didn't want

them to see my car parked in front of your place a lot."

Sounds like a really good idea, Boomer thought. He held her at arm's length and looked her directly in the eyes. "Or we can do the right thing, like we talked about, and not sleep with each other anymore."

"Oh, I know we talked about that," Sondra said with a little pout, putting her arms over his shoulders and her hands behind his neck, "but I can't help myself. You are such a hot hard-body, and you have that roguish little grin and that give-a-shit attitude that just drives me nuts. Not to mention you're a tiger in the sack."

"Thank you," Boomer said. "You're pretty hot too."

"Thank you."

"But your boyfriend, Brad, is becoming a friend, and if he found out about us, it'd be hard to work with him in the near future. His Starfire project just got approved for funding."

"Then I'll break up with him."

Boomer blinked in surprise. "Just like that?"

"When it's time to break up with you, it'll be just as quick," Sondra said. "I like Brad, and he's a hard-body too like you, but he's way younger than me, and he's away to college, and lately he's been too busy to come visit me, and I'm lonely being away from home.

Besides, I don't like getting tied down. I want what I want, when I want it, and right now I want you."

"And when Brad's here, you'll want him too?"

Sondra shrugged. "Maybe. I don't think he'd take me back after the breakup—he's a little immature about women and relationships, and I don't think he could handle just being friends or casual sex partners." She drew him closer. "How about it, stud? Fire up the engines and take me for a ride?"

Boomer smiled, but he shook his head. "I don't think so, Sondra," he said.

She took a step back and ran her hands down her blond hair, which was draped across her chest. "You don't want me anymore? I said I'd break up with Brad."

"We had sex once, and we talked about it afterward and both decided it wasn't right," Boomer said. "We'll be training together for another twelve months. I'm your instructor. Sleeping together is not a good idea."

"If you say so," Sondra said in a soft voice. Then, slowly and seductively, she pulled off the T-shirt, revealing her breathtaking body, firm breasts, and flat tummy. She held the T-shirt out, being careful not to let it block Boomer's view of her exquisite body. "Do you want your T-shirt back, Dr. Noble?"

Boomer reached out and took the T-shirt from her . . . then flipped it over his shoulder. "Shit, I'm going to hell anyway," he said, and he took Sondra in his arms and kissed her deeply.

FOURTEENTH BUILDING, THE KREMLIN, MOSCOW
RUSSIAN FEDERATION

Days later

President Gennadiy Gryzlov's primary official offices in the Kremlin government complex were in the Senate Building, also known as the First Building, but he much preferred the more isolated president's reserve working office known as the Fourteenth Building. Recently he had completely renovated the building, making it a high-tech copy of his oil company's offices in St. Petersburg, with several layers of security, sophisticated surveillance and countersurveillance systems, and ultrasecure communications, all of which rivaled and in many ways exceeded the best Russian technology; it also had an underground emergency escape railway that could whisk him to Chkalovsky Airport, eighteen miles northeast of Moscow, which was his cosmonaut training airfield serving Star City and now had a contingent of military transport planes that could get him safely away if necessary.

He was determined not to be trapped inside an underground command post during an air raid, the way his father had been: at the first warning of any danger, Gryzlov could be out of Fourteenth Building in less than a minute, out of the city in less than five, and stepping aboard a jet ready to take him anywhere in Europe in less than thirty.

Gryzlov rarely conducted meetings in Fourteenth Building, preferring that all official and high-level cabinet meetings be in his office in First Building, but he had summoned Foreign Minister Daria Titeneva to his office in Fourteenth Building early in the morning. She was escorted into the office by Chief of Staff Sergei Tarzarov, who then assumed his "out of sight, out of mind" position in the president's office, but was dismissed with a glance from Gryzlov. "*Privetstviye, Daria*," Gryzlov said from behind his immense desk. "Welcome. Tea? Coffee?"

"No, thank you, Mr. President," Titeneva said. She took a moment to look around the office. Behind Gryzlov's desk were picture windows with spectacular panoramic views of the Kremlin and Moscow, and on the walls before the desk were large-screen, high-definition monitors displaying a variety of information, from international news to feeds from government proceedings, to stock-market price and volume tickers from around the world. A conference table for twenty was to the president's left, and a comfortable seating area for twelve, surrounding a coffee table, was on the right. "I have not seen your private office here since you finished remodeling it. Very businesslike. I like it, Mr. President."

"I cannot get very much work done in the Senate Building with the staff running amok," Gryzlov said. "I go to First Building to hear the hens cluck, then come back here and make decisions."

"I hope I am not one of those hens you speak of, Mr. President," Titeneva said.

"Of course not," Gryzlov said, crossing around his desk, stepping up to Titeneva, and giving her a light kiss on the cheek, then receiving a polite one in return. "You are a trusted friend. You worked with my father for many years, ever since you served together in the air force."

"Your father was a great man," Titeneva said. "I was privileged to serve him."

"He brought you along the whole way with him, did he not?" Gryzlov said. "You both rose through the ranks in the air force together, and then he led you through the ranks of government, yes?"

"Your father knew that it was important to have trusted individuals with him, both in and out of the military," Titeneva said. "He was also careful to make sure I learned from the best experts in the Kremlin."

"You were his chief of staff for a short while, before the traitor Nikolai Stepashin, if I recall correctly," Gryzlov said. "I am curious: why did you leave him and join the Foreign Service? You could have been prime minister or even president by now."

"We both thought that my talents could better be utilized in Washington and New York," Titeneva said casually. "Back then, women did not take on most high-level positions in the Kremlin."

"I see," Gryzlov said. He turned directly to her. "So the rumors I have heard about a long-running sexual affair with my father are untrue?" Titeneva said nothing. Gryzlov stepped to her and kissed her lips. "My father was a lucky man. Maybe I can be as lucky."

"I am almost old enough to be your mother, Mr. President," she said, but Gryzlov leaned forward to kiss her again, and she did not back away. Gryzlov smiled at her, let his eyes roam up and down her body, then returned to his desk and took a cigar from a desk drawer. "You invited me to your private office to kiss me, Mr. President?"

"I cannot think of a better reason, Daria," he said, after lighting his cigar and blowing a large cloud of fragrant smoke to the ceiling. "Why not come visit more often?"

"My husband, for one."

"Your husband, Yuri, is a good man and an honored veteran, and I am sure what he does when you are away from Moscow is of no concern to you, as long as he does not jeopardize your position in the government," Gryzlov said. Titeneva said nothing. Without turning to her, he motioned to a chair in front of his desk with his cigar, and she took it. "You are receiving the reports of the American spaceplane flights?"

"Yes, Mr. President," Titeneva said. "The flights to the military space station have increased in number slightly, from three a month to four."

"That is a thirty percent increase, Miss Foreign Minister—I would say that is significant, not slight," Gryzlov said. "Their cargo?"

"Intelligence reports suggest that some major improvements to the station, possibly to the laser-beam control and power-distribution systems," Titeneva said. "Optical sensors can see very little change to the outside of the station."

"You personally and officially inquire about the contents of those spaceplanes, yes?"

"Of course, Mr. President, as soon as I am notified that a launch is imminent," Titeneva replied. "The Americans' usual replies are 'personnel,' 'supplies,' and 'classified.' They never give any details."

"And unofficially?"

"Security is still very tight, sir," she said. "The space-plane flights and most operations aboard Armstrong Space Station are done by civilian contractors, and their security is very sophisticated and multileveled. None of my contacts in Washington know much at all about the contractors, except as we have seen, many of them are ex-military officers and technicians. It is very difficult for me to get much information on the contractor-run space program, I'm afraid. Minister Kazyanov might have more information."

"I see," Gryzlov said. He fell silent for a few moments; then: "You have been granted permission to speak before the Security Council prior to the vote on our resolution about the American's outrageous space initiative, correct?"

"Yes, Mr. President."

Gryzlov blew a cloud of smoke into the air above his desk, then set the cigar in an ashtray and got out of his seat, and as protocol dictated, Titeneva immediately rose as well. "You left my father's side, Daria, because you could not handle the level of responsibility and initiative that my father wanted to give you," Gryzlov said, walking over to her and impaling the woman with an icy, direct stare. "You were not tough enough to be with him, even as his lover. You left Moscow for the high-society parties in New York and Washington rather than help him fight in the political ditches in the Kremlin."

"Who told you these lies, Mr. President?" Titeneva asked, her eyes flaring in anger. "That old goat Tarzarov?"

In a blur of motion that Titeneva never saw coming, Gryzlov slapped her across the face with an open right hand. She reeled from the blow, shaking stars out of her head, but Gryzlov noticed that she did not retreat or cry out, and in moments had straightened her back and stood tall before him. Again, in a flash he was on her, his lips locked onto hers, pulling her head to him with his right hand while his left roamed her breasts. Then, after a long and rough kiss, he pushed her away from him. She rubbed her cheek, then her lips with the back of her hand, but again stood tall before him, refusing to back away.

"You are going to New York City and addressing the United Nations Security Council," Gryzlov said, boring his eyes directly into hers, "but you are not going to be this mature, wise, respected, demure diplomat any longer, do you understand me? You are going to be the tigress my father wanted and trained but never had. I can see that tigress in your eyes, Daria, but you have been mired in a comfortable life in the Foreign Ministry with your war-hero husband, tolerating his little dalliances because you want to keep your cushy job. Well, no longer.

"You will go to the Security Council, and Russia will get all that I demand, or we will have nothing more to do with the United Nations," Gryzlov said. "You will get that resolution passed, or you will blow that place up. You will show my displeasure and anger without any doubt in anyone's minds, or do not bother returning from New York."

"The United States will veto the resolution, Gennadiy," Titeneva snapped. Gryzlov noticed the change in the tone of her voice and smiled—like a champion Thoroughbred racehorse, she was responding well to a little discipline, he thought. "You know that as well as I."

"Then bring that place down," Gryzlov said. "That chamber, and the *entire fucking world,* should understand clearly how angry I will be if that resolution does not pass." He grasped the hair behind her neck, pulled her to him, and gave her another deep kiss, then pulled her away from him. "If you choose to be the bunny rabbit instead of the tigress, and you dare return to the Kremlin, then I will make sure you become someone's little bunny. Maybe even mine. And I guarantee you will not enjoy it. Now get the hell out of here."

Sergei Tarzarov entered the president's office a few moments after Titeneva departed. "Not a typical staff meeting, I assume, sir?" he said, touching his own lips as a signal.

"Just a little motivational pep talk before her trip to New York City," Gryzlov said gruffly, wiping lipstick off his mouth with the back of his hand. "Where is Ilianov?"

"On the secure phone from Washington, channel three," Tarzarov said.

Gryzlov picked up the phone, stabbed at the channel selector, and impatiently waited for the decryption circuitry to make the connection. "Colonel?"

"Secure, sir," Ilianov replied.

"What in hell happened out there?"

"It was completely unexpected, sir," Ilianov said. "Apparently McLanahan does have a security detail, because they took down my team, took McLanahan, and closed the house down before sunrise."

"Where is your team?"

"Unknown, sir," Ilianov said. "They are not in local civilian law enforcement custody, that much I know."

"Shit," Gryzlov swore. "Either FBI or private security. They will be singing like birds in record time, especially if they are in the hands of civilian countersurveillance operatives. I told you, Colonel, do not assume anything. Where is McLanahan now?"

"He has just now surfaced, sir," Ilianov said. "He has registered as a resident of one of the campus apartment complexes. He was injured during my team's invasion, but appears to be all right now. We are studying his movements, the apartment complex's security, and searching for the presence of his personal security forces. We will not be surprised again. So far, we have detected nothing. McLanahan appears to have resumed his routine movements since before the invasion. We can detect no security surrounding him."

"Look harder, then, Colonel, damn you!" Gryzlov snapped. "I want him taken down. I do not care if you have to send in an entire platoon to get him—I want him *destroyed*. Get on it!"

NORWEGIAN ROOM, UNITED NATIONS SECURITY COUNCIL CHAMBER NEW YORK CITY

A few days later

"This illegal, dangerous, and provocative push for American domination of space must end *immediately*," Russian foreign minister Daria Titeneva shouted. She was addressing a meeting of the United Nations Security Council in New York City, seated in the ambassador's chair beside Russian UN ambassador Andrei Naryshkin. "Russia has recorded a thirty percent increase in the number of spaceplane and unmanned boosted flights to the American military space station since President Phoenix made his announcement concerning American control of space. Russia has evidence that the United States is reactivating its constellation of space-weapon satellites called Kingfishers, and will also reactivate the space-based free-electron laser called Skybolt with improved aiming systems and increased power, making it capable of destroying targets anywhere on Earth. All this appears to be nothing more than an election-year show of power, but President Phoenix is playing a very dangerous game, threatening the peace and stability of the entire world just to gain a few votes.

"The Russian government has drafted a resolution for the Security Council's consideration that demands that the United States of America cancel plans to reactivate all its space weapons and that it destroy the ones already in Earth orbit, and orders President Kenneth Phoenix to reverse his stated position that any orbit occupied by an American spacecraft is sovereign American territory that can be defended with military force. Outer space is not, and should never be, dominated by any one nation or alliance. I ask for Council authorization for Russia's resolution to be presented to the procedural committee and then to the Security

Council for a vote, with immediate implementation thereafter—after an affirmative vote. Thank you, Mr. President." There was a faint round of applause after Titeneva finished her address—not exactly a resounding sign of approval, but a rather ominous signal of difficulties for the Americans.

"Thank you, Miss Foreign Minister," Sofyan Apriyanto of Indonesia, the rotating president of the United Nations Security Council, said. "The chair recognizes Ambassador Ells for ten minutes for rebuttal."

"Thank you, Mr. President," Paula Ells, U.S. ambassador to the United Nations, responded. "I shall not need ten minutes to refute the Russian foreign minister's allegations. Her claims and accusations are completely baseless and her facts are inaccurate at best and outright lies at worst."

"How dare you, Ambassador!" Titeneva shouted when she heard the translation. "How dare you call me a liar! The evidence is plain for the whole world to see! It is you and Phoenix's entire administration who are the liars and instigators here!"

Ambassador Paula Ells blinked in surprise. She had met, and spent time with, the veteran Kremlin bureaucrat many times in her career and knew her as a calm, intelligent, completely professional person, but since she had arrived in New York, she was almost unrecognizable. She had given several interviews to the world press, slamming President Phoenix and his space initiative, using words that Ells had never heard her utter before. That attitude was continuing here, with even greater acidity. "The only facts that you stated that are true are the increases in spaceplane and unmanned rocket flights," Ells said, "but as usual, you state only half-truths and formulate wild accusations that are not supported by the facts:

"Our spacecraft missions have increased, it's true, but only because Russia has decreased the number of Soyuz and Progress missions to the International Space Station, for some unknown reason, and the United States decided to step up and increase our missions to fill the void," Ells went on. "Our spaceplane and commercial missions are not just going to Armstrong Space Station, as the foreign minister claims, but to the International Space Station as well. If Russia thinks they can influence foreign affairs by postponing and canceling critical supply missions—missions that have already been bought and paid for, I should add—they are completely misguided.

"As to this draft resolution, Mr. President: the wording is so broad and vague that it could have been better written by a seventh grader," Ells continued. Titeneva slapped her hand on her desk and said something to

Naryshkin, angrily jabbing a finger first at Ells, then at him. "If this resolution were to be adopted, the United Nations could for all practical purposes shut down the American Global Positioning System, because it is an integral part of space-weapon systems, yet it makes no mention of the Russian GLONASS satellite navigation system, which has the same capability.

"In addition, the resolution seeks to ban any weapon system that has anything, however remote, to do with spacecraft traveling above the atmosphere, which means the United Nations could ground all American heavy airlifters because at one time they test-launched ballistic missiles from aircraft, or beach cargo ships because they once carried parts for space weapons," Ells went on. "The resolution has nothing to do with peace and security and has everything to do with presenting a resolution to the Security Council that forces a veto from the United States, so that the Russian Federation can point to America with horror and tell the world that the United States is bent on dominating outer space. The United States hopes that the other members of the Council will see this tactic for exactly what it is: a cheap political ploy, using trumped-up evidence, distorted data, and fear-mongering. I urge the Council to reject introducing this resolution to committee and not give it any more consideration."

Ells turned directly to Titeneva. "Miss Foreign Minister . . . Daria, let's sit down with Secretary Morrison and work out a compromise," she implored, raising her hands as if in surrender. "President Phoenix's initiative is not a rearming of space. The United States stands ready to do whatever the international community wishes in order to verify our intentions and assets in space. We should—"

"Do not address me as if we are sisters, Ambassador Ells!" Titeneva snapped. "Show some respect. And it is far, far past the time for verification—the United States should have thought of that before Phoenix's proclamation from the military space station! The United States has just one option for demonstrating its sincerity, openness, and genuine desire for peace: dismantle the entire space-weapon infrastructure immediately!"

Ells's shoulders slumped as she perceived Titeneva's rising anger. There was simply no talking to her. It was as if she had turned into some sort of snarling monster in a Daria Titeneva costume. Ells turned to the Security Council president and said, "I have nothing further to add, Mr. President. Thank you."

"Thank you, Ambassador Ells," President Sofyan Apriyanto said. "Are there any more comments on the motion to introduce the Russian resolution into committee?" There were a few more brief speeches, both in favor and against. "Thank you. If there are no more comments, I shall entertain a motion to send the resolution to committee."

"So moved, Mr. President," Russian ambassador Andrei Naryshkin said.

"Seconded," said the ambassador from the People's Republic of China immediately, obviously prearranged so that China would be on record as supporting the measure.

"The resolution has been moved and seconded," Apriyanto said. "I offer one more opportunity for discussion with your governments or to offer any amendments." There were no takers, and the secretary-general moved along quickly: "Very well. If there are no objections, I call for a vote. All in favor, please signify by raising your hand, and please keep your hand raised so an accurate count may be made."

Every hand went up, including those of the representatives from Great Britain and France . . . except one, that of Ambassador Paula Ells from the United States. "All those opposed, please signify by raising your hands." All hands went down except Paula Ells's. "The chair recognizes a nay vote from the United States of America," Apriyanto observed, "and as such, the resolution is not carried."

"*This is an outrage!*" Russian foreign minister Titeneva shouted. "The Russian Federation protests this vote in the strongest terms! The resolution was voted in favor by all but one nation! *All* have voted in favor save one! This cannot stand!"

"Madame Foreign Minister, with all respect, you have not been recognized by the chair," President Apriyanto said. "The Security Council granted you the privilege of addressing its members on this matter in place of your ambassador, but has not granted you the right to make any remarks regarding the outcome of any vote. As you well know, the United States of America, as well as the Russian Federation and the other permanent members of the Council, exercise their privilege of great power unanimity when they cast a nay vote. The Russian Federation, and the Union of Soviet Socialist Republics before it, exercised the same privilege many times in the past. Thank you. May I call the Council's attention to the next item on the—"

"*Do not dismiss me like some child!*" Titeneva shouted. "Mr. President, *this will not stand*! President Kenneth Phoenix is about to grab complete and unfettered control of space, and the Security Council will do nothing to stop him? This is madness!"

Apriyanto picked up a small gavel and tapped its handle lightly on its sounding block, attempting to calm the Russian foreign minister without gaveling her into silence . . . or worse. "Madame Foreign Minister, you are out of order. Please—"

"No, this Council is out of order! This entire *body* is out of order!" Titeneva shouted. "Russia will not stand for this!"

"Madame Foreign Minister, please—"

"Mr. President, President Phoenix's declaration is clearly a violation of Chapter Seven of the United Nations Charter, which prohibits member nations from threatening the peace or conducting acts of aggression," Titeneva said loudly. "Chapter Seven authorizes the Security Council to act to preserve the peace and stop aggression."

"The United States is not threatening anyone, Madame Foreign Minister," Ells said. "President Phoenix's program is a technology laboratory to advance peaceful access to space. We are not activating any space weapons. We want—"

"You can say that all you want, Ells, but your words do not make it so," Titeneva said. "Mr. President, the veto does not apply in this matter because the resolution directly involves the United States, and a permanent member nation of the Security Council cannot veto a resolution against itself. They must abstain, and therefore the resolution passes."

"The Parliamentary Committee has already ruled that the resolution, although obviously aimed at the United States' recently announced space program, applies to any spacefaring nation, and is therefore subject to veto," Apriyanto said. "Madame Foreign Minister, you are out of order. You may file a protest with the secretary-general and appeal to the General Assembly, but the resolution did not carry and the matter is closed. You may continue to observe our proceedings, but—"

"I will not continue to sit and observe this farce," Titeneva said, shooting to her feet and throwing the translation earpiece on the table before her. "Listen to me very carefully. If the Security Council will not act, Russia will. Russia will not cooperate with any nation that opposes our desire for security against the American military space program, and if Russia detects that the United States is militarizing any aspect of their space hardware, Russia will consider that an act of war and will respond accordingly.

"Russian president Gryzlov has authorized me to inform you that Russia will no longer support manned or unmanned supply missions to the International Space Station," Titeneva thundered on. "Further, Russia demands that the modules on the International

Space Station that belong to Russia must be disconnected and made ready to transport to their own orbits
immediately. The Russian modules are hereby considered sovereign Russian territory and must be vacated
and surrendered to Russian control."

"Detach the Russian modules?" Paula Ells retorted.
"It's not a Lego toy up there, Daria. The modules were
Russia's contribution to an international partnership.
That partnership pays for the modules' upkeep, and
the partnership pays Russia for use of the modules and
for Soyuz support missions. You can't just take your bat
and ball and go home—we're talking about twenty-ton
modules traveling thousands of miles an hour orbiting
hundreds of—"

"I do not want to listen to your tiresome American
aphorisms, Ells," Titeneva said, "and I told you never
to call me by my first name in this or any other venue!
Russia will not allow the so-called partnership to use
modules built by Russians if the international community will not do something to assure Russia's national
security interests, and we certainly do not want any
nation antagonistic to Russia to freely use our modules.
You will vacate and surrender them to Russia immediately, or we will take action." And at that, Titeneva
turned and departed the chamber, followed closely by
Naryshkin.

SAN LUIS OBISPO, CALIFORNIA

One week later

James Ratel entered the back room of his *dojang* south of the city of San Luis Obispo to find Brad McLanahan already doing push-ups on the linoleum. "Well well, five minutes early . . . much better," Chief Ratel said. "And you came ready for a workout. Maybe you are trainable after all."

"Yes, Chief," Brad replied, hopping to his feet and standing nearly at attention at the edge of the blue mat.

"Are you warmed up?"

"Yes, Chief."

"Good," Ratel said. "So far we've been concentrating on strength training, and I've seen progress. From now on you will continue these exercises on your own, on your own time. You don't need to go to a gym for a good workout. Push-ups, crunches, dips, and pull-ups, all to muscle failure, with no more than ninety seconds rest in between. Every week I'll test you again, and every week I expect to see improvements."

"Yes, Chief," Brad responded.

"Today will be your first self-defense lesson," Ratel went on. He handed Brad a package. "From now on, you will wear a *beol,* or training outfit, what is called a *gi* in Japanese. Once we start more practical training, we'll do it in street clothes so you'll learn the feel in a more realistic way, but for now you'll wear this. You have thirty seconds to change." It took Brad less than fifteen. Ratel showed him how to properly tie the white belt, and then they were ready.

"We'll start with the most basic self-defense tool first." Ratel picked up a simple wooden walking cane with a pointed crook and two grooved grips carved into the wood, one near the crook and another farther down the shaft. "Many years ago, after the First Korean War, a South Korean master taught a school of self-defense called 'Joseon,' in which he used canes and farm tools for self-defense. The style was taught because during the Japanese occupation of Korea during World War Two, and during the North Korean occupation, South Korean citizens were not allowed to carry knives or guns, but canes, walking sticks, and farm implements such as rakes, saws, and thrashers were very common. A U.S. Army serviceman noticed that the canes were used by the locals as very effective self-defense weapons, and he developed a method for training others on how to use a walking cane for self-defense. It became known as Cane-Ja, or cane-discipline. For the next several weeks you will walk with a cane and carry it with you at all times, even if you travel on an airplane or go into a school or courthouse. After you learn Cane-Ja, you will advance to other, more violent forms of self-defense, where the cane may not be necessary, or that can be used if you lose or break it."

"A cane? You mean, like an old guy?" Brad protested. "I'm supposed to act like an old crippled guy and walk with a stupid cane, Chief?"

"You should not act like an old man," Ratel said. "Never try to be something you're not—most people can't pull it off, most others can detect it, and you'll call attention to yourself. Act normally. You don't have to walk with a limp, put any weight on it, or even have the tip of the cane on the ground all the time, but you should carry it with you, have it at the ready, and never set it down. Loop it over your arm or belt, but never set it down because you'll forget it. You can loop it through straps on your backpack as long as it's easily within reach. And never refer to it as a weapon or as something that is necessary for self-defense. It is a walking stick—you will just happen to know how to use it as something else."

"This is stupid, sir," Brad said. "I'm supposed to carry around a stick with me? On the bicycle? In class?"

"Everywhere," Ratel said. "Everyone around you must associate you with the cane and the cane with you. It must be your constant companion. People will see that bruise on your head and face, see the cane, and add one plus one, and that correlation will survive long after the injury is healed. Aggressors, on the other hand, will see the two and think you are weak and vulnerable, and that gives you an advantage."

Ratel held up the cane. "Notice that the cane has a round crook that is pointed at the tip, and grips cut into the shaft at two places and a grip cut into the crook," he said. "There is also a ridge along the back spine of the cane. We will adjust this cane for your height, but I estimated this one so it should fit well." He gave it to Brad. "As with any cane, it should be long enough to provide support for your body if you lean on it, but not too short to diminish its striking power or have you assume a weak stance. Hold it alongside your body." Brad did as he was told. "Good. Your arm is not quite straight. We want just a slight bend in your elbow. If you did lean on it, it should look natural, like you can really put a little weight on it."

Ratel picked up his own cane, a well-worn version of Brad's, for a demonstration. "You normally stand with one or two hands on top of the crook and form a triangle with your legs, like so," he said, standing casually before Brad. "This is the 'relax' position. You're not really relaxing, but the idea is to appear relaxed and casual yet let a potential attacker that you have identified by your observations or instincts see that you have a cane, which might either deter him or embolden him. Obviously, with the kind of attackers we're preparing for, the sight of a cane is not going to deter them, but they might think you are weak. If you need your hands you can hook the cane on to your belt, but return to the 'relax' position when you can. This is the first warning position to an attacker, the green light."

He slid his hand off the crook down the shaft to the uppermost set of grip ridges, with the open end of the crook facing downward. "Now your attacker is coming toward you, and you see him, so you take this position, which we call 'regrip,' the yellow light. The crook of the cane is in front of you, and you are holding the upper grip. The crook is facing downward. This is the second warning. To a casual observer or adversary this may not seem like a warning position.

"From here, there are a number of things you can do," Ratel went on. "The easiest, of course, is to use the cane to keep someone away simply by poking at him." He took a couple stabs at a mannequin that had been stationed nearby. "These, along with verbal warnings, are usually effective enough to deter an aggressive pan-handler or young would-be robber. Obviously, with the adversaries we are preparing for, that would probably not be enough. I will teach you later on how to counter someone who grabs your cane.

"From the 'regrip' position, if you are attacked with fists or a knife, you swing the cane from the outside, striking your attacker's arms between the wrist and elbow, as hard as you can. That twists his body away from you, and you have the advantage. You can strike with the crook on his knee, hip, or groin. Be warned, a blow to the head with the crook of the cane will probably kill or seriously wound. Killing in self-defense is permissible, but exactly what is 'self-defense' is debatable in a court of law. Defend yourself at all times, but always be aware that your actions have consequences."

Ratel had Brad practice the moves against the mannequin, doing each move on Ratel's orders, increasing speed as they went. Soon sweat was glistening on Brad's forehead. After just a few seconds of practice, Brad's arms were definitely getting weary. "Break," Ratel said finally. "Once we build up those arms and shoulders, you should be able to both speed up and increase your hitting power."

"But I won't be hitting an opponent for a long time, will I, Chief?" Brad asked.

"Our objective is to build up muscle memory so your moves become second nature," Ratel said. "It'll take time and practice." He motioned Brad away from the mannequin, then assumed the green-light position with both hands on top of the crook. He then assumed the yellow-light position, and then the red-light position with a loud *"Stop!"* command, the cane held out straight at the mannequin. The next instant the cane was nothing but a blur of motion as Ratel pummeled the mannequin from seemingly every possible angle, striking for an entire minute before assuming the three stances all the way to the relaxed green-light position.

"Holy crap," Brad exclaimed. "Incredible!"

"There are more strikes and techniques we will learn," Ratel said. "Until then, your primary assignment is to simply get accustomed to carrying the cane. That is the hardest task for new Cane-Ja students. You must learn the best place to keep it when it's not in use, remember to retrieve it after you set it on a bus or car seat, and always keep it with you. I guarantee, you'll lose your cane more than once. Try not to."

"Yes, Chief," Brad said. Ratel had Brad practice the swinging and striking moves on the mannequin until their session was up; then Brad changed back into his workout clothes, left the *beol* in a small storage box in the *dojang*, and headed back to Cal Poly.

Finals week was fast approaching, so after a quick shower and a change of clothes, Brad headed over to Kennedy Library to study. He found a desk, plugged his laptop in, and started going over lecture notes and PowerPoint slides provided to him by his professors. He had been at it for about an hour when Jodie Cavendish walked up to him. "Hello, mate," she greeted him. "Well well, look at the conchy. Thought I'd find you here. Ready for a smoko?"

"I don't know what you just called me," Brad said, "but I'm hoping it's something good."

"Just that you're a hardworking dude, and I think it's time for a coffee break."

"Then I'm in." Brad locked his computer up in a small cabinet next to the desk and stood up to follow Jodie.

"Do you need to take that?" she asked, motioning back to the desk.

Brad turned and saw that he had left the cane at the desk. "Oh . . . yeah," he said, and they headed to the stairs. "I knew I'd forget it."

As they went downstairs, Jodie noticed that Brad really wasn't using the cane to help him walk. "What's the cane for, mate?" she asked. "You look like you're moving fine to me."

"I still get a tiny bit dizzy once in a while, so I thought I'd carry it," Brad lied.

"But you're still on the bike and jogging, aren't you?"

"Yes," Brad said. "I don't need it all the time. In fact, I mostly need it just standing still."

"I hope nothing's wrong with your noggin, mate," Jodie said. "The bruise has gone away, finally, but maybe you're still affected by the whack."

"I've had an MRI done, and they found nothing," Brad said. He tapped his head and added, "In fact, they *literally* found nothing." Jodie laughed at the joke and changed the subject, and Brad was happy about that. Maybe it was time to ditch the cane, he thought. Chief Ratel said he was going to start unarmed martial-arts training soon, and when he got as good with that as he was getting with Cane-Ja, maybe the cane wouldn't have to be with him all the time.

The coffee shop on the first floor was almost as crowded as it was in the daytime, and they had to take their coffee outdoors. Fortunately, the early-evening weather was ideal. "How's the studying going?" Brad asked after they found a bench.

"It's apples," Jodie said. "I can't believe I used to study for finals without a laptop computer and all my professors' PowerPoint presentation slides—I actually relied on my own notes to pass finals back then! Insane!"

"Same with me," Brad admitted. "I take lousy notes." His cell phone beeped, indicating he had a message, and he looked at the number. "Someone in

Administration, but I don't recognize it. Wonder what's going on?"

"Why are they calling so late?" Jodie wondered aloud. "Better return the call."

Brad tapped the number on the smartphone and waited. "Hello, this is Brad McLanahan, returning a call from a few minutes ago. I just picked up the message . . . who? President Harris? You mean, the *university* president? Yes, of course I'll hold for him."

"What?" Jodie asked. "President Harris wants to talk to you?"

"Maybe this is what we've been waiting for, Jodie," Brad said. "Yes . . . yes, this is he . . . yes, sir, in fact, I'm here with one of the team leaders . . . yes, sir, thank you." He tapped the screen and put the call on speakerphone. "I'm here with Jodie Cavendish, sir."

"Good evening to both of you," university president Marcus Harris said. "I have good news. The news actually came in about a week ago, but we have just finalized the agreement and signed the papers. Your Starfire project was one of three projects selected for research and development funding by Sky Masters Aerospace. Congratulations." Jodie and Brad jumped to their feet, Jodie let out a yelp of glee, and she and Brad hugged each other. Harris let them celebrate for a few moments, then said, "But that's not all."

The students sat down. "Sir?"

"I am also pleased to tell you that your project received half of the Sky Masters Aerospace grant money—twenty-five million dollars," Harris went on. "That makes Starfire the highest-awarded undergraduate aerospace engineering research project in the history of Cal Poly."

"Twenty-five million dollars?" Jodie exclaimed. "I don't believe it!"

"Congratulations, you two," Harris said. "Brad, find a time when your entire team can get together as soon as possible, call my office, and set up a time for a press conference. I know we're coming up on finals, and I don't want to take too much of your time, but we want to make a huge splash about this before everyone takes off for the summer."

"Yes, sir!" Brad said. "I'll contact everyone tonight. We usually have a team meeting every day at eleven A.M., so that might be the best time tomorrow."

"Perfect," Harris said, his voice sounding more and more excited by the second. "I'll get your schedules and drop e-mails to your professors telling them you will be late for class, because I'm sure the presser and photo ops will take some time. We're going to go international with this one, guys, and we're looking to break more funding records with it. Wear something nice.

Congratulations again. Oh, one more thing, as long as I have Miss Cavendish on the line."

"Sir?"

"Miss Cavendish has been awarded a full scholarship to Cal Poly to finish her undergraduate degree, including tuition, books, fees, and housing," Harris said. "We can't have one of our best undergraduate students leave when she was so instrumental in getting such a large grant, now, can we? I hope you'll accept, Miss Cavendish."

"Of course I will, sir!" Jodie cried in stunned glee. "Of course I accept!"

"Excellent," Harris said. "Congratulations to the entire Starfire team. Well done. Good night, Mustangs." And the connection was broken.

"I don't friggin' believe this!" Brad exclaimed after he hung up. "Twenty-five million bucks just dropped in our lap!" He gave Jodie a big hug. "It's unbelievable! And you got the scholarship you were looking for! Congratulations!"

"It's all because of you, mate," Jodie said. "You're the jackaroo. You're *my* jackaroo." And Jodie put her hands on Brad's face and gave him a big, deep kiss on the lips.

Brad savored every moment of that kiss, pulled back, then gave her one in return. When they parted after the kiss, Brad's eyes were telling Jodie something, something powerful and incredibly personal, and her eyes were immediately saying yes. But to her dismay, she heard Brad say, "I'd better contact the others. Tomorrow will be a big day."

"Yes," Jodie said. She was content, at least for the moment, to put an arm around Brad and sip her coffee while he texted on his phone.

Brad contacted the entire team leadership by text messaging, then included the Cal Poly engineers, professors, and students who had helped with the project, then decided to include anyone who helped with the project who was within a couple hours' driving distance of the university, as far away as Stanford and USC—he was determined to fill that press conference room with Starfire supporters. When he was done with that, he decided to text anyone who had supported the project, whether or not they could possibly make the press conference—everyone associated with the project should be aware of the presser and the impending worldwide publicity, he thought. Anyone associated with this project should not hear about the grant from anyone else but the team leader.

He read off all the text acknowledgents to Jodie, save one. It was the only Central Asia country code in all the messages he received, and it was from Kazakhstan, which had no Starfire contributors. The message read simply, *Congratulations. D.*

When Brad put the phone keypad letters against the numbers that appeared on the message screen, the sender's name spelled *Resurrection.*

It was a few days later, and the weather, which had been outstanding during most of April, still couldn't completely shrug off winter, so they had days of rather cold, damp mist and rain. For the past three days, Brad had taken the bus instead of riding his bicycle. It was an enjoyable and relaxing trek to the *dojang* south of the city: an easy jog from Poly Canyon to the Route 6B bus stop near the Kennedy Library; an easy seven-minute bus ride to the Downtown Transit Center; switch to the Route 3 bus line; a longer twenty-minute bus ride to Marigold Shopping Center; and then another easy run from there down Tank Farm Road to the *dojang,* which was just north of the airport. He had lots of time to do some reading or listen to audiobooks or lecture recordings on his tablet computer. Brad wished he could take the bus all the time—it was free for Cal Poly students—but he wanted the exercise, so he stuck with it whenever the weather was cooperative.

The week had started, along with the rain, with an introduction to Krav Maga. "Krav Maga was developed in Israel for the military," James Ratel had begun last Monday afternoon. "It is not a discipline, like karate or judo; it is not a sport, and will never be in the Olympics or on television. Krav Maga has three basic objectives: neutralize the attack through the use of arm and hand locks and parries, being careful to protect yourself; go from defense to offense as quickly as possible; and quickly neutralize the attacker by manipulating joints and attacking vulnerable spots on the body, using any tools that might be handy. We are assuming you have broken or misplaced your cane, so now you are left with having to defend yourself without a weapon and probably against a very angry attacker.

"Some teachers will tell their students that the amount of force needed to neutralize an attacker should be proportional to the force of the attack, which means, for example, you would use less force on an attacker that uses his fist than on an attacker with a bat or knife," Ratel went on. "I do not believe in that. Your objective is to put the attacker down so you can escape. In training, you will do three blows to demonstrate you can do them, but on the street you continue to attack until your attacker goes down. Forget all the Bruce Lee movies you've ever seen: it's not one parry, one blow, and then let the guy get up to go after you again. Once you've blocked or locked up the attacker, you keep attacking his soft vulnerable spots and joints until he goes down, and then you run like hell and get away from the situation as quickly as possible. Understand?"

"Yes, Chief," Brad said.

Ratel motioned to a folder that was lying on the counter outside. "That is some homework for you," he said. "We will train to attack soft spots on the body using numbers, going from head to foot. Learn the spots and the numbers. You will also learn about all of the two hundred and thirty joints on the human body, and specifically which way they articulate so you can attack them. Be prepared to demonstrate those to me by next Wednesday."

"Yes, Chief."

"Very well. Kick off those shoes and socks, then on the mat." Brad removed his sneakers and socks, bowed to the center of the blue mat, and stepped to the center, and Ratel followed. Brad was wearing his workout *beol*, now with a red and black belt, instead of the white, with first-level *poom*-rank markings on it, indicating that he had passed his first round of basic instruction.

"We start with the basics, and in Krav Maga that is parries," Ratel began. "Notice I didn't say 'block.' A block suggests that you might absorb some of the energy an attacker is using against you, like two football linemen smashing into one another. We use the term 'parry' instead, which means you divert most or all of the energy of an attack in a safe direction."

"Just like the basic moves with the cane, sir?" Brad observed.

"Exactly," Ratel said. "The key to the initial parry in Krav Maga is anticipation, and that means awareness of your surroundings. If a would-be attacker approaching you has his right hand in his pocket, the weapon is probably in his right hand, so your mental plan of action is to prepare to defend against a right-handed attacker." Ratel picked up a rubber knife from a shelf behind him and tossed it to Brad. "Try it."

Brad put his right hand with the knife behind him and approached Ratel, then swung his hand toward him. Ratel's left hand snapped out, pushing the knife past his chest and half turning Brad's body. "Foremost, the knife is not near your body, and if the attacker had another weapon in his left hand, he could not use it right now because I turned him away. Like the cane, you now see areas of the body that are exposed." Ratel made punching motions at Brad's torso and head. "Or, I can catch the right arm with my right arm and lock it, with the knife safely away from me, and with the arm in a lock, I control the attacker." Ratel grabbed Brad's right arm from underneath, put his hand on Brad's tricep, and pushed. Even with a slight bit of pressure, it felt as if the arm were going to snap in two, and Brad could go nowhere but toward the ground.

That was the first day's training, and after finishing the third, Brad was starting to wonder if he would ever be able to learn any of those Krav Maga techniques, let alone use them. But he reminded himself that he'd thought the same thing about Cane-Ja, and he figured he was getting pretty good at that. He exited the *dojang,* put up the hood of his green-and-gold Cal Poly Mustangs windbreaker, and started running east down Tank Farm Road toward Broad Street and the bus stop. Although not quite sunset, it was drizzly, cool, and getting dark quickly, and he wanted to be off this unlit road, on the main drag, and on the bus as soon as possible.

He was halfway to Broad Street, on the darkest part of the road, when a car approached, heading west. Brad left the pavement and stepped onto the uneven gravel "warning track" strip, but kept on running. The car shifted left a little bit and straddled the center line, and it looked as if it was going to pass by him with plenty of room to spare . . .

. . . when suddenly it swerved farther left, then began to skid to the right on the slick road, the car now perpendicular to the road, brakes and tires squealing— and heading right for Brad! He had almost no time to react to the sudden move. The car had slowed down quite a bit, but when it hit, it felt ten times worse than any blow he had ever received in high-school football.

"Oh, jeez, sorry about that, Mr. Bradley McLanahan," a man said a few moments later through the haze in Brad's consciousness. Brad was on his back on the side of the road, dazed and confused, his right hip and arm hurting like hell. Then, in Russian, the man said, "*Izvinite.* Excuse me. Wet road, I may have been going a little too fast, a coyote ran out in front of me, and I could hardly see you in the drizzle, blah, blah, blah. At least that is the story I will give the sheriff's deputies, if they find me."

"I . . . I think I'm all right," Brad said, gasping for air.

"*V samom dele?* Really? Well, my friend, we can fix that." And suddenly the man pulled a black plastic garden cleanup bag from a pocket, pressed it against Brad's face, and pushed. Brad couldn't breathe anyway with the wind knocked out of him, but panic rose up from his chest in terrifying waves. He tried to push the attacker away, but he couldn't make any part of his body work properly.

"*Prosto rasslab'tes'.* Just relax, my young friend," the man said, mixing English and Russian as if he were an expatriate or foreign cousin from the old country telling a bedtime story. "It will be over before you know it."

Brad had no power at all to move the plastic away from his face, and he was considering surrendering to the roaring in his ears and the fiery pain in his chest . . . but somehow he remembered what he needed to do, and instead of fighting the hands holding the plastic on his face or trying to find his cane, he reached down and pressed the button on the device around his neck.

The attacker saw what he did, and for a moment he released the pressure on Brad's face, found the device, snapped it off Brad's neck, and threw it away. Brad gasped in a lungful of air. "Nice try, *mudak*," the attacker said. He pressed the plastic over Brad's face before Brad could take three deep breaths. "You'll be dead long before your medic-alert nurses arrive."

Brad couldn't see it, but moments later a set of head-lights approached. *"Derzhite ikh podal'she,"* the man said over his shoulder in Russian to a second assailant, whom Brad had never seen. "Keep them away. Have them call 911 or something, but keep them away. Tell them I am doing CPR."

"Ya budu derzhat' ikh podal'she, tovarisch," the assistant acknowledged. "I will keep them away, sir."

The first assailant had to stop pressing the plastic bag over Brad's mouth and nose until the newcomers left, but he bent over Brad as if he were doing mouth-to-mouth resuscitation, but covering his mouth so Brad couldn't cry out. A few moments later he heard, "*Eto vo vsem*. It is all over."

"*Takoy zhe*. Same here," the first assailant said . . . and then his vision exploded in a sea of stars and blackness as the crook of the cane crashed against his left temple, rendering him instantly unconscious.

"Jesus, Dexter, you're as blue as a fucking Smurf," James Ratel said, shining a small flashlight at Brad's face. He pulled Brad to his feet and put him in the front seat of his Ford pickup truck. He then loaded the two Russian hit men into the cargo bed of the pickup and drove back down Tank Farm Road to the *dojang*. He put plastic handcuffs on the wrists, ankles, and mouths of the two Russians, and sent a text message on his phone. By then, Brad was starting to come around in the passenger seat of the pickup. "Dexter!" Ratel shouted. "Are you okay?"

"Wh-what . . . ?" Brad murmured.

"McLanahan . . . Brad, Brad McLanahan, answer me," Ratel shouted. "Wake up. Are you all right?"

"I . . . what . . . what the hell happened . . . ?"

"I need you to wake the hell up, McLanahan, *right now*," Ratel shouted. "We could be under attack at any moment, and I can't defend you if you're not awake and

able to defend yourself. *Wake the fuck up, right now.*
Acknowledge my order, airman, *immediately.*"

It took a few long moments, but finally Brad shook
his head clear and was able to say, "Chief? Y-yes, I'm
awake . . . I'm . . . I'm good, Chief. Wh-what should I
do? What's happening?"

"Listen to me," Ratel said. "We don't have a lot of
time. I anticipate that we will be attacked by the backup
strike team any second. We are completely alone and in
extreme danger. I need you alert and responsive. Are
you hearing what I'm saying, McLanahan?"

"Y-yes, Chief," Brad heard himself say. He still
wasn't sure where he was or what was going on, but at
least he was able to respond to Chief Ratel. "Tell me
what to do."

"Go inside and grab some mats and weights to cover
these guys up," Ratel said. They both went inside.
Brad found workout mats and barbell weights. Ratel
unlocked an ordinary-looking trophy display case in
the front of the *dojang*; a hidden drawer underneath
the case concealed a number of handguns, shotguns,
and knives.

"I covered them up, Chief," Brad said.

Ratel racked a shell into a shotgun's chamber and
handed it to Brad, then did the same with two pistols. "Stick the pistols in your waistband." He armed

himself with two pistols, an AR-15 rifle, and several ammunition magazines. "We're going to try to make it to the hangar in Paso Robles—it's easier to defend."

"Shouldn't we call the police?"

"I'd like to avoid doing that, but we might not have any choice," Ratel said. "Let's go."

They drove onto Highway 101 northbound. Darkness had fallen, and the rain continued to fall, greatly reducing visibility. They were on the highway for less than five minutes when Ratel said, "We're being tailed. One car, staying with us about a hundred yards back."

"What do we do?"

Ratel said nothing. At the Santa Margarita exit a few miles later, he left the freeway, and at the end of the off-ramp they armed themselves and waited. No car exited behind them. "Maybe they weren't tailing us," Brad said.

"More likely they have a GPS tracking device somewhere on my pickup so they don't have to follow very closely—there was no time for me to check," Ratel said. "They probably have more than one pursuit team. The first team will drive on, then pull off somewhere, and the second pursuit team takes over. We'll go the back way to the airport."

They stayed on county roads for another hour until they finally reached Paso Robles Airport. Once inside the security gate, they drove toward the team's hangar, but stopped about a quarter mile away. "There's still too much activity at the airport to drag those guys inside," Ratel said, laying the AR-15 rifle across his lap. "We'll wait until it gets quieter." They waited, on hair-trigger alert for anyone approaching them. About an hour later a small twin-engine airplane taxied close by, and the pilot parked a few hangars away. It took the pilot almost an hour to get his own car out of the hangar, park the plane inside, then gather his belongings and drive away, and the airport was quiet once again.

Thirty minutes later, after no more signs of activity, finally Ratel could wait no longer. He drove to the hangar, and he and Brad dragged the assailants inside. Ratel then drove the pickup about a quarter mile away and parked it, then jogged back to the hangar.

"Made it," Ratel said, wiping rain off his head and his AR-15. "The backup teams will track down the pickup, and then track us to here. Then they'll probably wait a few hours before they attack."

"How will they track us down to here?"

"I can think of a dozen ways," Ratel said. "If they're any good, they'll be here. I just hope help arrives before that."

Less than an hour later, amid the steady rain and an occasional gust of wind, they heard the sound of metal scraping on metal outside the main entrance door. "Follow me," Ratel whispered, and he and Brad retreated to the hangar. There was a small business jet inside, its black paint job signifying it belonged to Kevin Martindale's Scion Aviation International outfit. Ratel found a large cabinet-sized toolbox on wheels alongside a hangar wall, pushed it away from the wall, and they both got behind it. "Okay, your job is to watch that walk-through door over there," Ratel said, pointing to the large aircraft hangar door. "I'll be watching the door to the front office. Single shots only. Make them count."

A few minutes later they heard another sound of forced metal, and a few minutes after that they heard more sounds of metal on metal coming from the walk-through hangar door, a signal that the door was being jimmied open. A moment later the door opened and Brad could see a man wearing night-vision goggles, crouching low, come through the opening, carrying a submachine gun. The bizjet was now concealing him. A second attacker stepped through the door, closed it, and stayed there to cover it. At the same time Ratel could see two more attackers come through the office door, also wearing night-vision goggles and carrying submachine guns.

"Crap," he whispered. "Four guys. We've run out of time." He pulled out his cell phone, dialed 911, left it on, turned the volume all the way down, and slipped it under the toolbox. "Use the pistol. Get the guy by the door. The other guy will probably hide behind the jet's right wheel." Brad peeked out from behind the toolbox and aimed at the guy by the walk-through door, which was partially illuminated by a lighted emergency exit sign. Ratel took a deep breath, then whispered, "Now."

Brad and Ratel fired nearly simultaneously. Ratel's shot found its mark, and one attacker went down. Brad had no idea where his shot went, but he knew he didn't hit one thing except maybe a hangar wall. The guy by the door dashed along the hangar wall toward the conference room, crouching low. As Ratel had predicted, the other guy took cover behind the jet's wheel . . . and then the hangar erupted with automatic-weapon fire, seemingly coming from all directions at once. Ratel and Brad ducked behind the toolbox.

"Open fire when the shooting stops!" Ratel shouted. The toolbox was being raked with bullets, but it looked like the tools inside were absorbing the bullets. A moment later there was a momentary lull in the shooting, and Brad peeked over the toolbox, saw movement by the jet's tire, and fired. The round hit the tire, which instantly exploded, sending a concussion shock wave into the attacker's face. He screamed, clutching his face in agony. The bizjet looked like it was going to crash to the right, but the wheel hub barely kept it from completely tipping over.

Now the gunfire was shifting directions—more bullets were hitting the side of the toolbox instead of the front. "Watch your sides!" Ratel shouted. "They'll try to . . . *ahhh! Shit!*" Brad looked to see Ratel clutching his right hand, which looked as if it had been split wide open by a bullet. Blood spurted everywhere. "Take the rifle and hold them off!" Ratel shouted, clutching his injured hand, trying to stem the bleeding.

Brad tried to peek around the toolbox, but the moment he moved, the bullets began to fly, and now he could feel them getting closer and closer, like a swarm of bats buzzing past his head. He tried pointing the rifle around the toolbox and firing, but the rifle's muzzle was jumping around uncontrollably. Ratel had wrapped a rag around his right hand and was firing a pistol with his left, but the muzzle wasn't steady at all and he looked as if he was going to go unconscious at any moment. Brad heard boot steps and voices in Russian getting closer. This is it, he thought. The next shot he'd hear would be the last one ever, he was certain of it . . .

SIX

A lie never lives to be old.
—SOPHOCLES

PASO ROBLES, CALIFORNIA

Suddenly there was a tremendous explosion at the back of the hangar. The air was instantly filled with dust and debris. Voices were shouting in Russian . . . and soon the shouting was replaced by screaming, and a moment later the screams fell silent as well.

"All clear, Brad," came an electronically synthesized voice. Brad looked up, and there behind the bizjet was a Cybernetic Infantry Device.

"Dad?" he asked.

"Are you all right?" Patrick McLanahan asked.

"Chief Ratel," Brad said, shouting over the ringing in his ears from all the gunfire in the enclosed hangar. "He's hurt." A moment later two men hurried over and carried Ratel out. Brad ran over to the robot. He saw where his father had burst through the doorway, taking out most of the wall around the door between the hangar and the front office. All six attackers, the four who had attacked the hangar and the two who attacked Brad on Tank Farm Road, had already been taken away.

"Are you all right, Brad?" Patrick asked.

"Yes. I can't hear very well from all the gunfire, but otherwise I'm okay."

"Good. Let's get out of here. The Highway Patrol and sheriffs are about five minutes out." Patrick picked up his son and carried him across a large open field to a parking spot near the south end of the runway, where the black Sherpa cargo plane was waiting, its turboprop propellers turning at idle speed. Patrick put Brad down, crawled inside through the cargo ramp in the back, and sat down on the cargo deck, and Brad climbed aboard right after him. A crewmember steered Brad onto a cargo net seat, helped him buckle in, and gave him a headset. Within moments they were airborne.

"What about Chief Ratel?" Brad asked, assuming that his father could hear him through the intercom.

"He'll be evacuated and treated," Patrick replied.

"What will the cops do when they see that hangar? It looks like a war zone. It *was* a war zone."

"President Martindale will handle that," Patrick replied.

"How did you get here so fast, Dad?"

"I was in St. George when your alarm went off back in San Luis Obispo," Patrick said. "It's less than two hours away in the Sherpa. Thank God Chief Ratel got to you in time and got you out of town."

"St. George? Is that where we're headed now?"

"Yes, Brad," Patrick said. The CID turned to Brad and raised an armored hand, anticipating Brad's protests. "I know you want to go back to Cal Poly, Brad," Patrick said, "and now that you've received that grant from Sky Masters, your work is even more important. I want to see you continue your training too. So I'm going to assign Sergeant Major Wohl's team to detect and capture any more attack squads that come after you. They'll set up closer to campus so you won't have to travel all the way to the south side of the city for training. They'll take over your training until Chief Ratel is well enough to do so."

"You mean, they'll be my bodyguards or something?"

"Although I'm sure they can handle them, Wohl's teams aren't made for personal security jobs," Patrick said. "They train for countersurveillance and direct-action missions. But we've encountered four two-man teams of Russian hit men now. I'm not going to allow any hit squads to roam around the United States at will, especially ones that target my son. So we need to set up a plan of action. We'll interrogate the new guys, do some investigating, and figure out a plan."

"So I'll be like a decoy, sucking in the bad guys so the sergeant major can take them out?" Brad remarked. He nodded and smiled. "That's cool, as long as I can go back to Cal Poly. I *can* go back to Cal Poly, right, Dad?"

"Against my better judgment, yes," Patrick said. "But not tonight. Let the sergeant major and his teams interrogate the new prisoners, gather some information, and sweep the campus and the city. It'll only be a day or two. I know you do most of your studying for finals online, and your classes are basically over, so you'll be able to work at our headquarters. Before finals week comes around, you should be able to go back to campus."

"I'll just have to figure out an excuse to tell the Starfire team," Brad said. "The project is exploding, Dad. The university is getting money and support from all over the world."

"I know, son," Patrick said. "To the university's credit, they are keeping Starfire strictly a Cal Poly undergraduate project—other universities, companies, and even governments have offered to take over. Looks like you'll stay the head honcho for now. Just realize that the pressure to turn the project over to someone else as a for-profit operation will certainly build—most likely Sky Masters Aerospace, I'd wager, now that they've invested so much in it—and the university might be induced by the big bucks to let some company take it over. Just don't be offended if that happens. Universities run on money."

"I won't be offended."

"Good." The CID turned its massive armored head toward Brad. "I'm proud of you, son," Patrick said. "I've seen it in hundreds of e-mails from all over the world: people are impressed with your leadership in driving this project forward, building a first-class team, and gathering technical support. No one can believe you're a first-year undergrad."

"Thanks, Dad," Brad said. "I hope I can achieve even a little bit of the success you've had in the Air Force."

"I think your path will be totally different than mine," Patrick said. He turned back, facing the rear of the aircraft. "I always wished I had leadership skills like yours. My life might have been so much different if I had your skills and learned how to use them. You obviously learned them from someone other than your dad, or maybe from Civil Air Patrol."

"But you were . . . I mean, *are* a three-star general, Dad."

"Yes, but my promotions came about because of the things I did, not because of my leadership skills," Patrick said, the pensiveness in his voice still obvious despite the CID's electronic voice synthesis. "I had a couple command positions over the years, but I never actually acted as a real commander—I acted like I always did: an operator, an aviator, a crewdog, not a leader. I saw a job that needed to get done, and I went out and did it. As a field-grade or general officer, I was supposed to build a team that would do the job, not go off and do it myself. I never really understood what it meant to lead."

"I think getting the job done is the most important thing too, Dad," Brad said. "I'm an aerospace engineering student, but I can barely make sense of most of the science I'm expected to learn. I muddle my way through it by finding someone to explain it to me. But all I really want to do is fly. I know I have to get the degree so I can attend test-pilot school and fly the hot jets, but I don't care about the degree. I just want to fly."

"Well, it's working for you, son," Patrick said. "Keep fixated on the goal. You'll make it."

The Sherpa landed about two hours later at General Dick Stout Field, fourteen miles northeast of the city of St. George in southern Utah. The airport had been greatly expanded over the past few years as the population of St. George grew, and although Stout Field was still a nontowered airport, the west side of it had blossomed as an industrial and commercial air hub. The black Sherpa taxied to a very large hangar on the south side of the industrial side of the airport, and was towed inside the hangar before anyone was allowed to disembark. The massive hangar contained a Challenger-5 business jet, a Reaper unmanned aerial vehicle with weapons pylons under the wings, and a smaller version of the V-22 Osprey tilt-rotor aircraft, all painted black, of course.

Patrick led his son to an adjacent building. Brad immediately noticed that the ceiling was higher and all of the doors and corridors were wider and taller than normal, all obviously constructed to accommodate the Cybernetic Infantry Device that was walking through them. Brad heard a lock automatically click open as they approached a door, and they entered a room in the center of the building. "This is home," Patrick said. It was nothing more than a bare windowless room, with just a table with some of the nutrient canisters sitting on it, a spot where Patrick plugged himself in for recharging . . .

. . . and, in the far corner, another new-model Cybernetic Infantry Device robot. "I see I'm getting a replacement," Patrick said woodenly. "It usually takes another day or so for us to run a full set of diagnostics on the new CID before they do the transfer."

"Then I'll be able to see you, Dad."

"Son, if you're sure that's what you want to do, then I'll allow it," Patrick said. "But it's not pretty."

Brad looked around the room. "Sheesh, they don't even let you have pictures on the walls?"

"I can get all the pictures I want, anytime I want, played right inside my consciousness," Patrick said. "I don't need them on the wall." He replaced the nutrient canisters in his chassis with the new ones on the table, then stood in a specified spot in the center of the room, and power, data, hygienic, nutrient, and diagnostic cables automatically descended from the ceiling and plugged themselves into the proper places on the CID. Patrick froze in place, standing straight up, looking very much like the unmanned robot in the corner. "The sergeant major will be by in a few hours to get briefed and talk to you about what happened, and then he'll take you to a hotel," he said. "He'll bring you back in the morning, and we'll set you up so you can do some studying."

Brad thought about what he was going to say for a moment in silence; then: "Dad, you told me that you're still you inside that robot."

"Yes."

"Well, the 'you' I remember had awards, plaques, and pictures on the walls," Brad said. "Even in the little double-wide trailer back in Battle Mountain, you had your old flight helmets, display cases with memorabilia, airplane models, and random bits of stuff that I never even knew what they were, but they obviously meant a great deal to you. Why don't you have any of that here?"

The robot remained motionless and silent for several long moments; then: "I guess I never really thought about it, Brad," Patrick said finally. "At first I thought it was because I didn't want anyone to know it was me inside here, but now all of the people with whom I interact in this building know that it's me, so that really doesn't apply anymore."

"Well, the robot wouldn't have stuff on the walls," Brad said, "but my dad would." Patrick said nothing. "Maybe when everything calms down and gets back to normal—or the closest it will ever come to normal—I can fly out here and set up some stuff. Make it more like your room, rather than a storeroom."

"I'd like that, son," Patrick said. "I'd like that."

OFFICE OF THE PRESIDENT
FOURTEENTH BUILDING, THE KREMLIN
MOSCOW

Several days later

"Definitely signs of increased activity on the American military space station," Minister of State Security Viktor Kazyanov said over the video teleconference link from his intelligence center to the president's office. He was showing before-and-after photographs of Armstrong Space Station. "There has been one heavy-lift rocket launch that delivered these long structures, along with many smaller pressurized and unpressurized containers. We do not know for certain yet what is in the pressurized containers, but these other unpressurized items resemble the batteries already mounted on the truss, so we assume they too are batteries."

"I want no more assumptions from you, Kazyanov," Russian president Gennadiy Gryzlov said, stabbing at the image of Kazyanov on a computer monitor with his cigar. "Find me the information. Do your damned job."

"Yes, sir," Kazyanov said. He cleared his throat, then went on: "There has been a great increase in spaceplane flights as well, sometimes three to four per month, sir." He changed slides. "The newest model of their single-stage-to-orbit spaceplane, the S-29 Shadow, has now completed operational tests and has made one flight to the station. It is similar in size and cargo capacity to our Elektron spaceplane, but of course does not need a rocket to be boosted into space."

"Of course not," President Gennadiy Gryzlov said acidly. "So. They have one Shadow spaceplane now that is similar in size to our Elektron. How many Elektrons do we have, Sokolov?"

"We have reactivated seven Elektron spaceplanes," Minister of Defense Gregor Sokolov replied. "One is standing by ready for launch in Plesetsk, and another spaceplane-rocket pair has arrived there and can be mated and placed into launch position within a week. We have—"

"A *week?*" Gryzlov thundered. "Minister, I told you, I want to fill Earth orbit with Russian spaceplanes and weapons. I want to be able to launch two spaceplanes simultaneously."

"Sir, only one launch pad at Plesetsk was stressed for the Angara-5 booster," Sokolov said. "Funds meant to build another pad there were diverted to the Vostochny Cosmodrome construction and to the extension of the Baikonur lease. We should—"

"Minister Sokolov, I am sensing a pattern here: I issue orders, and you give me excuses instead of results," Gryzlov said. "Does Vostochny have a launch pad suited for the Angara-5 booster, or not?"

"Vostochny Cosmodrome will not be completed for another two years, sir," Sokolov said. Gryzlov rolled his eyes in exasperation for the umpteenth time during the teleconference. "Baikonur is the only other launch facility available to accommodate the Angara-5 at this time."

"So why is there not an Elektron spaceplane at Baikonur, Sokolov?"

"Sir, it was my understanding that you did not wish to have any more military launches from Baikonur, only commercial launches," Sokolov said.

Gryzlov was struggling to contain his anger. "What I said I wanted, Sokolov, is to get as many spaceplanes on launch pads as quickly as possible so we can at least have a chance of challenging the Americans," he said. "We pay good money to use that facility—we will start using it. What else?"

"Sir, we are pressing ahead with upgrades and improvements at Plesetsk, Vostochny, and Znamensk spaceports," Sokolov went on, "but work is slowing down because of the cold weather, and must cease altogether in about a month or else the quality of the concrete castings will degrade."

"So we have just *two* launch pads available for our spaceplanes, and one is not even in our own country?" Gryzlov said disgustedly. "Perfect."

"There is another avenue we can take, Mr. President: launch Elektron spaceplanes from China," Foreign Minister Daria Titeneva interjected. "Thanks to American actions against both our countries, our relations with China have never been better. I have explored this possibility with the Chinese foreign minister, and I spoke with his military adviser, who suggested a base in China's far west: Xichang. With the opening of the new Wenchang spaceport on Hainan Island, all heavy launch operations have moved there from Xichang, leaving the base open and available, and their facilities are state of the art. They have two launch pads stressed for our Angara-5 rockets and our Proton series as well. There is great concern that a launch failure could bring debris down on nearby cities and factories downrange, but I think a little extra consideration to local and provincial politicians can alleviate their concerns."

"Well done, Daria," Gryzlov said, smiling for the first time in the meeting. "See, Sokolov? That is how it is done. Thinking outside the box."

"You object to launches from Baikonur but are considering sending our rockets and spaceplanes to China, sir?" Sokolov retorted. "I am sure the Chinese military would love to get an up-close look at Elektron and Angara-5."

"I ordered Russian spaceplanes on launch pads, Sokolov!" Gryzlov snarled, jabbing his cigar at the image of the defense minister on his monitor. "If I cannot launch them from Russian facilities, I will do it from somewhere else." He turned back to Titeneva. "Proceed with making the arrangements, Daria," he said. "What else did the Chinese talk about?"

"They talked of a trade for the use of Xichang, sir, along with cash, of course," Titeneva said. "They mentioned several things, a few political items such as support for their claims on the Senkaku Islands and in the South China Sea, and perhaps reopening talks about oil and natural-gas pipelines into China from Siberia, but they are most interested in S-500S mobile surface-to-air missiles, the newest model, capable of attacking satellites."

"Indeed?" Gryzlov said, nodding enthusiastically. "Trade launch facilities for S-500 missiles, which I would like to place at all Russian spaceports and military installations worldwide anyway. Excellent idea. I approve."

"Sir, the S-500 is the most advanced air defense weapon in the world," Sokolov said, his face a stunned mask, telling all that he couldn't believe what the president had just said. "It is at least a generation ahead of anything the Chinese or even the Americans have. The electronic, sensor, and propulsion technology used in the S-500 is the best in Russia . . . no, the best in the world! We will be giving them what they have been trying to steal from us for decades!"

"Sokolov, I want Elektrons and Burans on launch pads," Gryzlov snapped. "If the Chinese can do it, and they want S-500s, they will get S-500s." He scowled at Sokolov's shocked expression. "How are our other rearming programs proceeding? The Duma has

increased our defense appropriation by thirty percent—
that should translate into hundreds of S-500s, MiG-
31D antisatellite systems, and a lot more than just five
spaceplanes."

"It takes time to restart weapons programs that
were canceled years ago, sir," Sokolov said. "The S-500
was already in production, so we can expect one to two
systems per month for the next—"

"No, Sokolov!" Gryzlov interrupted. "That is unacceptable! I want at least *ten* per month!"

"Ten?" Sokolov retorted. "Sir, we can eventually
reach a goal of ten per month, but it takes time to accelerate production to that rate. Just having the money
is not enough—we need trained workers, assembly-
line space, a steady and reliable parts stream, testing
facilities—"

"If the S-500 was already in production, why is all
that not already in place?" Gryzlov thundered. "Were
you only planning on building one to two per month?
The most advanced air defense system in the world, or
so you say, but we are not building more of them?"

"Sir, defense spending was shifted to other priori-
ties, such as antiship missiles, aircraft carriers, and
fighters," Sokolov said. "The S-500 is primarily an
air defense weapon intended for use against cruise
missiles and stealth aircraft, and later adapted as an

antisatellite and antiballistic-missile weapon with the 'S' model. After our bomber and cruise-missile attacks on the United States that virtually eliminated their bombers and intercontinental ballistic missiles, air defense was not given a very high priority because the threat was all but gone. Now that space is a higher priority and the S-500S has proven successful, we can start to build more, but as I said, sir, that pivot takes time to—"

"More excuses!" Gryzlov shouted into the video teleconference microphone. "All I want to hear from you, Sokolov, is 'yes, sir,' and all I want to see are results, or I will get someone else to carry out my orders. Now get to it!" And he hit the button that terminated the connection with his defense minister.

At that moment Tarzarov sent the president a private text message, which scrolled across the bottom of the video teleconference screen: it read, *Praise in public, criticize in private.* Gryzlov was going to reply "Fuck you," but decided against it. "Daria, good work," he said over the teleconference network. "Let me know what you need me to do to assist."

"Yes, sir," Titeneva replied with a confident smile, and signed off. Gryzlov grinned. Daria Titeneva had definitely become a changed woman over the past several weeks: aggressive, creative, demanding, even vulgar at times . . . in and out of bed. Gryzlov continued the video teleconference with his other cabinet ministers for a few more minutes, then signed off.

"Your anger and temper will get the best of you eventually, Gennadiy," Tarzarov said once all the connections to the president's ministers were securely terminated. "Constantly warning you of it does not seem to help."

"It has been over ten years since the destruction of the American bomber and intercontinental-ballistic-missile fleet, Sergei," Gryzlov complained, ignoring Tarzarov's advice once again. "The Americans reactivated their military space station and made the switch to space-based weapons instead of rebuilding their bomber and missile weapons, and they made no secret of it. What in hell were Zevitin and Truznyev doing all those years—playing with themselves?"

"The former presidents had institutional, political, and budget problems during most of that time, Gennadiy," Tarzarov said, "as well as having to rebuild the weapons destroyed by the Americans in the counterattacks. It does no good to point fingers at past presidents. Very few heads of state, including you, are completely in control of their country's fate." He checked his smartphone, then shook his head in exasperation. "Ilianov and Korchkov are waiting outside. Are you not done with this project, sir? Ilianov is nothing but a thug in an air-force uniform, and Korchkov is a mindless automaton who kills because she enjoys it."

"I will be done with those two when their task is complete," Gryzlov said. "But for now, they are the right persons for this job. Get them in here." Tarzarov escorted the Russian officer and his assistant into the president's office, then took his "invisible spot" in the office and effectively blended in with the furniture. Ilianov and Korchkov were in military dress, Ilianov in his air-force uniform and Korchkov in a plain black tunic and trousers, with no decorations or medals, just insignia of rank on the epaulets, a characteristic of the elite *Spetsgruppa Vympel* commandos. She also wore a knife in a black sheath on her belt, Gryzlov noticed. "I expected to hear from you days ago, Colonel," he said. "I also have not heard anything in the news about the death of McLanahan's son, so I assume your squad failed."

"Yes, sir," Ilianov said. "Team One reported to Alpha, the command team, that they had McLanahan, and then Alpha lost contact with them. Teams Two and Three picked up McLanahan and an individual that McLanahan had been doing self-defense and conditioning training with driving out of the city."

"Who is this individual?" Gryzlov asked.

"A retired noncommissioned officer named Ratel, now a self-defense and firearms instructor," Ilianov said. "He makes occasional contact with several individuals that also look ex-military—we are in the process of identifying them now. One man looks as if he was burned by chemicals or radiation. He appears to be the one in charge of the ex-military men."

"This gets more interesting," Gryzlov said. "McLanahan's bodyguards? Some sort of private paramilitary group? McLanahan the elder reportedly belonged to such groups, both in and out of the military."

"Our thoughts exactly, sir," Ilianov said. "Team Two had to break off his tail because he thought that he had been detected, but the teams were using an electronic tracker on Ratel's vehicle, so they were ordered to break off the tail and wait for the tracker to stop. It stopped at a small central California airport. The teams found the vehicle abandoned, but they were able to find which building at the airport Ratel and McLanahan were hiding in, a large aircraft hangar. The command team ordered Teams Two and Three to wait for activity at the airport to cease and then attack from different sides, which they did."

"And failed, obviously," Gryzlov said. "Let me guess the rest: the members of all three teams are missing, are not in police custody, and McLanahan is nowhere to be found. Whom did the hangar belong to, Colonel?" He held up a hand. "Wait, let me guess again: some ordinary-sounding aviation company with unremarkable officers and few employees that had not been in the area for too long." Ilianov's expression told the president that he had guessed correctly. "Perhaps the hangar is this group's headquarters, or *was*. They will surely scatter to the four winds. Was your command team able to search the hangar?"

"The command team could not get inside because of the police and then because of a heavily armed private security guard," Ilianov said. "But the team leader did observe many men and women taking files and equipment out in trucks, and a business jet that had been inside the hangar during the operation taxied away and flew off the night after the operation. The business jet was painted completely black."

"I thought it is illegal in most countries to paint an aircraft all black—unless it is a government or military aircraft," Gryzlov said. "Again, very interesting. You may have stumbled onto some kind of mysterious paramilitary organization, Colonel. What else?"

"The command-team leader was able to observe that the front entrance to the aircraft hangar had been blown inward, possibly by a vehicle that had driven right through the front office and crashed all the way into the hangar itself," Ilianov said. "There was no sign of a damaged vehicle anywhere outside the hangar, however."

Gryzlov thought for a moment, nodding, then smiled. "So McLanahan's paramilitary friends effect a rescue by crashing a vehicle through the front door? That does not sound too professional. But they got the job done." He rose from his desk. "Colonel, ten of the men you sent in have been either killed or captured, supposedly by this countersurveillance or counterintelligence outfit around McLanahan. Whoever you are recruiting inside the United States are all but useless. You will stand down, and we will wait to allow conditions there to go back to routine. Obviously McLanahan has no intention of leaving that school, so it will be easy to pick him up again."

Gryzlov looked Korchkov's body up and down. "And when the moment comes, I think it is time to send in Captain Korchkov—alone," he added. "Your two-man teams are imbeciles or incompetent or both, and now this paramilitary team has been alerted. I am sure the captain can get the job done. She may have to eliminate a few of these ex-military men first before she gets McLanahan." Korchkov said nothing, but she wore a hint of a smile, as if already relishing the prospect of fresh kills. "But not right away. Let McLanahan and his bodyguards think we have given up the hunt. Spend some time putting the captain in the perfect cover, close to McLanahan and close enough to get a good look at this paramilitary team. Do not use her diplomatic credentials—I am sure all embassy and consulate staff members are going to be under intense scrutiny for a while."

"Yes, sir," Ilianov said.

Gryzlov stepped closer to Korchkov and stared into her unblinking eyes. She stared straight back at him with that tiny smile. "They let you in here wearing a knife, Korchkov?"

"Oni ne smeli vzyat' yego ot menya, ser," Korchkov said, the first words Gryzlov remembered ever hearing the beauty utter. "They dared not take it away from me. Sir."

"I see," Gryzlov said. He looked her body up and down once more, then said, "It would not bother me one bit, Captain, if you chose to torture McLanahan for a while before you executed him. Then you could come back to me and describe it all in great detail."

"S udovol'stviyem, ser," Korchkov said, "With pleasure, sir."

IN EARTH ORBIT

October 2016

"Wow, look at all the new bling," Sondra Eddington said. She and Boomer Noble were aboard an S-19 Midnight spaceplane, making their approach to the docking bay on Armstrong Space Station, which was about a mile away. This was her fourth flight in a spaceplane, her second in the S-19 spaceplane—the others having been in the smaller S-9 Black Stallion—but her first time in orbit and her first docking with Armstrong Space Station. Both she and Boomer were wearing skintight Electronic Elastomeric Activity Suits and helmets for prebreathing oxygen, just in case of an uncontrolled depressurization.

"Part of that Starfire solar-power-plant project," Boomer said. He could see Sondra shake her head slightly when he said the word *Starfire*. They were referring to two extra sets of solar collectors mounted on towers between the "top" modules on station, pointing at the sun. "Hard to believe, but those new photovoltaic collectors generate more electricity than all of station's silicon solar cells put together, even though they're less than a quarter of the size."

"Oh, I believe it," Sondra said. "I can almost explain to you how they're built and draw you the molecular structure of the nanotubes."

"Brad talked about them more than once to you, I suppose."

"Until it's coming out my ears," Sondra said wearily.

This part of Sondra's training to fly the spaceplanes was fully computer controlled, so both crewmembers sat back and watched the computers do their thing. Boomer asked questions about possible malfunctions and her actions, pointed out certain indications, and talked about what to expect. Soon they could only see one station module, and before long all they could see was the docking bull's-eye, and minutes later the Midnight spaceplane was stopped. "Latches secure, docking successful," Boomer reported. "Kinda boring when the computer does it."

Sondra finished monitoring the computer as it completed the postdocking checklist. "Postdock checklist complete," she said when the computer had finished all the steps. "There's nothing I like better than a boring flight—that means everything went well and everything worked. Good enough for me."

"I like to dock it by hand," Boomer said. "If we have extra fuel on Armstrong or on Midnight, I will. Otherwise the computer is much more fuel-efficient, I hate to admit."

"You're just a show-off," Sondra said. "Cocksure as ever."

"That's me." He paused for a moment, then asked, "How did the ascent feel? I sense you're still having a little difficulty with the positive Gs."

"I can stay ahead of them just fine, Boomer," Sondra said.

"It just looked like you were concentrating really hard on staying on top of them."

"Whatever gets the job done, right?"

"I'm a little worried about the descent," Boomer said. "The G-forces are heavier and longer. You only get about two or three Gs in the ascent, but four or five during the descent."

"I know, Boomer," Sondra said. "I'll be fine. I passed all the MiG-25 flights, and I did okay on the S-9 and other S-19 flights."

"Those were all suborbital—we can avoid the Gs easier because we don't have to decelerate as much," Boomer said. "But now we'll be slowing down from Mach twenty-five. To reduce the Gs I can shallow out the deorbit angle a bit, but then you'll have to go against the Gs for a longer period of time."

"I've heard the lecture before, Boomer," Sondra said a bit testily. "I'll be fine no matter what descent angle you pick. I've been practicing my M-maneuvers." M-maneuvers were the method for tightening the stomach muscles, inflating the lungs, and then grunting against the pressure in the chest to force blood to stay in the chest and brain. "Besides, the EEAS helps a lot."

"All right," Boomer said. "Is that like practicing your Kegel exercises?"

"Something you'd like to feel personally?"

Boomer ignored the intimate comment and pointed to the displays on the instrument panel. "This shows that the computer is ready to begin the 'Before Transfer Tunnel Mating' checklist," he said. "I'll go ahead and initiate it. Since the transfer tunnel will be mated by machine—that's why we wear space suits—in case the tunnel isn't secure when we want to exit, we can safely do a spacewalk to reattach it or reach station."

"Why don't we just do a spacewalk to get to the station, like President Phoenix did last spring?" Sondra asked. "That sounded like fun."

"We will do that in a later evolution," Boomer said. "Your job in this evolution is to learn how to monitor the ship and the station from the cockpit, be able to recognize anomalies, and take action."

"How long does the cargo transfer take?"

"Depends. There aren't that many cargo modules on this trip. Probably not long."

As the transfer tunnel was being mounted into place atop the transfer chamber between the cockpit and cargo bay, Boomer watched mechanical arms from Armstrong Space Station removing pressurized modules from the open cargo bay and carrying them to their proper destinations. The smaller modules were personal items for the crewmembers—water, food, spare parts, and other essential items—but the largest module was last. This was one of the last components of Project Starfire to come up to Armstrong Space Station: the microwave generator, which was to be fitted inside the free-electron laser already on the station to produce maser energy from collected solar-produced electrical energy.

A tone sounded in the astronauts' helmets, and Boomer touched a microphone button. "Battle Mountain, this is Stallion Three, go ahead," he said.

"Sondra, Boomer, this is Brad!" Brad McLanahan said excitedly. "My team members and I would like to say congratulations for bringing up the last major Starfire component."

"Thanks, buddy," Boomer said. "Pass along our congratulations to your team. Everyone on Armstrong and at Sky Masters is excited to be installing the last part of this project and preparing for a test-firing very soon."

"Same, Brad," Sondra said simply.

"How are you, Sondra? How was your first trip into orbit?"

"I'm more like a babysitter up here: everything is so automated that I don't do anything but watch the computers do all the work."

"Well, the takeoff was incredible, we watched your ascent from mission control, and the rendezvous was picture-perfect," Brad said. "We can see them loading the microwave cavity into the Skybolt module right freakin' now. And you just made your first trip into orbit. Awesome! Congratulations!"

"You sound like a little kid, Brad," Boomer said.

"The team and I couldn't be more excited, Boomer," Brad said. "I couldn't sleep at all last night—heck, not for the past *week*!"

"So when do we fire this bad boy up, Brad?" Boomer asked.

"It's coming together real well, Boomer, maybe in a week or so," Brad replied. "Construction of the first rectenna is complete, and it's being tested and readied for the test firing at the White Sands Missile Test Range as we speak. The computer chips and new software for the aiming controls are all online and tested. We've run into a couple glitches with the lithium-ion capacitors fully discharging into the Skybolt laser, but we have an army of guys working on them, and we recruit more experts and technicians for the project every day. I'm still trying to talk Dr. Kaddiri and Dr. Richter into letting me fly up to the station. Put in a good word for me, okay?"

"Sure, Brad," Boomer said.

"Sondra, when do you come back?" Brad asked.

"I can't tell you that, Brad, not on an unsecure transmission," Sondra replied testily. "I know I have some classes and exercises up here on station, and I don't think we're returning directly to Battle Mountain."

"I have to go back to Cal Poly tomorrow morning," Brad said, the dejection apparent in his voice. "I've missed enough classes already."

"Next time, Brad," Sondra said.

"Well, I'll let you guys get back to work," Brad said. "We're going to talk with the techs on Armstrong about beginning integration of the microwave cavity into Skybolt, and then the team is going to the city to celebrate the completion of Starfire. Wish you guys were with us. Thanks again for a thrilling and successful flight."

"You got it, buddy," Boomer said. "And I will talk to the brass about getting you up and other members of your team on a spaceplane flight to Armstrong. You should be up here when you make your first shot."

"Awesome, Boomer," Brad said. "Thank you again. Talk to you soon."

"Midnight clear." Boomer closed the connection. "Man, it's good to hear a guy so damned excited about something," he said on intercom. "And I like hearing 'the team this' and 'the team that.' He's the head of a project that has almost a hundred members and a budget of over two hundred million dollars at last count, but it's still about the team. Very cool." Sondra said nothing. Boomer looked over to her but couldn't read much in her face through the oxygen helmet. "Am I right?" he asked.

"Of course."

Boomer let the silence linger for a few long moments; then: "You still haven't broken up with him, have you?"

"I don't need to," Sondra said peevishly. "I've seen the guy just three weekends in six months, and when we do see each other, all he talks about is Starfire this or Cal Poly that, and all he does is schoolwork and Starfire stuff, and then he rides his bike or does hundreds of push-ups and sit-ups to work out. He did that every day I was visiting."

"He works out every day?"

"At least ninety minutes a day, not including the time on the bike riding to classes or the gym," Sondra said. "He's really changed, and it's a little creepy. He sleeps only four or five hours a night, he's on the phone or computer—or both at the same time—constantly, and he eats like a friggin' bird. I get home after visiting him and I feel like ordering a whole large cheese and pepperoni pizza just for myself."

"I have to admit, he looked really good when I saw him before takeoff today, a lot better than the last time I saw him when his dad was around," Boomer said. "He's lost a bunch of weight and looks like he's got some guns on him now."

"Not that I ever got to shoot any of them," Sondra said moodily.

Boomer didn't ask her to elaborate.

DOWNTOWN BATTLE MOUNTAIN, NEVADA

A few hours later

"The last piece of Starfire is in orbit!" Brad shouted to the team members assembled around him. "Excelsior!" All the team members echoed their newfound motto, which was Latin for "ever higher."

"I made reservations for us at Harrah's Battle Mountain steak house," Casey Huggins said, signing off on her smartphone. "They'll be expecting us at six."

"Thanks, Casey," Brad said. "I'm going for a little run. I'll see you guys at the casino concierge desk."

"You're leaving to go running?" Lane Eagan asked. "Now? Casey and Jerry's microwave cavity was just delivered to a space station and will be installed in a couple days, and then Starfire will be ready to go. You should be having fun, Brad. Starfire is almost ready to test-fire! You deserve it."

"I *will* be having fun, guys, believe me," Brad said. "But if I don't get a run in, I get cranky. I'll see you in an hour at the concierge desk at Harrah's." He trotted off before anyone else could object.

Brad ran back to his room, changed into workout clothes, did two hundred crunches and push-ups, then picked up his cane and went downstairs and outdoors. Early October in north-central Nevada was almost ideal weather, not quite as warm and with a little taste of winter in the air, and Brad found the conditions perfect. In thirty minutes he had run almost four miles around the hotel's RV park, which was a lot less congested than the parking lot, then headed back to his room to shower and change.

He had just started to undress when he heard a noise on the other side of the door. He picked up his cane, looked through the peephole in the door, then opened it. He found Jodie outside, tapping a note on her smartphone. "Oh! You're back," she said, surprised. Brad stepped aside, and she came inside. "I was just going to leave you a message to meet us at the Silver Miner's Club instead—they have a pretty good jazz band playing now." Her eyes roamed across his chest and shoulders and opened wide in surprise. "Crikey, mate, what in bloody hell have you been doing to yourself?"

"What?"

"These, mate," Jodie said, and ran her fingers across his biceps and deltoids. "Are you on steroids or something?"

"Heck no. I'd never do drugs."

"Then where did these spankin' flexors come from, Brad?" Jodie asked, her fingers running across the top of his chest. "I know you've been working out, but holy dooley! You've got some spiffy gams there too." She ran a hand across his abdomen. "And is that a six-pack I see, mate?"

"My trainers are pretty intense guys," Brad said. "We do weights three times a week, in between cardio. They throw in speed bag and even some gymnastics, just to mix things up." He still hadn't told her about the cane, Krav Maga, and pistol training, but he knew he should do so soon. They weren't officially a couple and hadn't actually been dating, just seeing a little more of each other outside of school. They'd taken a couple trips in the turbine P210 airplane, but they were all quick one-day trips to see a baseball game in San Francisco or do some seafood shopping in Monterey.

"Well, it's working for you, big boy," Jodie said with a smile. She traced her fingernail down the front of his chest, but when he didn't respond the way she hoped, she pulled back. "But I don't understand why you need that cane. You said you thought you needed it every now and then after that attack last spring just to help steady yourself. Are you still wobbly? You run and bike all the time."

"Yeah, every now and then I'll get a little vertigo," Brad lied. "Not enough to stop me from running or biking. I'm just used to having it with me, I guess."

"Well, it makes you look very dapper," Jodie said. "And I'll wager that folks let you ahead of them in line at the super too."

"I don't let it go that far, unless I'm really in a hurry," Brad said.

She went over and picked up his cane, tapping the crook against her hand. "Looks as mean as cat's piss, mate," she said, running a finger down the pointed tip of the crook and across the carved grips along the shaft. This one was a bit more ornate than the ones she had first seen him with; it had more ridges across it, and three channels that ran the entire length. "It's not my granddaddy's cane, that's for sure."

"I got it from Chief Ratel when he noticed me having a little dizzy spell," Brad lied again, using the excuses and stories he'd made up and rehearsed over the past several months. "I just never got around to getting another one, like the ones that stand up by themselves, and he never asked for it back."

By looking at her expression, Brad couldn't tell if Jodie was believing any of it or not, but she leaned the cane against the bed, gave another long glance at his body, and smiled. "See you downstairs at the club, spunky," she said, and departed.

The team members had an extraordinary dinner celebration. Afterward, Lane Eagan's parents took him to the airport to catch a flight back to California, so Brad, Jodie, Casey, and a few other team members decided to check out a new casino across Highway 50 that had a good comedy club. It was dark and starting to grow cooler, but it was still comfortable enough for a stroll. The regular crosswalk was blocked by sidewalk construction, so they were forced to go east about a half a block to the casino parking lot's secondary entrance, which was not quite as well-lit as the main entrance.

Just as they began to head back toward the casino, two men appeared out of nowhere from the darkness and blocked their path. "Gimme five bucks," one of the men said.

"Sorry," Brad said. "Can't help you."

"I didn't ask for your help," the man said. "Now it'll cost you ten."

"Get lost, creep," Casey said.

The second man lashed out, kicking Casey's wheelchair so she was spun around sideways. "Shaddup, gimp," he said. Brad, who had been helping push Casey when she needed him to, reached out to grab the wheelchair. The second man thought he was going after him, so he flicked open a knife and swung, slashing open Brad's shirt on his right upper arm and drawing blood.

"Brad!" Jodie shouted. *"Somebody, help us!"*

"Shut up, bitch," the man with the knife growled. "Now drop your purses and wallets on the ground *right fucking now* before I—"

The motion was nothing more than a blur. Brad grasped the crook of his cane with his left hand and spun it, cracking it down on the attacker's knuckles with the sound of splintering wood, causing him to drop the knife with a howl of pain. Brad immediately caught the end of the cane with his right hand and swung, hitting the first man on the side of his head. The mugger went down, but Brad's cane snapped in two.

"You motherfucker!" the second attacker shouted. He had retrieved his knife and had it in his left hand this time. "I'm gonna gut you like a fucking pig!"

Brad raised his hands, palms out. "No, no, no, no, please don't hurt me again," he said, but the tone of his voice sounded like anything but surrender—it was as if he was playacting in front of this attacker, teasing him with a mocking tone, as if he was actually urging the guy with the knife to attack! "Please, asshole," Brad said, "don't kill me." And then, to everyone's surprise, he wiggled his fingers at the attacker, as if making fun of him, then said, "Come and get me, big man. Try to take me."

"Die, asshole!" The attacker took two steps forward and the knife shot out toward Brad's stomach . . .

. . . but in another blur of motion Brad blocked the attacker's arm with his own right arm, reached under the attacker's arm and locked it straight, kneed the attacker in the stomach several times—no one watching this fight could count how many times he did it—until the attacker dropped the knife and was nearly bent over double. Then he twisted the attacker's left arm upward until they heard several loud *POP*s as shoulder tendons and ligaments separated. The attacker collapsed on the sidewalk, screaming insanely, his left arm bent back at a very unnatural angle.

At that moment two armed casino security guards rushed down the sidewalk, each grabbing one of Brad's arms. Brad offered no resistance. *"Hey!"* Casey yelled.

"He didn't do anything! Those guys tried to mug us!" But Brad was wrestled to the pavement, flipped over, and handcuffed.

"Crikey, coppers, can't you see he's been cut?" Jodie cried after the guards got off Brad. She applied direct pressure to the wound. "Get some first aid out here, *now*!" One of the security guards pulled out his radio, calling for the police and a paramedic unit.

"Looks like this guy's arm was almost twisted right off," the second security guard said after the paramedics arrived, examining the screaming man on the sidewalk. He checked the first mugger. "This guy's out cold. I've seen this guy around before panhandling, but he's never mugged anybody." He shined his flashlight at the pieces of the broken cane, then looked over at Brad. "What were you doing, kid—rolling drunks and panhandlers to impress your girlfriends?"

"They tried to mug us!" Jodie, Casey, and the others shouted, almost in unison.

It took more than an hour, during which time Brad was sitting with his hands cuffed behind his back to the door of a police cruiser after the gash on his right arm was bandaged, but finally surveillance video from two different casinos and a parking-garage camera showed what had happened, and he was released. They all gave statements for the police reports, and the group returned to their hotel.

While the others went to their rooms, Brad, Jodie, and Casey found a quiet bar in the casino and bought drinks. "Are you sure you're all right, Brad?" Casey asked. "That bastard got you pretty good."

"I'm fine," Brad replied, touching the bandages. "It wasn't a very deep cut. The paramedics said I probably won't need stitches."

"So how did you learn all that stuff with the cane, Brad?" Casey asked. "Is that the self-defense stuff you've been working on since that home invasion attack back in April?"

"Yes," Brad said. "Chief Ratel and his other instructors teach Korean self-defense and Cane-Ja, self-defense with a cane, as well as physical fitness. It came in handy."

"I'll say," Casey said. "It was still a fun night. I'm going to hit some slot machines, maybe see if that guy I met at the club is still around, and call it a night. See you guys in the morning." She finished her glass of wine and rolled away.

Brad took a sip of his Scotch, then turned to Jodie. "You've been real quiet since the altercation, Jodie," he said. "You okay?"

Jodie's face was a mix of confusion, concern, fear . . . and, Brad soon realized, disbelief. "Altercation?" she said finally after a long, rather painful moment. "You call that an 'altercation'?"

"Jodie . . . ?"

"My God, Brad, you nearly killed one guy and almost snapped off the other guy's arm!" Jodie exclaimed in a low voice. "You broke your cane over a guy's *skull!*"

"Damn right I did!" Brad shot back. "That guy slashed my arm! What was I supposed to do?"

"First of all, mate, the guy that slashed you was not the guy that you conked over the head," Jodie said. "All he did was ask for money. If you'd given him what he asked for, none of that would've happened."

"We got mugged, Jodie," Brad said. "That guy pulled out a knife and slashed me. He could've done that to you or Casey, or worse. What was I supposed to do?"

"What do you mean, what were you supposed to do?" Jodie asked incredulously. "You Yanks are all alike. Someone confronts you on the street and you think you have to leap into action like Batman and kick someone's arse. Are you drongo? That's not the way it works, Brad. Someone gets the drop on you like that, you give them what they want, they go away, and everybody's safe. We should have dropped our purses and wallets, backed away, and called the cops. We were the stupid ones for going off into the dark areas instead of sticking to the lighted and protected areas. If they tried to get me into a car with them, I'd fight with everything I have, but five or ten or a *million* lousy bucks is not worth anyone's life. It's not even worth a gash on your arm. And then after you broke your cane on the first guy's head, you took on a guy with a knife, and you were *unarmed.* Are you daft? You even sounded as if you were *teasing* the guy to attack you! What is with that shit?"

Wow, Brad thought, she's really upset about this—it was a reaction he completely didn't expect. Arguing with her wasn't going to help one bit. "I . . . I guess I just didn't think," he said. "I just reacted."

"And it looked like you were trying to kill both guys!" Jodie thundered on, her voice rising enough to get the attention of others nearby. "You were pummeling that second guy so bad I thought he was going to puke up his guts, and *then* you nearly twisted his arm off! What in bloody hell was that?"

"The self-defense classes I'm taking . . ."

"Oh, so that's it, eh?" Jodie said. "Your new buddy Chief Ratel is teaching you how to kill people? I think the farther you get away from that guy, the better. He's brainwashing you into thinking you're invincible, that you can take on a guy with a knife and stove a guy's head in with a cane." Her eyes widened in realization. "So that's why you carry that scary-looking cane? Chief Ratel taught you how to attack people with it?"

"I didn't attack anyone!" Brad protested. "I was—"

"You cracked open that poor guy's head with that cane," Jodie said. "He didn't do anything to you. The other guy had a knife, so it was self-defense—"

"Thank you!"

"—but it looked like you were trying to kill the bloke!" Jodie went on. "Why did you keep on beating him like that, and why twist his arm so far back?"

"Jodie, the guy had a knife," Brad said, almost pleading for her to understand. "An attacker with a knife is one of the most dangerous situations you can get into, especially at night and against a guy who knows how to use it. You saw how he came after us with his left hand after I knocked the knife out of his right—he obviously knew how to fight with a knife, and I had to take him out. I—"

"*Take him out?*" Folks at nearby tables were starting to notice the rising tone in Jodie's voice. "So you *were* trying to kill him?"

"Krav Maga teaches countermove, control, and counterattack, all in—"

"I've heard of Krav Maga," Jodie said. "So you're training to be an Israeli killer commando now?"

"Krav Maga is a form of self-defense," Brad said in a softer tone, hoping Jodie would follow suit. "It's meant to disable attackers, without weapons. It's meant to be quick and violent so the defender doesn't—"

"I don't know you anymore, Brad," Jodie said, rising to her feet. "That attack in your house in San Luis Obispo must've screwed you up a little, I think—or did you lie to me and the others about *that*?"

"No!"

"Ever since then you've become this compulsive type A, whirling-dervish kind of guy, exactly the opposite of the guy I met at the beginning of the school year. You don't eat, you don't sleep, and you don't hang out with your friends or network around campus anymore. You've turned into this . . . this *machine,* working out and learning Israeli commando beat-down tactics and carrying a cane so you can crack some skulls. You lied to me about the cane. What else have you lied to me about?"

"Nothing," Brad said immediately—probably too immediately, because he saw Jodie's eyes flare again, then narrow suspiciously. "Jodie, I'm not a machine." I *know* one, Brad thought, but *I'm* not one. "I'm the same guy. Maybe that home invasion did freak me out a little. But I'm—"

"Listen, Brad, I've got some thinking to do about us," Jodie said. "I really thought we could be more than friends, but that was with the Brad I met long ago. This new one is scary. It seems like you're scarfing up everything this Chief Ratel is feeding you, and you've turned into a monster."

"A *monster!* I'm not—"

"I suggest for your own sake that you tell this Chief Ratel guy to piss off and maybe get some counseling, before you go completely off the deep end and start roaming the streets in a mask and cape looking for blokes to beat up," Jodie said, jabbing a finger at Brad. "In the meantime, I think it's best for me to keep my distance from you until I feel safe again." And she stormed away.

MARICOPA, CALIFORNIA

Later that night

A woman with long dark hair wearing a leather jacket, dark slacks, and rose-tinted sunglasses was fueling her rental car at a deserted-looking gasoline station when a new-looking windowless van pulled into a dark parking spot beside the station's office. A tall, good-looking man in jeans and an untucked flannel shirt got out of the van, took a long admiring look at the woman at the pump, and went inside to make a purchase. When he came out a few minutes later, he walked up to the woman and smiled. "Evening, pretty lady," he said.

"Evening," the woman said.

"Nice night, isn't it?"

"It's a little cold, but pleasant."

"My name's Tom," the man said, extending a hand.

"Melissa," the woman said, shaking his hand. "Nice to meet you."

"Same, Melissa," the man said. "Pretty name."

"Thank you, Tom."

The man hesitated, but only for a second, before stepping a bit closer to the woman and saying, "I have an idea, Melissa. I have a bottle of bourbon in the van, some nice leather seats in back, and a hundred dollars burning a hole in my pocket. What do you say we have a little fun together before we get back on the road?"

The woman looked Tom directly in the eye, then gave him just a hint of a smile. "Two hundred," she said.

"Done this before, have we?" Tom said. "That's a little steep for a half-and-half in my van." The woman removed her sunglasses, revealing dark seductive eyes and long lashes, then unzipped her leather jacket, revealing a red blouse with a plunging neckline and a deep sexy cleavage. Tom fairly licked his lips as he took in the sights. "Park beside me."

The woman parked her rental car beside the van, and Tom opened the side door for her. The interior of the van was very well appointed, with a leather couch in back, rear-facing leather captain's chairs behind the driver's seat, a television with a satellite receiver and DVD player, and a wet bar. Melissa took one of the captain's chairs while Tom poured two glasses of bourbon. He handed one to her, then tipped his glass to hers. "Here's to a pleasant evening, Melissa."

"It will be," she said. "But first?"

"Sure," Tom said. He reached into his jeans, pulled out a money clip, and shook out two hundred-dollar bills.

"Thank you, Tom," Melissa said, taking a sip of bourbon.

Tom motioned behind him, and it wasn't until then that the woman noticed a sports camera in the corner, pointed at her. "You don't mind if I turn on my little camera there, do you, Melissa?" he asked. "I like to keep a souvenir collection."

The woman hesitated for a moment, a little confusion in her eyes, then gave him her tiny smile. "No, go ahead," she said. "I like performing in front of cameras."

"I'll bet you do, Melissa," Tom said. He turned, made his way to the camera in back, and pressed the button to turn it on. "I have another one up front that I want to get also." He turned . . .

. . . and found himself face-to-face with Melissa, looking into her dark, hypnotic eyes. He smiled, admiring her high cheekbones and full red lips. "Hey, baby, I can't wait either, but let me . . ."

. . . and that's when the knife plunged through his abdomen, up through his diaphragm, through his lungs, and all the way into his heart. A hand went over his mouth, but he did not cry out—he was dead before he hit the carpet.

The woman pulled the rear sports camera down from its mount, took the money clip, cracked open the side door, saw there were no onlookers, and quickly left the van, got into her own car, and drove away. By the time they found the body, she was hundreds of miles away.

THE WHITE HOUSE
WASHINGTON, D.C.

Days later

"There it goes," Vice President Ann Page said. She was in the White House Situation Room with President Kenneth Phoenix; National Security Adviser William Glenbrook; Harold Lee, the undersecretary of defense for space; and Air Force General George Sandstein, commander of Air Force Space Command, watching live video being broadcast from space on the Situation Room's wall-sized high-definition monitor. They watched in stunned amazement as a large section of the International Space Station separated from the rest of the structure and began to drift away from the ISS. "For the first time in almost twenty years, the International Space Station is vacant," Ann breathed, "and for the first time ever, there aren't any Russian components on it."

"What is being taken away, Ann?" the president asked.

"That is called the Russian Orbital Segment, or ROS, sir," the vice president replied, not needing to refer to any notes—as an ex-astronaut and aerospace and electronics engineer, she was an expert on all American and American-involved space stations dating back to Skylab. "There are three docking and airlock modules, one docking and storage module, one laboratory, one habitation module, one service module, four solar arrays, and two heat radiators."

"Any critical modules being taken away? If we sent crews back up there, would they be in any danger?"

"The most important Russian module was Zvezda, or 'star,' the service module," Ann replied. "Zvezda is the large module all the way in the 'back' as the station flies, and as such provides attitude and navigation control and is used to boost the station to a higher orbit when necessary. It also produces power, oxygen, and water, among many other critical functions."

"And now?"

"Zvezda will eventually be replaced by two American modules, the ISS Propulsion Module and the Interim Control Module," Ann explained. "These two modules were built back about twenty years ago when Zvezda was delayed in construction and were meant to serve as backup control and propulsion systems in case Zvezda failed or was damaged; the Propulsion Module was also designed to deorbit the ISS when the time came."

"That time might be coming sooner than we expected," National Security Adviser William Glenbrook commented.

"Both modules have been in storage at the Naval Research Laboratory," the vice president went on. "When the Russians made the announcement that they were going to take the ROS off the ISS, the NRL initiated functional checks of the two modules. That has just been completed, and now we are just waiting to have the modules mated to a booster and sent to the ISS. The problem with that is that the two modules were built to be transported to the ISS aboard a space shuttle, so some reengineering will have to be done to get them on a rocket. That might take a few more weeks."

"So that's why the station had to be abandoned?" the president asked. "They couldn't make power, water, or oxygen, or control the station?"

"The Harmony module on the ISS can make consumables, but for only two astronauts, not six," Ann said. "Unmanned and manned spacecraft can resupply the ISS and dock to the ISS to control and boost it higher if necessary, so station control and provisions should not be an issue. For safety reasons, it was decided to evacuate the ISS until the Russians' de-mating procedure was—" Ann suddenly stopped and was staring at the high-def monitor. "Oh, my Lord! Well well, our Russian friends sure seemed to be very busy over the past several months, haven't they?"

"What is it?" Phoenix asked.

"This," Ann said, rising from her seat, going to the screen at the front of the Situation Room, and pointing at a small triangular-shaped object on the screen. "Freeze that," she ordered, and the computer responded by pausing the live feed. "That, Mr. President, if I'm not mistaken, is a Soviet-era Elektron spaceplane."

"The Russians have a spaceplane, like the one I flew in?" President Phoenix asked incredulously.

"It's more akin to a small space shuttle, sir," Ann explained, "in that it's carried atop a booster, and then reenters the atmosphere and glides unpowered to a runway. Although it's smaller than the shuttle and carries only one cosmonaut, its payload is almost twice that of our S-19 spaceplanes, about fifteen thousand pounds. They were armed with guided missiles, specifically designed to hunt down and destroy American satellites and Silver Tower. The plane hasn't been seen since the Soviet Union collapsed. The Soviets said they were going to build hundreds of them. Maybe they did." Ann paused, distracted by painful memories of decades past. "I was aboard Armstrong Space Station when the Soviets attacked with three of those bastards. They almost took us out."

"Did we know they were going to launch a spaceplane, General?" the president asked.

"Not exactly, sir," Air Force General George Sandstein, commander of Air Force Space Command and deputy commander for space of U.S. Strategic Command, replied. "About three days ago we received a notification of a launch from Plesetsk Cosmodrome Launch Site 41 of a Soyuz-U rocket with an unmanned Progress payload to assist in the ROS de-mating process, sir. Nothing was mentioned about a spaceplane. We tracked the payload and determined it was indeed going into orbit and on course to rendezvous with the ISS, so we classified it as a routine mission."

"Isn't it unusual for the Russians to use Plesetsk instead of Baikonur, General?" Ann asked.

"Yes, ma'am—Plesetsk was almost abandoned after the Russians made a deal with Kazakhstan for the continued use of Baikonur," Sandstein replied. "Plesetsk was mostly used for intercontinental-ballistic-missile tests and other light and medium military projects—" Sandstein stopped, his eyes widened with shock, then he said, "Including the Elektron spaceplane and BOR-5 Buran test articles."

"Buran?" the president asked.

"The Soviets' copy of the space shuttle, sir," Ann said. "Buran was designed from the start as a military program, so test launches of the subscale test articles were from Plesetsk, which is well inside Russia instead of Kazakhstan. The Buran spaceplane itself made only one launch from Baikonur Cosmodrome before the collapse of the Soviet Union, but the mission was highly successful—a completely autonomous unmanned launch, orbit, reentry, and landing. Five Burans were built; one was destroyed, and three were in various states of completion."

"If the Russians are launching spaceplanes again, this could be the start of a new Russian initiative to push back into space," Glenbrook said. "They have the ROS, and it's not going to be attached to a Western space station anymore, so they can do what they want without a lot of close observation. If they are starting to fly Elektrons, they might be gearing up in many more areas, all related to building up their own capabilities as well as countering our own."

"An arms race in space," the president said. "Just what we need right now. Aren't we required to notify the Russians if we're going to launch a spaceplane into orbit?"

"Yes, sir, and we do, each and every time," Sandstein replied. "Date and time of launch, initial orbital path, destination, purpose, payload, and date and time of return."

"We give them all that?"

"Our spaceplanes are much more than orbital space-craft, sir," Sandstein explained. "Their flight paths are much more flexible than a launch from an Earth launch pad, as you yourself experienced. To avoid conflict, we agreed to give them information on each flight so they could monitor the flight and react to any unexplained diversions."

"So the Russians knew I was flying in the spaceplane?"

"We don't give them that much detail, sir," Sandstein said with a hint of a smile.

"So we should be getting the same information on the Russian spaceplanes, correct?"

"If we want to reveal that we know about it, sir," Ann said. "It might be better if we didn't reveal that we know about Elektron right now. We can assume that they know, but we don't have to reveal all we know about their activities. Silence is golden."

President Phoenix nodded—now that the discussion was beginning to move from the military into the geopolitical arena, he needed a different mix of advisers. "What can the Russians do with that section of the space station?"

"All by itself, the ROS is already a fully functioning space station for two or three persons," Ann said. "They could probably use a few more solar arrays for power, and they don't have as sophisticated space and Earth sensor systems or communications as the ISS, but they can have other spacecraft dock with it for resupply; it can maneuver, boost itself when it needs to, produce power, water, and oxygen, everything."

"And they undocked it just because Gryzlov is ticked off at me?" the president remarked. "Unbelievable."

"Unfortunately, his tactic may work, sir," National Security Adviser Glenbrook said. "It's possible that the European Space Agency will undock their Columbus research module rather than risk irritating the Russians—they have had plans to cooperate with Russia on building a presence in space long before they decided to cooperate on the ISS. If they do that, or if the replacement modules we plan on sending up don't do the job, the Japanese might undock their Kibō modules and abandon the project as well. Canada has its remote arms still on the station, but we're not certain if they'd keep them on ISS if the Russians, ESA, and Japan pulled out."

"So if all the other ISS partners leave, what are we left with?"

"The ISS is still a very important part of American scientific research, even without Kibō, Columbus, or the ROS, sir," Ann Page said. "We have a huge investment in it already, and we gain tons of knowledge and experience in living and working in space. If we want to eventually go back to the moon or send astronauts to Mars or beyond, the ISS is the best stepping-stone for that. The Japanese in particular have a very extensive scientific research program on the ISS, so I think they would want to keep the ISS aloft for as long as possible until they launch their own station, or partner up with someone else. And the ISS, as well as Armstrong Space Station, would be the best platforms to get your already-announced industrialization-of-space initiative going."

"Good," the president said. "I want to speak with the Japanese prime minister and the prime ministers of the European Space Agency countries, and I want to assure them that we are committed to maintaining the ISS and continuing all the work we're doing, despite the hissy fit the Russians are having."

"Yes, Mr. President," Ann said.

"Bill, if the Russians are indeed gearing up to push back into space," the president said to his national security adviser, "I need to find out what else they are developing, and how much—military, industrial, scientific, everything. I don't want to be surprised by any more spaceplanes suddenly popping up around our space stations. I'd like an update on all the Russian and Chinese spaceports. The Russians cooperated with the Chinese before, in the Indian Ocean and South China Sea—they might be getting ready to do it again."

"Yes, sir," Glenbrook responded.

"General, I need a rundown of all the assets we have to support the ISS and Armstrong Space Station in the light of this de-mating process and a possible Russian push into space, and what we might need and how soon," the president said to Sandstein. "If there's going to be an arms race in space, I want to win it."

"Absolutely, sir," Sandstein said. The president shook hands with the four-star general and dismissed him.

"Speaking of the space-industrialization initiative," the president went on after the general had departed, "what's going on with Armstrong Space Station and our other space projects?"

"On track, Mr. President," Undersecretary Lee said proudly. "Based on your outline, sir, we have three programs we're supporting: successful flight testing of the XS-29 Shadow spaceplane, a larger version of the spaceplane you flew in; support for larger commercial rocket boosters to bring larger payloads into space, including some reusable booster technologies; and the first industrial program: installing a solar power plant aboard Armstrong Space Station."

"A solar power plant?"

"It will collect sunlight, transform it into electricity, and store it," Lee explained. "When it gets within range of a ground collector, called a rectenna, it will transform the electricity into a form of electromagnetic energy called a maser—a combination of a microwave and laser—and shoot the energy to Earth to the rectenna, which transforms the maser energy back into electricity, then stores the power in giant batteries or puts it into the electrical grid. If what they are planning comes true, in a single four-minute shot—the maximum time it takes for the space station to go from horizon to horizon—they can transmit enough power to supply a remote research facility or village for a week or more."

"Incredible," the president remarked. "Well done."

"And, as you directed, sir," Lee went on, "the federal government is only providing support in the form of using federal facilities such as national laboratories, launch pads, and computer networks—things that are already being used for other projects. We're not loaning money to anyone. The companies and universities involved in these programs have to invest themselves big-time, and they are. If they're successful, they hope to get reimbursed with government contracts to operate the systems they develop."

"Excellent," the president said. "Please keep me informed, Mr. Undersecretary." He stood, shook Lee's hand, and dismissed him as well, and soon afterward Glenbrook departed. After the two had left, the president said to Ann Page, "Once the video of that Russian section of the ISS separating from the station gets out, Ann, we're going to take one hell of a shellacking in the press, with a little less than a month to the elections."

"I'm a little more optimistic, Ken," Ann said. She knew it was time to take off her vice president's hat and put on Ken Phoenix's chief political adviser's hat, something that she always enjoyed doing very much. "Secretary Barbeau criticized your space initiative as another Reagan 'Star Wars' folly. When the public sees the Russians starting to push back in space, they'll know that Barbeau is on the wrong side of the issue."

"I hope so," Phoenix said, "but it's been several months since I announced the initiative on board the space station, and so far only the Russians have made good on their promise to take their modules off the ISS. Are any of those space programs going to be available to us to use in the campaign?"

"Absolutely, Ken," Ann said. "The XS-29 space-plane has made its first orbital test flight and has already done a mission both to the ISS and Armstrong Space Station. The solar-power-plant project might go online before the election, and we could describe it as another project that Barbeau doesn't support, is not taxpayer funded, and will be an example of what will wither and die if you are not reelected. The new advanced rocket boosters are not quite as far along, but we could do tours of the assembly buildings and remind the voters about how important those things are."

"Where are we on the solar power plant?"

"It's all assembled—they're just doing last-minute testing and checking," Ann said. "About a dozen space-plane missions and one heavy-lift rocket, all assembled by remote control with just two or three spacewalks. It was designed that way from the beginning by a team of college students, supported by scientists and engineers from all over the world . . . led, by the way, by one Bradley James McLanahan."

"*Brad McLanahan?*" the president exclaimed. "You're kidding! Patrick McLanahan's son? I was sorry for him when he dropped out of the Air Force Academy and when his father was killed—I guess he's landed on his feet. Good for him." He paused, thinking hard, then said, "How does this sound, Ann: let's get Brad McLanahan and maybe one or two others on his team up to Armstrong Space Station."

"As long as you don't tell me *you* want to go up there again, sir."

"I think I've had my share of excitement for a lifetime," the president said. "Would this make Brad the first teenager in space?"

"Unless you don't count the dogs and chimps that have already been sent up, yes," Ann said. "I hear Brad's been asking to go up on station for a while." Her expression turned serious. "Initial thoughts, sir: risky. If the flight fails, the son of a very popular and high-value figure gets killed, and your space initiative might go out the window, like after *Challenger* and *Columbia*. Not good."

"But if it succeeds, it could be awesome, yes?"

"Yes, it certainly could, sir," Ann Page said.

"Then let's make it happen," the president said. "We'll send McLanahan and maybe a female member of his team up for the first use of the thing." He shook his head. "I remember the first time Patrick brought Brad to the White House. He looked around and said, 'Boy, Dad, you sure work in an old place.'" The president's expression turned serious. "Speaking of Brad McLanahan . . ."

"Yes, sir?"

"I didn't tell you this, because I thought the fewer who knew the better, but back last spring Brad McLanahan found out, so I think you should too."

"Found out what?"

Phoenix took a deep breath, then said, "Last year, right after the Chinese attack on Guam, a private counterintelligence group led by former president Martindale went out to Guam to collect information on the hacked utilities and to see if there was any other evidence of a Chinese intelligence presence on Guam."

"Scion Aviation," Ann said. "I remember. What does that have to do with Brad McLanahan?"

"One of Scion's teams had Brad under surveillance after that break-in at Patrick McLanahan's columbarium in Sacramento," the president said. "They wanted to make sure that the same Russian agents that broke into the crypt wouldn't target Brad. Turns out they did target him and actually attacked three times. Scion's guys saved him."

"Well, that's good," Ann said, "but I'm still confused. Why is Scion Aviation International doing surveillance on Brad McLanahan? Isn't that a job for the FBI? If he's a target of a foreign direct-action team, he should be under full FBI counterespionage protection."

"It's because of one of the members of Scion," the president said. He looked directly into the vice president's eyes and said, "Patrick McLanahan."

Ann's only visible reaction was simply a few blinks. "That's impossible, Ken," she said in a toneless voice. "You got some bad information. Patrick died over China. You know that as well as I."

"No, he didn't," the president said. "Martindale found and revived him, but he was in bad shape. In order to keep him alive, they placed him in a Cybernetic Infantry Device, one of those big manned robots." Ann's face was beginning to transform into a mask of stunned disbelief. "He's still alive, Ann. But he can't live outside the robot. Unless they can heal him, he'll be in there for the rest of his life."

Ann's eyes widened and her mouth formed an astonished O. "I . . . I can't believe it," she breathed. "And he can operate the robot? He can move around, communicate, everything?"

"He has some incredible abilities," Phoenix said. "He operates sensors and all the robot's capabilities, and can communicate with anyone in the world—I wouldn't be surprised if he's listening in on us right now. Patrick McLanahan and the robot is a one-man Army platoon—maybe an entire Army battalion and Air Force division combined." Phoenix sighed and looked away. "But he can never leave the fucking machine. It's as if he's trapped in the Twilight Zone."

"Amazing. Just amazing," Ann said. "And Martindale has got him doing operations with Scion?"

"Skating on the very edge of the law, I'm sure, like he always did," Phoenix said.

"Ken, why did you tell me this?" Ann asked. "I might never have found out."

"I know you and Patrick are friends," the president said. "But the main reason is that I feel bad that I didn't let you in on it from the beginning. You're my closest political adviser and my closest friend, except for my wife, Alexa. The whole stuff with Brad McLanahan reminded me of the mistake I made when I didn't trust you with my decision to keep Patrick alive and not tell anyone. I wanted to correct that mistake."

"Well, thank you for that, Ken," Ann said. She shook her head, still in a state of disbelief. "What a thing to keep bottled up. No one else knows except Brad? Not even his family?"

"Just Brad and a few of Martindale's guys," Phoenix said.

"Glad you got that off your chest, aren't you, sir?"

"You bet I am," the president said. "Now, let's get back to the other, unreal world: politics and elections. I want to really push the space initiative hard in the closing days of the campaign. I want to talk with teenagers in space, make lots of visits to, and give speeches in front of, hypersonic spaceplanes and rocket boosters, and help throw the switch on electricity fired from space. We may be down in the polls right now, Ann, but we're going to pull this out—I can *feel* it!"

SEVEN

He is not worthy of the honeycomb. That
shuns the hives because the bees have stings.
—WILLIAM SHAKESPEARE

REINHOLD AEROSPACE ENGINEERING BUILDING
CAL POLY

The next day

"This is our mission control room, otherwise known as one of our electronics labs," Brad McLanahan said. He was standing before a group of foreign journalists, bloggers, photographers, and their translators, giving for the umpteenth time a tour of the Starfire project at Cal Poly. With him were Jodie Cavendish, Kim Jung-bae, Casey Huggins, and Lane Eagan. The room was stuffed with a dozen laptop computers, control and communications gear, and network interface boxes with hundreds of feet of CAT5 cables snaking away into walls and under the climate-controlled floor. "It's not as large or as nice as NASA mission control, but the functions are very similar: we monitor the major components of Starfire such as the microwave generator, nantenna and rectenna steering, power control, and beam control, among many others. Although the astronauts on board Armstrong Space Station have ultimate control, we can issue some commands from here—namely, we can pull the plug if something goes wrong."

"Are you collecting solar energy now, Mr. McLanahan?" one reporter asked.

"We've been collecting and storing solar energy for about three weeks now," Brad replied. "The solar-energy-collection-and-storage systems were the first to be attached to Armstrong Space Station." He motioned to a large model of the station that the team had set up for the press. "These are the nantennas, or nanotube sunlight collectors, designed by Jodie Cavendish, assisted by Kim Jung-bae, whom we call Jerry around here. They are double-sided so they can collect sunlight directly from the sun or reflected off the Earth. Here on the truss are ten two-hundred-kilogram lithium-ion capacitors, each capable of storing three hundred kilowatts, designed by Jerry Kim. We're not going to fill them up for this test, but you can see we have the capability of storing three megawatts of electricity on the station, just with this small experimental system."

"How much energy will you fire on this test?"

"We're planning on shooting a total of one-point-five megawatts," Brad said. "The station will be in range of the rectenna for approximately three minutes, so you can see we're going to send a lot of juice to Earth in a very short period of time." He pointed to a large poster-sized photograph of a round object sitting in a desert landscape. "This is the rectenna, or receiving antenna, which will collect the maser energy, designed by Jodie Cavendish along with Casey Huggins," he said. "It is two hundred meters in diameter, installed out on the White Sands Missile Test Range because it's a large secure area that can be easily cleared of aircraft. As you can see in this photo, we only have the rectenna and some pointing controls and data-monitoring equipment—we're going to measure how much electricity is being received, but we're not going to store or put any electricity into the grid on this first test. Lane Eagan here wrote the software and programmed the computers here on Earth and up in Armstrong to allow us the precision we need to hit that rather small target from two hundred to five hundred miles away."

"Why do the test in a large isolated area, Mr. McLanahan?" a reporter asked. "What would happen if the maser energy from the space station hit an aircraft or object on the ground, like a house or a person?"

"It would be like putting a metal dish in a microwave oven," Brad said. "The maser beam is mostly microwave energy, designed and built by Casey Huggins and Jerry Kim, but collimated with Armstrong's free-electron laser subsystems to strengthen and help aim the energy."

"You're going to fire the Skybolt laser?"

"No, not at all," Brad replied. "The Skybolt laser system uses a series of electromagnetic gates to channel, strengthen, and align the free-electron laser beam. We've disconnected the free-electron laser and have installed Casey Huggins's microwave generator, power by the stored solar energy. We're going to use the Skybolt subsystems to do the same thing with the microwave energy: strengthen, collimate, and focus it, and then we use Skybolt's aiming subsystems, thanks to Jerry Kim, to send the energy earthward.

"But to answer your question: We really don't know what would happen exactly, so we don't want anyone anywhere near the beam when we fire," Brad went on. "We're going to close a lot of airspace before we set Starfire off. Obviously Starfire is more suited for firing the energy into isolated areas, to spacecraft, or even to the moon, so firing the maser into populated areas won't necessarily be an issue, but we will be making the aiming control and beam propagation better and better as we go on, so the rectenna can be smaller and the dangers greatly reduced."

Brad fielded a few more questions, but the last one was a doozy: "Mr. McLanahan," a very attractive female reporter standing in front, with long jet-black hair, dark eyes, full red lips, a killer body, and a very slight European accent began, "you are very good at giving credit to the others on your team for all the things they have done to contribute to this project . . . but what have *you* done? Which components have you built? What are *you* with this project, if I may ask?"

"To tell the truth, I haven't built any components," Brad admitted after a long moment of consideration. "I consider myself the scrounger, like the character Flight Lieutenant Hendley in the movie *The Great Escape.*" The woman blinked in confusion, obviously not knowing whom he was referring to but making a note to find out. "I came up with an idea, found the best students, scientists, and engineers I could find and had them explain the science to me, contributed a few ideas of my own, put them to work, and repeated the process. I get the team whatever they need for their phase of the project: money, assistance, computer or lab time, equipment, parts, software, whatever. I also conduct progress meetings and helped prep the team for our presentation to the school for summer lab space, before our project received funding from Sky Masters Aerospace."

"So you're more like a coach or project manager," the woman said. "You aren't really the quarterback: you don't actually pass the ball, but you train the team, get the equipment, and supervise the coaching staff." She didn't wait for a response, and Brad didn't have one to give her in any case. "But you *are* a freshman student of engineering, are you not?"

"Sophomore student of aerospace engineering, yes."

"Perhaps you should consider a different field of study?" the woman said. "Business, perhaps, or management?"

"I want to be a test pilot," Brad said. "Most of the best test-pilot schools in the United States require a degree in the hard sciences, like engineering, computers, math, or physics. I chose aerospace engineering."

"And are you doing well in it, Mr. McLanahan?"

Brad was a little surprised to find himself being asked so many personal questions—he had prepped to answer technical questions from foreign science and space journalists and bloggers, not answer questions about himself. "I managed to finish my freshman year and start my sophomore year," he said. "I guess my grades are average. If I need help, and I do, I ask for it. If I don't understand something, I'll find someone to explain it to me." He looked around the lab for any more upraised hands, then turned back to the woman and found her looking directly at him with a slight smile, and he gave her one in return. "If that's all, folks, thank you for—"

"I have one more surprise announcement that I would like to share with all of you," Cal Poly president Dr. Marcus Harris said from the back of the room. He stepped up to the lectern next to Brad. "The station manager of Armstrong Space Station, retired Air Force general Kai Raydon, recently spoke with the White House, and has received authorization from the president of the United States to fly two Starfire team leaders to Armstrong Space Station to observe the Starfire test shot." The reporters broke out in applause.

Harris put an arm around Lane. "I'm sorry, Lane, but you're too young, but it will happen soon. The flight will be in just one week, and they'll be aboard Armstrong Space Station for approximately three days. In the case of Brad, Jodie, and Casey, if they accept this offer, they would become the first teenagers in space, and if Jung-bae accepts, he will be only the second Korean to fly in space, and by far the youngest." More applause, then frantic scribbling.

"The White House said that their preference is a male and female team leader," Harris went on, "but that's up to the Starfire team to decide. The selectees will need to pass a comprehensive physical exam, but as we saw last spring with President Phoenix, you seem to just need to be a healthy and courageous person to fly in space—and, I'm proud to say, that includes Casey Huggins, who, if she accepts, will not only be the first female teenager in space but will also be the first paraplegic in space." The applause was even louder and longer this time.

"I will let the team talk amongst themselves and their parents, and then I'd like to meet with them myself," Harris said. "But this is an outstanding opportunity and a rare honor for our Mustangs, and we couldn't be prouder." More applause, led by Harris, and the press conference broke up.

"Holy crap!" Brad exclaimed when the Starfire team was alone in the lab. "What an opportunity! How should we decide this? Sorry, Lane."

"No problem," Lane said. "I get airsick anyway."

"Who wants to go?"

"You *have* to go, Brad," Lane said. "You're the project leader. We couldn't have done this without you."

"Damn straight," Casey said.

"Besides, just like your new friend—that pretty female reporter in front who was making goo-goo eyes at you—said: what the bloody hell else do you do around here?" Jodie quipped, and everybody got a good laugh out of that. Jodie gave Brad an accusing and inquisitive—and maybe a jealous? Brad wondered—eye but said nothing more. "And where did that *Great Escape* thing come from?" She then switched her voice to that of James Garner playing the character Hendley in the movie. " 'You want to talk about hazards? Let's talk about hazards. Let's talk about you. You're the biggest hazard we have.' " Another round of laughter.

"All right, all right, very funny," Brad said. "Let's see how this works out. I'm going to fly in space soon enough anyway, I can guarantee you that, so if anyone else wants to take this opportunity, I'll defer. Jodie?"

"Not me, mate," Jodie said. "I like sand and surf and sea level—even Cal Poly is almost too high above sea level and too far from the beach for me. Besides, I don't want to be anywhere else but right here in this lab watching the monitors when Starfire lets loose."

"Jerry?"

The thought of going up into space didn't seem to make Jung-bae too comfortable. "I don't know," he said uneasily. "I would like to design and test spacecraft someday, but as far as flying in orbit in one . . . I think I will pass. Besides, I want to be out at White Sands monitoring the rectenna and maser output. We are still having problems with the lithium-ion capacitors. We are storing plenty of power, but we occasionally have problems transferring the power to the microwave cavity."

"I'll get some more experts to help you with that, Jerry," Brad said. He turned to Casey. "Then it's just you and me, Casey. What do you say? It's your maser—you should be up there."

Casey's face was a mixture of apprehension and confusion. "I don't think so, Brad," she said. "I don't like people looking at me at airports or department stores—a paraplegic around a dozen astronauts on a space station? I don't know . . ."

"Well, just think, Casey—the last things you need in space are legs, right?" Brad said. "You'll be just like everyone else up there. No wheelchairs in space, lady."

She looked down at her wheelchair, her eyes averted, for a long moment . . . and then her head and arms snapped up and she shouted, *"I'm going into space!"*

The team went through a dry run of the test-fire procedures until late in the afternoon, then had a meeting with university president Harris and passed along the news of who was going to fly to Armstrong Space Station. Harris immediately scheduled the flight physicals for the next morning, after which he would make the announcement to the media. It wasn't until early evening that they were able to go home. Brad had just arrived at his apartment building in Poly Canyon and was about to carry his bike and backpack up the stairs when he heard, "Hey, stranger."

He turned and found Jodie, her laptop backpack in hand. "Hi, you," he said. "We're not strangers. I see you every day."

"I know, but only at school. We live in the same complex, but I hardly see you around here." She nodded toward Brad's bicycle. "Were you just going to carry your bike and backpack up five flights of stairs, mate?"

"I always do."

"Wow. Good onya." She glanced around him. "I noticed you don't carry the cane anymore."

"I just never replaced it."

"Won't Chief Ratel get mad at you?"

"He got hurt last spring, closed up shop, and moved away—to Florida, I think," Brad said. That was entirely true—afraid that the Russians would target him as well as Brad, Kevin Martindale had urged him to take his wife and get out of town, which he reluctantly did. "I should have let you know about that, but . . . you know how things were."

"Wow. I guess it's been a while since we've caught up," Jodie said. "So you don't go to the gym anymore?"

"Every now and then I'll do a self-defense refresher at a gym downtown," Brad said. That was mostly true, but it was every week, sparring with a member of Chris Wohl's team—and he would do firearms refresher training every other week. Brad had a permit that allowed him to carry a pistol on campus—he never told Jodie or anyone else on the Starfire team about that. "Most of the rest I do in my living room, on the bike, or doing stuff like carrying the bike up to my apartment."

"Great." They stood silent for a few long moments; then: "Hey, want to grab a cup of coffee before they close? My shout."

"Sure." They walked to the little coffee shop on the ground floor of the next apartment building and took their coffee outside. Late October was still ideal weather on California's central coast, although fall had definitely arrived. "Man, it's been a long day," Brad said after several minutes of silence. "Are you keeping up with your classes okay?"

"Mostly," Jodie said. "The profs are giving me a break until after the test firing."

"Same with me," Brad said.

They fell silent again for a few minutes, and then Jodie set her coffee down, looked at Brad directly, and said, "I apologize for my rant at the hotel in Battle

Mountain, mate. I guess I was shook up, and I took it out on you. You did protect us from the guy with the knife."

"Forget about it, Jodie," Brad said.

Jodie looked at her coffee, then at the tabletop. "Going up to the space station in just a couple days," she said in a low, halting voice, "made me realize that . . . what I mean is, if . . . if something went wrong, I . . . I'd never see you again, and I wouldn't have had a chance to apologize."

Brad reached over and took her hands in his. "It's okay, Jodie," he said. "Nothing's going to happen. It'll be a successful flight and test firing, and I'll fly back. It'll be an adventure. It already *has* been an adventure. I wish you were coming with me."

"Brad . . ." She squeezed his hands and lowered her head, and when she raised it again Brad could see the glistening in her eyes, even with just the light from the streetlights. "I'm . . . I'm scared, mate," she said, a slight catch in her voice. "I know how badly you want to fly in space, and I'm happy you got this opportunity, but I'm still scared."

Brad crossed over to a chair on Jodie's side of the table, put his arms around her, and held her tightly. When they parted, he lightly touched her face and kissed her. "Jodie . . . Jodie, I want—"

"Come with me," she whispered when the kiss ended. Her eyes opened wide and locked on to his, silently begging. "Mate, don't you dare bloody leave me alone again. Please, Brad. Take me before you leave me."

This time, in their next deep kiss, there was no hesitation in Brad McLanahan's mind whatsoever.

THE WHITE HOUSE SITUATION ROOM
WASHINGTON, D.C.

The next morning

"It's a good thing you decided to have me check other launch pads and spaceports, Mr. President," National Security Adviser William Glenbrook said after President Ken Phoenix and Vice President Ann Page entered the Situation Room and took seats. "The Russians have indeed been very busy."

"What did you find, Bill?" Phoenix asked, setting his coffee mug down, his second of the morning. His coffee intake had definitely risen as Election Day drew closer.

"A massive and rapid Russian outer-space rearming program under way, sir," Glenbrook said. He hit a button and the first photograph appeared on the screen at the front of the Situation Room, showing a rocket with a winged lifting-body aircraft on the very top, replacing the rocket's nose cone. "This is the Plesetsk spaceport in northwestern Russia. The spaceplane we observed when the ROS was undocked from the ISS was confirmed as an Elektron spaceplane, likely launched from Plesetsk.

"There is another spaceplane already on the launch pad there," Glenbrook went on, reading from the notes on his tablet computer, "and we believe these containers and this large storage facility near the launch pad is another Elektron and its Proton booster. We think it's a Proton and not an Angara-5 booster because of a lack of cryogenic oxygen storage nearby. The Angara-5 uses liquid oxygen and RP-1 kerosene, while the Proton uses hypergolic liquids: dimethylhydrazine and nitrogen tetroxide, two very toxic chemicals that burn when mixed, without need for an ignition source. The Angara-5 booster is more powerful, but its liquid oxygen needs to be replenished once it's aboard the booster because it boils off; the fuels in the Proton last almost indefinitely, so it can sit on the launch pad without needing service."

The photographs changed. "This is the Baikonur Cosmodrome in Kazakhstan," Glenbrook went on, "and as you can see, there appears to be another Elektron on a launch pad, on an Angara-5 booster this time. That's two that can be launched in fairly short order, maybe within days or even hours. The Elektron that was already launched when the ROS undocked from the ISS landed at the shuttle recovery airstrip at Baikonur yesterday. So we've accounted for possibly four Elektrons. We believe there are five in the inventory, although there might be more. So we set out to look for the fifth Russian spaceplane. It's nowhere to be seen in Russia . . ."

Glenbrook changed photos, and another picture of an Elektron spaceplane atop a large Russian rocket appeared. "We found it—not in Russia, but in the People's Republic of China," he said. "This is Xichang spaceport in western China. Xichang was used for the largest, most powerful, and most reliable Chinese Long March rocket launches, but all those missions moved to Wenchang spaceport on Hainan Island, so Xichang wasn't being used that much."

"So the Chinese are allowing Russian spaceplane launches from Chinese launch pads?" Ann remarked.

"Yes, ma'am," Glenbrook said. He zoomed in the photograph. "Not only that, but these buildings are identical to the buildings in Plesetsk. It's possible that these are buildings either housing or meant to house a second Elektron spaceplane launch system, and if so, that means there are possibly six Elektrons out there, and there may be more. We're watching all these sites for future launches and recoveries, but based on our intelligence when those things were first deployed, the Russians can relaunch a spaceplane every ten to fourteen days after recovery. That is extraordinarily fast. It could be faster now."

He stayed with the Chinese photograph but zoomed in on a different area. "Here's another interesting development." He highlighted some objects with a laser pen. "The Russians usually install sophisticated S-400 Triumph surface-to-air antiaircraft missiles at all their spaceports and at major military bases," he said, "but here we're looking at the S-500S, the world's most sophisticated surface-to-air missile, several times more capable and powerful than the S-400 or even our own PAC-3 Patriot. An S-500S is more akin to a medium-range ballistic missile than a regular surface-to-air missile, designed for extreme long-range air and space attack. This marks the first deployment of an S-500S outside of the Russian Federation, and the fact that it is on a Chinese military base is astounding—we assume that now the Chinese can access technical information on the best SAM system ever built.

"The 'S' model indicates that it is designed to be effective against space targets—specifically, American space stations, spacecraft, and weapon garages in low

Earth orbit, as well as ballistic missiles, low-flying cruise missiles, and stealth aircraft," Glenbrook went on. "We searched the known S-500 launch sites around Moscow and elsewhere, and our suspicions are confirmed: they're moving some S-500s normally placed around some of their cities and dispersing them to spaceports. We're also studying the Almaz-Antney production facilities near Moscow and St. Petersburg to see if there's any evidence that the Russians are upping their S-500 production. We anticipate they will quadruple S-500S production very shortly, and every Russian military installation in the entire world will have at least one S-500S battery assigned to it."

"Looks to me like they're preparing not just for operations in space, but to fight off another assault on their isolated bases," Ann said. She and Phoenix exchanged knowing glances—the last American attack on a foreign military base from the air was the B-1B Lancer bomber raid on military targets in the People's Republic of China, led by Patrick McLanahan, whom everyone thought perished in the attack.

"So the intel guys thought as long as we're looking at other antispacecraft weapons that the Russians or Chinese are deploying, they'd look for fighter-launched antispacecraft missiles," Glenbrook said. "There are three known bases for the Mikoyan-Gurevich 31D aircraft, which carries the Russians' frontline anti-aircraft and antisatellite missile. We counted a bit more than their usual observed number, and we also counted more Ilyushin-76 aerial refueling tankers at each base. All of the bases are active, and the Russians fly patrols around the clock—at least two antisatellite flights are airborne twenty-four/seven. The bases at Petropavlovsk-Kamchatsky, Yelizovo Air Base, in the Russian Far East, Bolshoye Savino Airport in west-central Russia, and Chkalovsky Air Base near Moscow are particularly active. They fly patrols and do many training mock launches, zooming the fighters almost straight up to very high altitudes.

"The MiG-31 has been out of production for almost forty years, but it has some upgrades," Glenbrook went on. "The plane itself is one of the fastest in the world. Carrying the ASAT missile turns it into a sluggish pig, but the system still works. It fires one modified 9K720 missile, the same as on the latest model of the Iskander theater ballistic missile, but with a millimeter radar-guided warhead with a high-explosive warhead for outer-space operations. There are about a hundred of the D-models in service—maybe more, if they are converting other models into antispacecraft models, or taking some out of storage." He closed the cover on his tablet, signifying that his briefing was over.

"So it appears the Russians are responding to my space initiative by gearing up their space forces, and the Chinese are assisting them, at least with launch pads and support," President Phoenix summarized. "Thoughts?"

"Not unexpected," Ann said. "We've seen all of that stuff in action over the past several years, except the spaceplanes."

"We have to assume they'll arm those Elektron spaceplanes the same as they did back fourteen years ago," Glenbrook said. "They carried ten laser-guided hypervelocity missiles. No warhead, but a warhead is unnecessary—if an object hits the station or a satellite traveling several miles a second, it will definitely cripple it, and most likely destroy it. And the land-based missiles could very well carry a micronuclear warhead as well, the same used in the American Holocaust attacks, which, if it explodes within a mile of the station, could blow it right into oblivion. Even if it missed by more than that, the radiation and electromagnetic pulse would probably severely damage the station."

"Our spacecraft are pretty well shielded against radiation, Bill, especially our manned spacecraft—they operate in cosmic radiation for years, sometimes decades," Ann said. "But any kinetic weapon directed against the station is a serious danger."

"The station has defensive weapons it can use, yes?" the president asked. "I got the tour of the command center on Armstrong. They said they could activate the big laser, Skybolt, in a matter of days, and they talked about a smaller chemical laser they could use, but the orbiting weapon garages are not active."

"That's correct, sir, after the Starfire experimental stuff is removed," Ann said. "Perhaps we should activate the Kingfisher weapon garages and place the inactive ones back in orbit."

"I'm not quite ready to do that yet, Ann," Phoenix said, "but I want to be ready in case we detect any movements toward our space assets, especially Armstrong. The rockets and air bases with those antisatellite MiGs can be targeted by sea-launched ballistic or cruise missiles, correct?"

"Yes, sir," Glenbrook replied, "but it will take time to move a sub in position, and an attack by Russia against Armstrong Space Station can happen very quickly. If Russia can overwhelm the station's defenses, they could knock it out of the sky. A combination of an Elektron spaceplane attack, air-launched missiles, and ground-launched antisatellite missiles all attacking at once could do just that."

The president nodded but remained silent for several long moments; then: "Let's give diplomacy and cooler heads a chance before we activate any more space weapons," he said finally. "Knocking down Armstrong would be like attacking an aircraft carrier or a military base: an act of war. Gryzlov's not that crazy."

"Russia has done both in the past, sir," Ann reminded the president. "Gennadiy's father was the master of the sneak attack against the United States in the American Holocaust, with almost ten times more casualties than Pearl Harbor."

"I know that, Ann, but I'm still not prepared to escalate this situation if I can avoid it," Phoenix said. "I'll authorize use of all defensive weapons currently deployed, including the chemical laser, but no offensive weapons."

"May I suggest we activate the magnetohydrodynamic generator on board Armstrong Space Station, sir?" Ann asked. Ann Page was the designer and builder not only of the Skybolt missile defense system but also of one of its many high-tech features: the MHD, or magnetohydrodynamic generator, a nuclear-powered device that produced hundreds of megawatts of power for the Skybolt free-electron laser without disrupting Armstrong Space Station's attitude controls or orbital path. "It's been in virtual mothballs for a couple years, and it will take a day or two to power it up and test it. If things do turn nasty it would be good to have Skybolt available as soon as possible."

"You're talking about the generator that powers the big Skybolt laser?" Phoenix asked. Ann nodded. "I know we never ratified the treaty banning offensive space weapons, but we've been acting as if the treaty is in force. Would this violate the treaty?"

Ann thought for a moment, then shrugged. "I'm no arms-control expert or lawyer, sir, but to me a power generator is not a weapon, even if it is pumped with a nuclear reactor. Skybolt is the weapon, and some of its components are being used by those Cal Poly students to fire electricity down to Earth." She hesitated, then added, "They could provide us some diplomatic security, should the need arise, sir."

"They're not going to use the big generator, are they? I never authorized that."

"The microwave-laser beam in Starfire is powered by the energy collected by the students' solar cells," Ann explained. "The MHD generator is still physically hooked up to Skybolt, but the free-electron laser cannot be fired without disconnecting the Starfire components and plugging the Skybolt parts back in place. I have no idea how long that would take, but the students got Starfire bolted into place pretty quickly, so if it's needed I think we can get Skybolt back online fairly quickly."

The president thought about it for a few moments, then nodded assent. "As long as the big ship-killing laser isn't operable without my order, I'll authorize the generator to be activated and tested," he said. "I think we'll hold off advising the Russians that we tested the big generator until sometime in the near future."

"I agree," Ann said. "But if you want to deal with the Russians, you may have to reverse yourself on your space policies and military drawdowns. Do away with declaring occupied orbits sovereign American possessions, for example—Gryzlov seemed particularly peeved at that one."

"I will if I need to—hopefully not before the elections, though," the president said. "That's more ammunition for Barbeau."

"We could leak the information Bill just briefed us on," Ann said. "If we show Russia's space-weapon buildup, your space policy looks like a legitimate national defense imperative."

"But Barbeau could say that Russia is just responding to my space initiative," the president said. "I'd rather not go down that road. I'll consider toning down my policies, especially regarding the defense of our space assets and orbits— You're right, I think that's the part that got Gryzlov hot and bothered. Hopefully it can wait until after the election." He turned to his national security adviser. "Bill, I need to know exactly how long it would take to deploy those Kingfisher weapon garages, and I want to put as many of those spaceplane boosters under our crosshairs as possible. I don't want any forces moved, but I want to know how long it will take to take out anything that threatens our space assets. I remember we had a whole array of space-launched weapons at one time—I want to find out what Joe Gardner did with them."

"Yes, sir," Glenbrook said, and departed.

After he left, the president poured himself his third cup of coffee of the morning—that, he thought, was not a good sign. "I hate interjecting politics into these decisions, Ann," he said. "That's not the way it's supposed to be done."

"Maybe not, but that's life in the real world, Ken," Ann said. "The president of the United States probably can never divorce himself from politics, especially around election time. That's just the way it is."

"Then let's get back to the campaign, Ann," Phoenix said. "What's on the agenda for today?"

"You have the day off, and I suggest you spend it with your family, because you'll be on the campaign trail almost every day until Election Day," the vice president said. "The final West Coast swing starts tomorrow morning. We have Phoenix, San Diego, and

Los Angeles booked, but the campaign staff suggested a few stops in northern and central California too. It's late—the FAA likes to have more than two days for notification to close down the airspace around the airports you fly into for Air Force One—but if we notify them this morning it should be okay.

"I suggest three stops before we hit Portland and Seattle," Ann went on, reading from her tablet computer. "First, the NASA Ames Research Center near San Jose, which is doing wind-tunnel tests on a variety of space technologies; the Aerojet Rocketdyne facility east of Sacramento, which is building the motors for a new class of heavy-lift boosters; and San Luis Obispo to attend the test firing of the Starfire solar orbiting power plant. There's one meet-and-greet in each city and one fund-raising dinner in San Jose. After that, it's on to Portland and Seattle, a memorial service at the former Fairchild Air Force Base near Spokane for the American Holocaust anniversary memorial, and then Boise to wrap up the West Coast. Then you work your way eastward. Three cities a day until Election Day. I'll make a few stops on the East Coast, and then I'll head out west when you come east."

"Whew," the president said. "I'm glad this will be my last campaign—it's exciting to meet the folks, but it sure takes it out of you." He thought about the change in plans, but not for long: "Go ahead and add the Northern California stops, Ann. I'll rest when I'm dead."

"Yes, sir," the vice president said, and she picked up a phone and alerted her staff to make the necessary arrangements. When she finished, she asked, "Before we alert the FAA, sir, I have a question: Do you want to postpone that orbiting solar-power-plant test firing and that trip up to the station by Brad McLanahan and Casey Huggins, the college students from California? It's starting to get tense with space issues, and that test firing is receiving an awful lot of attention around the world. A lot of folks, including the Russians and a bunch of antiwar and environmentalist groups, want that test canceled and the space station to be allowed to burn up in the atmosphere."

"I read about those protests," the president said, shaking his head. "It seems to be more of the same stuff we've heard from far-left liberals for decades: technology advancements are just plain bad for humans, animals, world peace, the poor, and the planet. Armstrong especially gets a lot of negative press, mostly I think because it's so noticeable in the sky, and the left thinks we are spying on everyone on Earth and ready to use a death ray to gun anyone down. They have no idea what they do on Armstrong Space Station. I can talk until I'm blue in the face about my experience and the technology that made it possible, but I'd be wasting my breath."

Ken Phoenix thought about it for a moment, then shook his head. "Ann, I'm not stopping my space technology and industrialization initiative because the Russians or some left-wing wackos think this is the beginning of the end of the planet," he said. "Let's try to anticipate and prepare for what these groups or even the Russians might do after that test firing, but I'm not going to cancel it. That would be an insult to the hard work those students put into this project. It's a peaceful project: sending energy to someone who needs it almost anywhere in the world. That's a good thing. The left can say whatever else they want about it, but that's what it is. No, we press forward."

SAN LUIS OBISPO REGIONAL AIRPORT

That evening

Brad was seated at a desk in an aircraft hangar at San Luis Obispo Regional Airport, watching the progress on his computer as the latest navigation, charts, terrain, and obstacle data were being broadcast via satellite directly to his father's Cessna P210 Silver Eagle aircraft parked behind him. The Silver Eagle was a small but extremely powerful Cessna P210 modified with a 450-horsepower turbine engine, plus a long list of high-tech avionics and other systems, making the thirty-year-old plane one of the most advanced anywhere in the world.

His cell phone beeped, and he looked at the caller ID, not surprised to not recognize it—he had been answering so many media requests that he just answered without screening: "Hello. This is Brad, Project Starfire."

"Mr. McLanahan? My name is Yvette Annikki Svärd of the *European Space Daily*. We spoke briefly at your press conference in your laboratory a few days ago."

He didn't recognize the name, but he sure recognized the sultry accent. "I don't think I caught your name at the press conference," Brad said, "but I remember seeing it on the media list. How are you this evening?"

"Very well, thank you, Mr. McLanahan."

"Brad, please."

"Thank you, Brad," Yvette said. "I have just returned to San Luis Obispo to attend your congratulatory party tonight and to observe the test firing of Starfire, and I had a few follow-up questions for you. Are you still in town?"

"Yes. But I leave for Battle Mountain early in the morning."

"Oh, of course, the flight to Armstrong Space Station aboard the Midnight spaceplane. Congratulations."

"Thank you." Damn, that voice was mesmerizing, Brad thought.

"I do not wish to disturb you, but if you are available I would very much like to ask some questions and get your thoughts about flying to the space station," Yvette said. "I can be on campus in a few minutes."

"I'm not on campus," Brad said. "I'm preflighting my airplane, getting ready to fly to Battle Mountain."

"You have your own plane, Brad?"

"It was my dad's. I fly it every chance I get."

"How exciting! I love the freedom of flying. It is so wonderful, being able to hop into your own plane and go somewhere on a moment's notice."

"It sure is," Brad said. "Are you a pilot?"

"I have only a European Light-Sport Aircraft pilot's license," Yvette said. "I could not fly from San Luis Obispo to Battle Mountain. I suppose that is a very easy trip in your plane."

"Driving takes about nine hours," Brad said. "I can do it in a little over two."

"Wonderful. It must be a very nice plane."

"Would you like to see it?"

"I do not want to impose on you, Brad," Yvette said. "You have a very big few days coming up, and I have only a few questions."

"It's no problem," Brad said. "Go south on Broad Street, right turn on Airport Road, and stop at the gate that's marked 'General Aviation' on the left. I'll come out and open it for you."

"Well . . . I would love to see your plane, but I do not wish to disturb you."

"Not at all. I'm just waiting for the plane to update itself. The company would be nice."

"Well, in that case, I would be happy to join you," Yvette said. "I can be there in about ten minutes. I am driving a rented white Volvo."

Ten minutes later on the dot, a white Volvo sedan pulled up to the terminal building. Brad stepped through the walk-through gate and swiped his access card on the reader, and the drive-through gate began to open. He jumped on his bike and headed back to his hangar, with the Volvo not far behind.

Brad had left the bifold hangar door open and the inside lights on, so Yvette could see the Silver Eagle as soon as she pulled up. "Nice to see you again, Brad," she said as she emerged from the car. She shook his hand, then offered him a business card. "I hope you remember me?"

"Yes, I certainly do," Brad said. Damn, he remarked to himself, she's even hotter than last time. He turned and motioned to the plane. "There she is."

"It is beautiful!" Yvette remarked. "It looks like you keep it in immaculate condition."

"I still consider it my dad's plane, so I work on it every chance I get and clean it up after every flight," Brad said.

"Your father was such a great man," Yvette said. "I am so sorry for your loss."

Brad always had to remember to play along with these sentiments offered to him all the time from the media—it was tough, but he was getting better and better at playacting that his father was indeed dead. "Thank you," he replied.

Yvette stepped inside the hangar and began admiring the plane. "So. Tell me about your sexy plane, Brad McLanahan."

"It is called a Silver Eagle, a Cessna P210 Centurion which had its 310-horsepower piston gasoline engine replaced with a 450-horsepower jet-fuel turboprop engine," Brad said. "It has a bunch of other mods to it as well. About two hundred and fifty miles per hour cruise speed, a thousand miles range, twenty-three-thousand-foot ceiling."

"Ooo." She gave Brad a naughty smile and said, "That would make it eligible for the four-mile-high club, not just the mile-high club, yes?" Brad tried to chuckle at her quip, but it just came out as a crude snort as he distracted himself thinking about how in the world he could manage to join that club in the cockpit of a Silver Eagle. "And you said the plane was updating itself?"

"Updates are broadcast by satellite," Brad said, shaking himself loose from his fantasizing. "When they're needed, I just plug the airplane into external power, turn it on, and wait."

"That does not sound like a normal way of updating avionics and databases."

"This plane has a few upgrades that are not yet available to the rest of the general aviation community," Brad said. "My dad used his plane as a test bed for a lot of high-tech stuff." He pointed to a tiny ball mounted midway along the underside of the right wing. "He used this plane for surveillance missions with the Civil Air Patrol years ago, so he had those sensors mounted on the wings. They're about the size of tennis balls, but they can scan twenty acres a second day or night on both sides of the aircraft with six-inch resolution. The images are broadcast to ground receivers, or they can play on the multifunction displays in the cockpit, with flight or navigation information superimposed on it. I've made several landings in pitch-black with no lights using that sensor."

"I've never heard of that before with a sensor so small," Yvette said.

"I can do stuff on this plane that won't be available to the public for at least five years, and maybe ten," Brad said. "Completely automated clearances, air-traffic-control advisories, automated flight planning and rerouting, voice-actuated avionics, lots of stuff."

"Can I write about this, Brad?" Yvette asked. "Can I tell my readers about this?"

Brad thought for a moment, then shrugged. "I don't see why not," he said. "It's not classified top secret or anything—it's just not available to general aviation yet. It's all been approved by the feds, but it's not yet being manufactured or offered for sale."

"But it represents the future of general aviation," Yvette said. "I am sure my readers would love to read about this. May I get copies of the Supplemental Type Certificates and approvals for these wonderful systems?"

"Sure—it's all public information," Brad said. "After I get back, I can collect all that stuff for you."

"Thank you so much," Yvette said. "I can see I must make another visit to San Luis Obispo after your return . . ." She fixed her eyes on his and gave him a mischievous little smile. "Not just so you can tell me about your trip into space but to tell me more about your fascinating plane. May I take a peek inside the four-mile-high-club headquarters?"

"Sure," Brad said. He opened the entry door for her, then glanced at her business card while she admired the interior—and yes, admired a peek at her exquisite ass that was shaking at him as she looked inside the plane. "You're based in San Francisco? That's an easy flight too. Maybe I could pick you up in San Carlos, we can do a test flight, and maybe have lunch in Half Moon Bay?"

"That sounds wonderful, Brad," Yvette said.

"Yvette. Pretty name," Brad added.

"Thank you. French mother and Swedish father." She turned to him. "You are very generous with your— Oh!" Brad turned to where she was looking and was surprised to find Chris Wohl standing just a few feet away, his hands in his jacket pockets. "Hello, sir. May we help you?"

"He's a friend of mine," Brad said. "Yvette, meet Chris. Chris, Yvette, a reporter from the *European Space Daily.*" The two looked directly at each other. "What's going on, Chris?"

Wohl remained silent for a few long moments, looking at Yvette; then: "There's a few necessary items we have to cover before you depart, if you got a minute."

"Sure," Brad said, blinking in surprise. Something was going on here—why didn't Brad detect it . . . ? "Yvette, will you—"

"I have taken up enough of your time, Brad," Yvette said. "I can e-mail you the questions I have. If you have time before takeoff, please reply; otherwise, they can wait until we meet again after your trip." She extended a hand, and Brad took it, and then Yvette leaned forward and gave him a kiss on his cheek. "Good luck with your flight and the test firing. I hope you have a safe trip and much success." She then extended her hand to Wohl. "Nice to meet you, Chris," she said. After a few rather awkward heartbeats, Wohl slowly took his right hand out of his pocket and shook her hand, never taking his eyes off hers. Yvette smiled and nodded, gave Brad another warm smile, entered her car, and drove off.

When she was out of sight, Brad whirled toward Wohl. "What's going on, Sergeant Major? You gave the warning code-phrase 'necessary items.' What's happening?"

"Who is she?" Wohl asked in a low, menacing voice.

"A reporter for the *European Space Daily*, an aerospace blog based in Austria." Brad gave him Yvette's business card. "I've spoken to her before, at a press conference."

"Did you check her out before inviting her out here to meet with you one-on-one?"

"No, but she was cleared by the university and given press credentials and access to the campus," Brad replied, carefully studying Wohl, who looked genuinely worried about that encounter.

"A chimpanzee can get press credentials and campus access with enough bananas, Trigger," Wohl said, using Brad's new call sign, given to him after the shoot-out in Paso Robles—he didn't know if it referred to the shoot-out or to the fact that he was a horse's ass. "You didn't check her out, but you invited her out to your hangar, at night, alone?"

"Dad checking in on me," Brad said. He had forgotten that his father could access the security cameras in the hangar and monitor his cell-phone calls, and realized that Patrick had undoubtedly called whoever was closest to head out to the airport immediately and check out the reporter.

"Probably saved your ass, Trigger," Wohl said.

"All right, all right, I violated standard security and countersurveillance procedures," Brad said. "You and your team have been in town for months without one alert, one warning. Now why suddenly the warning code-phrase? How do you know she's a threat?"

"I don't know for sure—yet—but I have a very strong suspicion, and that's all I need," Wohl said. For the very first time since Brad had been working with Chris Wohl, he saw the big retired sergeant major hesitate, as if he was . . . *embarrassed?* Chris Wohl, retired sergeant major of the U.S. Marine Corps, caring what the hell anyone thought of him . . . ?

"What the hell, Sergeant Major?" Brad said.

"I get a standard and . . . expected response from persons when I first encounter them, especially . . . especially women," Wohl said.

"Let me guess: they recoil in abject gut-wrenching horror at the very sight of your radiation burns," Brad deadpanned. "Pretty much the same reaction I had when I first saw you."

"With all due respect, Trigger: fuck you," Wohl said. *That,* Brad thought, was the real Chris Wohl he knew. "You didn't notice it with your friend Yvette, did you? You've been lax in your countersurveillance tactics, haven't you?"

"What in hell are you talking about, Sergeant Major?"

"Did you see the reaction from your friend Yvette when she saw me?" Wohl asked.

"Yes. She was . . . surprised. A little." But Brad was thinking back and reevaluating his response. "And nice."

"You think so, Trigger?" Wohl asked.

"I . . ." Brad paused. Boy, he thought, I completely missed something that has the big ex-Marine concerned, maybe even . . . scared? He thought hard, then said, "She was actually very collected. True, she didn't react in shock or surprise to you, like I've seen even grown men do. But she was polite."

"Polite, yes," Wohl said. "What else? What was she really going for, being nice to the ugly weird-looking stranger that had suddenly appeared right behind her that she didn't expect? What else was she computing, Trigger?"

"She . . ." Brad's mind was racing, trying to catch up with the things that Chris Wohl obviously had already divined way earlier, the things he himself should have discerned if he hadn't been distracted by outside— meaning sexual—factors. "She . . . she was trying to decide how she was going to . . . to deal with you," Brad said finally.

" 'Deal' with me?"

Brad hesitated again, but the answer was painfully obvious: "Eliminate you," he corrected himself. Holy fucking shit, Brad thought, his eyes bugged out, shaking his head in disbelief. "She was after my ass, but you came along and surprised her, and she didn't know what to do," he said. "She had to make a last-second decision about whether to attack or withdraw, and she decided to withdraw. Oh, *shit . . . !*"

"Finally, you're thinking tactically," Wohl said. "You think that you if spend a few months with nothing happening that you are safe? You couldn't be more wrong. Time always favors the patient hunter. It gives the enemy more time to do surveillance, plan, replan, and execute. You think that since the bad guys haven't attacked in six months they've given up? Wrong. Moreover, you can't *afford* to be more wrong." Wohl frowned, deepening the lines in his face even more. "Tell me, Trigger: Will you ever see your friend again?"

"Sure—when she's done stalking me and closes in for the kill," Brad said. "But as a reporter? No way. She's going to dive deep underground."

"Exactly," Wohl said. "She's not done hunting, but you won't see her interviewing anyone ever again, at least not in North America." He looked around at the gathering darkness. "She had several opportunities to take you down out here at the airport from a distance, without being seen by security guards or cameras, and she didn't take them. What does that tell you, Trigger?"

"That she doesn't want to do it from a distance," Brad said. "She prefers to do it up close."

"What else?"

Brad thought for a moment; then: "She's not afraid of being photographed. She believes she can escape, or she has a network behind her that she's confident can get her out."

"Or both," Wohl said. He looked at the business card. "*Svärd.* Swedish for 'sword.' She picked that cover name for a reason, I'll bet." Brad swallowed hard at that. "She's pretty brazen, that's for sure: she picked a cover that puts her in rooms with lots of cameras and microphones, and she's not afraid to dress in a way that calls attention to herself—exactly the opposite of what is taught. She's either really stupid, or a very talented assassin. She's definitely a cool cucumber. I'll bet there are lots of pictures of her. I'll have the team start tracking her down." He thought for a moment. "Huggins is already in Battle Mountain, yes?"

"Casey had to go early so they could fit a space suit for her," Brad said.

"How's the weather between here and Battle Mountain for tonight?"

"Clouds over the Sierra, maybe a little turbulence over the summit, but okay otherwise."

"You had something planned for tonight back on campus, yes?"

"The college of engineering was going to throw a little party for the Starfire team."

"Something came up, and you had to report early to Battle Mountain to prepare for the flight to the space station," Wohl said. "Make your apologies later. Your new friend Yvette was invited to that party, yes?" Brad said nothing, but the realization was clear on his face. "If I was brazen enough to try again on the same day, that's where I'd lie in wait. You're not going back to that campus." He got no argument from Brad—who knew how close he had come to being the woman's next victim, if she was indeed who they thought she was. "Do your preflight, then get going as soon as you can. I'll wait here until you're airborne."

Brad nodded and stepped inside the hangar. But before beginning his preflight, he turned to the security camera up in the corner and said, "Thanks, Dad."

Seconds later, he received a text on his smartphone. It read, *You're welcome, son. Fly safe.*

OVER CENTRAL NEW MEXICO

The next day

"Pressure disconnect," Boomer announced. Brad McLanahan pulled off some power and let the S-19 Midnight spaceplane slip back into precontact position behind and underneath the Sky Masters Aerospace's B-767 aerial refueling tanker. The refueling boom retracted back up underneath the tanker's tail.

"Showing you clear, Midnight Seven," the computerized female voice of the robotic boom operator said. *"Is there anything else we can do for you, Seven?"*

"A cup of coffee would be nice," Boomer said, "but failing that, we'll say adios."

The 767 tanker started a steep left turn. *"Masters Three-One is clear, Seven,"* the voice said. *"Have a nice day."*

Boomer raised the visor on his Electronic Elastomeric Activity Suit's oxygen helmet, observed the Midnight spaceplane's computers run the "After Refueling" and "Before Hypersonic Flight" checklists, then looked over at Brad in the mission commander's seat. Brad was wearing an ACES orange partial-pressure space suit and helmet; his gloved hands were on the sidestick controller and throttles on the center console, and he was comfortably seated, staring straight ahead as if he was watching TV on the sofa. Brad raised the visor on his helmet when he noticed Boomer had done so.

"You know, Brad, you're the second passenger in a row that I've had that has watered my eyes."

"Say again?" Brad said.

"First President Phoenix, and now you: both you guys are acting as if you've been astronauts for years," Boomer said. "You fly the spaceplane like a pro. You look totally at home."

"It's really not that much different than the B-1B bomber, Boomer," Brad said. Sky Masters Aerospace under Patrick McLanahan had refurbished a number of retired B-1B Lancer bombers and returned them to service, and Brad had trained to ferry the planes from Battle Mountain to Guam to counter the People's Republic of China's aggressive moves against its neighbors in the South China Sea. "It's a lot sprightlier at higher airspeeds, but subsonic it handles very much like the Bone, and the sight picture at the contact position under the tanker is almost exactly like the B-1."

"Well, I'm impressed," Boomer said. "You've been hand-flying it for almost the entire flight, and from the right seat no less, and wearing a space suit and bulky space-suit gloves to boot. Ready for the next step?"

"You bet I am, Boomer," Brad said.

"I'll just bet you are," Boomer said. "Now, up until now the worst G-load you've pulled was about two, but now it's going to get a little more intense. We'll only pull about four Gs maximum, but you'll feel them for a longer period of time. I'll let you hand-fly it, but if the Gs get to be too much, let me know and I'll let George the autopilot fly it. Remember the weight of your fingers will be almost a pound each. Don't try to tough it out—say something and I'll turn the autopilot on."

"I will, Boomer."

"Good. Casey?"

"Yes, Boomer?" Casey Huggins replied. She was in the spaceplane's passenger module in the cargo bay with Jessica "Gonzo" Faulkner. Casey was wearing her partial-pressure space suit with her visor closed; Gonzo was wearing her skintight EEAS.

"Remember what we told you about the G-forces," Boomer said. "If you've been on a roller coaster before, you've felt pressure like you're going to feel, only it'll last longer. Your seat will help you stay ahead of the pressure. Ready?"

"I'm ready, Boomer."

"Gonzo?"

"Ready."

"Brad?"

"I'm ready."

"Then prepare for some fun, mission commander," Boomer said to Brad. "You've got your flight director in front of you. I've got your throttles. Keep the flight director centered, just as if you were flying an instrument-landing-system cue. We'll start out at around twelve degrees nose up, but as the speed picks up it'll go higher. Like you said, the S-19 likes to go fast, so it'll feel very light on the controls the faster it gets until we're above the atmosphere and the control sticks switch to reaction-control mode, and then it'll be kind of a pig. I show us at the insertion window now. Checklists are complete. Here we go."

Boomer slowly advanced the throttles. Brad forced himself to remain calm as he felt the acceleration and the G-forces starting to build. He saw the flight-director wings move upward, and he pulled back on the controller a little too hard, and the wings dropped down, meaning their nose was too high. "Nice and easy, Brad. She's slippery. Light touches on the controls." Brad relaxed his grip on the controller and gently guided the flight-director wings onto the pyramid. "There you go," Boomer said. "Don't anticipate. Nice easy inputs."

The Mach numbers were clicking off very rapidly, and they transitioned from turbofan to scramjet mode faster than Brad could have imagined. "Sixty-two miles up, Brad and Casey—congratulations, you are American astronauts," Boomer said. "How's everybody doing?"

"Pretty . . . good," Casey said, obviously straining through the G-forces. "How . . . much . . . longer?"

"A few more minutes, and then we'll switch to rocket mode," Boomer said. "The Gs will jump from three to four—a bit higher G-forces, but it won't last as long." He looked over at Brad, who hadn't moved much at all during the boost. "You doing okay over there, mission commander?"

"I'm doing okay, Boomer."

"You're doing great. You got some competition up here, Gonzo."

"I haven't had a vacation in a while—Brad can take my shifts," Gonzo said.

A few minutes later the scramjets fully spiked, and Boomer kicked the "leopards" into full rocket mode. He noticed a few more dips and swerves in the flight director, although Brad was still sitting straight and didn't look like he was moving a muscle. "Doing okay, Brad?"

"I . . . I think so . . ."

"Walk in the park," Boomer said. "Just don't think about the fact that if you slip or skid more than two degrees, you can send us tumbling and skipping off the atmosphere for two thousand miles until we break up and crash to Earth in little fiery pieces."

"Thanks . . . thanks, buddy," Brad grunted.

"Took your mind off the Gs, I see," Boomer said, "and your course has straightened out considerably." And at that moment the "leopards" shut down and the G-forces stopped. "See? No problem, and we're right on course. I'll flip George on so you can take a minute to relax and breathe normally again." For the first time in many hours, Brad took his hand off the controller and throttles. "It'll take us about half an hour to coast up to station."

Brad felt as if he'd just spent two hours getting beat up by Chris Wohl and his strike team in the gym. "Can we raise visors?" he asked.

Boomer checked the environmental readouts. "Yes, you can," he said. "Cabin pressure in the green, clear to raise visors. We'll let Brad rest up a minute—he's had a good little workout, hand-flying a spaceplane from zero to Mach twenty-five. After a couple minutes, I'll have him come back to the passenger module, and have Casey come up for docking. Nice and easy moving about the cabin, everyone."

Brad raised his visor, then found his squeeze bottle of water and took a deep squirt, being careful to keep his lips sealed around the tube and to squirt the water deeply into his mouth so the throat muscles could carry it into his stomach—gravity would no longer do that for him. That helped settle his stomach, but only a little. He put the water bottle away, then said, "Okay, Casey, I'm ready."

It took a lot of grunting, groaning, bumping, and helmet-knockers, but Brad finally managed to get out of his seat and over to the airlock. "Not bad for the first time, Brad," Boomer said, "but President Phoenix was better."

"Thanks again, buddy," Brad said. The zero Gs felt really weird—he almost preferred the positive Gs, he thought, even the crushing ones. He opened the airlock door, stepped through, and closed the cockpit hatch. "Hatch secure," he said.

"Checks up here," Boomer acknowledged.

The passenger-module door swung open, and Casey was right on the other side, floating horizontally like an orange-clad fairy, a huge grin on her face. "Isn't this wonderful, Brad?" she said. "Look at me! I feel like a cloud!"

"You look great, Casey," Brad said. I wish I felt the same, he thought. He backed away from the hatch to let Casey pass and was rewarded with a crash against the bulkhead, a few pings off the deck and ceiling while he tried to steady himself, and yet another head-knocker.

"Nice, easy movements, Brad," Gonzo told him. "Remember . . ."

"I know, I know: no gravity to stop me," Brad said.

"Watch Casey and you'll learn," Gonzo said with a smile.

"See ya, Brad," Casey said gaily. With barely perceptible touches along the bulkhead, she glided like a wraith into the airlock.

"Show-off," Brad murmured as he helped close the airlock hatch. He couldn't wait to get into his seat, fasten his safety belts and shoulder harness, and crank those straps down as hard as he could.

EIGHT

There are a lot of dark sides to success.
— ANITA RODDICK

**PLESETSK COSMODROME
ARKHANGELSK OBLAST,
NORTHWEST RUSSIAN FEDERATION**

That same time

"Tri . . . dva . . . odin . . . zapusk . . ." the launch-center master controller announced. The spaceplane shuddered, then shook, then rumbled as if it were going to shake itself to pieces, but then the cosmonaut felt the hold-down towers separate. The rumbling stopped, and very soon the G-forces started to build as the Angara-A7P booster began its ascent.

"Main thrusters at one hundred percent power, all systems nominal," reported the lone cosmonaut. Colonel Mikhail Galtin was the number one active cosmonaut in the Russian Federation and commander of the astronaut training corps at Star City near Moscow. He was a twenty-two-year veteran of the Soviet and Russian space corps, with four public trips to space, including the first transfer from one space station to another. He also had several flights into space with classified projects, including two military space stations based on Salyut-7 and Mir. But he was known in cosmonaut circles as a member of the design team, one of the first spaceplane pilots, and now the most experienced pilot of the Elektron spaceplane, the only spacecraft specifically designed as an attack plane—a space-borne fighter.

Galtin was a protégé of the then–Soviet Union's most gifted and skillful cosmonauts since Yuri Gagarin: General-Lieutenant Alesander Govorov, Colonel Andrei Kozhedub, and Colonel Yuri Livya. Govorov was the true pioneer, the father of the Soviet Union's Space Defense Force, the first military branch in the world dedicated to manned space operations in defense of the homeland. No military cosmonaut stepped aboard any spacecraft unless Govorov had done it first, even if it was just another copy of an Elektron or Salyut. Kozhedub and Livya were the "Red Barons" of the Soviet Union's Space Defense Force, Govorov's wingmen on attack missions, and feared adversaries in space or on Earth. Galtin was just a young trainee when these space giants had taken on the United States and Armstrong Space Station in combat.

The Elektron spacecraft occupied the top stage of the Angara booster, mounted vertically atop the booster with its tail and wings folded, within a protective shroud that would open after orbital insertion and allow the spaceplane to fly free. Although Galtin had plans for a two-seat version of Elektron, all of the spaceplanes now flying were single-seaters, and they were the only spacecraft in the world that flew just one passenger into space.

In less than ten minutes, Galtin was in orbit. He performed several functional checks of his Elektron spaceplane and its payload while he waited for his objective to come into range.

"Elektron One, this is Control," the mission controller radioed about two hours later. "Range to Kosmos-714 is inside one hundred kilometers."

"Acknowledged," Galtin said. He activated Elektron's radar, and a few seconds later found his objective. "Elektron One has radar contact." Kosmos-714 was an electronic eavesdropping satellite that had malfunctioned and had been in a decaying orbit for several years—it would make a perfect target. It was in a different orbit than Galtin's; their orbits would cross about five kilometers from each other at their closest point.

As was the case for any fighter pilot, it was necessary to do a little gunnery practice every now and then.

Galtin entered commands that opened the cargo-bay doors atop the fuselage and extended a large canister, called *Gvozd'* or "Hobnail," from its stowed and locked position. At fifty kilometers he entered commands into his autopilot that would take control of the Elektron's attitude thrusters and rotate the spacecraft to track the satellite as it passed by. The two spacecraft were converging at over thirty thousand kilometers per hour, but that wouldn't matter for this weapon.

At thirty kilometers' range he activated the weapon. Outside Elektron there was nothing to see, but on the radar screen Galtin noticed the bloom and shaky path of the target satellite on radar, and in seconds he noticed that there were multiple objects on radar now—the satellite had been broken apart.

Hobnail was a one-hundred-kilowatt, carbon-dioxide, electric-discharge coaxial laser. It had a maximum range of more than fifty kilometers, but even at that range the laser could burn through a centimeter of solid steel in seconds—the skin on Kosmos-714 was far thinner. The batteries for the laser allowed it to be fired for about thirty seconds maximum, no longer than five seconds per burst, which equated to about six to seven bursts depending on how long the laser was activated. That was about half the number of attacks as in the Elektron's current weapon, the Scimitar hypervelocity missiles, but Hobnail had much greater range and accuracy and could engage targets in any direction, even targets crossing at very high speeds. That was Hobnail's first successful test in space, although the laser had been used successfully in a laboratory for many years. Every Elektron spaceplane would eventually get one, as would the Russian Orbital Section, the Russian-built segment of the International Space Station that had recently been separated from the ISS.

Galtin entered commands into his computer to stow the Hobnail back into the cargo bay and deactivate his attack radar. He would not begin his deorbit for another seven hours, but there was one more task to accomplish.

Three hours later, he reactivated the radar, and there it was, exactly where it was supposed to be, just thirty kilometers away, well within range of Hobnail: Armstrong, the American military space station. It was at a much higher altitude and in a completely different orbit—there was never any danger of a collision—but surely the Americans would squawk about a deliberate flyby like this.

Too bad, Galtin thought happily. Space does not belong to the United States. And, if necessary, it will become a battleground once again.

ARMSTRONG SPACE STATION
The next day

"Oh my God, I can't believe what I'm seeing!" Jodie Cavendish exclaimed when the monitor came to life. A round of applause broke out behind her from the spectators who had been cleared by the American Secret Service to watch the test firing—they were expecting the president of the United States to arrive in a couple hours. What they saw were Brad McLanahan and Casey Huggins, both wearing blue flight suits with patches of Armstrong Space Station and Project Starfire, floating in free fall at a console. Behind them were Kai Raydon and Valerie Lukas. "You made it! You made it!"

"Hi, Jodie; hi, Jerry; hi, Lane," Brad said. "Greetings from Armstrong Space Station!"

"I just can't believe what I'm seeing," Jodie said, tears of joy streaming down her cheeks. "I never would have believed this would ever happen, mates."

"You guys look great," Lane said. "How was the spaceplane trip?"

"Awesome, Lane," Brad replied. "The G-forces weren't as bad as I was expecting."

"Speak for yourself, buster," Casey said. It was so strange to see the young woman floating in zero-G with legs extended underneath her, exactly like every other astronaut—it was almost jarring *not* to see her in a wheelchair. "I thought I was going to be squished inside out."

"You guys feeling okay?"

"Not bad," Brad said.

"He was puking his guts out," Casey said with a giggle.

"Just twice," Brad said. "I got a shot, and I'm feeling okay now."

"I get dizzy every now and then, but I'm feeling great, Lane," Casey said. "I still have my barf bag handy, though."

"We heard you got to fly the spaceplane and even dock it on the station," Lane said. "How cool! How was it?"

"I had a few shaky moments, but it went great," Brad said. "I wish Boomer the pilot was here, but he had to take the spaceplane to the International Space Station—since the Russians disconnected their service module, they can't make as much water and oxygen as before, so some techs have to leave. How's everything looking from down there, Jodie?"

"Apples, Brad," Jodie replied. "However, we're still getting that intermittent fault on the lithium-ion capacitor output relay, the same one we've been working on for a couple weeks now."

"Is Jerry up on the channel with us?"

"He's meeting with his team on a video teleconference to try to come up with a solution," Jodie said. "He's thinking it's a temperature issue—he says when the station is in sunlight the relay works fine, but then when they go into shadows the problem sometimes crops up."

"Unfortunately, that means a spacewalk to change out the relay or its temperature-control unit," Kai Raydon said. "That could take a day or two."

"It won't affect our positioning with the rectenna, will it, sir?" Brad asked.

"A delay will degrade the test a little, depending on how many days it takes for the fix," Kai said. "We moved Armstrong into what is called a sun-synchronous orbit for this test, which means we pass over the same spot on Earth—the rectenna site at the White Sand Missile Test Range—at the same mean solar time every day. But because our altitude is lower, we move a few degrees away from the ideal spot every day, so our time within view of the rectenna will get shorter and shorter, all the way down to less than a minute. The situation reverses itself eventually, but it takes twenty-four days to get back to the ideal position. We're in that ideal time right now, with the maximum exposure available at the target's latitude. We just have to hope the relay works when it's time to open fire."

"God, it had better," Jodie said, patting her laptop. "C'mon, baby, you can do it."

"It might be a little embarrassing if it won't fire, with the president due to observe the test," Brad said. "Is there something else we can try?" He looked around the command center and noticed the empty control console for the Skybolt laser. "What about Skybolt?" he asked.

"Skybolt is a free-electron laser, Brad," Kai said. "It's been deactivated so we could install your microwave cavity."

"What about Skybolt's power source, the magneto-hydrodynamic generator?" Brad asked.

"You mean, use power from the MHD instead of the solar energy you've collected?" Valerie Lukas asked with a hint of a smile. "Wouldn't that be like cheating?"

"We've been collecting power with the nantennas and storing electricity in the capacitors, Sergeant, so we know all that works," Brad said, "and we've done discharge tests on the microwave cavity, so we know we can produce maser energy. All we need to do now to validate the project is hit the rectenna with a maser and have it produce electricity on the ground. Maybe we can do that with the MHD instead of the energy in the capacitors that we can't get to."

Valerie turned to Kai and shrugged. "We did get permission to activate the MHD and test it," she said. "We've run several full-power tests on it." To Casey, she asked, "What sort of power do you need, Casey?"

"We were planning on sending five hundred kilo-watts per minute through the microwave cavity," Casey replied.

Valerie shrugged again. "We've done ten times that amount, but for much shorter periods of time," she said. "But I don't doubt the MHD can do it. We'll have to watch the heat levels in your microwave generator and in Skybolt's magnetic reflectors, collimator, and electrical assemblies, but we've already determined that the Skybolt subsystems can handle the energy coming from the lithium-ion capacitors—I'm sure they can handle the same power level and discharge dura-tions from the MHD generator."

"Just one last thing to do, then: get the go-ahead from the man himself," Kai said.

They did not have long to wait. About ninety min-utes later, President Kenneth Phoenix entered the lab and greeted all who were there, ending with Lane and

Jodie. Cal Poly president Marcus Harris made the introductions. Phoenix shook Jodie's hand first. "How do you do, Miss Cavendish?"

"Fine, Mr. President. I'm the nanotechnology team leader. Lane Eagan is the team leader for computers and software."

The president shook Lane's hand. "And how are you today, young man?"

"Great, Mr. President," Lane said. He handed the president a silver-ink Sharpie, then stretched out a blank spot on the front of his blue-and-red Project Starfire nylon windbreaker. "Please, Mr. President?" Phoenix smiled and autographed the front of Lane's jacket in big cursive letters.

"May I introduce you to the other Project Starfire team leaders, Mr. President?" Jodie said. She motioned to the large monitor on the wall. "Inset at the upper left is Jerry Kim, team leader for power and control systems, hooked up via satellite from the White Sand Missile Test Range, where the receiving antenna is located; and in the main window aboard Armstrong Space Station are Casey Huggins, directed-energy team leader, and our overall team leader—"

"Brad McLanahan, I know," the president interrupted. Most everyone in the lab blinked in surprise—Brad McLanahan was an acquaintance of the president of the United States? "We've met many times, although you were pretty young and probably don't remember."

"No, sir, I remember," Brad said. "Nice to see you again, sir."

"You guys having fun up there?" the president asked. "I know my trip up there was an experience I'll never forget."

"We're having a blast, Mr. President," Casey said. "Thank you so much for allowing us this awesome opportunity."

"So along with brains, the whole world knows you guys have incredible courage," the president said. "The first male and female teenagers, and the first paraplegic, in space, and they're Americans. Congratulations. The whole country is proud of you, and the whole world is impressed, I'm sure. Where are we on the test firing, Brad?"

"We've run into a potential problem that we're hoping you can help fix, sir," Brad said.

"Me? How?"

"We've collected the energy that we'd like to beam to Earth," Brad explained, "but we're afraid we won't be able to get it out of the storage units and into the microwave cavity to shoot it Earthward."

"That's too bad, guys," the president said. "I hope it's an easy fix for you."

"Everything else works, sir, and we've proven we can form a maser beam," Brad said. "The only thing we haven't proven is getting the beam to Earth and transformed into electricity."

The president looked over to his traveling campaign director and lead Secret Service detail, silently signaling them to start preparations to form up and move his convoy, then checked his watch. "I'm really sorry about this, guys," he said, "but I don't know how I can help, and we do have a schedule to—"

"Mr. President, we think we have a workaround," Kai Raydon said.

"What's that, General?"

"Instead of using the energy stored in Starfire's capacitors, we'd like your permission to use Skybolt's magnetohydrodynamic generator," Kai said. "The MHD is still plugged into Skybolt, but the free-electron laser is disconnected so the students' microwave generator could use Skybolt's subsystems. We can route the power from the MHD to Starfire in exactly the same quantity as the capacitors. The only thing that's changed from the students' original plan is the source of the energy. You've already given us permission to test the MHD generator, and it's fully operational. We'd like permission to use it to power Starfire."

The president's face turned somber, and he looked around at all of the faces in the lab and on the monitor. "General, you are absolutely sure that the big laser is disconnected and will not fire?" he asked, his voice low in great concern.

"Yes, sir, I'm positive."

"Not one watt of laser light?"

"None, sir," Kai assured him. "It would take a long time to plug Skybolt back in. No, sir, Skybolt won't fire. I'm absolutely positive of that."

He looked around again, then pulled out his secure cell phone. "I need to consult a few folks," he said. "I'm afraid some might believe that your maser is really the Skybolt laser. I'd like to get a legal opinion before—"

"Excuse me, sir," Jodie said, "but we need a decision pretty quickly—the station rises above the target's horizon in about ten minutes." She looked at the large teleconference monitor. "Sergeant Lukas, can you tell me how long it will take to connect the MHD to Starfire?"

Valerie turned to a computer console and typed in commands. "The hardwire connection is already there," she said. "Testing the circuitry should take just a few minutes unless we find problems. No guarantees, but I think we can do it in time."

Jodie turned to the president. "Sir?"

Phoenix looked even more grim-faced than before, but after a few tense moments he nodded and said, "Do it. Good luck."

"Thank you, sir," Jodie said. Her hands flew over her laptop's keyboard, and Lane was actually punching instructions into two laptops at once. "Sergeant Lukas, you have the cavity power-control program on checklist page two-twelve bravo."

"Got it," Valerie said. "Engineering, this is Operations, spin up the MHD, switch to page two-twelve bravo, power on system seventeen red and the MHD power-control subsystem and cross-check."

"Standing by," came the response from Alice Hamilton in the Engineering module, waiting for validation from the station commander.

"Engineering, this is Command," Kai said on intercom. "Authorized to spin up the MHD and plug it into Starfire. Advise when ready." He hit the all-stations intercom switch. "Attention on the station, this is the director. We will be activating the MHD generator and using it to send Project Starfire's maser energy to Earth via Skybolt's subsystems. As at any time we activate the MHD, I want all modules sealed up, on-duty crewmembers on oxygen, and off-duty crews to damage-control stations and into space suits. Report by department when ready."

"Roger, Command," Alice acknowledged. "Operations, MHD is spinning up. Stand by."

"Roger," Valerie said. She entered commands into her keyboard. "Henry, Christine, get ready to do your thing."

"Yes, *ma'am!*" Henry Lathrop said. He and terrestrial-weapons officer, Christine Rayhill, were at their stations in their oxygen masks, running checklists. A few minutes later, the command monitor switched from an overhead still satellite image of the rectenna to a live image from Armstrong Space Station, clearly showing the large, dark, circular device all by itself in the New Mexico desert. "Combat is locked on to target," Rayhill said. "No other secondary sensors available except the Project Starfire cameras."

"We want this one right on the mark, Christine," Valerie said. "Use everything you got."

It was very close. After several faults were discovered and corrected, and about thirty seconds after the station had passed above the rectenna's horizon, they heard, "Operations, Engineering, link established and tested. You have power, and the feed levels are programmed. Engineering has switched MHD control to Operations and is ready."

"Roger," Valerie said. "Command, permission to switch Starfire control to Combat."

"Verify that Skybolt is cold, Valerie," Kai ordered.

After a few moments, Valerie replied, "Verified, sir. Skybolt is cold."

"Switch Starfire fire control to Combat, Valerie," Kai said. He looked over at Brad and Casey. "Release authorized. Good luck, guys," he added.

"Combat, you have control," Valerie said after entering instructions into her computer.

"Roger, Combat has control. Starfire, how's it look?"

"Everything is go, Armstrong, except for the capacitor discharge subsystem, and it has been deactivated," Jodie said, nervously twisting her long blond hair. "Starfire is ready."

"Roger that, Starfire. Good luck." Rayhill entered a command. "Starfire is alive, guys."

Absolutely nothing changed either on Armstrong Space Station or at the lab at Cal Poly for several long, tense moments. The only indication of anything happening was the suddenly excited face of Jerry Kim as he checked his readouts: *"Rectenna receiving power, Control!"* he shouted. "Point two . . . point four . . . point five . . . *it is working, guys, it is working!*" The control center at Cal Poly erupted into cheers and applause, and Brad and Casey almost flung themselves into an uncontrollable spin as they tried to hug each other.

"Microwave cavity is getting warmer, but it should still be within limits by the time we shut it down," Jodie said. "Reflectors, collimators, and beam control temps are higher but still in the green. Engineering?"

"Everything is in the green, Starfire," Alice reported. "We'll hit the yellow temperature range in about three minutes."

"One megawatt!" Jerry shouted a little more than a minute later. He was jumping around for joy on camera so much they could not see his face. "We have just received *one megawatt of power from Starfire!* The rectennas are right on their temperature curves— they should reach their yellow line in four minutes. Jodie, you did it! The rate of conversion is well past what we predicted! We could possibly get two megawatts before we hit the temperature limit! We could even—"

"I've received a warning from White Sands range control, guys," Valerie announced. "Unauthorized aircraft entering the range. Shut Starfire down, Combat. Engineering, secure the MHD and reactor."

"Roger," Henry said. His finger was already on the "kill button," and he entered the command instantly. "Nose is cold, crew."

"Starfire is off-line," Alice said. "MHD spinning down. Reactor is secure. Everything is in the green."

"Congratulations, guys," Kai said, removing his oxygen mask. "You pulled it off. You shot electrical power from space to Earth." On intercom he said, "All personnel, this is the director, you may secure from MHD stations. Join me in extending congratulations to the entire Starfire team for a successful test firing." Applause broke out in the command module.

"We couldn't have done it without you and everybody on station, sir," Brad said after removing his oxygen mask. He hugged Casey again. "It worked, Casey. Your microwave generator worked!"

"*Our* microwave generator," Casey said. "*Our* Starfire! It worked! *It worked!*" And to celebrate further, she pulled out her barf bag and threw up in it.

Despite the sudden shutdown, the celebrations continued at the lab at Cal Poly, and President Phoenix was applauding just as enthusiastically as everyone else. "Congratulations, Miss Cavendish, Mr. Eagan," he said. He was directed by his traveling campaign manager where to stand and face, and he had the two team leaders at his side and the large monitor showing the others over his shoulder when the cameras started to roll.

"I was privileged to attend and watch an amazing occurrence here at Cal Poly: the first successful transmission of electrical energy from space to Earth," he said. His staff had prepared several sets of remarks for him, including a speech in case Starfire didn't work, the spaceplane was lost, or the device destroyed the space station. He was overjoyed—and relieved—to be giving this version. "Although just in its infancy, this is a remarkable achievement, made no less remarkable by the fact that a team of undergraduate college students designed, built, installed, and operated it. I'm very proud of these young people for their achievements, and it highlights perfectly what an investment in education, technology, and space sciences can produce. Congratulations, Jodie, Brad, Casey, and Jerry, and to the entire Starfire team." The president stayed for several minutes longer for pictures, then departed.

WHITE SANDS MISSILE TEST RANGE
ALAMOGORDO, NEW MEXICO
That same time

"How far are we from that antenna, man?" the pilot of a Cessna 172 Skyhawk asked, sweeping rows of brown dreadlocks out of his eyes. "Everything looks the same around here."

"About ten more minutes," the man in the right seat said. He was using a map application on his smartphone to navigate the little plane. Like the pilot, he had long, shoulder-length, dirty-looking hair, a beard, mustache, and thick glasses. The pilot was wearing a Hawaiian shirt, knee-length Bermuda shorts, and sneakers; the right-seater wore a T-shirt, cutoff jeans, and sandals. "Stay on this heading."

"All right, all right," the pilot said. They had lifted off from Alamogordo–White Sands Regional Airport about a half hour earlier and headed northwest, entering Holloman Air Force Base's Class-D airspace without talking to anyone on the radio. "You sure you got the right spot, man?" the pilot asked.

"The news reports about the test pointed it out pretty clearly," the other man said. "We should see it when we get closer—it's pretty big."

"Man, this is loco," the pilot said. "They said on the news that no aircraft will be allowed to fly near the antenna."

"What are they going to do—shoot us down?" the navigator said.

"I don't want to get shot down, man, not by the military or this . . . phaser beam, laser beam, whatever the fuck it is."

"I don't want to fly over the antenna, just close enough so they'll cancel the test," the navigator said. "This is an illegal test of a space weapon, and if the federal government or the state of New Mexico won't stop it, we'll have to do it."

"Whatever," the pilot said. He strained to look out the windows. "Are we getting . . . *holy shit!*" There, off to their left, not more than a hundred feet away, was a green military Black Hawk helicopter with U.S. AIR FORCE in large black letters on the side, flying in formation. The helicopter's right sliding door was open, and a crewmember in a green flight suit, helmet, and lowered dark visor was visible. "We got company, man."

The helicopter crewmember in the open door picked up what looked to be a large flashlight and began blinking light signals at the Cessna pilot. "One . . . two . . . one . . . five," the pilot said. "That's the emergency distress freq." He changed his number one radio to that frequency.

"High-wing single-engine Cessna, tail number N-3437T, this is the United States Air Force off your left wing, transmitting on GUARD," they heard, referencing the universal VHF emergency frequency. "You have entered restricted military airspace that is active at this time. Reverse course immediately. The area is active and you are in great danger. Repeat, reverse course immediately."

"We got a right to be here, man," the pilot radioed. "We ain't doin' nothin'. Go away."

"November 3437T, this is the United States Air Force, you are putting yourself in great danger," the helicopter's copilot said. "Reverse course immediately. I am authorized to take any action necessary to prevent you from proceeding into restricted airspace."

"What are you going to do, man—shoot us down?" the Cessna pilot said. The helicopter did have a long tube thing on its nose that looked like a cannon—he didn't know it was just an air refueling probe. "Listen, we just want to stop the Starfire test, and then we'll go back home. Go away."

At that, the Black Hawk suddenly accelerated and did a steep right turn, passing in front of the Cessna not more than one hundred feet away, its rotor disk filling the Cessna's windscreen. The startled pilot cried out and yanked the control yoke back and to the left, then had to fight to regain control as the little airplane almost stalled. They could hear the helicopter's rotor beats thumping against the Cessna's fuselage as it circled around them.

The Black Hawk appeared off his left wing seconds later, closer this time, the beat of the rotor blades now thunderous, as if a giant invisible fist were beating on the side of their little airplane. "N-3437T, reverse course immediately! This is an order! Comply immediately!"

"Is that dude crazy, man?" the pilot said. "I nearly crapped my pants!"

"I see it! I see it, I see the antenna!" the right-seater said. "A little to the right, on the horizon! Big round sucker!"

The pilot followed his passenger's pointing finger. "I don't see nothin', man, I don't— Wait, I got it, I got it," he said. "That big round thing in the desert? I'll head over to it." He put the little Cessna into a steep right bank . . .

. . . and as soon as he did so, the Black Hawk helicopter made a steep left turn, blasting the Cessna with its powerful rotor wash. The action flipped the Cessna completely upside down. It entered an inverted flat spin and crashed into the New Mexico desert seconds later.

SEATTLE, WASHINGTON

A few hours later

"Congratulations, Jung-bae, on a successful test of Starfire," Dr. Toshuniko "Toby" Nukaga, professor of aerospace engineering at Cal Poly, said via a video teleconference hookup on his laptop computer from his room at an upscale hotel in Seattle, Washington. "I just heard the news. I'm sorry I couldn't be there, but I am chairing a conference up in Seattle."

"Thank you, sir," Jerry said. He was in a trailer about a mile from the Starfire rectenna site in the White Sands Missile Test Range northwest of Alamogordo, New Mexico, surrounded by laptop computers used to monitor the power and steering systems aboard Armstrong Space Station. Seven team members were with him, high-fiving one another as they began analyzing the mountain of data they had received. "I am sorry you could not be here as well, sir. You were the driving force behind this project from the very beginning."

"The credit belongs to you and the others on the project team, Jung-bae—I was only the facilitator. So, how much energy did you transfer?"

"One-point-four-seven megawatts, sir."

"Outstanding! Well done!"

"It had to be cut short because an unauthorized aircraft entered the range."

"I had heard that some protesters were going to try to disrupt the test by flying a private plane over the rectenna," Nukaga said.

Jerry blinked in surprise. "You did, sir?" he asked incredulously.

"Jung-bae, I'm here in Seattle at the annual conference of the International Confederation of Responsible Scientists," Nukaga said. "There are over a hundred groups represented here of scientists, politicians, environmentalists, and industry leaders from all over the world—we even have the presidential candidate, former secretary of state Stacy Anne Barbeau, here to give the keynote later today.

"We also have a few rather radical groups here too, and one of them, Students for Universal Peace, approached me to complain that Cal Poly was involved in a weapons development program with Starfire," Nukaga went on. "I assured them we were not, but they insisted. They said it was their duty to do anything they could to stop the Starfire test firing, even if it put their lives in jeopardy—I actually think they were *hoping* someone would get shot down by the maser just to prove it really was a weapon."

"That is unbelievable, sir," Jerry said. "Why did you not tell us about this?"

"I only half believed it myself, Jung-bae," Nukaga said. "Frankly, the kids that confronted me looked like they didn't know where their next meal was coming from, let alone having the wherewithal to hire a plane to fly over a government restricted area hoping to get shot down by a maser beam from space. So." Nukaga was obviously anxious to change the subject. "Mr. McLanahan and Miss Huggins looked good aboard the military space station. I saw one of their press conferences last night. Are they doing well?"

"Very well, sir."

"Good. Any problems? Any difficulties with the equipment or software?" Jerry hesitated and averted his eyes from his camera for a brief moment, and Nukaga noticed it right away. "Jung-bae?"

Jerry wasn't sure if he was supposed to be talking about anything having to do with Starfire and the space station on an unsecure network—the team leaders had decided to discuss among themselves what got released and what didn't—but Nukaga was one of their professors and an early but somewhat reluctant supporter of the project. "There was a potential problem with the relay I designed that allowed power to flow from the lithium-ion capacitors to the microwave generator, sir," he said finally.

"A 'potential' problem?"

"It did not fail today, but . . . it was not one hundred percent reliable," Jerry said uneasily, "and with the president of the United States attending the test firing at Cal Poly, we wanted to ensure we could hit the rectenna with maser energy."

"Well, you did so," Nukaga said. "The test was a success. I don't understand."

"Well, we . . . we did not use the energy we collected with the nantennas and stored in the capacitors."

"Then what energy did you use?"

"We used power from the . . . the magnetohydrody-namic generator," Jerry said.

There was silence on the line for several long moments, and on the video monitor Jerry could see the growing expression of disbelief on Nukaga's face; then: "You mean, *you activated the laser aboard Armstrong Space Station*, Jung-bae?" Nukaga asked in a breath-less, low, incredulous tone.

"No, sir," Jerry said. "Not the laser. The free-electron laser itself was deactivated so we could use the laser's subsystems for Starfire. We just used its energy source to—"

"That MHD generator was *still operational?*" Nukaga asked. "I was led to believe that all of the components of the Skybolt space laser had been deac-tivated." Jerry had no response to that. "So the one-point-four megawatts you collected with the rectenna came from the MHD and not from Starfire?"

"Yes, sir," Jerry replied. "We had validated every-thing else: we collected solar energy, stored the elec-tricity, powered the microwave generator with it, and shot maser energy with the Skybolt's reflectors, colli-mators, and steering systems. We just needed to hit the rectenna with maser energy. We wanted to do it on the first try, with the president of the United States watch-ing. The MHD generator was our only—"

"Jung-bae, you fired a beam of directed energy at a target on Earth," Nukaga said. "You shot one megawatt of energy for over two minutes at a distance of over two hundred miles? That's . . ." He paused, running the calculations in his head. "That's over *three million joules* of energy fired by the MHD from that military space station! That's *three times* the legal limit, at a distance almost *four times* the allowed range! That's a serious violation of the Space Preservation Treaty! That's an offense that can be prosecuted by the International Court of Justice or heard by the United Nations Security Council! Space weapons, especially directed-energy weapons, are not allowed to be employed by anyone, even students!"

"No, sir, that cannot be right!" Jerry said, confused, afraid he had said too much and betrayed his colleagues, and afraid of raising the anger of his favorite professor and mentor. "Starfire is a solar power plant, not a space weapon!"

"It was, Jung-bae, until you abandoned using solar power and used the illegal military space laser's power source!" Nukaga cried. "Don't you understand, Jung-bae? You can use fireworks to celebrate the New Year, but if you use a Scud missile to do so, it changes and contaminates the very nature of the spirit you were trying to express, even if you don't attack anyone or blow something up. That's why we have laws against using such things for *any* purpose." He saw the panicked expression in Jerry's eyes and immediately felt sorry for him. "But you were in New Mexico, were you not?"

"Yes, sir."

"Did they consult with you on the decision to use the MHD generator?"

"No, sir," Jerry said. "There wasn't time, and I was on a teleconference with my team trying to come up with a solution to the relay problem."

"Do you know who came up with the idea to use the MHD?"

"I believe it was Mr. McLanahan, sir," Jerry said. Nukaga nodded knowingly—he could have easily guessed that. "He brought the idea up to General Raydon, the station commander, and to Sergeant Lukas, the station's operations officer."

"These are all members of the military?"

"They are all retired, I believe," Jerry said, "but knowledgeable in space-station operations and hired by a private defense contractor to operate it."

" 'Private defense contractor,' eh?" Nukaga sneered. "Was it that company in Nevada, the one that presented the university with the seed grant money?"

"Yes . . . I . . . yes, sir, it was," Jerry said . . . and moments later the realization began to sink in.

"You're beginning to see now, aren't you, Jung-bae?" Nukaga asked, seeing Jerry's expression change. "Bradley McLanahan, the son of General Patrick McLanahan, a retired Air Force officer and former officer of that Nevada company, comes up with an idea for a so-called space-based solar power plant, and in just a few months' time he's assembled an engineering team and made several significant science and technological breakthroughs. Is it then a coincidence that Cal Poly gets the grant money? Is it just a coincidence that Mr. McLanahan wants to use Armstrong Space Station for Starfire, the station being managed by the *very same Nevada defense contractor*? I don't believe in coincidences, Jung-bae. Neither should you."

"But they received permission from the president of the United States to use the MHD," Jerry said, "only and unless the Skybolt free-electron laser was not capable of being fired."

"Of course. They couldn't fire the laser without breaking the Space Preservation Treaty, so they got the next best thing: a maser, built by a bunch of college students, all very neat, uplifting, and innocent—hogwash, all hogwash," Nukaga spat. "It seems to me that the so-called problems with your relay could have been easily contrived so they *had* to use the MHD generator to demonstrate the power of the maser weapon.

Three million joules! I'll bet the military was very pleased with this demonstration."

"I designed the power relay system, sir, and only I was in charge of monitoring it," Jerry said. "I assure you, no one deliberately tampered with it."

"Jung-bae, I am very glad that you told me of this," Nukaga said. "I am not implicating you of anything. It seems that Mr. McLanahan had his own agenda when he put this project together. As I suspected from the beginning, Mr. McLanahan was working with this defense contractor, and quite possibly the military itself, being the son of a prominent and infamous military officer, to build a space weapon and hide it from the world. He obviously had help from this contractor and the government—how else could a freshman gather all the resources needed to put together such a project in so short a time?"

"I . . . I had no idea, sir," Jerry said, his eyes darting back and forth in confusion. "Mr. McLanahan, he . . . he seemed to possess extraordinary leadership and organizational skills. He was always very open and transparent about everything. He shared all of his resources with every member of the team. We knew every moment of every day what was needed and how he intended to get it."

"Again, Jung-bae, I'm not implicating or blaming you for being taken in by this . . . this obvious huckster," Nukaga said. He nodded, satisfied that he was on the right track. "It makes perfect sense to me. Our university has been taken in by a coordinated plot by McLanahan—more likely by his late father at first, then adopted by the son—supported by that defense contractor, the military, and their government supporters like President Kenneth Phoenix and Vice President Ann Page, to surreptitiously build a space-based directed-energy weapon and disguise it as nothing more than a student engineering project. How horrifyingly clever. How many other progressive, peace-loving universities have they perpetrated this scheme on? I wonder."

Nukaga's mind was racing for several moments before he realized he was still on the video teleconference with Jung-bae. "I'm sorry, Jung-bae," he said, "but I must attend to a very important matter. You should leave that project immediately. In fact, if I find out that the university had anything to do with this military program, or if the university does not disavow any participation in the project and return the money it got from that defense contractor, I will resign my position immediately, and I would urge you to transfer to a different school. I'm sure we'd both be very happy at Stanford University. I look forward to seeing you soon." And he terminated the connection.

My God, Nukaga thought, what an incredibly diabolical scheme! This had to be exposed immediately. It had to stop. He was the chair of this conference, and it was being beamed around the world—he certainly had access to cameras, microphones, and the media, and he intended to use them.

However, he admitted to himself, his audience, although global, was not that large. Most of the world considered the attendees as nothing more than tree-hugging Occupy Wall Street peacenik hippie wackos—one of the reasons he was asked to chair the conference was to try to lend a lot more legitimacy to the organization and the conclave. He needed some help. He needed . . .

. . . and in a flash he remembered, and pulled a business card out of his pocket, then pulled out his smartphone and dialed the Washington number of a man he knew was just a few flights upstairs. "Mr. Cohen, this is Dr. Toby Nukaga, the chair of the event . . . fine sir, thank you, and again, thank you and Secretary Barbeau for attending.

"Sir, I just received some very disturbing information that I think the secretary should know about and perhaps act upon," Nukaga went on almost breathlessly. "It is in regards to the Starfire project . . . yes, the so-called space solar power plant . . . yes, I say 'so-called' because I have learned today that it is not by any stretch of the imagination a solar power plant, but a well-camouflaged space-weapon program . . . yes, sir, a military directed-energy space weapon, disguised as a student engineering project . . . yes, sir, the information was told to me by someone very high up in the project, *very* high up . . . yes, sir, I trust the source completely. He was taken in, just as I and my university and hundreds of engineers and scientists around the world were sucked into cooperating with it, and I wish to expose this frightening and outrageous program before any more harm is done . . . yes, sir . . . yes, sir, I can be upstairs in just a few minutes. Thank you, Mr. Cohen."

Nukaga had hurriedly starting packing up his tablet computer when a text message came across its screen. It was from the head of Students for Universal Peace, one of the international environmental and world peace groups attending the conference, and the message read: *Our protest plane was shot down by Starfire space weapon near rectenna site. We are at war.*

INTERNATIONAL CONFEDERATION OF RESPONSIBLE SCIENTISTS CONCLAVE KEYNOTE ADDRESS SEATTLE, WASHINGTON

Later that evening

"It is my pleasure and honor to introduce a person who certainly needs no introduction, especially to this assemblage," Dr. Toshuniko Nukaga began, reading from the script that had been provided for him from Secretary Barbeau's campaign office. "Stacy Anne

Barbeau describes herself first and foremost as an Air Force brat. Born at Barksdale Air Force Base near Shreveport, Louisiana, she said that the roar of the B-47 and B-52 bombers outside her family's home just lulled her to sleep, and the smell of jet fuel surely seeped into her blood. The daughter of a retired two-star Air Force air-division general, she moved residences a total of ten times with her family, including two postings overseas, before moving back to her home state of Louisiana to attend college. Undergraduate degrees in prelaw, business, and government from Tulane, a law degree from Tulane, then work in the public defender's offices in Shreveport, Baton Rouge, and New Orleans, before running for Congress. Three terms in Congress were followed by three terms in the U.S. Senate, the last four years as majority leader, before being selected as the sixty-seventh secretary of state. Today, she is a candidate for president of the United States, and if she wins, she will be the first woman to hold that office. I cannot think of a person more suited for that position, can you?" There was a tremendous standing ovation that lasted almost a full minute.

"That's her official background, my friends and colleagues, but let me tell you a few things about this extraordinary woman you may not know," Nukaga went on. "There are two sides to Secretary Barbeau.

There is the fierce but caring advocate for green technology, the environment, actions to counter global warming, and carbon control. But she is equally strong and dedicated to the strength and responsible modernization of our military. No surprise, she is a strong voice for the Air Force, but is also a supporter of our country maintaining its leadership on the world's oceans and of maintaining a force that stands ready to help other countries in time of need with rapid, sustained, and powerful yet compassionate humanitarian assistance. I know her as having a strong, caring, and dynamic personality, but she is undoubtedly someone Humphrey Bogart might have called a 'classy broad.' " Nukaga was relieved to get a peal of laughter and some applause for that line—it was one he would have deleted from the prepared introduction, if he had been allowed to do so.

"Stacy Anne Barbeau speaks five languages fluently. Stacy Anne is a scratch golfer. Stacy Anne knows Washington inside and out, but her roots and her heart are with the folks, you and me. Stacy Anne knows and cares about the U.S. military, the force that protects our nation and the free world, but Stacy Anne knows that the military is a force not just for war, but for defending those who cannot defend themselves." Nukaga let his voice rise as he wound it up, and the growing applause from the audience helped tremendously—so much so that he found himself raising his arms and clenching his fists, something he thought he'd never do. "Stacy Anne Barbeau is a leader, a fighter, and a protector, and with our help and support, Stacy Anne Barbeau will be the next president of the United States of America!" Nukaga's next words could not be heard because of the rumbling, ear-shattering standing ovation that erupted just then. "Ladies and gentlemen, friends and colleagues, please join me in welcoming the former secretary of state and the next president of the United States of America, Stacy Anne Barbeau!"

With a beaming smile and enthusiastic wave of both hands, Stacy Anne Barbeau strode onto the stage. She did something Stacy Anne Barbeau knew how to do with perfection: look professional, presidential, and seductive all at once. Her wavy blond hair and makeup were flawless; her dress was tight, which accentuated her curvaceous body without looking too trampy or obvious; her jewelry caught lots of attention, but just enough to make her look successful without looking flashy.

"Thank you, thank you, ladies and gentlemen!" Barbeau shouted into the microphone after she reached the lectern. She then recited her well-known and oft-repeated campaign motto in a very loud and Cajun-laced voice: "Let's get the future started together, shall we?" The applause and shouting were deafening.

Barbeau stood silent at the podium until the shouting and applause died down, and then waited nearly an additional minute so that the audience was waiting for her words with breathless anticipation. Finally, she began: "My friends, as I begin I am going to deviate from my prepared remarks, because serious events have happened in the last several hours that I think you should know about.

"I'm sure you are all aware that I am not a big fan of President Kenneth Phoenix's new so-called industrial space initiative," she said. "I give the president all the credit in the world for flying up to the military space station to make his big announcement—despite costing the American taxpayer tens of millions of dollars for what turned out to be the planet's most wasteful and unnecessary junket—but frankly, my friends, it's all been downhill from there: relations with the Russians and many nations in Europe and Asia are at an all-time low and threatening to explode into diplomatic friction at best and a return to the Cold War at worst; the military no longer trusts the president because of all these looming wholesale cuts he plans to make to our proud military forces; the Russians have abandoned the International Space Station, and the European Union and Japan are considering doing the same; and the economy is still in the tank four years after he came to office, this despite an austerity campaign that has seen entire cabinet-level departments nearly eliminated. Is this what we want to see continue for another four years?" The audience started chanting a familiar phrase, one that had been repeated over and over during Barbeau's campaign: "*Dites-moi la vérité* now, Ken Phoenix, or get down from the car!" a mixture of Cajun and Creole expressions.

After letting this go on for a few seconds, Barbeau raised her hands, smiling broadly, until the chanting finally ended. "But while he's been warning us of his plans to cut the military in a time of ever-increasing danger to our country and our allies; while he's warning us he's ready to cut social safety-net programs and benefits meant to assist the most vulnerable of us; while he threatens to run up huge deficits to try to deploy these pie-in-the-sky space things, do you know what he did earlier today, my friends? Today, he fired a directed-energy weapon from space, a microwave laser, in direct violation of the Space Preservation Treaty. While the treaty has not yet been ratified by the Senate—an omission I will remedy when I take over the White House, I promise you—its terms have been closely followed for the past eight years so as to ensure peace. And do you know the worst part? In order to hide his program from the world, he disguised this act as an innocent undergraduate college experiment.

"That's right, my friends. You've heard or read about the first teenagers in space, and of course, Casey Huggins, the first paraplegic in space, gifted young scientists who have the courage to travel in space to conduct this experiment. Well, it's all a big lie. With the help of a Nevada defense contractor and the support of President Phoenix and Vice President Page, these students built a directed-energy weapon that orbits above our heads right now, and today was successfully fired at a target on Earth, all in the guise of a solar power plant that can deliver electricity to any part of the globe to help underprivileged communities or researchers in far-off parts of the world. Like we say down on the bayou, my friends: That dog don't hunt.

"They tried to fool us, my friends," Barbeau went on. "They tried to trick us. But one member of the so-called Project Starfire team couldn't stand the hypocrisy any longer, and he called our conference chairman, Dr. Toby Nukaga, and told him the truth. That brave young man's name is Kim Jung-bae, a gifted engineering student from United Korea, who was a team leader on the project but was not allowed to voice his opposition to the test firing. He is a hero for exposing this charade."

Her face turned somber. "We also learned today that a terrible tragedy has occurred related to this directed-energy weapon—maybe you have already heard about it," Barbeau went on. "One of the groups represented here, Students for Universal Peace, organized a protest over the Starfire test site. They hired two brave men to fly a small plane near the Starfire target. They knew the danger, but they wanted to do anything they could to stop the test. I'm sorry to report . . . the plane was shot down by the illegal space weapon. Yes, shot down by a microwave-laser beam from Armstrong Space Station. The two brave individuals aboard were killed instantly." The room became completely silent except for a few sobs and gasps of horror, and all the attendees at one table immediately shot to their feet in shock and anguish and headed out of the hall.

Barbeau let the silence linger for a few moments. Then, slowly, gradually, her expression changed: no longer somber, but red-hot angry. "Enough of the double-talk, Mr. Phoenix," Barbeau said, aiming her words and pointing a finger directly at the network and cable news cameras that had hastily been set up at her suggestion for her speech. "Enough of the lies and deception, enough of wasting our hard-earned tax money on dangerous and illegal weapons programs, and enough of killing innocent Americans who wanted nothing more than to voice their outrage and do something, anything, in the name of peace. Deactivate that space weapon immediately, abandon it, and allow it to deorbit, burn up, and crash into the ocean. Do it *now*." More thunderous applause and chanting, *"Do it now! Do it now! Do it now!"*

"When I become president of the United States, my friends," Barbeau went on after a minute of cheering and chanting, "I will restore faith and honor to this country, our military, the White House, and in the eyes of everyone around the world who yearns for freedom and prays for a helping hand. Our military will be number one again, not struggling to stay number three. When the oppressed and peace-loving people of the world look overhead, they won't see rockets from their own government being fired at them, and they certainly won't see an American military space station ready to turn their village into ashes or blast an airplane out of the sky with an invisible beam of light— they'll see a transport plane flying the red, white, and blue of the flag of the United States of America, carrying food, water, medicine, doctors, and peacekeepers to assist them. And when Americans look for help and ask their government for assistance in feeding their children and getting jobs, they won't hear about their president spending hundreds of millions of dollars taking a joyride into space or secretly building death rays—they'll get the help they desperately need. That I promise!"

The applause and chanting were even louder than before, and this time Stacy Anne Barbeau let it go on and on and on.

THE KREMLIN
MOSCOW, RUSSIAN FEDERATION
Several hours later

"My remarks will be short and direct this morning, my fellow Russians," President Gennadiy Gryzlov said into the camera from the television studio in the Kremlin. He wore a somber, stern expression, as if he were about to announce the death of a beloved person. "By now you should have heard about the remarks made by American presidential candidate and former secretary of state Stacy Anne Barbeau earlier today about the test firing of a directed-energy weapon from space at a target on Earth from the American military space station, and the downing of an American aircraft by the weapon. I and my ministers were horrified to hear of this. We are working to verify this information, but if it is true, these actions would be a serious threat to world peace—in fact, they are a treaty violation, a warning to the rest of the world, a provocation, and a virtual act of war.

"When we considered our options, we were concerned about creating a panic throughout Russia, and indeed the world. But we felt that we had no choice, and that is why I am speaking to you this afternoon. Moreover, we decided to act in a deliberate and immediate way to protect the lives of Russians and our friends and allies, as follows:

"First: beginning immediately, the Russian Space Defense Force will continually broadcast the predicted position of the American military space station and the potential range and azimuth of its directed-energy weapon, and give warnings of when and where the directed-energy weapon may threaten Russians, our allies, and our friends on the ground," Gryzlov went on. "When the weapon is a threat to you, we ask that you take shelter underground or in the strongest building to which you can quickly evacuate. The exact properties of the weapon are unknown, so we do not yet know what the best shelter may be, but you may have a better chance of surviving an attack if you are indoors rather than outdoors. The threat may last as long as four minutes. You and your loved ones may be under threat from the weapon several times a day.

"Electronics may be affected by a blast from this weapon, so prepare your households and places of business to be without power for days or even weeks: stock blankets, food, and water; gather wood for a fire; and organize your neighborhoods to band together to help one another," he went on. "If at all possible, avoid flying in aircraft, riding an elevator or electric train, or operating heavy machinery while the weapon is within the danger zone, because, as we have seen, the weapon can easily take down an aircraft and may be able to disrupt or even destroy electrical circuits.

"Second: I demand that all of the American space weapons on Armstrong Space Station be deactivated and destroyed immediately," Gryzlov said. "This includes the Skybolt free-electron laser, the Hydra chlorine-oxygen-iodine laser, and the Kingfisher orbiting weapon garages; Starfire, the so-called college-student experiment which turned out to be in reality a microwave-laser weapon; and any other space-based weapons, their power sources, and all their components, whether or not the Americans classify them as defensive weapons only. In particular, Russia demands that the Skybolt module be separated from Armstrong Space Station within forty-eight hours, and that, when it is no longer posing a hazard to anyone or anything on Earth, it be deorbited and sent to burn up in Earth's atmosphere or crash into the ocean. We have powerful ground sensors to detect if this is done. If it is not done, I must assume that the United States intends to continue to use the weapons, and Russia will immediately take all necessary steps to protect itself.

"Third: I hereby announce that, beginning in ten days, if the Americans do not destroy all of their space weapons, all airspace around the Russian Federation from the surface to five hundred kilometers' altitude is now restricted airspace and closed to all unauthorized spacecraft or aircraft," Gryzlov went on. "For decades, all nations recognized that only the airspace below twenty kilometers' altitude could be restricted or controlled, but no longer. Our scientists estimate that the Americans can fire their directed-energy weapon as far as five hundred kilometers with enough power to kill a person on the ground, so that is the airspace that we will defend. Any unauthorized flight over the Russian Federation below that altitude, regardless of type of aircraft or spacecraft, will be considered hostile and be subject to neutralization. I know this impacts many nations, but the Americans have changed the world's security dynamic for the worse, and we have no choice but to act. Ten days should be sufficient time for all unfriendly nations to alter the orbits of their spacecraft or provide us with details on the type, purpose, and orbits of aircraft and spacecraft overflying Russia in order to comply with this order.

"This restriction is especially true of one spacecraft in particular: the American single-stage-to-orbit spaceplanes," Gryzlov said. "Because of their hypersonic flight capabilities in the atmosphere and their ability to boost themselves into Earth orbit, as well as their demonstrated ability to release weapons or insert weapon-carrying satellites into orbit, they are a particularly dangerous threat to the Russian Federation.

"Therefore, beginning in ten days, in order to allow time for the spaceplanes to evacuate any personnel from the International Space Station or Armstrong Space Station, the S-series of American spaceplanes will not be welcome over Russian airspace and will be engaged and shot down without further warning," Gryzlov went on. "Let me repeat this so there is no confusion or doubt: beginning ten days from today, the American spaceplanes will be engaged if they overfly the Russian Federation. The threat of attack by these hypersonic aircraft is simply too great a threat to the Russian people. The United States possesses many man-rated commercial spacecraft that can service the International Space Station and perform other such tasks, and it will be allowed to do so after requesting permission to overfly Russia, but the spaceplanes will not be granted permission to fly over Russia under any circumstances.

"I was reluctant to take such drastic measures, my fellow Russians, but, after consultation with my counselors and after much prayer, I felt I had no choice if I was to protect Russian citizens from the danger they now face above their heads," Gryzlov concluded. "I urge all Russians to take all necessary precautions to protect themselves and their families from the danger of space-weapon attack. If the Americans do not respond to my demands, I assure you, Russia will act. Stay informed and stay safe, my fellow Russians. May God bless the Russian Federation."

Gryzlov rose from his seat and strode out of the Kremlin television studio, followed closely by his chief of staff, Sergei Tarzarov. He did not greet anyone or stop to chat, but quickly made his way back to his official office. Waiting for him inside were Foreign Minister Daria Titeneva, Minister of Defense Gregor Sokolov, and chief of the general staff General Mikhail Khristenko, who all rose when Tarzarov opened the door for the Russian president. "Excellent address, sir," Sokolov said. "I think ten days will be sufficient for the Americans to begin negotiating for access to Russian airspace for their spacecraft."

Gryzlov sat at his desk and glared at Sokolov. "I am not going to give anyone ten days," he snapped, lighting a cigar, "and I will not negotiate for anything with anyone."

"Sir?"

"Forty-eight hours, Sokolov," Gryzlov said. "If I do not see that Skybolt module disconnected from that space station, I want that space station attacked the next time it flies over Russia, with every weapon in our arsenal. The same with any of their spaceplanes. I am not going to sit back and do nothing while the Americans fly over my head with a directed-energy weapon. I will take this country to war before I allow that to happen."

Sergei Tarzarov picked up the telephone at the other side of Gryzlov's office, listened, then put it back. "President Phoenix for you, sir," he said.

"That did not take long," Gryzlov said. He motioned for those in the room to pick up dead extensions so they could listen in on the translation, then picked up the phone on his desk. "What is it, Mr. Phoenix?"

"It wasn't a directed-energy weapon, Mr. President," Phoenix said through a translator. "It was a college engineering project, a space-based solar power plant. And that airplane wasn't shot down by Starfire—it lost control while trying to evade an Air Force patrol helicopter after it had violated restricted airspace, several minutes *after* the test was terminated. I don't know where Secretary Barbeau got her information, but she's wrong, and you were misguided to believe it. She's campaigning for president, and she wants headlines."

"Wait." Gryzlov hit the hold button and turned to those in the room with him. "Well well," he said, "Phoenix starts this conversation with an attempt at an explanation. This could be interesting."

"He could be willing to negotiate," Tarzarov said. "Let him give something, and then you give something in return."

"The hell you say, Tarzarov," Gryzlov said angrily, but with a smile on his face. "I will not give one inch to this weak-kneed excuse for a head of state." He hit the hold button again. "Are you saying Barbeau is lying, Phoenix?" he asked, no longer using Phoenix's title or even addressing him as "Mister"—Phoenix's opening move was a defensive one, and Gryzlov wanted there to be no doubt about who was now in control of this situation.

"I'm telling you the facts, Mr. President: Starfire is not a directed-energy weapon," Phoenix said. "It is an experimental space solar-powered power plant designed by some California engineering students. The Skybolt free-electron laser was deactivated. The students' experiment was to beam electricity from space to Earth. That's *it*. The small plane crashed because its pilot was stupid, not because it was hit by the maser. The solar power plant is not a threat to anyone on the ground and will certainly not disable airplanes, elevators, trains, or anything else. You're creating a panic over a harmless college experiment. Neither that project nor the space station is any threat to you."

"Phoenix, I simply do not believe you any longer," Gryzlov said. "You can do one thing only to restore my faith in your words: detach the laser module from the space station immediately. If you do this, I will not implement the enhanced restriction of Russian airspace, and I will enter in negotiations with you to create a permanent treaty on space weapons. All I care about is offensive weapons in space that might be a threat to Russia. Perhaps I received bad information about the nature of the device, but it still does not alter the fact that you have used the Skybolt module to shoot directed energy at the surface of the Earth, and that cannot be tolerated."

Gryzlov noted the long silence on the other end of the line; then: "I will consult with my advisers, Mr. President," Phoenix said finally.

"Very well," Gryzlov said. "You have two days, Phoenix, and then Russia will defend its airspace and low Earth orbit as we would our motherland, with every man, woman, and child, and every weapon in our arsenal, at our disposal. That I promise, Phoenix." And with that, he threw the phone back onto its receiver.

Sergei Tarzarov put the dead extension back on its cradle. "I think he will do as you ask and detach the laser module from the military space station," he said. "He will certainly concede that. May I suggest—"

"No, you may not, Tarzarov," Gryzlov interrupted. He turned to Minister of Defense Sokolov and Chief of the General Staff Khristenko. "I will give the Americans their two days to detach that Skybolt module from the space station, and I will allow them to fly manned capsules to their space station only if they inform us of their exact flight path and destination before launch, and if they do not deviate from that flight path by as much as a degree or meter. If they do not inform us, or if they deviate from their flight path, I want the spacecraft destroyed. The spaceplanes will be engaged whenever they come within range of our weapons."

"What about details of their cargo or passengers, sir?" Foreign Minister Titenov asked.

"I no longer care what they might be carrying," Gryzlov said. "From now on I am assuming that every spacecraft launched by the Americans carries a space weapon and is a danger to Russia. The Americans and that spineless president Phoenix are liars and a danger to Russia. I will treat them like the enemies they are, I will not concede anything, and I will work from the assumption that America is just waiting for the right opportunity to strike, so we must be ready to strike first."

NINE

Gun battles are caused by outlaws,
and not by officers of the peace.
—JOHN F. KENNEDY

ABOARD AIR FORCE ONE, OVER
NORTHERN CALIFORNIA

That same time

President Phoenix replaced the phone on its cradle. "That went swimmingly," he murmured wearily. He was heading north to Portland, Oregon, for his next day of campaign stops. "You guys hear all that?" he asked into his video teleconference camera. All three participants in the video teleconference—Vice President Ann Page, National Security Adviser William Glenbrook, and Secretary of Defense Frederick Hayes—responded in the affirmative. "I screwed the pooch. I should've called you guys up and asked your opinion before I authorized the Cal Poly students to use the nuclear generator. Thanks to Barbeau, Russia thinks I just fired a death ray. I don't feel as if I have any choice here, guys, but to detach that Skybolt module. Thoughts?"

"I would've advised going ahead with using the MHD generator test if you had asked me beforehand, Mr. President," Ann said. "All we did was allow the Cal Poly students to demonstrate their technology—we didn't fire a space weapon. Starfire *is not* a space weapon, no matter how much Barbeau and Gryzlov say it is."

"The question now is: Do we think Gryzlov will dare attack if we fly a spaceplane over Russia?" the president asked.

"He's taking steps to try to convince us that's exactly what he'd do," Glenbrook said. "Launching that Elektron spaceplane into an intersecting orbit with the space station? That was a deliberate action."

"They were miles apart," Hayes said. "There was no danger of collision."

"But a miscalculation of just a few seconds and things could have been far worse," Ann said. "Bill is right: it was a deliberate and dangerous action."

"You mentioned something else that happened before that flyby episode, didn't you, Fred?" the president asked. "What was it?"

"Before the Russian spaceplane flew past Armstrong Space Station, we observed it fly very close to a malfunctioning Russian satellite," Hayes said. "While we watched, we noticed the satellite suddenly breaking apart."

"The spaceplane attacked it? With what?"

"The preliminary data on the event was from radar images, and they did not spot any projectiles such as the Scimitar hypervelocity missiles they have used before," Hayes said. "We've asked the Air Force to look back through images from the Space-Based Infrared Satellite system taken during the incident to see if they can detect a laser."

"A laser?" the president exclaimed. "A satellite-killing laser on a spaceplane?"

"Very possible, sir," Hayes said. "We've had plans for small satellite-killing lasers for a long time, as have the Russians—it's possible they've mounted one in the cargo bay of an Elektron spaceplane."

"We could sure use something like that now," Ann said.

"We opted for the Kingfisher attack satellites, ma'am, because they could carry antisatellite, antiballistic-missile, and ground-attack weapons, whereas the laser satellites couldn't attack targets on Earth," Hayes said.

"Are we in agreement that the Russians at least appear to be ready, willing, and able to attack our spacecraft?" the president asked. His question was met with silence and a lot of somber faces. "I tend to agree, guys: Gryzlov is angry, and he's psychotic, and with that Starfire test he's seen his opportunity to push the issue of space weapons—and he could very easily have world opinion with him. He could attack one of our spaceplanes and argue that he was provoked into doing so." He looked at the stunned faces on the videoconference screen. "Anyone think that Gryzlov is going to negotiate any of this?"

"He's already told the world what he's going to do," Glenbrook said. "He's invoked the safety of his entire nation—he's even told his citizens to *take shelter* when the station flies overhead! Anything less than Skybolt becoming a meteorite would not be acceptable. He'd look weak if he started negotiating."

"What are my military options? Fred?"

"We haven't exhausted all our options, Mr. President," Secretary of Defense Hayes said resolutely. "Not by a long shot. The free-electron laser aboard Armstrong Space Station and the Kingfisher weapon garages are the best options to take out the Elektron launch sites, MiG-31D bases, and S-500S antisatellite missile launchers, sir. If we deploy the entire Kingfisher constellation, we can hold every Russian antispacecraft site and spaceport at risk twenty-four/seven. The Russians have deployed the S-500 air defense weapon at their launch sites, but they can't touch a Thor's Hammer precision-guided projectile coming in from space at ten thousand miles an hour—and of course Skybolt flies at the speed of light. If it gets into position and lets loose, it can't be stopped."

The president thought about that for several moments—it was obvious he wasn't comfortable with using the space-based weapons. "Other options, Fred?" he finally asked.

"The S-500 changes the game, sir," Hayes said. "The only other nonnuclear options are attacks by our six remaining B-2 stealth bombers, and cruise missiles launched from our few B-1 and B-52 bombers, plus ship-launched nonnuclear cruise missiles. To attack the Russian and Chinese spaceports, it means overflying Russian and Chinese territory—our nonnuclear cruise missiles have a range of only seven hundred miles, which means we could hit a few of those S-500 sites but not the spaceports. The S-500 is capable against both stealth and subsonic low-flying cruise missiles, highly capable against B-1 bombers, and deadly to a B-52."

"What would the chances be for the cruise missiles and stealth bombers, General?" Vice President Page asked.

"No better than fifty-fifty, ma'am," Hayes said. "The S-500 is that good. Our air-launched cruise missiles have twice the range of the S-500, but the S-500 is mobile and can be moved and set up quickly, so the chance of an inertially guided cruise missile targeting just a set of geographic coordinates at the battery's last known position and getting one is not very good. The extended-range version of the Joint Air-Launched Standoff cruise missile has an imaging infrared sensor, so it would be more capable against mobile and pop-up targets, but it's subsonic and the S-500 would be very capable against it. The twelve refurbished B-1 bombers we obtained are good, but we don't have experienced crews yet. B-52s would have zero chance. They would have to get past the Russian's primary air defense system, the S-400, and then take on the S-500s protecting the spaceports and launch sites." He turned to the president. "The space weapons are our best option, sir. We shouldn't deactivate the Skybolt module—in fact, my recommendation is to activate Skybolt and the Kingfisher satellites already in orbit, send up spaceplanes, and have them place the garages that are in storage back into their orbits to complete the constellation."

It was obvious the president didn't like that recommendation. "I don't want the Russians taking potshots at our spaceplanes, Fred," he said after a long moment of consideration.

"They could still do that if we detached the Skybolt module, sir, and then we would've given up a major weapon system that could help fight off an attack on the station or the weapon garages."

The president nodded. "How long will it take to deploy the Kingfisher garages back into orbit?"

"Several weeks, sir," Hayes said after consulting some notes on his tablet computer. "The garages are being stored on Armstrong. They would have to load the modules aboard a spaceplane, then either wait for the proper moment or fly into what is called a transfer orbit to get into the proper position to insert the module into its orbit."

"And the Russians will be observing this activity the whole time, I suppose?"

"Undoubtedly, sir," Hayes replied. "They can see as well as anyone what orbits need to be occupied in order to complete the coverage—all they have to do is monitor those orbits. In the meantime, they can place S-500s and MiG-31Ds in the right places to take shots at the garages whenever they please, and of course they can do that now with Armstrong—in fact, we believe they have as many as six S-500s and MiG-31Ds with antisatellite weapons targeted against Armstrong right now in its current orbit. If we move the station's orbit, they simply move the antisatellite weapons wherever necessary."

"So Armstrong is vulnerable to attack?" the president asked.

"The Hydra COIL defensive laser is operational, and the Kingfishers currently in orbit and the Skybolt laser can be activated fairly quickly," Hayes replied. "Each Kingfisher garage carries three antisatellite weapons as well as three land-attack projectiles. I believe the station can defend itself very well once all systems are back online." He spread his hands. "After the two-day deadline, the Russians would see that we have not disconnected Skybolt, and that's when we see if they make good on their threat."

"Gryzlov has already gone on international television—if he backs down, he loses face in the eyes of the whole world," National Security Adviser Glenbrook said. "He could do a minimal attack to try to look serious . . ."

"Gryzlov doesn't strike me as a guy who would do something halfway," Ann said. "I don't think he's concerned about losing face—the guy is just plain maniacal. I think if he decides to go, he'll go all-out."

"What would we lose if we lost Armstrong, Fred?"

"Fourteen personnel, including the two college students," Hayes said. "A multibillion-dollar investment. Several different weapons and sensors with advanced capabilities. We'd still have control of the weapon garages from U.S. Space Command headquarters, however."

"Armstrong is a pretty powerful presence, sir—it's like an aircraft carrier sitting off someone's coast," Glenbrook added. "If we lost it, that could paint a very ominous picture around the world. We wouldn't be totally defeated, but definitely taken down a few notches."

Ann could see the absolute agony in the president's face as he struggled with the decision. "Sir, the main thing we'd lose is the high ground," she said. "Gryzlov wants it, and he's hoping we'll just hand it over to him. I believe Armstrong has the weaponry to fight off a Russian attack. I don't want to knuckle under to Gryzlov's bullying. Starfire is not a space weapon and it doesn't threaten Russia. Gryzlov can't dictate what we do with our forces. What's he going to demand next—we do away with all of our nuclear subs and aircraft carriers because they *might* threaten Russia? My suggestion: Tell the bastard to go pound sand."

"Shit," Phoenix muttered. This was the moment he had feared all of his presidential life: the future of the republic, dependent on the words he might utter moments from now. Yes or no, go or no go, attack or not attack. If he ordered his forces to stand down, they might survive to fight another day. If he ordered his forces to escalate and prepare to fight, that's probably exactly what they'd have to do very soon.

"I hate to knuckle under to Gryzlov, guys," he said after a long moment's consideration, "but I feel I have no choice. I want the Skybolt laser deactivated and the module detached from Armstrong Space Station." Glenbrook and Hayes looked relieved; Ann looked dejected. "What are we left with on the station after Skybolt is deactivated, Ann?"

"The Skybolt laser module has a few targeting sensors and lasers that will be off-line when the module is detached," Ann replied, "but station will still have the Hydra short-range laser, the Trinity modules that are stored on station's truss, and the weapon garages of the Kingfisher constellation already in orbit."

"All defensive weapons?"

"The Trinity modules each contain three land-attack reentry vehicles and three antisatellite vehicles," Ann said. "Those could be considered offensive weapons. Sir, I wish you'd reconsider your decision," she added. "We can't deactivate every military system Gryzlov wants."

"Unfortunately, I made the decision to allow a military weapon system to be used for that college experiment," the president said. "A lot of people are making up stories, expressing outrage and horror, and threatening war, but the fact remains that I decided to turn a college experiment into a weapon. I have to live with the consequences. Shut it down and detach it, Fred."

"Yes, sir," Secretary of Defense Hayes said.

"Mr. President, I would like to go to station to help deactivate Skybolt," Vice President Page said.

"*What?*" Phoenix's eyes bugged out in absolute shock. "That request is *denied*, Miss Vice President! That station is already in Russia's crosshairs, and it could come under attack at any moment!"

"Sir, no one knows more about that module than I do. I spent three years designing it and two years building it. I know every circuit and rivet, because I personally drew them by hand on a real drawing board and did everything but operate the soldering iron and riveter myself." The president didn't look convinced one bit. "One more ride in space for the old lady. If John Glenn can do it, I sure as hell can. What do you say, sir?"

The president hesitated, studying Ann's smiling face carefully. "I'd rather have you close to the White House or out campaigning for our reelection, Ann," he said, "but I know Skybolt is your baby." He shook his head woefully, then nodded. "I might be crazy for doing this, but your request is approved. The first president,

first Secret Service agent, first teenagers, first paraplegic, and now the first vice president in space, all in one
year. My head is spinning. God help us."

"Thank you, sir," Ann said.

"I'll head back to Washington right away," the
president said. "I'll plan on going on television to
explain that Starfire was not a space weapon and that
the United States will deactivate and detach the laser
module right away."

"Very good, sir," Ann said. "I'll see you from station. Wish me luck." And the video teleconference was
terminated.

"We're all going to need some luck," the president
said half aloud, then reached for the phone to call Air
Force One's flight crew. In moments, the president's
plane was heading east toward Washington.

Next, the president called Moscow. "What did you
decide, Phoenix?" Gryzlov asked through the interpreter without any pleasantries or preamble.

"The United States agrees to undock the Skybolt
module from Armstrong Space Station," Phoenix said,
"and at an appropriate time deorbit it and allow it to
reenter the atmosphere. Any parts that survive reentry
will splash down in the ocean."

"Then Russia agrees not to restrict its airspace above
twenty kilometers," Gryzlov said, "to all spacecraft . . .

except your S-series spaceplanes and your Kingfisher weapon garages."

"We need those spaceplanes, Mr. President," Phoenix said.

"They represent as much a danger to Russia as your Skybolt laser, Phoenix," Gryzlov said. "Maybe even a greater danger. No, sir. The United States flew in space for decades without a spaceplane, and you now have several commercial operators who can service the space stations and do other tasks. The commercial spacecraft are permitted to overfly Russia, as long as they report their mission details before they launch. But after ten days' time from today's date, we will consider any overflight by the spaceplanes or the weapon garages to be a hostile act and will respond accordingly. Do we have an agreement, Phoenix?"

"No, you do not, sir," Phoenix said. "The space-planes allow us access to Earth orbit and to our in-orbit assets. They are not military weapons. We will agree to keep informing you of future launches and their flight paths, and we will keep the spaceplanes from overflying Russia in the atmosphere if possible, but we insist on access to space for all our vehicles, including the spaceplanes. Are we agreed, Mr. President?"

After a long pause, Gryzlov said, "We will be watching your military space station for signs that the laser module has been deactivated and detached. Then we will speak again." And the call was terminated.

Phoenix pressed the button for the communications officer. "Yes, Mr. President?" she answered immediately.

"I want to speak with the national security team back at the White House again," he said. A few moments later, the vice president, national security adviser, and secretary of defense appeared again on the video teleconference screen. "I made a deal with the devil, guys," he said. "I want the Skybolt module detached from Armstrong Space Station as soon as possible. Ann, get up there as quickly as you can."

ABOARD ARMSTRONG SPACE STATION

A short time later

"Is he insane?" Brad exclaimed. "Gryzlov wants us to detach Skybolt and deorbit it? And now he's going to restrict all the airspace over Russia out to *three hundred miles up*? That's craziness!"

"Guys, I am so sorry about this," Kim Jung-bae said over the satellite videoconference feed from the White Sands Missile Test Range. "I never said it was a space weapon—that was Dr. Nukaga's conclusion. I'm sorry I told him we used the MHD generator, but all I did was admit to him that my power transfer relays did not work, and he asked me what power source we did use. I am so sorry, guys. I had no idea this would blow up like this."

"It's not your fault, Jerry," Brad said. "I think Dr. Nukaga thought it was a weapon from day one. But he supported the project because of you, and then when Cal Poly won that big grant and we went international, he was fully on board." Jerry still looked ashen and dejected, as if he had just lost his best friends in the world by getting caught stealing from them. "The question is: What do we do now?"

"That one's easy, Brad; as soon as we can, we're going to bring a spaceplane up and get you and Casey off station," Armstrong Space Station's director Kai Raydon said. He was seated at the command position, and every other combat position was manned as well—including the Skybolt station, even though the Starfire microwave generator was still installed. "After that, I want to get this station ready for war, not only on the ground but imminently in space."

"Can any orbiting body completely avoid overflying Russia?" Casey Huggins asked.

"Any orbit less than about thirty-five degrees inclination will not overfly Russia," Valerie Lukas said. "We can still look pretty deeply into Russia, although we miss most of their farthest north regions, depending on the altitude. In contrast, if we put up the same restriction, Russian spacecraft would be limited to no more than about twenty-five degrees. But except for geosynchronous orbits or for ocean surveillance, equatorial orbits are mostly useless because so little of Earth's population lives on the equator."

"But that's not the point, Valerie," Kai said. "There are thousands of spacecraft that overfly Russia every day—Gryzlov can't simply tell everyone that they have to move them. It's all bluster. Even if he had enough weapons to attack satellites that overflew Russia, he knows he could spark a world war if he even attempted to shoot down a foreign satellite. Gryzlov is making wild accusations, and using his trumped-up scenarios to try to institute an emergency edict and circumvent international law." His serious expression turned even darker. "Casey, how long would it take to get your microwave generator off Skybolt?"

"Less than two days, sir," Casey replied, "with at least one spacewalk."

"Plus another two days, maybe three, to plug in the free-electron laser, with at least one spacewalk," Valerie Lukas added. "Plus a day or so to test it. We could sure use some technical assistance and more hands to help."

"Trevor, get Alice together with the Starfire people and start to work getting the microwave generator uninstalled," Kai said. The station manager, Trevor Shale, turned to his communications panel and started making intercom calls. "I'll call U.S. Space Command and start getting some help and permissions to reinstall the free-electron laser and get it ready to go."

"Do you really think Gryzlov would attack the station, sir?" Brad asked.

"You heard him, Brad; the guy thinks we're going to start razing towns, villages, and the countryside with death rays," Kai replied. "He's given us an ultimatum of just ten days, and anyone that overflies Russia will be subject to what he calls 'neutralization,' whatever that means. Those are some pretty serious threats. I want this station fully operational just in case he's serious."

Kai heard the incoming-call alert tone and hit a button on his command console. "Just getting ready to call you, General," he said after the encryption channels locked in.

"I take it you've heard Gryzlov's remarks, Kai," General George Sandstein, commander of Air Force Space Command, said.

"Pretty outrageous, General," Kai said, "but I'm believing every word. I want to reactivate the free-electron laser and start rebuilding the Kingfisher constellation right away."

"Unfortunately, the order from the White House is to deactivate Skybolt and detach the module from the station, Kai," Sandstein said.

"Say again, General?"

"That's the order from the president himself," Sandstein said. "We're launching an S-19 and an S-29 as soon as possible to get the students off the station and bring up some extra personnel—including Skybolt's designer."

The entire command module occupants gasped in surprise. "They're sending up the vice president?"

"You heard me right, Kai," Sandstein said. "It sounds a little loco, but she's an experienced astronaut, and there's no one who knows Skybolt better. Sorry about Skybolt, Kai, but the president wants to defuse the situation before things get out of hand. Everything else in the green?"

"The Hydra laser is operational," Kai said, shaking his head in disbelief. "We are also able to use the Kingfisher modules on the central truss for station self-defense."

"Excellent," Sandstein said. "Good luck up there. We'll be watching. Hopefully everyone will stay nice and cool, and this will all blow over soon."

MCLANAHAN INDUSTRIAL SPACEPORT, BATTLE MOUNTAIN, NEVADA

Later that day

"Thanks for coming in so quickly, guys," Boomer said as he strode into the crew briefing room. Seated around the room were the six spaceplane student pilots and four instructor spacecraft commanders, along with mission support and maintenance technicians. "This might sound like some cheezy World War Two novel, but I'm sure you heard Gryzlov's nonsense, and I think we are inching toward war with the Russians. The president has canceled the rest of his campaign and is on his way back to Washington to make an address about the Starfire thing. He has ordered the deactivation of the Skybolt laser and detaching it from Armstrong."

Everyone in the briefing room looked horrified. "This is bullshit!" Sondra Eddington exclaimed. "Gryzlov spouts off, makes all kinds of outrageous claims, and threatens us, and we kowtow to him? Why don't we tell him to bugger off instead?"

"I agree with you, Sondra, but we've got our orders, and time is of the essence," Boomer said. "We've been tasked to bring up supplies and technicians to help detach the Skybolt module, and we'll also be flying more supplies to the ISS as well. I think we'll be doing a lot of flying in the next couple weeks." He looked over the spaceplane crewmembers before him. "John, Ernesto, and Sondra, you have a year of training or more and are checked out as mission commanders in at least two of the spaceplanes, so you're going to go operational and fly as mission commanders before graduation." All three of them wore excited smiles and gave each other high-fives, and the others looked dejected. "Don, Mary, and Kev, you guys might not get much spaceplane time for a few weeks, but you can keep up your studying and double up on the simulator and MiG-25 time. Kev, you're closest to the one-year cutoff and you're checked out as MC in the S-9 and S-19, so you may be called upon if this thing drags on.

"Now, Russian president Gryzlov threatened to attack any spaceplanes overflying Russia after ten days," Boomer reminded them all. "I think the guy is doing nothing but chest-thumping, but we just don't know for sure. So if you think there might be too much danger—even more than we normally have in store on every flight—you don't have to fly. No one will criticize you at all if you decide to bug out. We're not in the military: we're contractors, and although we put our butts on the line every time we step into those flying machines, we're not expected to work in a combat zone. We take enough risks already to not have to fly with missiles or lasers being fired at us, right? You don't have to tell me now—tell me in my office, in private, and we'll redo the schedule."

"I'll tell you right now, Boomer: I'm flying," Ernesto Hermosillo, one of the senior student pilots, said. "Gryzlov can *besar mi culo peludo.*" The others in the briefing room all clapped and said they would go as well.

"Thank you, all of you," Boomer said. "But I know you haven't spoken about this with your families, and it has to be a family decision. After you talk with your families, if you want to cancel, just tell me. Like I said, no one will think less of you.

"We have one S-29 and one S-19 on the line, and two more 19s ready to go in a few days, so here are the assignments," Boomer went on. "Gonzo and Sondra in the S-19, and myself and *culo peludo* Ernesto in the S-29. Because I anticipate doing some spacewalks when we arrive, I'll be prebreathing." He handed out the other assignments, always pairing up an experienced spaceplane commander with a student mission commander. "Get your physicals, we'll all be in EEAS or ACES suits, and will probably stay in them for several days. Ernesto, we'll brief right after we suit up during my prebreathe. Questions?" Boomer fielded several questions and shared a little nervous banter with his crews. "Okay, guys, the countdown has started for the first two birds. Let's pay attention, work smart, work as a team, and everyone comes home. Let's go."

Sondra stayed behind after the others left, a little flash of anger in her eyes. "Why am I flying with Gonzo?" she asked. "Why can't I fly with you?"

"You're not checked out as MC in the S-29, Sondra," Boomer said. "Ernesto is. Besides, I'm giving you and Gonzo the stop in Washington. You'll get to meet the vice president and take her up to Armstrong."

Instead of being surprised or happy about flying the vice president, Sondra was still angry. "I'm just a couple months from finishing the S-29 mission commander course," she said petulantly. "I'm a better MC now in any of the spaceplanes than Ernesto will *ever* be."

Boomer's eyes rolled in surprise. "Whoa, whoa, Sondra. We don't talk smack about fellow pilots, even in private. We're a team."

"You know it's true," Sondra said. "Besides, the damn thing practically flies itself—it doesn't even need an MC. You did it because you're pissed because we're not sleeping together anymore."

"I did it because you're not checked out as an MC in the S-29, Sondra, simple as that," Boomer said. "Besides, *I* made the decision not to sleep with you. Brad and I were working closer and closer together on Starfire, and I didn't think it was right."

"But it was okay when I started training here, wasn't it?" Sondra spat. "You knew I was seeing him back then."

"Sondra, I'm not changing the schedule," Boomer said. "Fly with Gonzo or don't fly." He looked at his watch, then at her. "The countdown has started. Are you going or not?" In reply, she gave him an angry scowl, spun on a heel, and stormed out.

Boomer ran an exasperated hand across his face, confused and conflicted about what to do in this situation. But he resolved to put this personal matter out of his mind and concentrate on the task at hand.

Every crewmember was required to get a physical exam before flight, so that was Boomer's first stop. Afterward, he stopped at Mission Planning to check on the flight schedule, which was being set up and verified by computer and then loaded into the spaceplane's computers. His own S-29 Shadow spaceplane was being loaded with much-needed supplies for Armstrong and the ISS, so he would arrive first. Gonzo's S-19 Midnight spaceplane had the passenger module on board in the cargo bay. She would take off, arrive at Joint Base Andrews near Washington just a couple hours later, pick up the vice president and her Secret Service detail, and fly her to Armstrong about four hours after he arrived at Armstrong.

Next stop was life support. While Hermosillo needed help to get into his Advanced Crew Escape Suit, suiting up was relatively easy for Boomer. The EEAS, or Electronic Elastomeric Activity Suit, was like a heavy union suit, made of silvery radiation-proof carbon-fiber threads that covered every part of the body from the top of the neck to the bottoms of the feet. After putting on electronically controlled insulated underwear, which would control his body temperature during a spacewalk, Boomer slipped into the EEAS, then into boots and gloves, locking in the connectors for each, plugged his suit into a test console, then put on his pre-breathing mask.

After making sure there were no deep folds or crinkles and that his testicles and penis were arranged properly, he plugged the suit into a test console and hit a button. The suit instantly constricted tightly around every square inch of his body that came into contact with it, making him involuntarily grunt aloud—the source of the suit's nickname and pseudonym for EEAS, "EAHGHSS!" But moving about and especially space-walking would be much easier for him than it would be for someone in an oxygen-inflated ACES, because the suit would automatically readjust around his body to maintain pressure on the skin without creating any binding or causing changes in pressure. The human body's vascular system was already pressure-sealed, but in a vacuum or at a lower-atmospheric pressure, the skin would bulge outward if it were not constrained; the ACES did it with oxygen pressure, while the EEAS did it with mechanical pressure.

"I always think I'd like to try one of those things," Ernesto said on intercom, smiling and shaking his head while he watched Boomer preflight his suit, "and then I watch you hit the test switch, and it looks like you get kicked in the nuts every time, so I change my mind."

Boomer shut off the test switch to relax the suit. "Takes a little getting used to," he admitted.

They finished getting suited up, then sat in comfortable chairs while they received a crew briefing by the chief mission planning officer, Alice Wainwright, via video teleconference. The route of flight got Boomer's attention right away. "Uh, Alice? Given the reason we're doing all this, is this really the route of flight we should be taking?" he asked over the intercom.

"The computers don't know about politics or Gryzlov, Boomer—all they know is desired final position, bearing, velocity, gravity, orbital mechanics, thrust, position of station, and all that good stuff," Alice said. "Station needs the equipment as soon as possible."

There was a process called the "accident chain," Boomer knew: a series of minor and seemingly unrelated incidents that combine to cause an accident—or in this case, an encounter with a Russian antisatellite weapon. One of the more common incidents was "get the mission done—it's important; disregard safety and common sense and just get it done." That's what was happening right now—link number one in the accident chain had just appeared. "It can't wait one more day or even a few hours?" Boomer asked.

"I mapped out all of the launch windows and flight paths, Boomer," Alice said. "All of the others fly over populated areas, and people have complained about the sonic booms." Link number two. "Since the Russians disconnected the ROS from the International Space Station, both Canada and Mexico and a bunch of other countries are expressing deep reservations about allowing spaceplanes to fly over their territory until above the Kármán level. It's this flight or nothing for two days."

That alarm bell was going off in his head as link number three joined the others, but he knew Armstrong and the ISS needed the supplies, and those left on the ISS needed them badly—or was he now forging his own links in the accident chain? "Are we going to notify the Russians of our missions?" he asked.

"That's standard procedure," Alice said. "Apparently Space Command thinks Gryzlov is bluffing. We're going to keep on normal protocols."

The fourth link in the accident chain had just been forged, Boomer thought—this was not looking good. He turned to Ernesto. "*¿Qué te parece, amigo?* What do you think, buddy?"

"*Vamos, comandante,*" Ernesto said. "Let's go, Commander. Gryzlov doesn't have the cojones." Was that yet another link? Boomer wondered.

"Any other questions, Boomer?" Alice asked a little impatiently. "You step in ten minutes, and I still have to brief Gonzo and Sondra."

The fifth link in the accident chain had just been connected, but Boomer didn't recognize it. He was the spacecraft commander—it was his final decision . . . but he didn't. He thought about it for a moment, then nodded to Ernesto. "No questions, Alice," he said on intercom. "We press." Ten minutes later Boomer picked up his portable air-conditioning and oxygen pack, and he and Ernesto headed out to the crew van that would take them to the flight line.

The S-29 Shadow was the third and largest model of the spaceplanes, with five "leopards" engines instead of four, and a fifteen-thousand-pound payload. With the preflight already accomplished by the techs, Boomer and Ernesto entered the spaceplane through the open cockpit canopies, connected their umbilicals to the ship, and strapped in. The Shadow was even more automated than its sisters, and it was just a matter of checking the computer's progress as it handled the preflight checklists, acknowledging each checklist complete, then awaiting their start-engines, taxi, and takeoff times.

At the preprogrammed time the engines automatically came alive, the after-engine-start checklists were run, the taxi lane was cleared, and precisely at the taxi time, the throttles automatically came up and the Shadow began to taxi itself to the main runway at Battle Mountain for takeoff. "I'll never get used to the plane just taxiing by itself," Ernesto said. "Kinda creepy."

"I know what you mean," Boomer said. "I've asked several times to be allowed to fly it myself, without the automation, but Richter always turns me down, with a stern warning not to try it. After there's more than one of these, I'll ask again. Kaddiri and Richter don't want their newest and brightest daughter defiled by someone like me. They do enough defiling to each other, *corregir*?" Ernesto gave Boomer a fist bump and nodded agreement.

The two astronauts literally just sat there for the rest of the voyage, chitchatting, monitoring checklists and acknowledging completions and starts, and watching the Shadow do its thing: it flew itself to the refueling anchor, this time over northern Minnesota; refueled itself with another computer-controlled tanker aircraft; turned to the orbital insertion point over Colorado, turned northeast, and hit the throttles at the appropriate time. They watched all the readouts and acknowledged the checklist executions and completions, but in the end they were just babysitters.

But now, as they headed into orbit, they stopped chatting and were on guard, because their track would take them across northwestern Russia . . .

. . . just three hundred miles northwest of Plesetsk Cosmodrome, and practically right over the Russian Red Banner Northern Fleet naval headquarters at Severomorsk.

"Talk about twisting the tiger's tail, comandante," Ernesto commented. "Or, in this case, the bear's tail."

"You got that right, amigo," Boomer said. "You got that right."

THE KREMLIN
MOSCOW, RUSSIAN FEDERATION
That same time

"Sir, an American spaceplane has just been detected overflying Plesetsk Cosmodrome!" Minister of Defense Gregor Sokolov shouted into the phone when Gryzlov picked it up.

"What in hell did you say?" Gryzlov grunted into the bedroom phone. Foreign Minister Daria Titeneva, lying naked beside Gryzlov, was instantly awake, and she rose out of bed and hurried to get dressed—she didn't know what the call was about, but anyone daring to call President Gennadiy Gryzlov in the middle of the night had to have a damned serious reason for doing so, and she knew she would be called into his office immediately afterward.

"I said, the Americans have launched a spaceplane into orbit—and it came within a few hundred kilometers from Plesetsk Cosmodrome!" Sokolov repeated. "It directly overflew the Red Banner Northern Fleet headquarters in Severomorsk. It is definitely going into orbit, and is on course to intercept Armstrong Space Station within the hour."

"*Vyyebat'!*" Gryzlov swore. "How dare those sons of bitches do that after I just issued my orders? Are they fucking ignoring me? Were we notified of any spaceplane flights?"

"We are checking with the air attaché's office in Washington, sir," Sokolov said. "No response from them yet."

"*Those bastards!*" Gryzlov shouted. "Phoenix is going to pay for this! Summon the entire security council to my office *immediately*!"

Twenty minutes later Gryzlov strode into his office, his longish dark hair streaming behind his neck in his hurry. Only Tarzarov and Sokolov had arrived. "Well, Sokolov?" he shouted.

"The American Space Command reported to the air attaché in Washington that one S-29 Shadow and one S-19 Midnight spaceplane will be sent into orbit within the next six hours," the defense minister reported, handing the president some charts and radar plots. "The S-29 will go to Armstrong, drop off supplies and pick up passengers, go into a transfer orbit, transition to the International Space Station to drop off supplies and pick up personnel, then return the next day. The S-19 will fly to Joint Base Andrews near Washington, pick up passengers, then fly to Armstrong. They also announced that they will send several manned and unmanned commercial cargo modules to both stations over the next seventy-two hours."

"*Two* spaceplanes?" Gryzlov thundered. "They are launching *two spaceplanes*? And one is already in orbit, not within six hours? That is unacceptable! And their flight paths?"

"Any flight path that travels to either space station will overfly Russia, sir," Sokolov said.

"That is *unacceptable!*" Gryzlov shouted again. "I ordered spaceplanes to *not* overfly Russia! Is there any evidence that they are working to detach the Skybolt module from the military space station?"

"No, sir," Sokolov said. "We scan the station when it passes near a space surveillance site, about every four to six hours, and we have not noticed any external change in the station."

"It has not been that long since you made your speech or spoken to President Phoenix, sir," Chief of Staff Tarzarov said. "Maybe the purpose of these flights is to do as you ordered. And, sir, you said you would give the Americans two—"

"Stop making excuses for the Americans, Tarzarov," Gryzlov said. "I will not be disregarded like this! I will not be made a patsy, like that tottering fool Phoenix!" He looked at the radar plots of the spaceplane's flight path. "This looks to me like a trial attack run on our cosmodrome! *That is not acceptable!*"

"Shall I get President Phoenix on the phone for you, sir?" Tarzarov asked. "This must be explained."

"No need, Mr. Tarzarov," Daria Titeneva said as she walked quickly into the president's office, after waiting a discreet length of time after leaving Gryzlov's bedroom. She held up a folder. "Text of an address Phoenix gave on American television just a short time ago. He again denies that it was a space-based directed-energy weapon and that the civilian airplane was downed by the weapon; no mention of deactivating the Skybolt laser; and he says that no nation has the right to restrict any movement of any aircraft or spacecraft above the Kármán line, which is the altitude above which aerodynamic lift cannot be—"

"I know what the hell the Kármán line is, Daria—I trained as a cosmonaut, remember?" Gryzlov interrupted acidly. He nodded, then turned back to his desk and looked out the windows. He was suddenly acting remarkably calm, they all noticed—they had expected him to continue the rant that started this meeting. "So. This is unexpected. Kenneth Phoenix has somehow grown a spine in recent days, despite his surprising agreement to detach the Skybolt module. We have much to discuss, my friends. Let us move to the conference room. Coffee and tea?"

JOINT BASE ANDREWS, NEAR WASHINGTON, D.C.

Several hours later

Inside a large aircraft hangar, Jessica "Gonzo" Faulkner and Sondra Eddington stood at the base of the boarding stairs of the S-19 Midnight spaceplane as the limousine pulled up. Gonzo was wearing her EEAS space suit, while Sondra had an orange ACES suit. Neither was wearing a helmet. On either side of them were two plainclothed Secret Service agents, who had already inspected the interior and exterior of the S-19 space-plane they were standing beside—they freely admit-ted they didn't know what in hell to look for, but their job was to inspect any area the vice president might occupy, so they did it. The spaceplane was parked on a secure section of the aircraft parking ramp at Joint Base Andrews, formerly Andrews Air Force Base, the main military airport used by high-ranking members of the U.S. government when they travelrd on military aircraft. The ramp was surrounded by several layers of security, both on the ground and overhead.

A Secret Service agent opened the limousine's doors, and out stepped two persons, both wearing orange ACES space suits: a female Secret Service agent, and the vice president of the United States, Ann Page. Ann came over to Gonzo and extended a gloved hand. "Colonel Faulkner?"

"Yes, ma'am," Gonzo said, shaking her hand. "Nice to meet you. I'll be your spacecraft commander today. This is Sondra Eddington, our mission commander." Sondra and the vice president shook hands as well. "Welcome aboard."

"Thank you. I'm looking forward to this," Ann said, her eyes glistening with excitement. "This is Special Agent Robin Clarkson, my Secret Service detail." Clarkson shook hands with the pilots. She looked a little nervous, Gonzo thought, but not nearly as much as poor Special Agent Charlie Spellman did when he flew with the president. Ann stood and admired the S-19 Midnight with a big smile on her face. "My first time in an S-19 Midnight. I've got a few flights in an S-9 Black Stallion, but that was in the very early days."

"I don't think you'll find many differences at all, ma'am," Gonzo said. "The passenger module is very comfortable, but I assumed you'd want to be in the cockpit for this flight."

"Hell yes," Ann said. "I hope you don't mind, Miss Eddington. I never turn down an opportunity to ride in the cockpit."

"Of course not, ma'am," Sondra said, but it was rather obvious that she did mind. I never turn it down either, she thought, but I guess I just don't matter around this place anymore.

"Shall we go?" Ann asked excitedly. "I can't wait to see station again."

"We have plenty of time, ma'am," Gonzo said. "No hurry at all. Our launch window opens in about an hour."

"Very good, Colonel Faulkner," Ann said.

"Gonzo, please. I don't respond to rank anymore."

"Gonzo it is." She looked at the EEAS space suit. "I love this suit," she said. "It accentuates your figure very well, a lot better than this old thing. You like it?"

"When it's activated it's a bit of a kick in the pants," Gonzo admitted, "but it makes moving around and working so much better."

They made their way up the stairs to the airlock entry hatch atop the Midnight spaceplane, then down a ladder and aft to the passenger module, and Gonzo helped Clarkson and Sondra strap in and don their helmets, then briefed them on normal and emergency procedures. "I know the drill, Gonzo," Sondra said, sounding perturbed when Gonzo tried to help her attach her umbilicals.

"I gotta go through the routine with everybody, Sondra—you know that," Gonzo said in a low voice, giving the young woman a warning stare and looking to see if Clarkson was noticing any of this. "Play nice, okay?" To Clarkson she said, "For safety reasons, we'll be wearing helmets and gloves, but you can keep your visors open. If necessary, all you need to do is close them, and you'll be secure. Sondra will help you. Have a nice flight." Clarkson nodded but said nothing.

After technicians made sure everything in the passenger module was secure and ready, they helped Ann Page into the Midnight's right front seat and strapped her in, connected her up, and helped her with her helmet. "I can't wait, I can't wait," she said excitedly when the intercom was activated. "I miss traveling in space so much. With you guys it probably seems so routine, but back in the shuttle and early spaceplane days, it seemed every flight was a test flight. The media always reported it as 'just another shuttle launch,' but we were so clueless. You have no idea."

"Oh, I do, ma'am," Gonzo said. "I know the guy who designed our 'leopards' engines, and he can be a real flake-ozoid sometimes. Our lives are in that guy's hands on every flight."

"Please call me Ann on this flight, Gonzo," Ann said. "I want to feel like a crewmember and not a passenger who's allowed to ride shotgun."

"Okay, Ann."

"Hunter 'Boomer' Noble," Ann said. "I remember I was the cat's pajamas in aerospace engineering until he came along. His reputation blew past mine like a freakin' hurricane."

"The students working on the Starfire project will blow past Boomer soon, I guarantee it," Gonzo said, "and their school, Cal Poly, isn't even the best engineering school in the country. I think we'll see some amazing advances very soon."

The two continued chatting until it was time for taxi and takeoff. Gonzo found that the vice president was very familiar with the spaceplane's checklists and switch positions, and she performed very well as a mission commander. "I'm impressed, Ann," she said. "You know as much about Midnight as a student MC."

"I helped design the S-9 spaceplanes and trained to fly them, although most times I was just a passenger," Ann said. "I guess it's like riding a bicycle: once you do it, you never forget."

Takeoff, repositioning to the air refueling track, and the acceleration using the scramjets were normal. Because their takeoff time was several hours different from the S-29s, the flight paths of the two spaceplanes were several thousand miles apart—as the S-19 Midnight ascended on scramjets, they overflew India, China, and the Russian Far East.

"I love it, I love it, I love it," the vice president intoned as they started their steep ascent. There was absolutely no hint of the G-forces in her voice, just a big smile on her face. "This is the *only* way to fly!"

OVER YELIZOVO AIRPORT
KAMCHATKA KRAI, EASTERN RUSSIA

That same time

"*Garpun* flight, this is *Uchitel,* your order is *solnechnyy svet,* repeat, *solnechnyy svet,*" the senior controller radioed. "Sunshine, sunshine. Proceed as planned."

"Harpoon flight leader acknowledges," the pilot of the lead formation of two MiG-31D Foxhound fighters radioed in reply. "Break. Harpoon Two, did you copy?"

"*Da, vozhd'*," the second MiG-31's pilot responded. "Two is ready."

The lead pilot completed his before-release checklists, turned to center the flight-director bars in his heads-up display, gradually fed in power until he was in afterburner zone, waited for airspeed to build up past Mach 1, then pulled up into a steep climb and continued feeding in power until he was in zone-five afterburner. Now climbing at ten thousand feet a minute, he punched through fifty thousand feet. The airspeed had hit Mach 1.5, but now it was in a gradual decline as the pilot traded airspeed for altitude, but that was not a concern for him: keeping the flight-director bars, which depicted his necessary course and climb angle as broadcast from the headquarters tracking station, was his main job.

"Datalink has downloaded final targeting data," the weapon-systems officer behind the pilot reported. "Data transmission to *Osa* commencing. Ten seconds to go."

At sixty thousand feet the pilot received his first low-fuel warning—the two huge Soloviev D30-F6 engines in full zone-five afterburner were gulping fifty thousand pounds of fuel an hour, yet it carried only thirty thousand pounds total—airspeed had decreased to just three hundred knots, and climb rate was down to three thousand feet per minute. "Data transmission complete, five seconds to launch," the weapon-systems officer said. The pilot was relieved—in ten seconds, if they didn't pull out of this climb, they were going to stall and drop out of the sky like a rock. "Three . . . two . . . one . . . missile away."

The MiG-31D made a shallow turn to the left, and both crewmembers were able to watch as the Wasp missile ignited its solid-propellant motor and began its climb into space on a long yellow-and-red column of fire and smoke. The Wasp was a derivative of the 9K720 Iskander short-range theater ballistic missile. It received flight-path data from a ground tracking station, used its inertial guidance system to follow the flight path, then activated an imaging infrared terminal guidance system to home in on its target. Even traveling nearly vertical, it traveled well over a mile per second. Twenty seconds later, the second MiG-31 launched its own Wasp missile . . .

. . . on an intercept course for the S-19 Midnight spaceplane that was hurtling through space over Russia to rendezvous with Armstrong Space Station.

ARMSTRONG SPACE STATION

Moments later

"Missile launch detection!" Christine Rayhill, the terrestrial-weapons officer on Armstrong Space Station, shouted. "Two Russian Wasp ASATs launched from Kamchatka!"

Kai Raydon mashed the "all-call" button on his console. "Combat stations!" he shouted, trying to keep his voice under control. "All personnel to combat stations, this is not a drill!" To Valerie Lukas he said, "All defensive systems to auto, Valerie—we'll have to put it back in MANUAL when the spaceplane approaches. What's the status of Skybolt?"

"Still deactivated," Valerie said. "We've just started disconnecting Starfire."

"Connect it back up—we might need it," Kai said. "Where are the students?"

"I'm right here," Brad said, attached to a bulkhead beside Valerie's console. "Casey is in the Skybolt module. What should I do?"

"Keep watch over the monitors and sing out if you see something that looks dangerous," Kai replied. "Point it out to Sergeant Lukas, or anyone else, if she's busy. I can always use another set of eyes."

"Should I get into a space suit?" Brad said on intercom once he'd donned his oxygen mask and activated it.

"It's too late," Kai said. "All the modules should have been sealed up by now. Command-module personnel have to rely on damage-control crewmembers to assist." Kai didn't want to think about what would eventually happen to all of them in the case of a major hull breach, oxygen or no, but one hundred percent oxygen was the best they had. He hit another intercom button. "Boomer, say your status?"

"We'll be off in ten minutes, General," Boomer replied. He and Ernesto Hermosillo had docked with Armstrong Space Station and were supervising the off-loading of supplies from the cargo bay and refueling, and as soon as the alert was sounded they had terminated off-loading and began preparing to undock.

"All defensive weapons except Skybolt are active and on auto," Valerie reported. "Starfire, can you give me a—"

"*It's the S-19!*" Christine Rayhill shouted. "*The Wasp is targeting the S-19!* Intercept in two minutes! Two missiles inbound!"

"Shit!" Kai swore. He hit a button on his console. "Midnight Two, this is Armstrong, *red Wasp, repeat, red Wasp.*" On intercom he asked, "What's their range to station?"

"Beyond Hydra range," Valerie replied.

"Crank the range up to maximum," Kai said. The Hydra chlorine-oxygen-iodine laser, which had a maximum range of three hundred miles, had been detuned to sixty miles in compliance with the treaty, but Kai Raydon wasn't going to pay attention to treaties now. "Get the Kingfishers on station ready to go. They're released as soon as you have a firing solution."

"The Midnight is accelerating and climbing," Henry reported. In orbit, speed meant only one thing: altitude above Earth. Go faster and your altitude increased; slow down and altitude decreased.

"Computing a firing solution now," Valerie reported. The Kingfisher weapon garages being stored on Armstrong's central truss had been connected to the combat system and its missiles made available for station defense.

Moments later Henry Lathrop shouted, "Got it! Intercept course set! Six interceptors ready!"

"Combat, batteries released," Valerie said. "Nail those suckers!"

"Weapons away!" Henry shouted. Two of the weapon garages on the station's truss released all three of their satellite interceptors. They were simple nonaerodynamic boxes—since they would never fly in Earth's atmosphere, they could be in any shape— six feet long, with a radar and imaging infrared seeker in front, maneuvering rocket nozzles around the body at both ends, and a large rocket engine in back. The interceptors used steering signals from Armstrong to maneuver until they could lock on to targets with their own sensors. "Good track on all Trinities. Sixty seconds to intercept. I think we'll be in time, sir. The Midnight is going higher and faster. The inbounds will be within range of Hydra in seventy seconds."

Kai wasn't going to relax until both those Russian Wasp missiles were goners. "Trev, contact Space Command, tell them what's going on," he ordered. "Tell them I want permission to take out every antisatellite airfield and launch site that we—"

"*Pop-up orbiting bogey!*" Henry Lathrop shouted. A new icon had appeared on the large tactical display. It was in an orbit offset from Armstrong's by more than a hundred miles and in a completely different declination, but that was a very near miss in orbital terms. "It came out of nowhere, sir! Designate Oscar one." It did not seem to be a threat to the station or the S-19 Midnight, but the fact that they had not detected it until it was very close was troubling, very—

"*Sir, I'm losing the Trinities!*" Henry shouted.

"*What?*" Kai shouted. "What in hell's going on?"

"I don't know, sir!" Lathrop shouted. "Lost contact with one . . . two . . . three, sir; three Trinities, negative contact!"

"What is that newcomer?" Valerie shouted. "Can you get a visual on it?"

"All electro-optical trackers are being used on the Trinity intercepts," Lathrop said. "I've got a good radar track but negative visual." A heartbeat later: "Lost contact with four Trinities. Am I cleared to engage bogey Oscar-one, sir?"

"It's not a threat to station or the S-19, it's not at our altitude or orbit, and we don't have a visual identification," Kai said. "Negative. Do not engage. Launch more Trinities to get those ASAT missiles, *now.*"

ABOARD THE RUSSIAN ELEKTRON SPACEPLANE

That same time

They could not have timed it better, and Colonel Mikhail Galtin knew it was as much fate and luck as it was design, but it didn't matter—it was going to work perfectly. After four orbits intersecting Armstrong Space Station's, but at a lower altitude and offset about sixty kilometers, he had gotten himself in perfect position to arrive at the exact spot to engage the American space station's defensive missiles. He knew he had only seconds to act . . . but seconds were an eternity to the Hobnail laser weapon.

As soon as the American antisatellite weapons were launched from Armstrong Space Station, Galtin's Elektron's fire-control radar had begun tracking them from a range of one hundred kilometers: six American interceptors—nothing but a steerable rocket engine with a seeker on it, but simple and effective as an anti-satellite and antiballistic-missile weapon. That the interceptors were fired from the station itself was inter-esting: the report that President Joseph Gardner had destroyed all of the Kingfisher constellation's weapon modules was not quite true. Apparently there were others, attached to the military space station and fully operational.

No matter. The Fates had placed him in perfect position to intercept the interceptors. Galtin marveled at the luck involved, marveled at the boldness and courage of his president, Gennadiy Gryzlov, to order this attack, marveled at the thought of what was going to happen. Russia was about to attack a spaceplane belonging to—arguably—the most powerful nation on Earth. They were attacking a $3 billion spacecraft with American civilians on board. That was ballsy. There was no other term for it: ballsy. To say that the ante had just been raised in the war for control of space was a vast understatement.

Galtin raised the red guarded cover of the weapon arming switch and moved the switch underneath from SAFE to ARM. The attack computer was in control now. In seconds, it would be over. Three spacecraft and six missiles, traveling at tens of thousands of kilometers an hour hundreds of miles above Earth, would intersect at this point in space. It was nothing short of breathtaking. The science, the politics, the sheer courage, and yes, the luck, was all on the side of the Russian Federation right now.

Attack.

ABOARD THE S-19 MIDNIGHT SPACEPLANE

That same time

As soon as she heard the "red Wasp" warning, Gonzo had fired the main rocket engines. "What is it? What happened?" Ann Page asked. "What's a 'red wasp'?"

"Russian antisatellite weapon," Gonzo replied. "Our only hope is to outrun, outclimb, or outmaneuver it. Everybody, lower visors, lock them down, and make sure your oxygen is on. Sondra, check Agent Clarkson." Gonzo and Ann began running checklists in preparation for a possible collision.

"Midnight, be advised, we've lost contact with four of the interceptors we launched at the Wasp," Kai radioed. "Two are still tracking. We have an unknown pop-up target above and to your right, about forty miles, doesn't look like it's on an intercept course."

"It's a Russian spaceplane," Ann said. "We were briefed that the Russians were using a laser aboard at least one of their Elektrons. It shot down a satellite and is probably attacking the Trinity interceptors."

"Shit," Gonzo swore. "Armstrong, this is Midnight. Our passenger said that bogey is probably an Elektron and it's firing a—"

"Gonzo, maneuver!" Kai cut in. *"Wasp on your tail! Maneuver!"*

Gonzo immediately hit the maneuvering thrusters, throwing the spaceplane into a sharp sideways maneuver, then hit another set of thrusters that moved it "up"—away from Earth. She then began to translate backward, maneuvering to point the nose opposite the direction of flight to present the smallest possible profile to . . .

. . . and halfway through the maneuver, the Wasp antisatellite missile struck. It had a small ten-pound fragmentation warhead, which ignited jet fuel and BOHM oxidizer that leaked out of ruptured fuel tanks, creating an explosion that tore through the spacecraft.

· · ·

"It hit! It hit!" Valerie shouted. *"The first Wasp hit the spaceplane!"* The command-module crew watched the electro-optical image of the stricken spaceplane in horror as the tremendous explosion filled the screen.

"Second Wasp missile intercepted and destroyed," Henry Lathrop reported in a quiet voice on intercom. "Scope is clear."

"Boomer?" Kai radioed.

"I'll be off in five minutes," Boomer said.

"Have you been prebreathing?"

"Yes, I have," Boomer replied. "Not my MC."

"Trev, find out if anyone on station is suited up and has been prebreathing."

"Stand by," Trevor Shale responded. A moment later: "Sorry, Kai. We've got three suited up but none were prebreathing."

"Get them on oxygen right away," Kai said. On the radio he said, "Looks like you're the one, Boomer. We don't see any survivors from here, but go take a look. Be sure to rig for towing."

"Roger," Boomer said. A few minutes later: "We're ready to get under way." As soon as he was detached from the station, he received vectors to the Midnight spaceplane's last location and began to make his way toward it—luckily, because the S-19 was approaching Armstrong in preparation for docking, they were all in the same orbit, so it was just a matter of maneuvering laterally over to it rather than launching into a different orbit with a different altitude or direction.

"Valerie, get the Kingfisher constellation activated, and get Starfire online as soon as possible," Kai said. "It's time to do some hunting." He called up U.S. Space Command headquarters from his console. "General, we lost the S-19 spaceplane," he said when the secure channel was linked. "It had the vice president on board. We're checking for survivors, but so far it looks like a total loss."

"My God," General George Sandstein groaned. "I'll notify the White House immediately."

"Request permission to attack the entire fucking Russian space force, General," Kai said angrily.

"Negative," Sandstein said. "Don't do a thing except protect yourself. Do not fire unless fired upon."

"I'd say we've been fired upon, General," Kai said. "I don't know if the spaceplane was the target or if station was and the spaceplane got in the way. Either way, we're under attack."

"Let me notify the president first and see what his response is, Kai," Sandstein said. "In the meantime, I'm authorizing you to activate every defensive-weapon system you have and begin putting the Trinity modules you have stored on the station back into orbit. You have a spaceplane with you right now, do you not?"

"Yes, an S-29," Kai replied. "It's searching for survivors, and then we need to off-load supplies for here and for the ISS."

"What other spaceplanes are available?"

"Two S-19s will be available in a few days, and we have two S-9s that can be made ready in a few weeks," Kai said, checking his spacecraft status readouts. "General, I have ten weapon garages in orbit, which places much of the Russian antispacecraft force in the crosshairs, and they'll be activated shortly. I began the process of disconnecting the Starfire maser device from Skybolt, but I'm having my crews reconnect it. That should be ready soon. I request permission to lay waste to any Russian antisatellite facility that gets within range."

"I get the intent of 'lay waste,' Kai," Sandstein said. "I want permission from the White House before you start bombarding Russian targets from space. Your orders are: Protect your station with everything you have, and *await further orders*. Repeat my last, General Raydon."

Kai hesitated, and even thought about not replying; instead: "Roger, General," he said finally. "General

Sandstein, this is Station Director Raydon aboard Armstrong. I copied: my orders are to protect the station with everything we have, and await further orders."

"I'll be in touch, Kai," Sandstein said. "This won't go unavenged. Stand by." And the connection was broken.

"Shit," Kai swore. "The vice president of the United States was just maybe blown into space debris, and I'm supposed to just 'stand by.'" He checked his monitors. "Valerie, what is the status of the on-orbit Kingfishers?"

"We have six of the ten online and expect the rest in about an hour," Valerie Lukas reported.

That was just a fifth of the complete constellation, but it was better than what they had just minutes ago. "Put up the Russian and China-based terrestrial targets within range of our land-attack weapons."

"Roger." Moments later a list of targets appeared on the main command-center display as well as a list of available weapons that might be capable of defending against them. The list included targets other than antispacecraft ones: any militarily significant target was on the list, and as the Kingfisher weapon garages or Armstrong Space Station passed beyond range, the target disappeared, only to be replaced by another that had crossed over a weapon's horizon somewhere else on the globe. With only ten weapon garages plus Armstrong Space Station, the target list was very short, but every few minutes a new potential target popped up, would stay for two to four minutes, then disappear again.

One line on the target list turned from green to yellow. "Xichang Spaceport," Kai observed. "What's going on at Xichang?"

"S-500S 'Autocrat' Echo-Foxtrot-band search radar from Xichang Spaceport swept us," Christine reported. "Ever since the Russians set up the S-500S in China, they've tracked and sometimes locked us up on radar when we pass overhead. I think it's just calibration or training—it's just a long-range scan. Nothing ever happens."

"'Locked us up,' eh?" Kai muttered. "Anything beyond just a scan?"

"Once in a while we'll get a squeak of a 30N6E2 India-Juliet band missile-guidance uplink radar, like they've fired a missile at us," Christine said, "but all signals disappear within seconds, even the search signals, and we don't detect a motor plume or missile in the air—it's obvious they don't want us to think they're steering an interceptor toward us, using radar or optronics or anything else. It's all cat-and-mouse crap, sir—they shoot us radar signals to try to frighten us, then go silent. It's bullshit."

"Bullshit, huh?" Kai said. "Report if it happens again."

"Yes, sir," Christine replied.

Kai was silent for a few moments, thinking hard. "Christine," he said, "I want some detailed imagery of that S-500S unit. Give me a narrow-beam SBR scan from our big radar. Max resolution."

Christine Rayhill hesitated for a moment, then commented, "Sir, a spotlight scan could—"

"Do it, Miss Rayhill," Kai said tonelessly. "Narrow-beam scan, max resolution."

"Yes, sir," Christine said.

Things were quiet for about sixty seconds; then: "Sir, detecting S-500S target-tracking radar, appears to be locked on to us," Christine said. "Azimuth, elevation, and range only—no uplink signals." It was precisely what she had been concerned about: if the S-500S battery detected that they were being tracked on radar from Armstrong, they might think they were under attack and could retaliate.

"Designate target and send to Combat, Christine," Kai ordered. "Continue scanning."

There was a bit of confusion in Christine's voice: this was certainly no big deal, not worth a target ID badge. "Uh . . . designate target Golf-one, sir," she replied after entering commands into the attack computer. "Target locked into attack computer."

"Command, this is Operations," Valerie reported. "Verifying that target Golf-one is locked into Combat. Two Hammers ready from Kingfisher-09, one remaining, forty-five seconds until out of engagement envelope."

"Verified," Kai said. "Christine, warn me if the target's designation changes."

"Wilco, sir," Christine said. Her palms started to get a bit sweaty: this was starting to look like a prelude to—

Suddenly the signal identification changed from TARGET TRACK to MISSILE TRACK. The shift was instantaneous, and it didn't stay on the board for more than one or two seconds, but it was long enough for Christine to call out, "Command, I have a missile tr—"

"Combat, Command, batteries released on Golf-one," Kai ordered. "Repeat, batteries released."

"Batteries released, Roger," Valerie said. "Combat, target Golf-one, engage!"

A Kingfisher weapon garage almost four thousand miles away from Armstrong—although Armstrong Space Station was much closer to the target, the missiles needed time and distance to reenter Earth's atmosphere, so a Kingfisher weapon garage farther away got the tasking—maneuvered itself to a computer-derived course, and two Orbital Maneuvering Vehicles were ejected from the weapon garage thirty seconds apart. The OMVs flipped themselves over until they were flying tail first, and their reentry rockets fired. The burns did not last too long, decelerating the spacecraft by just a few hundred miles an hour, but it was enough to change their trajectory from Earth orbit to the atmosphere, and the OMVs flipped back over so their heat-protective shields were exposed to the onrushing atmosphere.

As the spacecraft entered the upper atmosphere, the glow from friction burning the air changed colors until it became white-hot, and streams of superheated plasma trailed behind each vehicle. Tiny hydraulically controlled vanes and maneuvering thrusters on the tail of the OMV's body helped the spacecraft make S-turns through the sky, which helped not only to increase the time they had to slow down through the sky but also to confuse any space tracking radars on their intended target. One of the steering vanes on the second OMV malfunctioned, sending it spinning wildly out of control, mostly burning up in the atmosphere, and what was left went crashing into the Siberian wilderness.

At a hundred thousand feet altitude, the protective shrouds around the OMVs broke free, exposing a two-hundred-pound tungsten-carbide projectile with a millimeter-wave radar and imaging-infrared-seeker head in the nose. It followed steering signals from its weapon garage until the radar locked on to its target, then refined its aiming, comparing what it saw with its sensors with the target images stored in memory. It took only a fraction of a second, but the images matched and the warhead locked on to its target—the transporter-erector-launcher vehicle of an S-500S surface-to-air missile system. It struck the target, traveling almost ten thousand miles an hour. The warhead didn't need an explosive warhead—hitting at that speed was akin to being armed with two thousand pounds of TNT, completely obliterating the launcher and everything else in a five-hundred-foot radius.

"Target Golf-one destroyed, sir," Christine reported moments later, her voice muted and hoarse—that was the first time she had destroyed anything in her entire life, let alone a fellow human being.

"Good job," Kai said stonily. "Trev, I want a two-person team to suit up and begin prebreathing, going on six-hour emergency standby duty. The rest of the off-duty crew can stand down from combat stations. Eyes and ears open, everybody—I think we'll be busy. What's the status of Starfire? How much longer?"

"I don't know, sir," Casey Huggins responded from the Skybolt module. "Maybe an hour, maybe two. I'm sorry, sir, but I just don't know."

"As quickly as you can, Miss Huggins," Kai said. He hit a button on his communications console. "General Sandstein, urgent."

THE KREMLIN
MOSCOW, RUSSIAN FEDERATION
A short time later

"Those American bastards struck my spaceport with a missile from space!" Zhou Qiang, president of the People's Republic of China, thundered through the secure voice teleconference link. "I am going to order an immediate launch of a nuclear ballistic missile against Hawaii! If they kill a hundred Chinese, I am going to kill a *million* Americans!"

"Calm yourself, Zhou," Russian president Gennadiy Gryzlov said. "You know as well as I that if you launch an intercontinental ballistic missile, or anything that looks like one, anywhere near the United States or its possessions, they will retaliate with everything they have, against both our nations. They are on a hair trigger now, thanks to your attack on Guam."

"I do not care!" Zhou snapped. "They will regret the loss of one Chinese a thousand times, I swear it!"

"My commanders on the ground say that your S-500S battery locked on to the space station with missile-guidance radar," Gryzlov said. "Is that true?"

"Then I suppose you know that the Americans locked on to the S-500 launcher with their microwave weapon?"

"I know they scanned you with a simple synthetic-aperture radar, Zhou, the space-based radar mounted on the station itself," Gryzlov said. "I have technicians and intelligence men on the ground there, remember? They know exactly what you were scanned with. It was not the directed-energy weapon. They obviously meant to goad you into responding, exactly like your stupid ill-trained men did."

"So are they now trying to goad us into widening the conflict, to turn it into a nuclear exchange?" Zhou asked. "If so, they are succeeding!"

"Calm yourself, I said, Zhou," Gryzlov repeated. "We will respond, but we must be patient and plan this out together."

"This is all because of your foolhardy attack on their spaceplane, is it not?" Zhou asked. "You tell me to be calm, but then you do an insane act like destroy one of their spaceplanes! We tracked those fighters and your antisatellite weapons. Who is the crazy one now? You want to prohibit unauthorized spacecraft from overflying Russia? That is even more crazy! What has gotten inside your head, Gryzlov? You are even more unstable than that idiot Truznyev before you."

"Do not talk to me about insane acts of war, Zhou!" Gryzlov retorted. "We are lucky we are not at war with the United States after that crazy General Zu attacked Guam!"

"I could say the same about your father's cruise-missile attack on the United States itself!" Zhou shot back. "Ten thousand, fifteen thousand Americans vaporized? One hundred thousand wounded? Your father was—"

"Tread carefully, I warn you, Zhou," Gryzlov spat menacingly. "Be careful of your next words if they even remotely concern my father." There was complete silence on the other end. "Listen to me, Zhou. You know as well as I that the only American non-nuclear weapons that can reach our spaceports and other antisatellite launch sites are either cruise missiles launched from penetrating bombers or weapons launched from their military space station or weapon garages," Gryzlov went on. "The military space station is the key because it controls all the weapon garages, uses its space-based radar for surveillance and targeting, and has the Skybolt laser, which is impossible to defend against. It must be disabled or destroyed before the Americans employ their weapons."

"Disabled? Destroyed? How?" Zhou asked.

"We must pick the perfect time when the maximum number of Russia and China's antisatellite weapons can launch simultaneously," Gryzlov said. "The station has self-defense weapons, but if we can overwhelm them, we could succeed. My defense minister and chief of the general staff will inform me of when the American space station is in perfect position, and then we must attack at once. The station's orbit is well known. They changed it recently for the Starfire microwave-laser test, and they may change it again, but we will watch and wait. When the orbit stabilizes, we attack with everything that is in range.

"But I need your commitment, Zhou: when I say attack, we attack with every weapon in range, simultaneously," Gryzlov went on. "That is the only way we can hope to disable or destroy the military space station so it cannot retaliate against us, because if it does, it can destroy any target on the planet at the speed of light."

There was a very long silence on the other end of the secure connection; then: "What is it you want, Gryzlov?"

"I need the precise description, capabilities, status, and location of each and every antisatellite weapon system in your arsenal," Gryzlov said, "including your antisatellite missile submarines. And I need to establish a direct secure connection to each site and submarine so I can launch a coordinated attack against the American military space station."

"Nǐ tā mā de f engle?" Zhou shouted in the background. Gryzlov knew enough Chinese expletives to know he'd said "You fucking crazy?" From the interpreter, he instead haltingly heard, "The president strongly objects, sir."

"Russia has many more antisatellite weapons than China, Zhou—if I sent you a tiny bit of our data, you would be quickly overwhelmed," Gryzlov said. "Besides, I do not think your military or your space technicians have the capability to coordinate the launch of dozens of interceptors spread out across thousands of miles belonging to two nations against a single spot in space. We are much more experienced in orbital mechanics than China."

"Why do I not just turn over all the launch codes to all of our nuclear ballistic missiles to you, Gryzlov?" Zhou asked derisively. "Either way, China is dead."

"Do not be a fool, Zhou," Gryzlov said. "We have to act, and act quickly, before the Americans can place more weapon garages in orbit and reactivate the Skybolt laser, if that drivel about the college students' microwave laser replacing the free-electron laser is to be believed. Give me that data—and it had better be accurate and authentic—and I will determine the exact moment when the maximum number of antisatellite weapons is in range to strike at Armstrong . . . and then we will attack."

"And then what, Gryzlov? Wait until American nuclear missiles rain down on our capitals?"

"Kenneth Phoenix is a *weakling,* as are all American politicians," Gryzlov spat. "He attacked that S-500 site knowing we would retaliate. The minute he fired that microwave laser from the station, he knew the station would become a target. He did both thinking we would not respond. Now I have responded by destroying his spaceplane, and he has a choice: risk intercontinental thermonuclear war over this, or forfeit the military space station for peace. He is predictable, cowardly, and sure to be emotionally crippled. He is nothing. There is no threat to either of our countries except nuclear war if Armstrong Space Station is destroyed, and I do not believe Phoenix or anyone in America has the stomach for any kind of war, let alone a nuclear war."

Zhou said nothing. Gryzlov waited a few moments, then said, "Decide *now,* Zhou, damn you! *Decide!*"

TEN

The God of War hates those who hesitate.
—Euripides

IN EARTH ORBIT, THIRTY MILES FROM ARMSTRONG SPACE STATION

A short time later

From about a mile away, all Boomer and Ernesto could see was a dense cloud of white gas, as if a cumulus cloud had broken free of Earth's atmosphere and decided to float around in Earth's orbit. "Still can't see anything, Armstrong," Boomer reported. "Just a very large cloud of frozen fuel, oxidizer, and debris."

"Copy," Kai replied. "Get as close as you can, but mind the fuel and oxidizer—don't get close enough to ignite it. Even one spark of static electricity in that mess could set it off."

"Roger."

It took several minutes to close the gap, but the cloud still obscured the scene. "I'm about fifty yards away," Boomer said. "This is about as close as I dare get. I can't make anything out. Ernesto, you see anything in there?"

"Negative," Ernesto said. "It's a pretty dense— *Wait! I see it! I see the Midnight!* It looks like the right wing and part of the tail have been torn off, but the fuselage and cockpit look intact!"

"Thank God," Boomer said. "I'm going over there to take a look." He unstrapped and went back to the airlock. For a long-exposure spacewalk, in addition to wearing the EEAS for more protection against micrometeors and debris and for better temperature control, Boomer put on a lightweight unpressurized space suit resembling coveralls, then donned a large backpack-like device called a Primary Life Support System, or PLSS, and plugged his EEAS and environmental umbilicals into it. The backpack contained oxygen, power, carbon-dioxide scrubbers, environmental controls, communications gear, and a device called a "SAFER," or Simplified Aid For EVA Rescue, which was a smaller version of the Manned Maneuvering Unit device, which allowed tethered and untethered astronauts to move unassisted in space. SAFER was only supposed to be used in an emergency, in order to return an untethered astronaut to the spacecraft—well, this was definitely an emergency. "How do you hear, Ernesto?" he radioed.

"Loud and clear, Boomer."

"Cockpit hatch is secure," Boomer said after checking the readouts. "Depressurizing the airlock now." A few minutes later: "Opening cargo-bay hatch." He unlocked and opened the hatch and stepped inside the cargo bay, secured himself with a tether, then closed and sealed the hatch behind him.

The cargo bay was still mostly full, because they were carrying all of the supplies for the International Space Station and still had some untransferred supplies for Armstrong. Boomer brought out a one-hundred-yard length of cargo strap used for transferring items to a space station, made sure the end of the strap was secure to the spaceplane, attached the strap to a clip on his backpack harness, and unhooked himself from the cargo-bay tether. "Leaving cargo bay," he reported, then maneuvered himself up and out of the cargo bay and headed for the Midnight spaceplane, the cargo strap unreeling itself behind him.

A few minutes later he entered the fuel-oxidizer cloud—thankfully the jets on SAFER used inert gases for propulsion, so there was no danger of creating an explosion—and he could clearly see the spaceplane. The damage looked worse from up close, but the fuselage and cockpit looked intact. "I'm about twenty yards from Midnight," Boomer reported. "I'm going in." Using tiny puffs from SAFER, he moved in toward Midnight's cockpit . . .

. . . and through the cockpit canopy windows, he saw Jessica Faulkner and Vice President Ann Page, still seated, upright, and strapped in, heads bowed as if napping in an airliner seat, but not moving. "I see Gonzo and the vice president," Boomer said. "They're strapped in and upright. I can't see if their eyes are open." He took out a flashlight and tapped gently on the Midnight's cockpit canopies—no response. "Their suits look undamaged, and I can see LEDs on their suits' status panels—hot damn, they might be—"

And just then, Vice President Ann Page raised her head, then her right hand, as if waving. *"The vice president is alive!"* Boomer said. "I think she's waving at me!" He realized it could just be the motion of the spacecraft, but he had to cling to any drop of hope he possibly could. "Gonzo's still not moving, but the vice president is conscious! Power is out. The airlock hatch and cockpit look secure—no sign of damage or decompression. We've got to get them back to station."

He floated above Midnight to look at the cargo bay. "The right side of the fuselage at the wing attach point looks badly damaged." He maneuvered himself around to the right side of the cargo bay. "Shit," he murmured a few moments later. "Looks like the passenger module was breached. Stand by. I'll see if I can check the passengers."

Aboard Armstrong Space Station, Brad McLanahan held his breath. He knew Sondra was on that space-plane and had switched to the passenger module to allow the vice president to ride in the cockpit.

"Brad," Jodie radioed from Cal Poly—no one on the Project Starfire team had left their station since Stacy Anne Barbeau's explosive accusations. "I heard everything. Wasn't . . . wasn't your friend Sondra . . . ?"

"Yes," Brad said.

"Prayers," Jodie breathed.

Boomer was able to look through the breach in the hull and passenger module. "There's not enough room for me to get into the module," he said. He shined his flashlight at Sondra and the Secret Service agent. "They are unconscious, but I see indicator lights on their suits' status panel, and their visors are down and appear locked. We—"

And at that moment, as Boomer swept his flashlight's beam across her helmet visor, Sondra raised her head. Her eyes were open and wide with fear. *"Holy shit, Sondra's alive!*" Boomer shouted. "The Secret Service agent is not moving, but as far as I can tell, her suit is intact! We might have four survivors here!"

"Excellent!" Kai radioed. He and the rest of the crew had been watching Boomer's progress on video and audio streamed back from cameras mounted on Boomer's PLSS. "Get back here on the double. We'll widen the breach to get into the passenger module, and then we can recover the passengers and then gain access to the cockpit through the airlock."

"Roger." Boomer made his way to the front of the Midnight spaceplane, found a Reaction Control System nozzle on the nose, and hooked the cargo strap securely inside it. He then hooked a ring on his backpack harness to the strap and propelled himself back to the S-29 Shadow spaceplane, zip-lining down the strap. In minutes he was through the Shadow's airlock, set the PLSS in its cradle to recharge and refill, and made his way back into the Shadow's cockpit.

"Nice job, comandante," Ernesto said after Boomer had strapped in. They exchanged a fist bump. "Do you think we can get them out and transfer them to station, boss?"

"Not sure," Boomer said, taking a few moments to let his breathing and heartbeat start to return to normal. "The passenger module is definitely breached, but the cockpit looked intact. I saw LEDs on their suits, but I couldn't tell if they were warning lights or what. We might be able to get messages to the vice president on how to open the airlock or cockpit canopies, and then we hope they can survive the transfer. Let's get back to station."

It took them a half hour of careful maneuvering to tow the crippled S-19 Midnight spaceplane back to Armstrong Space Station. Crewmembers were already standing by with more cargo straps and cutters, and the remote manipulator arms were extended as far as they could to do whatever was necessary. Boomer docked the S-29 with the station.

"Good job, Boomer," Kai radioed as he studied the images of the stricken S-19 Midnight and the crewmembers working on gaining access to the passenger module. "I've ordered the S-29 refueled and as much cargo as possible unloaded. We can use one of the airlocks as a hyperbaric chamber. I'm going to have you and your MC stay with the spaceplane. We've got about three hours before we arrive at the next DB, so if you need to get out and use the 'wicks,' do it now." Ernesto waved a hand, signaling that's what he wanted. The "wicks," or WCS, was the Waste Containment System, or space toilet, on Armstrong Space Station.

"Roger," Boomer said. "Which duck blind are we coming up on?"

"The worst one," Kai said. "Delta Bravo-One. Downtown. Right up the middle." Boomer was very familiar with which ones they were: Moscow and St. Petersburg. They had overlapping kill circles from multiple antisatellite sites that extended coverage from the Barents Sea to the Gulf of Azov. "With the Russian Orbital Section detached and not having our own maneuvering module, we can't reposition station for a less dangerous orbit."

"Ernesto is clearing off to use the 'wicks,'" Boomer announced as Ernesto began unstrapping. "I want to supervise the refueling. I need someone in the seat to watch for faults."

"We're running low on spaceplane crewmembers, Boomer," Kai said. He turned to station manager Trevor Shale. "Trev, want to suit up and—"

"Send Brad McLanahan," Boomer said. "He's not busy. Hell, he's practically a spaceplane pilot already."

Brad had been silent ever since the S-19 Midnight had been hit by the Russian ASAT, watching out a window at the workers surrounding the Midnight and hoping to catch a glimpse of Sondra, but he brightened when he heard his name. "You bet I will!" he said excitedly on intercom.

"Report to the airlock—someone will help you into an ACES," Kai said. "You'll have to be fully suited up and on oxygen. There's no time to get you into an LCVG." The LCVG, or Liquid Cooling and Ventilation Garment, was a formfitting suit with water tubes running through it that absorbed heat from the body. "Trev, help Brad get to the airlock." Trevor led Brad to the hatch leading to the storage and processing module. Because he would not be wearing an LCVG, it was relatively quick and simple to don an ACES suit, gloves, and boots, and in just a few minutes Brad was on his way to the tunnel connecting the S-29 Shadow spaceplane to the station.

On the way into the docked spaceplane, Brad passed Ernesto Hermosillo heading to the Galaxy module. "Hey, good news about Sondra, man," Ernesto said, giving Brad a fist bump. "I hope she'll be all right. We'll know soon, amigo."

"*Gracias*, Ernesto," Brad said.

A technician helped Brad through the docking tunnel, and Brad made his way through the airlock and into the cockpit. Boomer handed him his umbilicals. "Hello, Brad," Boomer said on intercom. "Everything that can be done for Sondra and the others is being done. My guess is that she and the Secret Service agent will have to spend the night in an airlock pressurized with pure oxygen. They might be out for a while, but if they made it through the attack with their suits intact, they should pull out of it."

"Thanks, Boomer," Brad said.

"Thanks for doing this, Brad," Boomer said. "This is nothing but a simple babysitting job, but the regs—which I myself wrote—say that one person has to be behind the controls of an S-29 during space refueling, wearing a space suit and on oxygen. The Black Stallion and Midnight spaceplanes require both crewmembers because they're not as automated as the Shadow. I want to supervise the refueling and maybe hit the head, and Ernesto is heading to the 'wicks' now, so that's why you're here.

"The Shadow is highly automated, so it will tell you verbally and on this screen what's going on," Boomer continued, pointing at the large multifunction display in the middle of the instrument panel. Checklist items appeared in yellow, then several sublines of computer actions, with a yellow line turning green, and finally the end result, with a little yellow button on the touchscreen display asking if the computer could continue. "If something does happen, it'll notify you and wait for an acknowledgment, which you do by pressing the soft key that appears. Most of the time it'll just fix the problem itself, notify you that it's fixed, and wait for an acknowledgment. If it can't fix it itself, it'll let you know. Just tell me if that happens and I'll get the techs working on it. Like I said, you're babysitting, except the 'baby' is smarter and bigger than you. Any questions?"

"Nope."

"Good. I'll be able to hear the computer if it announces anything. I won't be far away. Just call if—"

And at that moment they heard, "Armstrong, this is Midnight One, how do you hear?"

"Gonzo?" Kai shouted. "Is that you?"

"Yes," Gonzo said. Her voice was hoarse and labored, as if she were trying to talk with a large weight on her chest. "If you can hear me, report in. Miss Vice President?"

"I . . . I can hear you . . . Gonzo." The vice president responded with the same low, hoarse voice and slow cadence. "I . . . I can't breathe very well."

"Help is coming, ma'am," Gonzo said. "Agent Clarkson." No response. "Agent Clarkson?" Still no word. "Sondra?"

"Loud . . . and . . . and clear," Sondra replied weakly. Brad took a deep breath, the first in many tense moments. "I'll . . . I'll try to check on Clarkson."

"We have power to the Midnight," Trevor reported. "We'll check the spacecraft's hull status, then figure out if we can do a pressurized tunnel transfer or we'll have to spacewalk them. Their breathing suggests their space suits might not be receiving oxygen from the spaceplane, so we'll have to hurry to see if we can—"

"Command, Surveillance, I detect multiple rocket launches!" Christine Rayhill shouted on all-stations intercom. "One launch from Plesetsk, one from Baikonur! Computing launch track now . . . stand by . . . *now detecting a second launch from Baikonur,* repeat, two launches from . . . *now detecting a rocket launch from Xichang,* Command, that's four rockets lifting . . . *now detecting a fifth rocket,* this one from Wenchang spaceport on Hainan Island. That's five rockets launching! No prenotifications of any launches."

"Combat stations, crew," Kai ordered on intercom. "All hands, man your combat stations."

Aboard the Shadow spaceplane, Boomer zoomed through the airlock faster than Brad had ever seen anyone move in space, maneuvered himself into the pilot's seat with incredible dexterity for someone who was in free fall, fastened his umbilicals, and started to strap in. "What do I do, Boomer?" Brad asked. "Do I get out and let Ernesto—"

"It's too late," Boomer said. "The outer airlock hatches are automatically sealed when we go into combat stations, in preparation for us detaching from station. They'll terminate fueling and unloading cargo, and as soon as they do, we'll be under way."

"You mean, *back into orbit*?"

"Yep," Boomer said, hurriedly getting strapped in and responding to notices by the computer. "We're going flying, as fast as we can. There's a paper checklist Velcro'd to the bulkhead by your right knee. Strap it on to your thigh. Follow along with the computer as it goes through each item. When it tells you to acknowledge, and you agree that it followed the steps correctly, go ahead and touch the button on the screen. If it goes out of order or you get an error message, tell me. It'll adjust how fast it goes through each section depending on how fast you acknowledge each action, but it also knows we're at combat stations, so it'll try to go quickly. Check you umbilicals and oxygen and strap yourself down as tightly as you can—this may be a hairy ride."

"It does not appear to be a ballistic-missile flight path," surveillance officer Christine Rayhill reported, studying her two computer monitors. "First two missiles staging now . . . they look like they're going orbital, Command, repeat, orbital flight paths."

"Russian spaceplanes," Valerie guessed. "A salvo of five nearly simultaneous launches."

"What's the status of Starfire?" Kai asked.

"Still working on it," Henry Lathrop reported. "I don't know how long it will be yet."

"As quick as you can, Henry," Kai said. "Valerie, status of the Kingfishers and Hydra?"

"Kingfisher-9 is minus two Mjollnir projectiles, and three Trinity modules on station have expended a total of six antisatellite projectiles," Valerie reported. "All other modules on station are ready. Six of the ten Trinity modules in orbit are ready. Hydra is ready, approximately thirty bursts remaining."

A few minutes later: "Command, the first two rockets appear to have released an orbital payload, believed to be spaceplanes," Christine reported. "Their orbits are not coincident with ours."

"They might have payload-assist modules that will boost them into a transfer orbit," Trevor Shale said. A payload-assist module was an extra booster stage fastened to the topmost payload section that could boost that payload into a different orbit at the right time without having to expend its own fuel. "We should expect those spaceplanes to move to intercept orbits within one to ten hours."

Kai Raydon looked around the command module and noticed that Brad wasn't in his usual position, attached to a bulkhead in the command module. "McLanahan, what's your location?" he asked on intercom.

"Mission commander's seat on Shadow," Boomer replied.

"*Say again?*"

"He was warming the MC's seat while Ernesto had to take a 'wicks' break, and now that we're at combat stations, he's pinned to it," Boomer said. "So far he seems to have a pretty good handle on things."

"Override the airlock lockouts," Kai said. "Get your MC back in there."

"There's no time, General," Boomer said. "By the time Ernesto gets his ACES back on, we'll be bye-bye. No worries. Brad's doing good. Looks to me like he has already started mission-commander training."

Kai shook his head—too many things that were out of his control were happening, he thought ruefully. "How long before you detach, Boomer?"

"Cargo-bay doors coming closed now, General," Boomer said. "Maybe two minutes. Will advise."

"Command, rockets three and four going orbital as well," Christine reported about a minute later. "Russian payloads one and two established in orbit. No further activity from any ground sites." That changed just moments later: "Command, detecting numerous high-performance aircraft departing Chkalovsky Air Base near Moscow. Two, maybe three aircraft airborne."

"Antisatellite launch aircraft," Trevor said. "They're putting on the full-court press."

"Radio all to Space Command, Trev," Kai said. "I don't know for sure who the target is, but I'll damned well bet it's us. Christine, I'm assuming their objective is to reach our altitude and a matching orbit to intercept us. I want orbital predictions on all those Russian spaceplanes—I need to know exactly when they will launch themselves into transfer orbits."

"Yes, sir," Christine replied. "Computing now." A few minutes later: "Command, Surveillance, assuming they want to jump to our orbital angle and altitude, I expect spacecraft Sierra-Three will reach a Hohmann-transfer-orbit jump-off point in twenty-three minutes, reaching our altitude and orbital plane seven minutes later. Sierra-One will do the same in forty-eight minutes. Still working on the other three spacecraft, but they could all be in our orbit in less than four hours. I'll compute where they'll be relative to us when they enter our orbit."

"Four hours: that's about the time we pass over Delta-Bravo One," Valerie pointed out, referring to the orbital display on the main monitor. "They timed this to perfection: they'll have five spacecraft, presumably armed, in our orbit when we pass over the antisatellite missile sites in Moscow and St. Petersburg."

"Trevor, I want to move station as high as we can, as fast as we can," Kai said. "Change our trajectory as much as possible, but I want to increase altitude as much as possible—maybe we can get out of the S-500S's envelope. Use every drop of fuel we have left, but get us up and out of the danger zone."

"Got it," Trevor responded, then bent to work on his workstation.

THE WHITE HOUSE
WASHINGTON, D.C.
A short time later

President Kenneth Phoenix entered the White House Situation Room at a fast walk, waving the others in the room to their seats. His face was gray and haggard, and he had a day's growth of beard, the result of staying awake and at his desk awaiting news of his vice president, chief adviser, and friend. "Someone talk to me," he ordered.

"The Russians have launched what are believed to be five Elektron spaceplanes into orbit," National Security Adviser William Glenbrook said. In the Situation Room with him was Secretary of State James Morrison, Secretary of Defense Frederick Hayes, chairman of the Joint Chiefs of Staff General Timothy Spelling, and director of the Central Intelligence Agency Thomas Torrey, plus some assistants standing by near telephones. The large monitor at the front of the room was split into several screens, with one showing the image of the commander of U.S. Strategic Command, Admiral Joseph Eberhart, and commander of the U.S. Space Command, Air Force General George Sandstein, joining the meeting via video teleconference. "They have also launched fighter jets believed to be carrying antisatellite missiles, similar to the one that hit the vice president's spaceplane."

"Get Gryzlov on the phone *right now*," Phoenix ordered. "What else?"

"We should know within minutes if the spaceplanes are going to be a threat to Armstrong Space Station," Glenbrook went on. "The personnel aboard Armstrong can predict when the spaceplanes need to adjust their orbital track to match the station's, or if they will go into an orbit that will intercept the station."

"Gryzlov on the line, sir," the communications officer announced a few minutes later.

Phoenix snapped up the receiver. "What in hell do you think you're doing, Gryzlov?" he snapped.

"It does not feel so good to have so many unidentified armed enemy spacecraft overhead, does it, Phoenix?" the interpreter said. "I am sure your orbital mechanics technicians will inform you very soon, but I will tell you now myself to save you the trouble: your military space station will intersect with all of our spaceplanes and antisatellite weapons in approximately three hours, at which time I will order my space forces to shoot down your military space station."

"*What?*"

"You have three hours to evacuate the station and save your men's lives," Gryzlov said. "I simply will not allow that monstrosity to fly over Russia again while its weapons are active—as we have just seen in China, the space station and the weapons it controls are a great threat to Russia."

"*Evacuate the space station?*" Phoenix retorted. "There are fourteen men and women aboard! How am I supposed to do that in three hours?"

"That is not my concern, Phoenix," Gryzlov said. "You have your spaceplanes and commercial-passenger-rated unmanned spacecraft, and I am told that the station has emergency lifeboats that can keep personnel alive long enough so they can be retrieved and brought back to Earth or transferred to the International Space Station. But it is not my concern, Phoenix. I want assurances that the space weapons have been deactivated, and the best way I can think of to do that is to destroy the space station."

"Armstrong Space Station is a U.S. possession and military installation," Phoenix said. "Attacking it will be like attacking any other American military base or aircraft carrier. That is an act of war."

"Then so be it—go ahead and declare it, Phoenix," Gryzlov said. "I assure you, Russia and its allies are ready for war with America. I consider the fact that America has been flying weapons over Russian territory now for years to be an act of war—now finally something will be done about it. I am doing nothing more than protecting Russia from a rampaging American military machine that tried to disguise itself as a college-student experiment. Well, I was fooled. I will be fooled no longer."

"Have you thought about what will happen if the station doesn't completely disintegrate on reentry, Gryzlov? How many people on the ground will be killed by falling debris and the core of the MHD generator?"

"Of course I have considered that, Phoenix," Gryzlov said. "The station will be struck over western Russia. We predict it will crash harmlessly in western China, Siberia, or the North Atlantic. And if it does not crash until it reaches North America, it would probably crash in western Canada or the western United States, all sparsely populated. This is fitting, no? Since all nations are responsible for their own spacecraft no matter how they reenter, your monstrosity might be returned right to your doorstep.

"Three hours, Phoenix," Gryzlov went on. "I suggest you tell your astronauts to hurry. And one more thing, Phoenix: If we detect any space-based weapons launched at any targets in Russia, we will consider that a commencement of a state of war between our two nations. You started this fight when you fired that directed-energy weapon—the price you will pay is the loss of that space station. Do not compound the misery you and your people will suffer by touching off a thermonuclear war." And the connection was terminated.

"Damn that bastard!" Phoenix shouted, throwing the phone back on its cradle. "Fred, put us at DEFCON Three. I want to know all possible spots in the U.S. where that station could come down."

"Yes, sir," the defense secretary responded, and his aide picked up his phone. DEFCON, or Defense Readiness Condition, was a graduated system for increasing the readiness of the U.S. military forces for nuclear war. Since the American Holocaust and the release of a nuclear depth charge in the South China Sea by the Chinese People's Liberation Army Navy, the U.S. had been at DEFCON Four, one step up from peacetime; DEFCON One was the most dangerous level, meaning nuclear war was imminent. "Do you want to order evacuations over the possible impact areas, sir?"

The president hesitated, but only for a moment: "I'm going to go on national TV and radio and explain the situation," he said. "I'm going to lay it out for the

American people, tell them the odds of station hitting North America, tell them we're doing all we can to stop it from happening, and let them decide if they want to evacuate or not. How long would it take for it to reenter, Fred?"

"About fifteen minutes, sir," Hayes said. "Normal ICBM flight time from launch to impact is around thirty minutes, so half of that would be about right."

"With less than four hours to evacuate, I think most Americans would stay put," National Security Adviser Glenbrook said.

"I just hope we don't create a panic," the president said, "but a few incidents or injuries in a panic would be better than having Americans killed by falling debris and we didn't tell them it was coming." He turned to Admiral Eberhart. "Admiral, what does Gryzlov have in western Russia that could bring the space station down?"

"Primarily the antisatellite air-launched missiles and the S-500S antiaircraft missile, sir," Eberhart replied. "Both Moscow and St. Petersburg have deployed one battery of the S-500S. Each battery has six launchers; each launcher has four missiles plus four reloads that can be inserted within an hour. There are two bases near Moscow and St. Petersburg that fly the MiG-31D, each with about twenty interceptors."

"And it can hit the space station?"

"The station is at the missile's maximum altitude, if what we know about the S-500S is true," Eberhart said. "The station is well within the air-launched antisatellite missile's maximum range."

"Can we move the space station to a higher orbit?"

"That is being done right now, sir," Eberhart said. "The station's director, Kai Raydon, ordered the station to the highest altitude it can attain before it runs low on fuel. They are also trying to alter its orbit to avoid overflying Moscow and St. Petersburg, but that might take too long."

"What else do we have to stop those missiles from being launched?" the president asked.

"In western Russia: not much, sir," Hayes responded. "We have one guided-cruise-missile submarine in the Baltic Sea that can launch against the antisatellite air bases in St. Petersburg, and that's it. We can destroy the base easily, but it's only one base, and our sub would be dog meat for Russian antisub patrols afterward—the Russians definitely control the Baltic Sea. The value of the loss of the sub would be twice that of the Russian base."

"Plus we run the risk of starting a nuclear exchange if those cruise missiles are detected," Glenbrook added. "We're lucky that attack from space didn't do the same."

"So we have no options?" the president asked. "The space station is history?"

"We have one option, sir: attack the air bases and antisatellite missile sites from space," Glenbrook said. "The station has defensive weapons, but it can also attack ground targets, as we saw at that missile site in China. They may not get all the sites, but they might get enough of them to save themselves."

"And start World War Three?" Secretary of State James Morrison retorted, his eyes wide with fear. "You heard Gryzlov, Bill—the guy just threatened the president of the United States with nuclear war! Anyone here think the guy is not crazy enough to do it? I'd be surprised if he wasn't heading for an underground command bunker right now. Sir, I suggest we get those students and all nonessential crewmembers off the military space station immediately and let the rest of the crew fight off any incoming missiles as best they can. If the station looks like it will be overwhelmed, the rest of the crew should evacuate."

"I disagree, sir," Secretary of Defense Hayes said. "To answer your question, Jim: I think Gryzlov is delusional and paranoid, but I don't think he's crazy enough to launch a nuclear war, even if we knocked out all his antisatellite bases from space. Gryzlov is young and has a long and comfortable life ahead of him. His father was killed by an American counterattack—that's got to be weighing on him. I think he cares more about political survival and maintaining his wealth than starting a nuclear war. Besides, his strategic nuclear forces are no better than ours."

"General Spelling?"

"Under DEFCON Three, we put all of our few remaining bombers and our nuclear-capable fighters on nuclear alert and send as many ballistic-missile and cruise-missile submarines as possible on patrol," the chairman of the Joint Chiefs of Staff said, referring to a tablet computer. "It would take one to three days to put our bombers on alert, three to seven days for the fighters, and one to three weeks to get available subs under way. Secretary Hayes is correct about the numbers, sir: American and Russian forces are roughly equal in strength. We have more surface ships and ballistic-missile submarines; they have more aircraft and land-based ballistic missiles."

"After Gryzlov's threat, we'd have to assume they're placing their nuclear forces on a greater readiness level as we speak," Hayes added. "Maybe even greater than ours."

The president was silent for several long moments, looking into the faces of his advisers. Finally: "I want to talk directly with General Raydon," he said.

A few moments later, after the secure video teleconference link was established: "General Raydon here, Mr. President."

"First of all: status of the vice president and the spaceplane crew."

"We were working to get inside the passenger module, but I canceled the spacewalks when those Elektrons launched," Kai replied. "Still no response from any of them."

"How much oxygen do they have?"

"Several more hours if their space suits or the spaceplane's environmental systems weren't damaged. We've examined the readouts on their suits and we think they are still receiving oxygen from the ship and not just from their own suits. If that turns out not to be the case, they haven't much longer."

The president nodded grimly. "Here's the situation, General: Gennadiy Gryzlov says flat out he wants to shoot down Silver Tower," he said. "He told me about the kill box and how he's going to position those spaceplanes in the same area as the antisatellite weapons around Moscow and St. Petersburg. My question is: Can you survive an attack on the space station?"

"Yes, sir, we can," Kai said immediately, "but not for long. We have sixteen engagements of antisatellite weapons and approximately thirty engagements with the Hydra COIL laser. We also have sixteen engagements on our weapon garages in orbit, but the odds are very long that they'll be in a position to defend station. After those are expended, we'd have to rely on refueling and rearming."

"And then Gryzlov could take potshots at our resupply spaceplanes and commercial cargo spacecraft," the president pointed out.

"Which is why I recommend we attack any antisatellite sites we can with our Mjollnir missiles," Kai said. "Our nine remaining weapon garages are within range of an ASAT site every twenty to thirty minutes. We have thirteen land-attack engagements with the orbiting weapon garages, plus fifteen from the stored-weapon garages on station. That would put a pretty big dent in Gryzlov's antisatellite forces."

"Gryzlov has threatened nuclear war if we attack any of his bases in Russia."

Kai's expression turned first surprised, then serious, and finally angry. "Mr. President, the question is considerably above my pay grade," he said, "but if anyone threatens the United States with nuclear war, I say we work to hand him his head on a platter."

The president looked at the expressions of his advisers once more—they ranged from outright fear, to determination, to blankness and bewilderment. He had the distinct impression that all of them were glad they didn't have to make the decision. "Secretary Hayes," the president said moments later, "put us at DEFCON Two."

"Yes, sir," the secretary of defense responded, reaching for the phone.

"General Raydon, I am authorizing you to attack and destroy any Russian antisatellite installations that present a risk to Armstrong Space Station," the president said grimly. "You will also use any weapons available to defend station from attack. Keep us advised."

ABOARD ARMSTRONG SPACE STATION

That same time

"Yes, sir," Kai replied. On the stationwide intercom he said, "All personnel, this is the director, we have been authorized by the president of the United States to attack any Russian bases that are a threat to us, and to use all weapons at our disposal to defend station. That is exactly what I intend to do. I want Casey Huggins on oxygen and into an ACES, and I want Life Support to teach her how to use a lifeboat."

"General, I'm almost done connecting up Starfire again," Casey responded. "An hour, maybe less. If I stop, you may not have it ready in time."

Kai thought about it for a moment; then: "All right, keep at it, Casey," he said. "But I want you on oxygen now, and as soon as you're done, I'm putting you in a space suit."

"I can't work with the oxygen mask on, sir," Casey insisted. "When I'm done I'll get suited up."

Kai knew this was not good, but he really did want Starfire activated again. "Okay, Casey," he said. "As fast as you can."

"Yes, sir."

"What's our next duck blind?" Kai asked.

"Chinese S-500S site on Hainan Island," Christine Rayhill announced. "In range of Kingfisher-Two in five minutes. Yelizovo Air Base, MiG-31D base, an S-500S site at Yelizovo, and an S-500S site at Petropavlovsk-Kamchatskiy Naval Base will be in range shortly thereafter, also for Kingfisher-Two."

"One Trinity against each of the S-500s and one against the air base, Valerie," Kai said.

"Yes, sir," Valerie said. "Combat, designate ground targets for—"

"Command, Surveillance, first Elektron spaceplane Poppa-One looks like it's altering course," Christine said. "It's accelerating . . . looks like a transfer-orbit maneuver, sir. Looks like it'll be the opposite direction from ours and offset slightly—can't tell the altitude yet.

I expect Poppa-Two to accelerate into a transfer orbit in a few minutes. Elektron spaceplane Poppa-Three should jump in fifteen minutes. Can't tell yet on Four and Five."

"Boomer, do you have enough fuel to transfer to the ISS, dock, then return to us?" Kai asked.

"Stand by. I'll check," Boomer replied. A moment later: "Yes, General, I do, but not enough to reenter afterward without refueling. How much fuel and oxidizer is still on station?"

Trevor checked his readouts. "Twenty thousand pounds of JP-8 and ten thousand of 'bomb.'"

"Should be enough, unless I have to do a lot of maneuvering," Boomer said. "I'd feel better if we could get a resupply mission up—"

"Missile launch detected reported by SBIRS, sir!" Christine shouted on intercom. SBIRS, or the Space-Based Infrared Surveillance, was the U.S. Air Force's newest infrared satellite system, capable of detecting and tracking missiles and even aircraft by their hot engine or motor exhausts. "Pop-up targets from over Novosibirsk. Two . . . three launches, definitely on an intercept course, not going ballistic. Intercept in six minutes!"

"Looks like they moved some MiG-31s to central Russia," Trevor said.

"Designate targets Poppa-Six, -Seven, and -Eight, Combat," Valerie said.

"We've been swept by target-tracking radar . . . switching to missile-guidance radar . . . *missile launch,* S-500S . . . salvo of four interceptors, seven minutes to intercept!" Christine reported. "Missiles tracking . . . *another salvo of four,* second launcher, looks like a . . . *third salvo* of S-500s lifting off, looks like a ring of S-500 launchers around Novosibirsk! I count . . . *a fourth salvo,* sixteen S-500s inbound from Novosibirsk! That's nineteen interceptors inbound, crew!"

"That's more than we ever did exercises against," Trevor said.

"Status of our defensive weapons, Valerie," Kai asked.

"All in the green, sir," Valerie replied. "Sixteen Kingfisher engagements on the keel plus approximately thirty Hydra shots."

"What's our altitude, Trev?"

"Two hundred and fifty-seven," Trevor replied. "Maximum slant range of an S-500S is supposed to be five hundred miles. We're going to be close."

"Four minutes on the Wasp interceptors," Christine said.

"Batteries released on all weapons, Valerie," Kai said.

"Roger, sir, batteries released, Combat, clear to engage."

"Roger, clear to—"

"Decoys!" Henry Lathrop shouted. "Warheads on the S-500 missiles splitting into two—no, three, three apiece!"

"Can you discriminate among them, Henry?"

"Not yet—too far away still," Henry said. "When they get within three hundred miles I'll get 'em with the infrared sensor first to see if there's a temperature difference, then with the optronic sensor to see if there's a visual."

"Three minutes on the Wasps."

"Missiles away," Henry Lathrop announced. "Two Trinities outbound, tracking. Next launches in ten and twenty seconds." Exactly ten seconds later: "Missiles away. Good track on first salvo—damn, lost control on second Trinity for the second engagement, launching a third salvo on second inbound . . . fourth salvo on third inbound away, good track . . . good track on first salvo, intercept looks good . . . Hydra is ready on all inbounds, good track, stand by . . . coming up on first intercept . . . now."

At that instant all the lights on Armstrong Space Station brightened to more than twice their normal level, then flickered and went dead. Several computer terminals went blank momentarily, but seconds later started an automatic reboot. "What was that?" Kai shouted. The intercom was dead. "What happened?" The crew remained calm, but they were staring at momentarily useless displays and readouts, then at each other—and a few were gauging their distance to the hatch for the life-boat spheres. "What do you got, Valerie?"

"I think it was an EMP, sir!" Valerie shouted. "I think the warhead on that Wasp interceptor had a nuclear warhead on it!"

"Shit," Kai cursed. He looked over at all the monitors around him. Thankfully they hadn't been fried—Armstrong Space Station was heavily shielded against cosmic radiation—but the power spike had reset all their computers. "How long before everything is back up?"

"Most will be back up in ninety seconds," Trevor shouted across the command module, "but the synthetic-aperture radar might take three minutes or more."

"Do you still have contact with the Trinities?"

"I got nothing until my computers reboot, sir," Valerie said. "About a minute. Hopefully that EMP took out the Wasp interceptors as well as all our stuff."

It was an agonizingly long wait, but soon the command module began coming back to life as computers rebooted and other systems were reset. "One Wasp missile remaining inbound!" Henry shouted when his computer monitor began displaying useful information. "All S-500 missiles still on course, about two minutes to intercept!"

"Nail that Wasp missile, Valerie!" Kai shouted.

"Trinities away!" Valerie said. "Hydra is not online yet—we can't back up the intercept with the Hydra on this engagement! Trinities will launch against the S-500s in fifteen seconds!"

"Crew, report to Command on damage or injuries," Trevor said on intercom. "Casey?"

"I just got my test computer back up," Casey said from the Skybolt module. "Another forty minutes."

"That's too much time," Kai said. "Casey, go on oxygen, put a space suit on, and report to your assigned lifeboat."

"No! I can do it in time!" Casey shot back. "I'll hurry. I can do it!"

Kai punched the air in front of himself. "Hurry, Casey," he said finally.

"Coming up on intercept on the third Wasp," Henry said. "Trinities away on the S-500 missiles—we're launching against everything on the screen, including what might be decoys. Wasp intercept in three . . . two . . . one . . ." Again, the lights flared brightly, then most of the lights and displays in the Command module went dark . . .

. . . but this time, not all of the computer monitors began rebooting automatically. "The Trinity fire-control computer didn't reboot," Henry shouted to the others in the Command module. "I've got to do a hard reset."

"Starfire fire control is rebooting," Christine said. "I have to do a hard reset on Hydra."

"Command, Engineering, hard reset under way on environmental and station attitude-control computers," the engineering officer reported. "Switching to backup environmental controls, but I can't monitor if they came up yet. I'll get a report in—"

At that moment there was a tremendous shudder throughout the entire station, and the crewmembers could feel a slight adverse spin. "Did we get hit?" Kai asked.

"All readouts still blank," Trevor said. "Pass the word through the other modules to look out the windows for evidence of damage." Seconds later they felt another shudder, and the station started a spinning motion in a different direction. "Do we have anything, Valerie? We're definitely getting hit by something."

"I should get the Hydra fire control back in a few seconds," Valerie replied. At that moment most of the module lights and intercom came back.

". . . hear me, Armstrong," they heard on the radio. "This is Shadow, how do you hear me? Over."

"Loud and clear now, Boomer," Kai said. "Go ahead."

"The number seven solar cell and the truss just inboard of number two solar cell were hit," Boomer said. "Station has started a slight adverse roll. Are your positioning systems working?"

"We're doing a hard reset," Trevor said. "We don't know the status yet."

"Radar is back up," Christine reported. "Scope is clear. No contacts. We're down to three engagements on the Kingfishers on the truss."

"I got another fault indication on Hydra," Henry reported. "I'm doing another hard reset." Kai looked at Trevor and Valerie, and their expressions wordlessly sent the same message: we're running out of defensive weapons, and we haven't reached the most deadly part of the orbit.

"Gonzo? How do you hear?"

"Loud and clear, General," Gonzo replied, her voice sounding almost normal. "We were getting oxygen and data from station, but that's cut off now."

"We'll get it back for you as soon as we can, Gonzo," Kai said. "Stay strapped in. Those attacks put a slight spin on station, and our attitude-control systems are down right now, but we'll get them back soon."

"Yes, sir."

"Update on those spaceplanes?"

"First Elektron is in a matching orbit to ours, about a thousand miles away," Christine reported. "No contact on four and five. Two and three seem to be in the same orbit and the same altitude as ours, but the orbit is different than ours. They'll make their closest approach to us in about an hour . . ." She turned to Kai and added, "About five minutes before we overfly DB-One."

"The Russians timed those spaceplane launches down to the nanosecond," Valerie exclaimed.

"Maybe we'll get lucky and they'll shoot down their own spaceplanes," Kai said. On intercom he spoke: "Attention on station. I want all off-duty personnel in space suits. Rehearse the lifeboat evacuation procedures and make sure you're ready to board the lifeboats as soon as I give the warning. We're down to just a few engagements with our defensive weapons, and the Hydra still hasn't come back up. Casey, time's up. I want you in a space suit right away. Someone in Life Support give her a hand."

"Thirty minutes to DB-One," Christine reported.

"Status of the Hydra?" Kai asked.

"Still down," Henry said. "I'll do another hard reset. Trinity fire control is back up, but the station's spin might be a problem launching interceptors."

"Command, this is Jessop in Life Support," came a call a few minutes later.

"Go ahead, Larry," Trevor responded.

"I can't open the hatch to the Skybolt module. It appears to be locked from inside."

Kai's eyes flared in surprise. "Casey, *what are you doing?*" he thundered on intercom.

"I can fix it!" Casey radioed. "I almost had it before the last brownout! Just a few more minutes!"

"Negative! Get out of that module *right now!*"

"I can fix it, sir! It's almost ready! Just a few more—"

"Radar contact, spacecraft," Christine interjected. "Same altitude, different orbit, range four hundred fifty miles! It will pass by at fifty miles!"

"Status of the Trinities and Hydra?" Kai asked.

"Hydra looks like it's coming up now," Henry said. "About ten minutes until ready. Trinities are ready, but with the station spin, they might have to expend extra fuel to steer an intercept—"

"Second radar contact, spacecraft," Christine reported. "Intersecting orbit, range four hundred eighty miles, passing approximately thirty miles!"

"Launch commit the Trinities, Valerie," Kai ordered.

"Trinities are ready, showing launch commit," Valerie said. "The computers should adjust the launch for the station spin."

"Three hundred miles on first spacecraft."

"Trinity one away . . . Trinity two away," Henry said. A moment later: "Trinities off course . . . wait, regaining course . . . back on course, good track . . . Trinities three and four away . . . good tr—" And suddenly there was a loud *BANG!* The station shuddered, and several alarms sounded. "Trinity four hit a solar panel!" Henry shouted. "Trinity five away!"

"Batteries not fully charging," Alice Hamilton in the Engineering module reported. "Discharge rate is slow, but the other solar panels can't compensate."

"Shut down nonessential equipment," Kai said. "Casey, get out of that module *now*! I'm going to power it down!"

"Hydra is reporting ready!" Henry said.

"Radar contact spacecraft!" Christine said. "Same orbit, four hundred miles and closing slowly."

"Lost contact with Trinities one and two!" Henry shouted. "May have been downed with a laser from that Elektron!"

"Two hundred miles and closing on spaceplane one."

"Engage with Hydra," Kai ordered.

"Roger, Combat, clear to engage with Hydra!" Valerie said.

"Combat copies," Henry said. "Hydra firing!"

"Missile launch detection!" Christine reported. "Multiple S-500 launches from near Chkalovsky Air Base!"

"Direct hit on spaceplane one!" Henry reported. "Nailed him! Shifting track to target two!"

"Command, Engineering, battery power down to seventy-five percent," the technician said. "You can fire Hydra two, maybe three more shots! Our solar panels are charging the batteries at only half rate—it'll take hours to fully recharge them even if you don't fire any more weapons!"

Kai thought quickly; then: "Take out that second spaceplane with the Hydra, and use any Trinities we have left on the third spaceplane," he said.

Just then they heard Casey shout, "It's ready! It's ready!"

"Casey? I told you to get out of that module!"

"It's ready!" she repeated. "Try it!"

"Hydra engaging second spaceplane!" Henry reported. This time the lights significantly dimmed in the command module.

"Hydra powered down!" Valerie said. "It drained the batteries below forty percent and shut itself down!"

"Second spaceplane still inbound."

"Try it, General!" Casey said on intercom.

"Valerie?"

"Starfire has full continuity," Valerie said. She looked over at Kai, a glimmer of hope in her eyes. "Permission to spin up the MHD, General."

"Go," Kai said. On intercom he said, "Engineering, Command, permission to spin up the MHD."

"Engineering copies," Alice acknowledged. A moment later the lights dimmed again. "Batteries down to twenty-five percent."

"Too bad we can't plug the MHD generator into station," Kai said. "We'd have all the power we'd ever need."

"Next time, we will," Trevor said.

"MHD at twenty-five percent," Alice said.

"Spaceplane two closing to one hundred miles," Christine said. "I'm picking up a target-tracking radar from that spaceplane—he's locked on to us with something. Spaceplane three closing to two hundred miles. Multiple S-500 missiles still inbound."

"*High hull temperature warning on the Galaxy module!*" Alice reported. "Temperature still rising!"

"Everyone in the Galaxy module, *get into your life-boats!*" Kai shouted. "*Move!* Engineering, make sure the Galaxy module is—"

"Hull temperature at limits!" Alice reported about thirty seconds later.

"Lifeboat one sealed," Trevor reported.

"Lifeboat two, seal it up *now!* Lifeboat two, do you—"

Suddenly alarms went off throughout the command module. "Galaxy module hull breached," Alice said.

Kai looked at Trevor, who shook his head—lifeboat two was still not sealed up. "Module pressure down to zero."

"Spaceplane two is headed away from us," Christine reported. "Spaceplane three closing to one hundred miles."

"Hobnail is locked on to target," Colonel Galtin reported to his command post. "Request permission to engage."

"Permission granted," the controller said. "Elektron Two had a successful attack. Good luck."

I need no luck, Galtin thought—I have Elektron and Hobnail. Seconds later, the radar reported in range and Galtin hit the switch to commit the Hobnail laser.

"Warning, hull temperature in command module *rising!"* Alice shouted. "It'll hit the limit in twenty seconds!"

"Lifeboats!" Kai shouted. *"Move!"* But no one moved. Everyone stayed at their stations . . . because Kai did not unstrap himself from his seat, they were not going to do so either.

"MHD is at one hundred percent!" Alice reported.

"Valerie, *go!"*

"Combat, Starfire commit! Shoot!"

. . .

The first indication that something had happened was the acidy smell of burning electronics, even though Galtin was sealed up in his space suit. The second was the astounding scene of his instrument panel sparking, arcing, and finally setting itself afire, all in the blink of an eye. The third was a warning tone in his head-phones indicating a complete system failure, although he could no longer see the status of any of his systems. The last thing he encountered was his space suit filling with smoke, then he briefly felt the oxygen in his suit explode . . .

. . . seconds before his Elektron spaceplane exploded into a billion pieces and spread across space in a fiery spear; then the oxidizer was consumed and the fire blanked itself out.

"**Spaceplane three** eliminated," Christine said. "Still multiple S-500 missiles inbound, about sixty seconds."

"Hull temperature stabilizing," Alice reported. "MHD and Starfire are in the green. Batteries are down to ten percent. At five percent the station will shut down to allow the remaining battery power to drive lifeboat release mechanisms, air pumps, emergency lights and alarms, and rescue beacons."

"Can we get the rest of those S-500s with the power we have left?" Trevor asked.

"We got no choice but to try," Valerie said.

"No, not the missiles—the S-500 radar and control truck," Kai said. "Maybe that will take out the missiles."

Valerie hurriedly called up the last-known S-500 site at Chkalovsky Air Base northeast of Moscow and used Armstrong Space Station's powerful radar and optronic sensors to scan the area. The S-500 transporter-erector-launchers had moved to the south side of the airport in three widely separated emplacements, but the radar truck, command vehicle, and power and hydraulic generator truck were in the same location as previously cataloged. The trucks were located in a vacant area of the large aircraft parking ramp, where long lines of Antonov-72, Ilyushin-76, and -86 transport planes were lined up; farther down the ramp were two rows of five MiG-31D antisatellite-missile launch planes, each with a 9K720 antisatellite missile waiting to be loaded aboard. "Target acquired!" Christine shouted.

"Combat, *shoot!*" Valerie ordered.

"Starfire engaged!" Henry shouted . . .

. . . and just seconds later, all power in the command module went completely out, leaving only emergency exit lights. Kai hit a button on his console, and an alarm bell sounded, along with the computerized words, *"All personnel, report to lifeboats immediately! All personnel, report to lifeboats immediately!"*

The maser beam from Armstrong Space Station fired for less than two seconds . . . but traveling at five miles every second, the beam was able to sweep across almost the entire length of Chkalovsky Air Base before extinguishing.

The S-500 command, power, and radar trucks sparkled as the beam swept across them, and moments later their fuel tanks exploded, setting all of them afire. Next were the transport planes, which one by one burst open like overripe melons, transforming hundreds of thousands of gallons of jet fuel instantly into huge mushroom clouds of fire. The same fate awaited the MiG-31D fighters, fed by ten exploding 9K720 solid rocket booster motors that launched several of the missiles spinning through the sky for miles—and spreading radioactive material from two of the missiles' micronuclear warheads. The beam shut down the base operations building, destroyed several more parked and taxiing aircraft, and then detonated several aircraft inside their maintenance hangars, obliterating each hangar in a spectacular fireball.

. . .

Casey heard the alarm and hurriedly began unstrapping herself from her seat in the Skybolt module. There was no lifeboat in the Skybolt module, but she knew that the closest one was in the Engineering module just "above" hers. She donned her emergency oxygen mask, then looked up and saw Larry Jessop the life-support guy looking through the window in the hatch waiting for her. She smiled and was about to unlock the hatch . . .

. . . when a tremendous explosion rocked the station. The destruction of the S-500 command and control vehicles at Chkalovsky had nullified guidance to all of the 9K720 missiles . . . except for the first four that had been launched and had locked on to Armstrong Space Station with their own terminal guidance sensors. All four made direct hits, and the fourth missile hit squarely on the Skybolt module.

Casey turned and saw nothing but planet Earth beneath her through the gaping, sparking hole that seconds ago was her Starfire microwave cavity and Skybolt. She smiled and thought it was the most beautiful thing she had ever seen in her life. As she watched, the spectacular blues and whites of the spinning planet below her feet slowly faded into shades of gray. It was not as beautiful as before, but she still marveled at her home planet *right there*—she even thought she could see her home, and she smiled, thinking of the next time she would go home and see her parents and her brothers and sisters and tell them about this incredible adventure. She smiled, her mom and dad's faces smiling back at her, and felt happy and a little euphoric, until her vision tunneled closed into blackness seconds later as the last of her oxygen seeped out of her body.

The S-500S missiles tore into Armstrong Space Station. Boomer and Brad watched in absolute horror as modules were either hit or ripped off when the station started to cartwheel through space. "Midnight, this is Shadow," Boomer radioed. "Hold on, guys. I'll be over there in a minute. We'll transfer you out through the cockpit and through the hole in the fuselage."

There was no reply for several long moments; then, a sleepy, tired voice radioed, "I don't think . . . even . . . the great spaceplane pilot . . . Hunter 'Boomer' Noble could . . . could match this spin," Vice President Ann Page said. "Save your fuel. Retrieve the lifeboats. I'm . . . I'm hypoxic, I don't see . . . see any lights on Gonzo's suit . . . save your fuel and . . . and retrieve the lifeboats, Boomer. That's an . . . an order."

"I'm not in your chain of command, Miss Vice President," Boomer said. "Hang on. Stay with me."

"Brad?" they heard. "Brad, can . . . can you hear me?"

"Sondra!" Brad exclaimed. "We're going to rendezvous with you! Hang on!"

There was silence for a long time, and Brad's mouth was quickly turning dry. Then they heard in the tiniest of voices: "Brad?"

"Sondra, don't worry," Brad said. "We'll be there as fast as we can!"

"Brad? I . . . I'm sorry. I . . ."

"Sondra!" Brad cried out. "Hang on! We'll rescue you! *Hang on!"* But as they watched the crippled space station spin away, they knew it would not be possible to try a rescue.

BLACK ROCK DESERT
NORTH OF RENO, NEVADA

One week later

Defying federal orders, thousands of vehicles of every description were parked at the edge of the Black Rock Desert in northwestern Nevada at the terminus of Highway 447 to witness something that no one believed they would ever see in their lifetimes. The Black Rock Desert was the home of the world-famous Burning Man Festival, where thousands of artists, adventurers, and counterculture free spirits gathered every summer to celebrate freedom and life . . . but this would be a day on the playa that would represent death.

"I guess it is returning home," Brad McLanahan said. He was seated in a lawn chair on the roof of a rented RV. Beside him on one side was Jodie Cavendish, on the other was Boomer Noble, and behind them, clearly separating himself from the others, was Kim Jung-bae. They had just concluded a series of press interviews with the dozens of news agencies that had come out to witness this incredible event, but now they had broken away from the reporters several minutes before the appointed time so they could be by themselves.

Jodie turned to Jung-bae and put a hand on his leg. "It's okay, Jerry," she said. Jung-bae lowered his head. He had been weeping ever since they had arrived on the playa and had refused to talk with anyone. "It's not your fault."

"It *is* my fault," Jung-bae said. "I am responsible for this." And for the millionth time since the test firing, he said, "I am so sorry, guys. I am so sorry."

Brad reflected back on the events over the past week. After realizing they could not rescue the persons trapped in the Midnight spaceplane, he and Boomer had returned to the area where the three lifeboats had been jettisoned before the Russian S-500S missiles had hit the station. Boomer had exited the cockpit, suited up, gone into the cargo bay, and jettisoned the last few remaining pieces of cargo. With Brad at the controls of the Shadow spaceplane, he had maneuvered them to each of the lifeboats, and Boomer reeled them into the cargo bay. After hooking up oxygen, power, and communications cables, they made a transfer-orbit burn and entered the International Space Station's orbit.

It took almost two days, but they finally rendezvoused with the ISS. Sky Masters had flown up two station technicians on commercial spacecraft to power up the station and bring supplies, and they used the robot arms to attach the lifeboats to docking ports. All of Armstrong's crewmembers had to spend a night in an airlock pressurized with pure oxygen to ward off nitrogen narcosis, but afterward they were all deemed fit to fly, and they returned to Earth the next day.

Brad's smartphone beeped a warning. "It's time," he said.

They watched and waited. Before long they could see what looked like a star grow brighter and brighter in the cloudless Nevada sky. It grew brighter and brighter, and everyone parked on the playa thought they could actually feel heat from the object . . . and then suddenly there was a tremendous earsplitting sound, like a thousand cannons going off all at once. Car windshields cracked, and cars rocked on their wheels—Brad thought he was going to be jostled right off the roof of the RV.

The star turned into a spectacular ball of fire that grew and grew, trailing fire behind it for a hundred miles, until the ball started to break apart. Seconds later there was another tremendous explosion, and twenty miles to the north the spectators saw a massive ball of fire at least five miles in diameter, followed by a rapidly growing mushroom cloud of fire, sand, and debris. They saw a huge wall of sand and smoke thousands of feet high rushing toward them, but just as they were thinking they should retreat inside their vehicles, the wall began to dissipate, and it thankfully disappeared long before it reached them.

"So long, Silver Tower," Boomer said. Jung-bae was openly and loudly sobbing behind them, crying in sheer anguish at the thought of his friend Casey Huggins in that maelstrom. "It was nice flying with you, old buddy."

SAN LUIS OBISPO COUNTY REGIONAL AIRPORT

The next evening

After observing the final flight of Armstrong Space Station, Brad McLanahan and Jodie Cavendish had done more media interviews in Reno and San Francisco, then they flew the turbine P210 Silver Eagle back to San Luis Obispo. Night had already fallen. They had just pushed the plane into the hangar and were unloading their few pieces of luggage when Chris Wohl appeared at the hangar door. "You must be Sergeant Major Wohl," Jodie said, extending a hand. After a moment Chris took it. "Brad has told me a lot about you."

Chris shot a querying expression at Brad. "Yes, a lot," Brad said.

"I'm sorry about your friends," Chris said. "I'm glad you made it back, Brad. Had enough of space travel for a while?"

"For now," Brad admitted. "But I am going back. Most definitely."

"Done with all the media stuff too for a while?"

"Definitely no more," Jodie said. "I can't wait for our lives to go back to normal. Crikey, I can't even *remember* what normal is."

"You need anything, either of you?" Chris asked. "The team will be back in the morning. When you feel up to it, you can start training."

"He's right back to his usual routines," Jodie said. "I might join him from now on."

"That would be fine," Chris said. "Ready to go back to the apartment?"

"We'll unload, and then I'll close it up," Brad said. "I'll wipe it down tomorrow."

"I'll drive with you back to Poly Canyon, and then I'm going to the hotel," Chris said. "I'll see you in the morning. We'll update your call sign then, I think." He gave Brad and Jodie a half smile, which was a big one by Wohl's standards, and then he put his hands in his pockets against the growing chill, turned on a heel, and . . .

. . . walked right into the knife held by Yvette Korchkov, which plunged deep into his belly. He had enough strength and wherewithal to head-butt his assailant before falling to the tarmac, clutching his abdomen.

"*Grebanyy ublyudok,*" Korchkov swore, holding her bleeding forehead. "Fucking bastard." Brad pushed Jodie behind him. "We meet again, Mr. McLanahan. Thank you so much for informing the world where you will be. It was child's play to track you down."

Brad pulled Jodie to the back of the hangar, then went over to a toolbox and found a Crescent wrench. "Call 911," he told her. To Korchkov he said, "Svärd, or whatever the hell your name is, if you don't want to get caught, you'd better leave. This place has security cameras, and Wohl's troops will be here any minute."

"I know where all of the sergeant major's associates are, Brad," Korchkov said. "They are hours away, and

I will be gone long before the police arrive. But my mission will be completed."

"What mission? Why are you after me?"

"Because your father made a terrible enemy in Gennadiy Gryzlov," Korchkov said. "He ordered all of your father's possessions to be destroyed, and you are at the top of the list. And I must say, after the destruction you caused near Moscow last week, he will have an even greater burning desire to see you dead."

"The police are on their way," Jodie called out.

"They will be too late," Korchkov said.

"Well, then, come and get me, bitch," Brad said, waving her on. "You like doing it up close and personal? Then give me a hug, bitch."

Korchkov moved like a cheetah despite the wound on her forehead, and Brad was far too late. He partially deflected the knife with the wrench, but the blade sliced across the left side of his neck. Jodie screamed when she saw the rivulet of blood forming between Brad's fingers as he tried to stop the flow. The wrench dropped from his hand as the room started to spin.

Korchkov smiled. "Here I am, handsome space traveler," she said. "Where is your tough talk now? You are perhaps a little weak from your space travels, no?" She raised the knife so Brad could see it. "Give me a good-bye hug."

"Here's your hug, bitch," a voice behind her said, and Chris Wohl broke a push-broom across Korchkov's head. She whirled and was about to knife him again, but Chris dropped to the floor and was still.

"Finish bleeding and die, old man," Korchkov said.

"That's not an old man—he's a sergeant major," Brad said, just before the Crescent wrench crunched on the back of Korchkov's head. She went down. Brad brought the wrench down hard against the hand holding the knife, pushed the blade away, then continued to beat her face with the wrench until he couldn't recognize it anymore. He collapsed on top of the battered body as Jodie ran up to him, rolling him away from Korchkov and pressing her fingers against the gash on his neck.

Brad opened his eyes to the sounds of sirens outside the hangar and found Jodie still crouched over him, her hands pressed against his bleeding neck. "Brad?" she asked. "Oh, God . . ."

"Hey," he said. He gave her a weak smile. "Who says I can't show my girl a good time?" And he thankfully dropped into unconsciousness once again.

EPILOGUE

There is a skeleton on every house.
—Italian saying

SCION AVIATION INTERNATIONAL HEADQUARTERS
ST. GEORGE, UTAH
Several days later

Brad stood at the head of the Cybernetic Infantry Unit as the straps began to slowly retract up toward the ceiling, and moments later Patrick McLanahan was pulled clear of the robot. His body was as pale as a bedsheet, and he was thinner than Brad could ever remember, but he was not as skeletal as he had feared—he looked wiry, with good muscle tone beneath the snow-white skin. His head was supported with a pillow attached to its own straps. Doctors and nurses rushed up to him, administering medications and attaching sensors all over his body. They placed an oxygen mask over his mouth and nose with a microphone in it.

Patrick turned and opened his eyes, looking at Brad, and he smiled. "Hello, son," he said. "Good to see you in person and not through an optronic sensor."

"Hello, Dad," Brad said. He turned a little to his right. "I'd like you to meet Jodie Cavendish, my friend and one of my Starfire team leaders. Jodie, please meet my father, General Patrick S. McLanahan."

Patrick closed his eyelids and even slightly bowed his head. "A pleasure to meet you, Miss Cavendish," he said. "I've heard a lot about you."

"It is a great honor to meet you, sir," Jodie said.

"I'm sorry about Casey Huggins and Starfire," Patrick said. "You did some amazing work."

"Thank you, sir."

Patrick looked at Brad. "So, you're headed back to school," he said. "I'm not sure if you can get any work done with all the publicity swirling around you guys."

"We're counting on fast news cycles and short memory spans," Brad said. "Cal Poly is a big place. We're the ones who lost a space station. We're not heroes."

"In my eyes, you are," Patrick said.

It did not take long. As Patrick was suspended above, the old CID was wheeled away, the new one wheeled into place. Patrick's body was lowered inside, the straps pulled free, and the rear hatch was closed. Jodie was awestruck as the CID stood up, wriggled its arms and legs as if waking up from a nap, then extended a hand to her. "It was a pleasure to meet you, Miss Cavendish," Patrick said in his electronically synthesized voice. "I look forward to seeing you again."

"We're coming up next weekend to decorate your room," Brad said. "I got a bunch of your Air Force stuff out of storage. We'll make this place feel like home."

"I can't guarantee I'll be here, Brad," Patrick said, "but you're welcome to do whatever you feel like doing. I'd like that." Brad gave his father a hug, and he and Jodie departed.

A few minutes after they left, with the CID plugged into power, nutrients, environmental, and data umbilicals, former president Kevin Martindale entered the room. "You actually approved Miss Cavendish to visit," he remarked. "I'm surprised."

"She promised to keep it a secret," Patrick said. "I believe her."

"Too bad about Phoenix losing the election to Barbeau," Martindale said. "That could be the end of a lot of government contracts."

"Many more clients out there," Patrick said. "Many more projects that we need to get under way."

Martindale shook his finger at Patrick. "Very clever of you, I must say," he said. "Injecting news articles and data to Brad about orbiting solar power plants and microwave lasers. You actually made your son believe Starfire was *his* idea."

"I planted the ideas—he had to run with them," Patrick said.

"True, true," said Martindale. "But when the idea came to life, it was so clever of you to secretly and carefully send him the experts, point him to Cavendish, Kim, Huggins, and Eagan, and line up Sky Masters to support him with that grant money."

"My son is a true leader," Patrick said. "He may be a terrible aerospace engineering student, but he's a good pilot and a great leader. All I did was place the resources at his disposal—it was up to him to put them together and build it. He did a good job."

"But you used your son to build an illegal directed-energy space weapon, in violation of international law," Martindale said. "Very, very clever. It worked. Unfortunately it was destroyed by the Russians, but it proved the value of microwave lasers. Good job, General." Martindale smiled and asked, "So what else do you have in store for young Bradley, may I ask?"

"We have to deal with a President Stacy Anne Barbeau now," Patrick said. "She will surely scrap the space initiative. But the good thing is, she wants to build bombers, aircraft carriers, arsenal ships, hypersonic weapons, and unmanned everything. I'm sure Brad can design and test most of those things. I'll get to work on it right away."

"I'm sure you will, General McLanahan," Martindale said with an evil smile. "I'm sure you will."

Acknowledgments

Information on Cane-Ja was taken from "Street Techniques" by Mark Shuey Sr. and Mark Shuey Jr., © Canemasters.com.

The P210 Silver Eagle, a Cessna P210 Centurion modified with a turboprop power plant (minus a lot of the high-tech stuff I added to it), is a product of O&N Aircraft, Factoryville, Pennsylvania, www.onaircraft .com.

Angel Flight West is a real charitable organization that matches needy medical or humanitarian recipients with pilots who donate their airplane, the cost of fuel, and their skills to fly them to wherever they need to go for medical or support reasons, with absolutely no cost to the passengers. I have flown for Angel Flight West for four years, and I think it may have been the ultimate reason I became a pilot: to use my skills to help others. Learn more at www .angelflightwest.org.

THE NEW LUXURY IN READING

We hope you enjoyed reading
our new, comfortable print size and found it
an experience you would like to repeat.

Well – you're in luck!

HarperLuxe offers the finest in fiction and
nonfiction books in this same larger print size and
paperback format. Light and easy to read, HarperLuxe
paperbacks are for book lovers who want to see
what they are reading without the strain.

For a full listing of titles and
new releases to come, please visit our website:

www.HarperLuxe.com